SUDDENLY BOUND

BOOK 3 IN THE DIRTY TEXAS SERIES

JA LOW

BOOK 3 IN THE DIRTY TEXAS SERIES

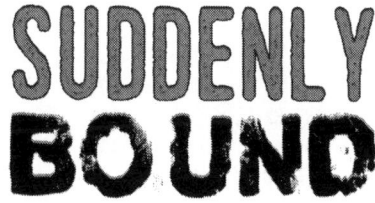

A DIRTY TEXAS novel

Copyright @ 2016 JA Low

All rights reserved. No part of this eBook may be reproduced or transmitted in any form, including electronic or mechanical, without written permission from the publisher, except in the case of brief quotations embodied in critical articles or reviews.

This is a work of fiction. Names, characters, businesses, places, events, and incidents are either the products of the author's imagination or used in a fictitious manner. Any resemblance to actual persons, living or dead, or actual events is purely coincidental. JA low is in no way affiliated with any brands, songs, musicians, or artists mentioned in this book.

This eBook is licensed for your personal enjoyment only. This eBook may not be re-sold or given away to other people. If you would like to share this eBook with another person, please purchase an additional copy for each person you share it with. If you are reading this eBook and did not purchase it, or it was not purchased for your use only, then you should return it to the seller and purchase your own copy.

Thank you for respecting the author's work.

Cover Design by Book Nerd Fan Girl

www.booknerdfangirl.com

Editor by Trish Bacher

www.editorinheels.com

❦ Created with Vellum

My family.

PROLOGUE
AXEL

"You have a fiancé?"

All I see is red. No, actually, all I see are his lips on hers, and that image alone kills me.

"I'm sorry, Axel... but it's not what you think."

Um, yeah, it is. She lied to me. "Do you or do you not have a fiancé?"

She stands there silently, choosing her words carefully. Her hazel eyes can't meet mine and are glued firmly to the floor. "Yes, yes, I do have a fiancé."

I'm seething and shocked. She looks so innocent. I never expected this from her, not after everything. She played me and played me good. I fell for the goddamn innocent act—hook, line, and sinker.

"I know I should've told you, it's just that..."

"There are no fucking buts, Olivia. You have a fiancé. You chose to continue whatever was happening between us, knowing full well that you were engaged to another. I can't stand to look at you. Was I just a convenient fuck? Or are you really a Dirty Texas groupie? Ha, groupie is too good a word for you. At least those women are honest when they fuck me."

I can see my words are hitting their mark.

"Go back to your fiancé. I never want to see you again." Turning my back on her, I walk out of the room, shaking my head.

Women, they're all the same. You can never trust them.

1
OLIVIA

I hear shouting as I enter my home, a little cottage just off in the forest beside my family's castle. My parents are currently staying with me, having a break from their home in Edinburgh, where my father is getting medical treatment for his heart problems.

"I don't care, Agnes," my father shouts. I follow the sound to where my parents are sitting in my office.

"What's going on?" Looking at the two of them, my father's face is red with anger. "Dad, you need to think of your heart." Tension is swirling around the room, and he doesn't need any more stress on his heart at the moment.

"Your sister has graced us with another scandal." I can see the disgust on my father's face as he points to the newspaper. My younger sister, Penelope, is, well, a bitch. I know it's not a nice thing to say about your sister, but it's the truth.

All my life I had to put up with her behavior, from stealing my dolls to getting me into trouble when she did something wrong. As we got older and grew out of toys, Penny loved to steal my friends and then, my boyfriends. I don't think there was one she didn't steal. Yes, as I said, a grade-A bitch. So, it's not surprising Penny is involved in another scandal. It is what she's known for.

"Who the hell is this man?" My father points to the picture and continues, "He's most certainly not from our circles."

I can hear the disdain dripping from his words, and when he says *not from our circles,* he means the aristocratic ones we come from. I take a look, and yes, there she is, sunning herself somewhere exotic with some footballer fondling her breasts. I'll say that the images look like they have been taken with a telescopic lens, so in her defense, and I don't know why I still defend her as she's the devil incarnate, she probably didn't think she was being photographed.

Who am I kidding, my sister loves the attention, and she adores the spotlight on her. That's why she hates the fact that I'm the older child because I get everything. By everything, I mean the vast estate we have and everything that comes with it, even working seven days a week, twelve or sixteen hours most days. All she sees is the money the estate makes and that I control her purse strings. God, if Penny were running the show, we'd have no money left, and she would be homeless.

"It doesn't look like she had any idea the camera was there." I know I'm covering for my sister. If the roles were reversed, there's no way in hell she would be doing it and would gladly throw me under the bus. But I need to calm my father down.

"Yes, dear, these vultures have preyed on poor Penelope for years, just like they did to Princess Diana."

I roll my eyes at my mother. She's always happy to excuse Penny's behavior. Penny is most definitely nothing like Princess Diana—she may be a *Lady* by title, but that's where it ends.

Father frowns and looks again at the paper. "Vultures, bloody vultures. Get Gregory, he'll sort it out." Gregory is our family lawyer and used to sorting out Penny's scandals. Not sure how he does it, but he can pretty much get a retraction from a magazine or newspaper within twenty-four hours. Luckily, we have him on staff because Penny definitely makes his job harder than it should be.

"Now, Olivia, we have something very important to discuss with you." My father turns to me, his face slowly losing the angry redness that was just there. My heart starts beating faster. What on earth could it be? My mind races through the estate's accounts—definitely not that, they're all good. Since I took over from my parents two years ago, I have turned this once money-sucking pit of rock into a glistening, shiny beacon as the UK's premier wedding venue. Yes, little old me with my business degree, turning a vast estate filled with castles, cottages, manors, villages, and one hundred thousand acres of land from the brink of bankruptcy into a multi-million-dollar company. Me. Not Penelope, even though she likes reaping the rewards from my efforts.

He points to one of the velvet seats, and I follow his order. My heart is pounding. Please don't let this be bad news, please.

"As you know, your thirtieth birthday is happening next year."

Yes, I am well aware that I'm getting older, I reply sarcastically to myself.

"And yet you're still single."

That shouldn't be surprising to anyone. I'm not sure how I can possibly meet someone when I am stuck in a castle in the middle of nowhere, working sixteen-hour days, seven days a week, trying to make sure the home that has been in our family for the past four hundred years stays that way.

"Your mother and I think that you should get married." I turn and look at Mother, who's nodding excitedly at this news.

"Of course, I'd like to get married, but at the moment, I'm so busy, I haven't had time to meet anyone."

"Yes, yes, we know all this." Father waves his hands in the air, dismissing my comments. "So, we have decided to find you a partner."

I think I just had a heart attack.

My parents want to set me up with someone.

No, no, no, absolutely not.

"No, you don't have to do that." I feel the panic rise through my body.

"Of course, we do. We can't trust you to choose the right person."

My jaw drops. "Excuse me?" I can't believe he just said that to me. I know my parents are old-school, but this is ridiculous. I'm a grown woman and can pick my own husband.

"Don't take that tone with me, young lady," my father cautions.

"Sweetheart, we have your best interests at heart," my mother adds.

"I can choose my own husband. I don't need my parents doing that for me. You do realize I am a grown adult, that I'm running a multi-million-dollar company all on my own." I jump to my feet and glare at my parents. It's rare that I stand up for myself, but this, this is too much.

"Sit down," my father scolds.

"No, I don't want to hear it. This, this has gone too far, even for you, Father." I storm out of my office, my father's voice bellowing behind me. I run up the stairs two at a time toward my bedroom and slam my door. I throw myself onto my bed and scream into my pillow like some moody teenager.

My life literally sucks. I'm stuck here in the English countryside, where my only companions are the staff who work for me, the tourists, and some cows. I don't complain because I live in one of the most beautiful parts of England. Although, I could be sunning myself somewhere being fondled by a footballer like my sister. God, for once in my life, I'm envious of her.

It stings that my parents don't trust me to find a suitable husband. They don't know that I'm too scared to bring anyone home because my sister likes to shag them behind my back.

That's why I am single. I know I'm not unattractive, but how can I ever trust a man around my sister when every single one of them has fallen for her seduction? *Ugh, God, I hate her.* She gets to gallivant around the globe with the world's hottest bachelors while I'm stuck here looking at spreadsheets and wondering if a man will ever touch me again. I mean, it's been two years, two very long years. I scream my sexual frustration into my bed again, dramatic yes, satisfying, well kind of.

"Olivia." My mother's quiet voice pulls me from my self-loathing. I turn my head and stare at her, looking every inch the duchess she is—the twin set, the pearls, the kitten heels, her honey-colored hair pulled into a neat bun, and her natural makeup perfectly done.

"Your father is just trying to look out for you."

I roll my eyes as I turn over and sit up on my bed. "But I'm an adult," I whine like a teenager, not the adult I am trying to portray.

"Sweetheart, we know… but your father is sick, and all he wants to do is see his oldest daughter get married."

Punch to the gut with that statement. "I want to give him that, I do, but it's kind of hard to meet men when I'm here." I wave my hand around the room.

"We know, sweetheart, and that's why he has found someone for you." I raise my brows at her. "I think you might even like this young man we have found. He's perfect in every way, plus your father just adores him."

I roll my eyes, but I'm curious.

"It would make your father so happy if you married this young man, he'd…" Mother pauses, and that's when I see it, she has tears in her eyes. "He would know that when he's gone, you're being looked after."

I feel sick. I can't imagine what life would be like without my father in it. I know he may not have been the traditional father like most people have. He grew up differently, where children were to be seen and not heard, that old-school kind of mentality, but he always did make time for us. He used to take us shooting and horseback riding, he'd read to us from one of the thousands of books in the library, but he could also be strict and cold. I love him even with his faults.

"Your father is sick, sweetheart." Mother pulls out her hanky and wipes her tears away. "I'm not going to have many years with him, Olivia." She breaks down, which is so unusual. She usually keeps all her emotions inside for no one to see. This is the first time I think I have ever seen her cry. I walk over and wrap my arms around her shaking body.

"Your father and I were an arranged marriage." This news shocks me. I had no idea. I thought they grew up together and fell in love.

"I know that isn't the story we told you, not because we were ashamed but because we fell in love, and saying it was arranged felt like it cheapened what we had." She sniffles.

"Most of the story of how we met is true. We knew each other growing up, our parents were best friends, and we saw each other at functions. I thought he was very good-looking, charming, and charismatic... everything I could've ever wanted in a man. My father approached me, told me that he had found a suitable husband for me, and it would strengthen the family estate, which, of course, it did. When they told me it was your father, I said yes straight away with no hesitation. I knew he was the one for me. It took your father a little more convincing, and he most certainly didn't want to give up his bachelor life." Mother winks at me. *Eww, father was a playboy?*

"But we both knew we had a duty to honor, plus we could've been paired with worse people to be married to. Anyway, what I'm saying is... we made it work, and it wasn't long until we both were in love and happily married. Some arranged marriages do work."

"So, what you're saying is that the man you have for me

could be the man of my dreams." Mother nods enthusiastically. "But what happens if I don't want to marry him?"

Mother frowns. "We won't force you, Olivia." Well, that's good to know. "But you would break your father's heart if you did." Nothing like emotional blackmail to force you into marriage.

"I know that to you modern-day women arranged marriages are so archaic." She's right there. "But sometimes they work."

"But what happens if we don't like each other?"

Mother sighs. "I'm pretty sure you'll like this young man, but if for some reason you both don't get along, then I'm sure you can come to some sort of mutual arrangement."

What? Yes, my mouth fell open at that comment.

"What... like see other people on the side?"

Mother raises her eyes wide at me. "It would be unsavory. However, if you both honestly don't like each other and mutually agreed, then I don't see why not, but you would still need to produce heirs."

"Can I think about it? Or do I have to give you an answer right away?"

Mother smiles at me. "Take your time, this is an important decision, sweetheart. I know you'll choose the right one, you always do."

And with that, she leaves me to ponder my future. Of course, she knows I am going to do the right thing. I'm the good child, the obedient child, the one who can't say no to her parents. I think this calls for a large bottle of wine.

"There she is." My father smiles as I make my way down the grand staircase, dressed in an emerald green evening dress my mother picked out for me. It's not really my style, but if it makes her happy, I'll wear it.

"You look beautiful, sweetheart." My father kisses my cheeks, showing a surprising amount of affection. He holds out his arm, and I link mine with his as he pats my hand.

"You made the right decision, Olivia. You have made me very proud." As his whole face lights up while he looks at me, I feel the full effect of my father's adoration, which is rare, and it makes me straighten myself up. He escorts me toward the dining hall, where I can hear chatter and laughter. I still for a moment when I hear *her* laugh.

"Penny is home?" I look at my father.

"Yes, of course, she wouldn't miss her sister's big night."

I hear her giggle again. It's like nails down a chalkboard and sends shivers down my spine. I can see exactly what's happening—Penny is introducing herself to my soon-to-be fiancé. I'm sure she has probably already made a move as she has always had a crush on him. The thought makes my stomach churn. I know Penny isn't going to let me have all this attention. She hates when the spotlight isn't on her, and my wedding planning will most definitely mean the spotlight is firmly set on me.

"Okay, let's do this."

My father chuckles. "Olivia, you aren't going to meet the executioner, you're meeting your husband-to-be. Put a smile on your face." And with that, I plaster on the biggest fake smile I can muster and walk into the dining room. Conversations stop as we arrive, and the people in the room stare at me. Mother has her public smile on and tells me I look beautiful.

Next, I see the Duke and Duchess of Roxburghe, whose estate borders ours to the north in Scotland. They have been best friends with my parents all their lives as they grew up together. I give them a warm welcome and engage in some polite conversation. I turn when I hear Penny's laugh again. Of course, she's sitting beside him, and, of course, they are getting on fabulously. Penny gives me a fake smile, and I can see the contempt hidden beneath it.

Then I see him, the man my father wants me to marry, Marquees Edmund Lumleyl, the social pages' favorite playboy, the man who's pictured with Victoria's Secret models and celebrities on his arm while he's partying in St. Barts or Ibiza. The same man who loves fast cars and likes to show them off on Instagram—#richkidsofinstagram—the same man who looks like he has stepped right off the pages of *Tatler* magazine under the title 'Hottest Royals of Europe.' The man is one of the most handsome men I have ever met, and he's going to be *my* husband. He stands up, ignoring Penny when he sees me, and walks around the table. The chatter in the room becomes nonexistent, his dress shoes clicking along the stone floor.

"Olivia, it has been too long a time." He smiles, and good gracious, he has the most amazing dimples—they just pop, enticing you closer. He grabs my hand, softly presses his lips to it, and gives me the barest of kisses. It lights my skin on fire, and I can feel my cheeks heat from a blush. *Ugh, this man is good.* I'm like a little lamb being led to slaughter by the worldly and charming wolf.

"It has been a while," I finally answer. We grew up together. We're about the same age, and with our parents being close friends, it was natural for us to all play together when we were younger. Once we were old enough, we were all sent to boarding school and never really saw each other much again, except the odd holiday.

"You're a vision." He smiles, and I'm pretty sure women drop their knickers for that smile. I may be one of them if he keeps laying on the charm. My eyes flick to where Penny is, and I can see she's shooting daggers my way. When we were growing up, she always had a crush on Eddie, as he likes to be called, but he was never interested in her.

"You don't have to woo me, I'm a sure thing," I whisper to him. As soon as the words come out of my mouth, I realize how that sounds. Eddie's eyebrows raise, and he smirks at me.

Stepping toward me and taking my arm, he whispers into my ear, "Just so you know, so am I." His heated words light my body on fire as he leads me to the spare seat beside him. Eddie is sitting in between Penny and me. This should be fun.

The food is amazing as always, and the conversation flows easily enough between Eddie and me, especially when Penny isn't hogging his attention. He seems intelligent, and we get along well, so that's definitely a good thing. But when he looks at me with hunger in his eyes, it gives me butterflies, so that's a good start, especially if we're going to be stuck with each other for a lifetime.

"Olivia, may I speak to you privately?" Eddie asks.

I look around the room and notice all eyes are on us. "Of course."

As Eddie pulls out my chair, he holds out his arm, and I slip mine in his. Just as we pass Penny, she sticks her foot out, tripping me up, and I stumble into Eddie's arms.

"Are you okay?" He looks at me, and I'm mortified, my face turning red.

"You should really slow down on the champagne, Livy. I'm sure Eddie doesn't want a drunk for a fiancée," Penny says sweetly.

Never in my life have I wanted to murder someone more than I do right now, looking at my sister's smug face.

Eddie ignores the tension between us. "Come, I have something for you." He pulls me away before I have a chance to crash-tackle my sister to the floor and beat the living daylights out of her. I'm not normally a violent person, but Penny likes to push my buttons.

We move through the stately home and out to one of the parlor rooms near the back. It looks out over the gardens, where fairy lights have been strung up through the bushes and are currently twinkling like tiny little stars against the darkness.

"I'm sorry about my sister, she's—"

"Don't apologize. I know exactly what she's like." He chuckles.

I take a deep breath. This is the first time we have been alone together, and it's a little awkward.

"Thank you for coming tonight. Our parents look happy about our arrangement." He stares off into the darkness, his hands shoved into his pockets.

"Can I ask you something?" He turns toward me.

"Of course, I guess we need to get to know each other before the wedding." My stomach sinks, thinking about the wedding. I still can't believe I'm doing this. He nods.

"Why are you doing this? I mean you're a beautiful woman, and I'm sure you have a ton of suitors at your door. Why me?"

I laugh at his comment. "Eddie, I live in the middle of nowhere, the closest person my age is probably across the border in another country. My days are filled with trying to set the estate up so that future generations don't have to go through what I'm going through. I want to be the last generation who has to struggle with this estate."

Eddie just stares at me and looks a little stunned by my comment.

"You're a special woman, Olivia." Moving toward me, I take a couple of steps back, feeling a little nervous at his sudden attention.

"When my father came up with this crazy idea, I was firmly against it, like strongly against it." He smiles at me, and I nod in agreement. I understood exactly what he was saying.

"But then I found out it was you." This stills me. I take a small gulp, nervous at what he's going to say. "And I knew that you were doing this out of duty to your father. That you weren't doing this with some sort of romantic notion that we would fall in love."

Okay, well, bollocks, that stings a little. "But most of all, I knew you would be rational about what I am going to ask."

Okay, now I'm a little worried.

Eddie reaches out and takes my hands, holding them in his. "I'm not ready to settle down yet, Livy. I am having way too much fun as a bachelor."

Well, good for him, but this is a semi-engagement party, so telling me he isn't ready to settle down is kind of weird.

"But I, too, am bound by duty, so I want to propose something to you." I'm pretty sure he's supposed to be proposing to me, but I don't think he will be asking me the right question.

"I think that we should still see other people, even when we're married. Discreetly, of course."

And there it is, my jaw hits the floor.

I'm in shock.

"You want to have an open relationship?"

Eddie moves closer, and his hand pushes away a small tendril of hair from my face. "Yes, but we would be the only ones who would know, and as I said, it would have to be discreet."

"But what happens about children? I mean, I don't want there to be any… you know… baby mamas knocking down our door."

This makes him laugh.

"Please, Olivia. I never go without protection. When the time comes for us to have children, we'll talk about our extracurricular activities then."

It all sounds very complicated. "What happens if you meet someone and fall in love? I don't want to be left a single mother."

"Livy, there's no way in the world I'd fall in love with any of the women I sleep with. They are just a good time. You, on the other hand, maybe… maybe I could fall for you. If I'm honest, I've always had a crush on you growing up."

"I don't believe you." Shock radiates throughout my body.

He smirks. "I remember everything about you. During the

summer, you wore that brown one-piece that used to ride up your bottom, and you were forever adjusting it."

We used to go swimming in the summer at one of the lakes, and he was right, that swimsuit was horrible, always giving me a wedgie as I swung on the tire rope and dropped into the cool water. I playfully slap his chest, a little embarrassed by his confession. His hand captures mine and holds it to his muscular chest.

"I wanted to kiss you so badly when we went horseback riding, you looked so beautiful, riding free through the countryside. The only time I ever saw you like that was on the back of a horse." Gosh, we were teenagers then, but I never saw him like that. *Okay, I'm lying. I was never allowed to see him like that because Penny would never allow me to.*

Eddie pulls me closer to him, the steady beating of his heart vibrating through my hand. "And now, now you're going to be my wife." The gravity of his words hit me. Dear God, he's going to be my husband, but neither of us is in love with one another. We're both doing this out of duty to our families. Can I seriously live like this?

Eddie's lips are suddenly on my neck, shocking me. "I like you, Livy." His lips make their way up to my jaw. "I trust you." His lips touch the sensitive area behind my ear, and I let out a whimper. It has been too long since a man has touched me. "I believe you'll be the perfect wife, perfect mother, and perfect duchess." His soft lips move ever so lightly against mine, gently kissing me, testing me. "I'm very lucky to be marrying you, Liv." His mouth opens against my own, urging me to open for him. My mind has gone blank at the sensations taking over. I feel the wetness of his tongue, teasing me, begging me to open, and I do because it has been too long since I was last kissed.

This man is going to be my husband, and I should at least check to see if I can stand kissing him. We're going to be doing a hell of a lot more than kissing once we're married. Eddie groans as his hand grips around my neck, pulling me in closer to him, holding me, his expert lips teasing me. "You taste amazing," he mumbles against my lips. He takes my hand that's still pinned against his chest and moves it down, pressing it against the bulge in his pants. I shriek and jump out of his arms.

Eddie looks confused.

"What do you think you're doing?" I question him.

"Having fun with my fiancée?" He gives me a boyish grin.

"Do you seriously think that I'd touch your... your..." I point to his considerable bulge because I can't finish my sentence.

"What? My penis? My cock? My dick?" His words shock me, making me gasp. "I didn't believe Penny when she said you were frigid. I thought the whole innocent look was for show, but now I see that it isn't."

My blood starts to boil. "What did Penny tell you?" My bloody sister, always meddling in my relationships.

"She told me you're very inexperienced. I like sex, Olivia. I need it all the time, and if I can't get it from you, then I'm going to get it elsewhere. Hence, why I asked about the open relationship. Actually, I wasn't asking, I was just trying to be nice because even if you had said no, I was still going to keep seeing other women."

I feel like I have been slapped in the face. I don't get how he can change so quickly.

"You know nothing about me," I argue back.

"Yes, I do. Your sister is a wealth of information. I couldn't shut her up. You have only been with four people, Liv, four people. I can't be stuck with a woman like that, a woman who doesn't know what she's doing. I'll not be stuck doing missionary for the rest of my life," he growls at me.

Now, I want to murder a second person tonight.

"Here." Eddie shoves a small velvet box into my hand. "This is for you." I open it up and see a huge diamond ring. "Wear it, don't wear it. I don't care." Shoving his hands back into his pockets, he continues, "But I suggest that you take up my offer of an open relationship, brush up on some experience so when it comes to the wedding night, I'm not disappointed." And with that, he walks away, whistling as if he hasn't just ruined me. I try and stop myself from crying, but it's useless.

What the hell have I gotten myself into?

2

AXEL

"Are you seriously inviting Ness up here?" I question Christian as I look at him. This is his goddamn bachelor party, and he's moping around missing his wife. Such a fucking pussy.

"She's bringing friends with her." He wiggles his eyebrows at me. I roll my eyes back at him, but he gets my attention. "And, I'm not stopping you guys going to The Paradise Club either, so don't worry, brother, there's plenty of time for you to wet your dick." As he says this, he throws a seven in craps and wins a shitload of money. Mind you, we have also lost a shitload of money as well.

We're currently in the high-rollers section of one of the casinos in Monaco. Christian's bright idea for a bachelor party was to 'James Bond' it up here. We're all dressed in monkey suits and basically throwing away large sums of money. At least Nate was here and had his super yacht filled with beautiful women to distract us.

"Angel," Christian calls out when he sees Vanessa enter the room. So much for guy time! My brother runs and picks up his wife, twirling her around, making her laugh. Evan has made his way over to Sienna and is kissing her, whispering things into her ear, making her blush. A tiny little pang of jealousy hits me, but I push it away.

Then my eyes fall on a petite brunette who Derrick has his arm wrapped around. *Who the hell is she?* I have never seen her before, but mind you, I haven't met all of Vanessa's friends. She's so tiny—in heels, she only makes it to Derrick's shoulder. They are laughing together. Her cheeks are pink, maybe from one too many cocktails. *Who is she?*

While Derrick has her attention, I take my time looking her over. She's wearing a red mini dress that shows off her curves, has long brown hair that falls like silky threads. I'm itching to wrap it around my hand and pull on it, maybe while I'm fucking her from behind. Her skin is like porcelain, and all I want to do is touch it to see if she feels as soft as she looks.

I shake my head.

No, I can't fuck her.

She's Ness' friend, and that always complicates things, but it doesn't mean I can't admire her.

She turns around, and she sees me, her big, hazel, doe eyes pull me in. We both still as we realize we're staring at one another. Derrick bends down and whispers something into her ear, and I watch as her skin turns pink, and her attention is pulled away again.

"So, how do you know Ness?" I ask Olivia when I get a chance to chat with the beautiful brunette who's caught my attention. She's incredibly quiet, timid even, especially around me. I don't think I'm that scary. Usually, I have the opposite effect on women, and they are always jumping all over me.

"We met through Camryn. She worked on one of my mother's charity functions in London. Cam was doing an amazing job, but my mother can be... well... a little much when it comes to entertaining, and I basically told Camryn to ignore her. Pretty much after that, we became friends.

"I'm best friends with her younger sister, Ivy. She couldn't make it this weekend as she had to go to Dubai for work. She's an interior designer, the best in London."

Olivia takes a breath as she kind of dumped all this information on me, her nerves getting the better of her. I love the fact that I make her nervous, the way she pushes her hair behind her ear and can't quite look at me full-on. She's got my attention without even trying.

"So, your mom does charity work?" I ask.

Olivia looks a little uncomfortable at my question. "Yes, she um... we are... um..." She's tripping over words.

My finger darts out under her chin, making her look at me, her cheeks pink at my touch. "You don't have to answer if you don't want to. I understand fully about keeping some things to yourself." I let my hand fall away.

"I'm surprised you don't already know," she says, giving me a slight smile.

Why would I know, I think to myself?

"Your brother is getting married at my home." She giggles, and my eyes widen. She's the friend who owns the castle.

"You're..." I'm a little speechless.

"I see that you didn't know."

Shaking my head, I reply, "No, all Christian said was a friend of Vanessa's owned a castle, but he never mentioned your name."

"Yes, it's been my family's home for four hundred years."

"Wow." I'm impressed. I don't think my family owns anything even close to that old. "And you live there?"

She nods. "I have my own cottage away from the castle, but yes, I live there. It's rather beautiful with rolling green countryside, peace, and tranquility."

"By yourself?" I just need to be sure she's single. Her eyes lower to the floor. "Yes, by myself." Stuck in a castle by yourself, and here I thought I was lonely. That must be hell.

"What do you do up there?"

"I run our estate."

"Estate?"

She blushes. "Yes, it's what we call our holdings... a castle, some country homes, manor houses, a village... that sort of thing." She shrugs.

"And you run all of it by yourself?"

"Yes, I'd love more help from my sister, but she thinks hard work is boring and would rather reap the rewards." I can hear the disdain in her voice when it comes to her sister, which is interesting.

"Guessing you two don't get on?"

"That's an understatement, but she's the youngest, and my parents like to indulge her."

"Christian's the youngest, and I totally get it."

She laughs. "But you're twins?"

"I'm older by a couple of minutes, and it makes all the difference when you're twins."

She gives me a broad smile. "You totally give off the older brother vibe."

Is she flirting with me?

"Older, wiser, more experienced." I wink, making her blush.

"Liv, come on, we're going dancing," Camryn calls from the dance floor.

She hesitates which makes me feel good. She wants to keep talking to me. We'll have time—the night is still young.

"Go, I'll see you down there. I'm sure we'll be following once the boys are finished here." She nods at me and joins the girls as they disappear out of the high-rollers' section.

"They are a beautiful bunch of women." Nate joins me at the

casino bar. His eyes are equally glued to the girls dancing on the dance floor. I nod in agreement, sipping my beer. "That petite brunette I saw you chatting with is pretty cute."

"That she is." I don't want to give anything away.

"Think she might want to come to The Paradise Club later?" He sips his whiskey on the rocks.

"I'm hoping so." Yes, that would be the perfect place to sample Olivia.

"So, talking about the club, my friend, Sam, who's an investor in the resort, is actually friends with Camryn and has hired her company to organize our launch."

"Really?"

"Yeah, small world. I have known him most of my adult life, and I have never run into her."

I can see that look in his eye. He wants to do more than business with her. "She's not single."

He nods. "Yeah, I've done my research now. I try not to screw around when it comes to business."

This makes me chuckle.

"Yeah, yeah, asshole, I'm just saying we have a working relationship now so… you know nothing would happen."

I nod, but I don't believe him. "And taking her to the club tonight is professional?"

"Probably not for conventional businesses, but I need to know that she's not going to freak out when she comes to the resort. The last thing I need is some uptight prude to make my guests uncomfortable."

He has a solid point, but the way Camryn and Vanessa are gyrating on the dance floor, I'm pretty sure he has nothing to worry about. I turn and look at him, and he's mesmerized by what he is seeing. Most men are.

"You guys go, I'm heading back to the hotel with Ness." Christian has his arms wrapped around Vanessa, nuzzling her neck. I need to stop being such a dick because my brother is happy. I mean, if he wants to stay with one woman for the rest of his life, then who am I to rain on his parade.

"I'm going back with Sienna, too," Evan adds. He's another one that shocked me. Evan was the worst of all of us, and he wasn't much into any of the kinks at The Paradise Club, but he was definitely into the free pussy. One look at Sienna, and he was a goner.

How the hell can my boys be dropping like flies?

At least Finn and Oscar are still going strong in bachelorhood. Maybe not so much Finn because he keeps hooking up with Isla, which I know is supposed to be some massive secret. I'd be pissed if I found out my best friend had been hooking up with my little sister all these years behind my back. I think Oscar is going to freak when he finds out. I still can't believe they have gotten away with it for this long, but I try and stay out of my friends' sex lives.

Well, not entirely true. A while ago, Oscar asked me to join him and Stacey at the club. She wanted to experience something that Oscar couldn't do alone. Oscar set boundaries, I kept to them, and we all had fun. We have done it a couple of times since, but it's just fun, nothing more. Stacey is a lovely girl. She's also beautiful, but I'm not interested in her.

I need and like control in the bedroom. I love it. I know there's a fucked-up reason why I like it, but that was a long, long time ago and something I don't want to dwell on. Shaking those dark thoughts from my mind, my eyes land on Olivia.

She has a British accent—hottest fucking thing in the world—and I think I could just come from listening to her. According to Derrick, she's royalty. I knew she had an estate, but I didn't realize it was because she was a royal. I thought she was just rich and came from old money. That's why Derrick keeps calling her princess. She's definitely not one, so she tells us. She's a lady and one day will be a duchess when she takes over the estate from her father. It's not like we haven't met royalty before, but none that were this hot.

I haven't been able to get back to her to continue chatting. Once the girls were on the dance floor, that's kind of where they stayed. I did notice that she kept taking sneaky looks my way during the night. And any time I caught her, her cheeks would turn pink. Fuck, if that didn't get my dick hard. I started to imagine what other things I could turn pink or what I could do to her to keep those rosy cheeks pink. My imagination is limitless.

"Limousines are waiting downstairs for us to take whoever would like to go to The Paradise Club," Nate tells the group. The boys are interested, and Isla, Stacey, Camryn, Yvette, and Olivia are coming as well. The girls say their goodbyes to Vanessa and Sienna and jump into the limousine. I find a spare seat beside Olivia, and when I sit down, I hear her gasp when my long leg touches her exposed thigh. *I affect her—nice.*

You can't touch. Remember that, Axel, *friends are off-limits.* I tell myself that's my mantra, even though I'm intoxicated by her fruity scent as we drive the small distance to the club.

"Axel, wait up," Derrick calls for me as the others follow Nate and head inside the club. "I need to talk to you."

"No, Derrick, you can't watch me."

"Cute, but one of these days, Mr. Taylor, I'm going to see you in action," Derrick flirts. "But right now, I need a favor."

"No, you can't suck my dick."

"Geez, you're full of sass tonight, Axel."

I give him a look.

"Ooh, the brooding Axel Taylor stare… it just gave me goosebumps."

His words make me laugh. "Okay, D, I'm all ears."

"Well, it has to do with princess Olivia."

Again, his words get my attention. "I know, hands off."

Derrick laughs. "Actually, I'm kind of asking for the opposite. I want your hands all over her."

I stare at Derrick, and I'm pretty sure I didn't hear him correctly. "What did you say?"

"She'll kill me for this, but I'm doing my civic duty to make sure everyone has a good time."

It's hard to follow Derrick when he's sober, and it's even harder to follow his train of thought when he's tipsy. He leans in and starts to whisper, but it's not as quiet as he thinks.

"Liv isn't very experienced, and well, most of the men she has been with have *not* treated her very nicely." I bristle at his words. "They have, you know, kind of ridiculed her for not being experienced."

"What the fuck!" Running my fingers through my hair, I become furious. Men can be such dickheads.

"She also said they were pretty crap in bed, and she's the only one that can give herself an orgasm." The words tumble out of his mouth quickly.

He can't say those kinds of things to me. I'm not meant to touch friends.

"Why me?"

"You're Axel Taylor, and there's no chance that you want anything more." His answer kind of pisses me off since maybe one day I could want more if I found the perfect woman. *As if that's going to happen.* Most women are after my money or the kudos of fucking me, so yeah, maybe Derrick is right. I don't want anything more.

"But I don't get what you're asking of me?"

"I need you to be her teacher, maybe not of the super kinky stuff that I know you like." Derrick gives me a smirk. "But, basically, give her a fucking orgasm. The poor girl needs it."

"I think I can handle that."

"You're such a giving man, Axel. But I must warn you, it's been two years since she last slept with someone."

"What?"

"Olivia has taken over her family's huge estate. Her family has owned it for like four hundred years or some crazy shit like that. She's like the first female descendant to get the estate. It was going belly up, so she took it over two years ago. It's in the middle of fucking nowhere with nothing but probably sheep around to entertain her, but she has turned it into this swank wedding venue. Hence, Ness and Christian's wedding is taking place there. That doesn't leave much time for you know… a good time because, as I said, she's surrounded by sheep and probably a shit-ton of ghosts."

Derrick is rambling, but I think I get the gist of what he's saying. She hasn't had sex in ages because she's super busy and lives in the middle of nowhere.

"How do you know if she is even interested?"

Derrick rolls his eyes. "You do own a mirror, don't you?" The question throws me, but I nod in agreement. "Well, then, hello… of course, she's going to want to jump on the Taylor train."

"Does she know about this?" I don't want to scare the poor girl.

"Kind of… no, not really, but maybe. I think she thinks I was joking when I suggested it, but I wasn't joking when I made her jerk off one of the strippers tonight, so I'm guessing she knows I'm not joking about this."

I still. "What did you say?"

"Well, Ness wasn't going to enjoy her bachelorette strippers, and I didn't want the three of them to go to waste."

"Three of them?"

"Oh, she only jerked off one… I didn't want to push her. God, baby steps, Axel."

"You're telling me that little miss innocent jerked off a stripper tonight?"

"She didn't finish it because, you know… we don't all need

to see that. I did offer the three of them to her for the night, but she declined. Luckily, one of them swung both ways, so I was able to get my money's worth." D

I shake my head because this chat is ridiculous. Mind you, most drunk chats with Derrick are.

"Anyway, enough about that, so are you still okay with helping her out? I mean the girl is stunning, and if I weren't gay, I'd totally tap that."

"Um... yeah, she's pretty."

"Hey, don't go all shy on me now, Axel. I saw the way you were eye-fucking her all night. Don't make out like this little request is going to be a hardship on you. Oh, ha-ha... something is going to be hard tonight."

"Please, stop talking. Fine, come on, but let me do it my way, okay?"

Derrick salutes me, and we walk into the club.

3

OLIVIA

What the hell am I doing at a sex club? It definitely doesn't look like some seedy, run-down place I envisioned a sex club to be like. This is nothing short of luxurious.

"Please select your bands for the evening," a beautiful hostess informs us.

"Bands?" I ask, looking confused.

"They are to tell people what you're into," Axel states behind me, making me jump. God, the man is so beautiful. With his caramel brown, shoulder-length hair currently pulled back into a man-bun, he looks gorgeous. Most days in his normal rock-star gear, he looks gorgeous—come on, who doesn't know who Dirty Texas is, they are everywhere—but tonight he's in a tuxedo that's molded to his muscles. The man could walk the runway for Tom Ford in that kind of suit. Oh, and his whiskey-colored eyes, the ones that pull you in and make you want to drop to your knees and do bad things to him. *Huh, what? Where did that come from?* Five minutes in a sex club, and I have already turned into a deviant.

"Now this one…" he holds up a pink band, "… this is if you like to play with women." He slips it over his wrist and pushes one toward me, and I shake my head. "Okay, so no girl-on-girl action. Such a shame, it's pretty hot to watch." I gulp because his voice is like silk and sin wrapped together, and it makes me want to please him.

"I've never been with a woman," I squeak out, not sure why I needed to tell him that.

"Have you ever wanted to play with a woman?"

"Haven't thought about it."

"Being with another woman is different than being with a man. She's softer, gentler, and she understands what turns you on. From a man's point of view, two beautiful women exploring one another is one of the most erotic things a man can see."

My body is humming, listening to Axel's words—it sounds kind of hot, but the inner prude in me pulls me back. *No, ignore it!* Remember you said this weekend is all about the new Olivia, the one who puts a pink band on her wrist to please a hot rock star in a sex club.

Axel quirks a brow at me. "I don't want to push you into something you aren't ready for."

I shake my head. "You painted an interesting picture for me."

Axel just stares at me, then shakes his head as if coming to his senses. "Blue is you play with men." He hands me the blue band. "White is no sexual intercourse, but all other play okay." He holds the white band in his fingers, and my heart is thumping.

Do I want to have intercourse with him? Well, of course.

But do I want to have intercourse with someone else? I'm not sure.

"Do what you feel comfortable with, Olivia." I hand him back the white band, and he smirks at me. He hands me a red band. "This means happy for intercourse." I quickly pop it on my wrist.

"Now things are getting a little more interesting with these next bands." My heart is thumping. What more could there be? "Yellow is if you would like to play with one person." I take it without thinking. "But the green one here is for multi-play." I still, and he twirls the band around.

Remember why you're here, Olivia. You're here to go wild, crazy, have fun, and get experience. Then, you can go back to your boring old life in your gilded cage. I take it from him and slip it on.

"Interesting." He smiles. "Now this one, I like." He slides the purple one to me. "Means you'll play in public."

I stiffen. "I'm not going outside on the street to do anything."

He chuckles. "No, darlin'. Once you're in the club, you are in, and only super select people get to come in here. You're perfectly safe. But public play is maybe on a stage."

Gulp. On a stage...

"Or maybe in a room, and there are many people around just enjoying watching you receive pleasure."

Gulp again. Having people watch me have sex...

"Or maybe you would like to go into the glass cube and let many people watch you. I bet you would have a crowd before you knew it. Everyone would want to watch you come."

Gulp, gulp, gulp. Glass cube? His words are heating my skin.

Remember, Olivia, you only live once. I grab the band.

"Orange is for play behind closed doors." He hands me that one. "And there's one more, but it's missing. It's black, and it is for staff. Now, staff who wear just black, they don't play, but staff who wear black with colors, they are allowed to play."

"What? You can sleep with the staff?" I didn't mean to yell that out so loudly, and it makes him laugh.

"Yes, most are professionals, so you're guaranteed a good time."

"So, you like this?" I shake my bands at him.

"Very much, very much indeed." Those whiskey eyes trail over my body. I can't believe I let Derrick talk me into this dress. I look like a slut, which is, of course, what he was going for. My tits are practically hanging out, and I don't have big boobs to start with. I thought he was a big-time stylist, and he puts me in this. At this moment, Axel's eyes are very much stuck on my mediocre breasts spilling out of the dress—maybe Derrick does know what he's doing.

"Hey, how are you doing?" Stacey wanders over, breaking Axel's gaze.

"I'll leave you ladies." Axel moves away and heads to where the others are standing.

"Are you excited?" Stacey asks.

"I'm so nervous."

Stacey laughs. "I know, everyone is the first time. I was, and then I had multiple orgasms and soon chilled out." We both laugh. I think I could handle that. "So, Axel seems interested," Stacey states.

My eyes find his as he talks to the boys. He winks at me and goes back to his conversation.

"He makes me nervous."

"Don't be. Axel is a sweetheart. He's very careful and considerate and the best person to walk you through this new adventure you're on tonight."

"But he's so... experienced." I sigh, feeling totally inadequate, especially when a beautiful, elegant woman walks past and captures every male's attention. "How can I compete with that?"

"You don't. This isn't a competition, Liv. This is about fun, safe sex, and exploring things you wouldn't normally do." Maybe Stacey is right, and I need to forget all about my hang-ups. Tonight is the only night in my entire life to experience something so far out of my realm. Maybe I can pick up some tips, so when I have to be with Eddie, I can surprise him with tricks of my own. *Ugh, I don't want to think of Eddie.*

"Okay, you're right. Let's do this," I tell her as we follow the rest of the crew inside.

Wow, this place is impressive. It looks like an old yacht club. The walls are white-washed with wood paneling, blue and white striped couches, and old driftwood sculptures. The bar is made to look like the hull of a ship and totally different than everything I ever thought a sex club would be like.

"The one in LA is completely different than this. It has a Gatsby theme about it, but this is very Mediterranean," Stacey whispers to me.

"Ladies, what would you like to drink?" Nate, the owner of The Paradise Club and good friends with the Dirty Texas boys, asks us. "Cocktails, champagne, beer?" He looks to us.

If you asked for a tall, dark, and handsome man, then he'd be it—brown, almost black hair, tanned skin, probably from spending his days laying in the sun. I bet he has no tan lines as well, probably from being naked on a yacht somewhere surrounded by women in bikinis. Nope, scratch that, they'd all probably be naked as well, and I'm sure he knows how to give them multiple orgasms. *What's wrong with me?* I have never had so many sexual thoughts in my life. Maybe that's what's wrong with me.

"Hit us with your best cocktails." Camryn decides for us. Nate gives her a smirk and talks to the bartender, the incredibly good-looking bartender. He looks like he could've walked off the runway in Milan and straight into this club. It's not long before I notice the colored bands on his wrist as he busily makes our cocktails. I watch the muscles in his arms twist and turn as he throws the shaker around.

Moments later, we're handed the most beautifully decorated cocktail I have ever seen. I take a sip, it's amazing, and before I know it, it is almost gone.

"You might want to slow down. You're going to need your wits about you tonight," Axel whispers as he passes by to grab another drink. His hand lightly touches the curve of my back, the tiniest connection, and my body feels on fire. Maybe I should slow down—my face already feels hot.

"Most of you know how the club works." Nate looks at our group. "But for those who don't, this level we're on now is for relaxing. There's to be no full playing going on down here, meaning no sex. If a hand wants to disappear up a skirt, that's fine," he says, giving me a wink. *Oh, that man is hot.*

"There are four levels to the club, and each one has a certain level of comfort. The first level is beginners, the second level is intermediate, and the top floor is experts. So just remember that, and you won't stumble into something more than you can handle." Again, Nate looks at me. I get it... I'm the inexperienced one.

"If you'll excuse me, Camryn and I have a meeting." Camryn smiles and disappears with Nate.

"Okay, well, I'm ready to go check things out," Derrick says excitedly.

Oscar and Stacey have already disappeared, Finn, Isla, and Yvette are talking at the bar, and that leaves Axel, Derrick, and me.

"Hey, Ax, do you mind keeping an eye on my princess while I go find myself a prince?" Derrick chuckles.

"Of course." Axel looks at me, and it sends shivers down my body. I'm so nervous but also a little bit excited.

"Okay, well, have fun, kids. Don't do anything I wouldn't do, which is pretty much nothing, so…" Derrick bounces away energetically and disappears up a staircase.

"You look nervous." Axel turns to me.

"I kind of am," I confess.

"You know you don't have to do anything at all, you can just watch." My eyes widen. "Watching is kind of hot." A dirty smirk plays on his face.

"Might be a good place to start… maybe." I gulp down any apprehension I have and take the hand he holds out for me, linking our fingers together.

4

AXEL

Having Olivia's hand in mine feels nice yet strange. I can't remember when the last time was that I held a woman's hand as we walked. I'm going to say never. There isn't one memory in my mind where I think I ever held a woman's hand other than my mom's. That sounds kind of sad, but that's just not the type of guy I am. *So why am I doing it now?* Because Derrick asked me to look after her, to protect her, and to teach her. Maybe that's it—my protective instincts have kicked in.

The security guard scans the membership band on my wrist to check-in and does the same for Olivia's guest band. We ascend the first set of stairs. The higher we go, the tighter her grip is on my hand. I like the fact that she trusts me to look out for her. *Remember, you're doing Derrick a favor, nothing more.*

We reach the top of the stairs, and Olivia lets out a gasp which makes me smile. Right in the middle of the floor is a huge glass cube room, and inside there's an orgy going on. I try to move her forward, but her feet are firmly planted to the floor.

"Olivia," I call out to her, but she's so zoned out she doesn't hear me.

"Olivia," I say her name again, trying to snap her out of whatever is happening in her mind, but still nothing. I step in front of her, my large form shadowing her, and this pulls her away from what's happening in the cube.

"Hey, stay with me. Are you okay?" I let my hand cup her cheek, my thumb gently rubbing across her soft skin. God, it's so soft. She shivers at my touch, and my dick responds. *Easy, boy, it's going to be a while before any action can happen, if any.*

"Sorry, I just wasn't expecting that." Those doe eyes stare widely at me.

"I guess for someone new, it could be confronting." My thumb caresses her cheek, the same cheek that now has a pink tinge to it.

"But I want to ask you something, and I want you to be honest with me. Can you do that?" I pause for a moment before she nods her head in agreement. "Good, did it turn you on?"

Olivia stills, and I can see her mind thinking over my question. "Um..." She rolls her plush, pink lip between her teeth nervously, and I want to suck on it. Maybe later I'll get a chance, and if I'm really honest, it kind of excites me. I don't remember the last time a woman excited me. I mean it's stimulating when I come to one of these clubs and have some fun, but the women here know exactly what they want and what to do. I guess you could say the sex, even though it's adventurous, is kind of the same.

Fuck, what's going on with me? Why the fuck is my head running away with crazy-ass thoughts? Now isn't the time to be having some sort of sexual life crisis. I can see she's having an inner battle with herself. She's a good girl, who wants to try some of the dark side, and she isn't sure if she should like it, but she does.

I pull my hand away, and the tiniest of frowns forms across her forehead, making me chuckle. I move behind her, place my hands on her shoulders, and lean down and whisper in her ear, "Tell me, Olivia, do you like what you see?"

I'm forcing her to look back at the cube. I want her to really take in what she's seeing, to push her to move past all the insecurities, social hang-ups, and innocence she has going on in her head, and just take in the sexual liberation side of her brain—the portion that registers that what she's seeing actually turns her on.

"Do you like the way the men have their hands all over that woman? Do you like that they are worshiping her incredible body? That they are taking their time with her, each one of them exploring every inch of her? Do you like how one man is lapping at her pussy like she's the sweetest thing he has ever tasted? Do you like the way she wriggles on the table, the way one of her hands tangle in his hair, pulling him close into her, pushing him against the spot she knows is going to have her exploding all over his tongue?"

I watch as Olivia swallows hard, her delicate throat moving against my breath. She's turned on. I know it, and I bet if I felt her, she'd be wet.

"Or do you like how the other man is sucking on her tits, using his teeth, the sharp sting of them against the cool heat of his lips, soothing her? Do you like the way his fingers twist her peaked nipple, turning it around and around, a little bit of bite adding to her pleasure?"

Another swallow. I'm fucking turned on, and my dick is rock hard against my tuxedo trousers. I let my lips touch her heated skin, and she gasps but still doesn't move. My lips make their way down her throat, then back up again until I reach that sensitive area behind her ear.

"Or maybe you like the way she has the third man's cock in her mouth, the way she's gagging on his thickness, and the way she loves the saltiness of his pre-cum? She's a good girl sucking him all the way down her throat. Are you a good girl, Olivia? Will you suck my cock all the way down your throat?"

My teeth sink into the fleshy globe of her ear, sucking on it, loving the way my words are making her squirm. Now, I press my hard self against her. Her gasp is audible, but still, she stays watching the scene play out before her.

"Would you like to be that woman? Would you like to have three men worship your body? Or would you rather be blindfolded and not know how many men are touching you and whose lips are on your neck?" I question as I suck on her flesh.

"Or whose hand is on your breast?" I tease as one of my hands comes out and squeezes one of her breasts. She lets out a tiny whimper as my thumb and forefinger find the peaked nipple through the thin fabric and twist.

"Or would you like multiple hands touching your sweet, wet pussy, or maybe touching that virgin asshole?"

She stiffens at the mention of her asshole. Yes, I think I want to be the man who shows her the wonders of anal. I want to be the first person to claim it. My hand just slides along the curve of her ass, my fingers dig into her fleshy globes, and I squeeze.

"You have me so turned on, Olivia, I want to take you right here, and I want to show the room how responsive you are. Your whimpers, your moans, I want to be the one who delivers them, and I want the men and women to be jealous of the way I make you come."

"Axel." My name is a soft moan on her lips.

"Yeah, darlin'."

"I think… I think I'm turned-on now."

Her confession makes me chuckle. "That's good, then. Shall we stay and watch the rest of this, or would you like to see more?"

She pauses for a moment thinking over my request. "I want to see more."

I grab her hand, and we move through the crowd surrounding the cube. There are people in various stages of undress, women and men on their knees sucking their partner's dicks, women with legs spread, and their partners lapping at their folds.

The smell of sex in the air, sounds of moaning, whimpering, and groaning hit our ears the further into the darkness we travel. We head toward one of the long hallways, where strips of neon lights line the floor and light streams in from some open windows.

We stop and look into the windows that don't have their blinds pulled, which means they want people to watch. There are some scenes like naughty schoolgirls getting fucked by the teacher while students look on as they jerk off. That is one of my favorites. Some of the other rooms are just sex—a couple enjoying people watching them and another room where they are enjoying multiple partners.

All the while, Olivia is still notably quiet, taking it all in. But for me, I'm dying. My dick is painfully hard pressed against the seam of my trousers. I need relief, but I have to be patient. My time will come, but only when she's ready. We get to the end, and there's a spare room.

"Shall we go in?" I ask her, making sure she's still with me on this adventure. She slowly nods her head. I push the door, and she follows me through. I pull the blinds, so no one can see in, as I'm unsure if she's ready for that. This room has a large, four-poster bed that dominates it, a sofa is to the left, and a sex chair is to its right. There's a chest I know will be filled with goodies, plus a large wooden cupboard which will have more toys for me to use.

"What do you think?" I watch as Olivia's chest rises and falls. Those doe eyes look up at me, and a big smile slowly forms across her pink lips.

"I think... I think this could be fun."

That's my girl.

5

OLIVIA

My heart is racing, but this room doesn't look as scary as I had imagined. It doesn't look that different than the rooms in some homes I've stayed in. Nothing screams out sex club. But I'm assuming underneath the luxury veneer there is. Axel hasn't moved. He's watching me, letting me explore the room in my own time. I open the cupboard, and a tiny gasp leaves my mouth as I stare at the contents contained inside.

"You'll enjoy them," Axel tells me. "I'll make sure of it."

My heart starts to beat quickly, his voice weaving lust through my veins. I pick up what I assume is a flogger and run my fingers over the soft leather. "That would make your ass a perfect shade of pink," Axel adds.

I look up at him and frown. "Why would I want my bottom pink?"

He chuckles. "Oh darlin', you have so much to learn."

My stomach churns, I guess I do. Turning, I put the flogger back into the cupboard.

"Hey." Axel is right behind me, his hands on my shoulder as he slowly spins me around. "What's the matter?"

I can't look at him, so I don't.

"No, eyes on me," he commands, and I slowly meet his wild, whiskey-colored eyes.

"I know I have so much to learn. I hate that I'm constantly a joke to other people because I am inexperienced. And I hate... I hate that I think I have been missing out on things that I might have liked."

Axel just stares at me. Maybe my truth shocks him, but before I can even apologize to him, his large hand reaches out and wraps around my neck. Using his strength, he pulls me closer to him as his lips slam against mine with force. This shocks me. His soft lips are opening mine while his hands are massaging my neck, urging me to let him in. The hesitation I feel all over my body I try to ignore, but Axel Taylor is kissing me. No, he's not just kissing me, he is devouring me.

I think I kind of want to be devoured.

His tongue finds mine, and they dance for a moment, tiny mews leaving my throat as his teeth sink into my lips. The sharp sting of pain is then softened by his tongue. I'm panting when he pulls away.

"You're so damn beautiful, Olivia."

I can feel my cheeks turn pink at the way Axel is looking at me.

"Never apologize for inexperience. Sometimes it's a good thing."

I chuckle. "Ha, yeah, right. Tell that to the men I've been with."

Axel growls, like full-on growls. "You have been with the wrong ones. Ones who don't understand the precious gift they have before them."

Huh, I'm a precious gift? Wow.

This makes me laugh. "Yeah, I know because each one of them has ended up in bed with my more experienced sister." *Oh shit.* That wasn't supposed to come out of my mouth. I don't want Axel to know what kind of loser I am, and my sister steals all my dates.

"What did you say?" Those whiskey eyes glowing with fire at me.

"Nothing, don't worry about it." I try to move away from him, embarrassed. But his hand halts me.

"Your sister has slept with all your boyfriends?"

I sigh. Tonight is supposed to be a one-night stand with a sexy, hot rock star, not a night telling him all the reasons why he shouldn't sleep with me.

"Don't worry about it." I try to move from his grip.

"But I do," he says softly, that tiny little confession calming me.

"But tonight is supposed to be about sex, not my messed-up history with my sister."

Axel gives me a big smile. "There's plenty of time for sex, Olivia, believe me. But I would like to know about your sister."

Of course, he does. He probably wishes my sexually adventurous sister was the one standing here with him and not me.

"Hey." He grabs my face between his large palms. "I'm not interested in your sister."

How the hell did he read my mind?

"Your face gives it all away."

There he goes again. Bugger. He gently kisses each of my cheeks, then lets me go. He walks toward the four-poster bed, sitting down on the fluffy duvet and pats the place beside him. "I want to get to know you."

Confusing thoughts run through my mind, but I silence them and decide to let it go as Elsa from *Frozen* would say.

"Seriously, you want to know?" I ask as I sit beside him. Axel nods his head in agreement. I let out a heavy sigh.

"Penny, that's her name. She's beautiful, the total opposite of me—"

"You're fucking beautiful," Axel interrupts.

I laugh. "Thanks." But I don't really believe him. If he saw Penny, he'd fall for her as well—they all do.

"No, you don't get it, do you? You're one of the most beautiful women I have ever met." His honest words steal my breath. "Has no one ever told you how beautiful you are?" he questions.

"No, not when my sister is standing with me. She kind of glows, whereas I'm kind of just... well, not as glowy compared to her."

Axel scoffs at my answer but doesn't interrupt again.

"Penny gets jealous. She likes the limelight to be on her all the time. She also wants what I have and has always gotten it. When we were younger, it was my toys, and as we got older, it was boys." Axel's hand reaches out and rests on my knee, sending goosebumps over my skin. "Each boy I have ever dated or has become serious she has slept with. It wasn't hard to find this out either." My throat has a knot in it. I don't like exposing myself like this.

"She sounds like a bitch."

Axel's comment makes me laugh, a deep belly laugh. Not sure why I find it so funny. It's probably all the nerves finally coming out of me.

"You'd be right, she is. But she's still my sister." I shrug because you can't pick your family. We both sit there in silence for a couple of moments.

"She's jealous of you, you know that? Not because you have things, but because there's something about you that draws people in. You are fascinating, you are beautiful, and you are good. Men just know that you're the woman they want to bring home to their mothers, a woman they want to marry, to have a family with. They look at you with their heart." I blush at his compliments.

I still and look at him. This conversation has gotten a little more serious, but he isn't looking at me, he's staring at the floor.

"But men look at your sister with their dicks. And most of the time that wins out."

"Or they just see a boring life of missionary with me and a life full of sex romps with my sister."

"That gets boring fast."

"Are you bored?"

Axel's silent for a moment lost in his thoughts. "Yeah, maybe I am."

"Does seeing Christian settle down change things for you?"

He turns and looks at me, those whiskey eyes flickering with something that I see in my own—loneliness. It's only there for a moment until they turn molten, and I watch as Axel's body changes. The next thing I know, I'm pinned under him, my back sinking into the fluffy duvet.

"I guess we're both looking for the same thing tonight," he whispers into my ear as he grinds his arousal against my body.

"Yeah, and what's that?" My mind is fogging up as his hands glide over my skin, tiny sparks of heat pulsating through my body.

"Not to be lonely." He stares at me, his full weight against me, those skillful hands tracing lines along my body.

"One night, Axel. One night, I don't want to be me anymore," I confess.

"I can help you, Olivia. Let me help you," he groans as he slowly grinds against me.

"Yes," I whisper as my hands automatically remove his tuxedo jacket. "Please, help me." Letting my hands run over his taut back, I feel every muscle straining against his shirt.

"Thank fuck, I need you, Liv. I can't wait, please don't make me wait. I need to sink so deep inside of you, it hurts."

I can hear the strain in his voice and feel the tension vibrating through his body.

"Take me, Axel." Those words are like a bomb has exploded between us. Hands and lips crash against each other, furious fingers pushing material off heated bodies, teeth clashing against their counterparts, and breasts pushed against hard muscles. I have lost my shoes at some point, and not long after, my dress is undone and falling away from me, all the while Axel is grinding against me, his heavy dress shoes hitting the tiled floor. My hands reach down for his belt, quickly undoing it as he concentrates on getting his dress shirt off. I wasn't able to wear a bra with this dress, just a tiny G-string.

"Fuck, your tits. Your tits are fucking natural and perfect," Axel groans as his lips wrap around one of my nipples. Pure white heat shoots through my body, and teeth gently tug my sensitive nipple, making me groan. Large palms tenderly play with my breasts.

"Best tits I have ever seen," Axel mumbles against them as he spends some time sucking and biting them. I close my eyes as the sensations are overwhelming. No one has ever lavished my breasts with so much attention before—maybe a couple of hard gropes but not this, not this reverence he's showing them. It's too much, and I could possibly come from his attention on them.

"Liv, please let me inside of you," Axel growls into my ear. My legs open on their own for him, letting his hips wedge against me. Now I can feel him, feel his want directly against my need. One of his hands disappears, and I can hear him rummaging around in the bedside table.

"Take your underwear off. Now," he demands before he goes back to my breasts. My arms aren't long enough to get to them, so I shimmy and wiggle, but I can't reach them. Then without warning, they are ripped down my legs. Within seconds, and ever so slowly, Axel is sinking deep inside of me.

Holy Shit! This man is splitting me in half.

What the hell does he have between his legs?

Can your hymen grow back after being vacant for so long?

"You're so fucking tight," Axel groans against me. "Your pussy is strangling me."

"Sorry."

Axel grabs my face, those whiskey eyes swirling like fire. "Never, ever apologize for being so fucking tight. It's the hottest thing I have ever experienced. You feel like paradise."

He's serious. Whatever I'm doing, he likes, so I nod in agreement.

"Believe me when I say your pussy is one of the best."

Should I be proud of that fact? This is Axel Taylor, lead singer for Dirty Texas, the hottest band in the entire world. He's a man women lust after, dream about, and fight over. He features in most women's fantasies, and he's here with me, telling me things that no man has ever told me before.

And I think I believe him.

6

AXEL

Shit, fuck, holy crap! Olivia is so fucking tight, it's like she's a virgin. I fucking love it. Now, I don't want to brag, but my dick is kind of big from what the chicks tell me. I'm guessing the men Liv has been with have, well, not been this big. God, I kind of wish I could feel her tight cunt bare.

What? Hold up a minute. *What the fuck am I thinking?* Never in the history of ever have I wanted to ride a chick bare. *EVER! Why the fuck am I thinking about it now?* Because that sweet pussy is choking my dick and making my balls ache like they have never ached before doesn't mean I have to throw everything like that out the window.

What kind of punk-ass, dumb-ass am I? I know that's how you end up with a kid and some gold digger taking you for all your money. But Olivia is rich. She's royalty. She probably has more to lose by getting knocked up by me than I do.

What? Why the fuck am I thinking about knocking up Olivia? No, no, no. I think I'm having a mental breakdown in the middle of some of the best sex of my life, and in missionary, for God's sake. Is this how Sienna, Vanessa, Stacey, and Isla weaved their magic with my boys? Now I get it, magic pussy does things to you. It makes you crazy.

Why the hell am I talking to myself while I'm fucking her?

"Yes," Olivia purrs, bringing me back out of my mind.

"Yes, shit, this feels so good," I moan as I pump into her. My eyes are closed, and I'm lost in her. I am about to come, and I have only been fucking her for five minutes. Five fucking minutes. I'm disgusted with myself. No, this is just the warm-up. I just needed her, the pent-up sexual chemistry between us was too much. *Why the fuck are we in missionary?* I don't remember the last time I was fucking in missionary. What's going on? I'm losing my mind.

"Oh my God," Liv groans as I find her magic spot. The place I know my dick finds because of its length. I concentrate on hitting that target over and over and over again. Oh shit, her pussy just got tighter. Is it cutting off my blood flow? I don't know, I think I'm seeing stars.

"Oh my God," Olivia screams as she comes hard.

Sweat is trickling down my body, my balls tighten, and I feel it—the orgasm quakes my entire body as I come. My body convulses from the intensity. I roll her on top of me as I'm spent. Her pussy has broken me. She squeals as I roll her over me, but it feels good. My hands rest on her lush ass, and I give it a little squeeze. I need to get this condom off before it breaks, but I don't want to pull myself from her.

"That was..." She looks at me in awe.

"Pretty fucking fantastic," I finish, and she nods enthusiastically.

"Want to do it again?" My dick twitches inside of her as she raises her eyebrows.

"You can go again so soon?" she questions me.

"Well, give me at least twenty minutes, and yeah, I most definitely could go again, especially if it's as good as it just was."

"It was good for you?" I can see the vulnerability in her eyes. Fuck, what douchebags has she been sleeping with?

"Darlin', you made me come like a damn teenager, so yeah, it was pretty fan-fucking-tastic." She smiles, and I can already see her confidence lift.

"Coming from you, that's a big compliment." Her statement makes me cringe a little, even though it's true. I'm not sure why now I am with her that my manwhore status bothers me. Maybe I need to see someone. I really don't understand what's going on in my head. It's all messed up at the moment. I slap her pert ass.

"Get up, sweetheart. I need to get rid of the condom."

She quickly jumps up and pulls the sheet over her.

"Hey, don't cover yourself. I need to see you, all of you." She smiles weakly, the confidence taking a small hit. I pull the sheet down, exposing her tits. "Perfect, let me get rid of this, and I'll be back to inspect more of you."

Jumping up, I quickly get rid of the condom in the special condom bins in the bathroom and return. Those doe eyes watch my semi-hard dick bounce as I walk toward her. When she realizes I have caught her staring, she looks away. "You can look all you want, sweetheart." The pink flush is back across her cheeks.

"I just..." she stutters.

"The night is young. I want you to get used to looking at me freely, just the same way I do you." I stay where I am standing, not joining her on the bed. "Liv, I'm all yours." *Why did that statement make my stomach somersault?* "For the night," I quickly add, more for my benefit than hers.

She sits up on her knees and moves closer to me, making my heart race. Maybe I'm sick? That has to be the only reason I'm being weird. She sucks her bottom lip between her teeth, and my dick twitches, which makes her smile. She reaches out a tentative hand and wraps it around my cock.

"It feels so..." She doesn't finish her words as her hand

glides over my cock. Those hazel eyes are staring at my dick like it's a priceless work of art. "Can I ask you a question?"

"You can do anything you like if you keep doing what you're doing." My dick starts to stand at attention with each glide across its skin.

"Why do you come to sex clubs?"

I still and stare at her. "I like certain things in the bedroom." She nods, pushing me to continue. "I like control, I must have control in the bedroom." She frowns a little. "Except for tonight." Those hazel eyes look up at me, worry laced behind them. "Tonight, for the first time, I didn't worry about control. I just went with the flow."

"To me, it felt like you were in control," she whispers.

"Believe me, darlin', what just happened is so far from me being in control."

She continues stroking my cock, a perfect rhythm, nothing that's going to make me come but enough that it makes me feel good.

"I want you to control me, Axel." I freeze at hearing her words. "I want you to show me this world." Those eyes again are pulling me in. "I want to experience everything tonight."

"Why?" I know I shouldn't ask a woman why she wants to try everything a sex club has to offer, but I want to double-check she's thinking this through.

"I have one weekend where I'm not me. What we just did was amazing, but now that my nerves have disappeared a little, I want to try more. I need to try more. For the first time in my life, I wasn't thinking about anything other than pleasure. I don't get to do that in my normal life. But the clock is ticking. I feel like Cinderella, and at the stroke of midnight, I'll turn back into a maid and go back to my restrained existence. I need this weekend so I have memories of a life I won't ever get to experience again."

A single tear falls down her cheek, and my thumb comes out and wipes it away.

"Okay then, Olivia. Tell me your deepest, darkest fantasies. Don't feel ashamed. If you want one weekend of doing things you have only ever dreamed of, then don't hesitate to tell me."

Olivia lets go of my dick and chews on her lip some more.

"I want…" Her cheeks turn pink again.

"Tell me." My voice changes to the one I usually use during sex. The one that makes women drop to their knees and give me whatever I want.

"I want to be tied up, maybe even spanked. I want to try all those toys I saw in the cupboard."

"That can be arranged. What else?"

Olivia hesitates, and I can see she's getting to her darker desires.

"I want a threesome." Her eyes quickly look back at the floor. My forefinger touches her chin, making her lift her head toward me.

"You want two men?" I have had many threesomes before, but the thought of sharing Olivia stabs me in the gut. But this isn't about me but about her. If I'm her teacher for the night, I should be able to give her whatever she desires.

"Yes," she whispers.

"Do you want double penetration?" She shakes her head no. "Do you want one in your mouth while the other fucks you?" Olivia nods yes. "Good girl, I think we can arrange that." She gives me a small smile, those cheeks still pink.

"What else do you desire?" My hand comes out and tweaks her nipple, making her shiver.

"Um…" Her neck is now going red. Shit, this next thing she's really embarrassed about.

"I've seen it in porn and well…"

Olivia watches porn. My dick springs to life thinking about that.

"Go on." My finger traces around the bumpy skin of her areola.

"I want to be blindfolded and not know who's fucking me," she quickly spits out. My hand pauses. My girl has a rather kinky side to her, especially with multiple men. I suppose when she's as inexperienced as she says she is, she's trying to catch up.

"How many men?" I question her. Again, her eyes look at the floor. "Look at me when I ask you a question, Olivia," I command. Her whole body responds to my voice, she sits up taller, her nipples pebble, and she moves uncomfortably on the bed.

"Actually, stand up." She quickly follows orders and stands before me. "Open your legs."

She hesitates but only for a second. My hand reaches between her thighs, she's drenched, and my fingers slip between her wet folds. "You're turned on." Those teeth sink into her lips again. I press a finger inside of her, making her moan.

"Tell me, how many men do you want to fuck you while you're blindfolded?" My finger wiggles around inside of her, teasing her G-spot.

"I… I'm… not sure." She stumbles over her words as I move inside of her.

"Would you object if I chose which men it will be?" I add another finger. She shakes her head. "Okay, another fantasy noted. Next?"

Her chest is heaving as my fingers work her over. "Olivia, I asked you a question."

She stills, trying to concentrate. "Maybe… maybe I'd like to kiss a woman."

My hand stops as I look at her. "A woman?"

She nods. "You said that it got you hot… and… I… I… want to please you."

My whole body is struck motionless by her words.

I want to please you.

Why is this woman making me crazy? How does she know what buttons to press? My fingers start again, and this time, I want to please her. In and out, they go easily through her slickness while my thumb strums her clit, and she shudders.

That's it, sweetheart, let go. Let me see you come.

Higher and higher I take her until I feel her pussy clench.

"Axel," she screams, falling forward toward me. I catch her as my fingers still work her over, and goosebumps lace her skin. When she has finished, I take my fingers out of her, her juices glistening in the light.

"Taste yourself."

Olivia's eyes widen, but she doesn't move. I bring my fingers to my lips and let my tongue run along them. "You taste so sweet." Olivia's eyes widen even more. "Here." I place my fingers against her lips, rubbing her sweetness along her bottom lip. A hesitant tongue comes out and tastes them along the same path as my tongue had been, and Olivia licks.

"See, so sweet." Those cheeks turn pink again. "Now suck off the rest."

She opens her mouth, pink lips wrapping around my fingers, and flashes of her lips wrapping around my dick filter through my mind. I need to see if reality is as good as the fantasy that's running through my mind.

"On your knees." Olivia quickly obeys, and fuck, that makes me feel good. "Now, take my cock and suck it until I tell you to stop." Olivia hesitates, her eyes looking at my hard dick. "Have you done this before?" I ask her.

"I tried it once, and he said I was bad," she whispers almost inaudibly.

Tilting her face up to me, I reply, "There's no way in this world that having these lips…" I pause, and my thumb rubs along her plump, pink lip. "Having your lips wrapped around my cock could ever be bad. Do you understand me?"

She smiles slightly but nods in agreement.

"Good, now show me how much you want it." She leans forward and ever so gently wraps her small hands around it. She strokes it a couple of times before her mouth wraps around the aching head of my cock. I let out a hiss which makes her stop.

"No, it feels so good."

My hands grip her hair, pushing her hot, wet mouth around my cock. She takes it in again, her tongue swirling around, caressing the underside of the head, hitting all the sensitive spots. One of her hands moves slowly to cup my balls before she moves them around, giving them a gentle tug, feeling the weight of them. How the hell did any man think this woman was bad at giving head? She's no porn star, but most men don't care as long as someone is sucking it. Olivia is gentle yet hard as she takes me further into her mouth. She tries to deep throat me but gags a little.

Before I can tell her not to worry about it, that most women can't, she tries again. Each time she takes me deeper into her mouth until I'm hitting the back of her throat, and she isn't gagging anymore. My fingers lace in her hair harder when I realize she has taken me all in, and I start fucking her mouth. She has given over control to me. Her hands move to my ass, her fingers digging into the flesh, trying to hold on as I punish her mouth. Saliva is dripping down her chin, her eyes are watering, and her mascara is smudging. Her eyes are closed, and she's the most beautiful creature I have ever come across. I quickly pull out before I come down her throat. I so want to, but I have to wait. We have so much to do tonight.

"Did I do something wrong?" she asks, looking worried.

"You could never do anything wrong when you're kneeling before me." I caress her cheek, wiping the mascara away. "I just wasn't ready to come yet," I tell her with a smirk. Her mouth forms an 'O' in surprise, and then she smiles.

"You, darlin', are just perfect. Don't ever let anyone tell you any different, do you hear me?" Olivia nods.

"Now, would you like to freshen up in the bathroom while I organize what's happening next? Because for the next couple of hours, you're going to be extremely busy."

Olivia's eyebrows raise, but she stays silent.

"I want to give you everything your heart desires this weekend." Leaning down, I give her a heated kiss.

7
OLIVIA

I can't believe I slept with Axel Taylor, and he liked it. Letting the steaming hot water run over my body, I go over the events of a few moments ago. From what Derrick explained, Axel likes to be in control. He also said he thought he was very Christian Grey regarding sex, but up until this moment, I haven't seen any of it. Well, actually, a little at the end when he demanded me to stand while making me come, then telling me to get on my knees and suck him off. I still can't believe I did that. Wow, it was kind of crazy, not something I have ever done before. I kind of liked it.

Maybe Axel has unlocked the inner sex goddess in me.

Ha, as if.

Me, a sex goddess?

No, I need to have more confidence in myself, especially tonight as I'll experience things I haven't before, and I'm going to need to find all my confidence. Bugger! Why did I tell Axel my fantasy? The one I had seen on Tumblr. I mean, they look all hot and sexy in black and white, staring back at me from the computer, but maybe in reality, it isn't like that. Who the hell is Axel going to find to be the third wheel? Do I really want to have sex with more than one man? I mean, Axel Taylor is kind of the holy grail of men. I don't need to downgrade from that.

"Olivia." I freeze at the female voice that greets me through the steam in the bathroom, my heart taking off at a gallop. "It's Stacey." I relax a little.

"Um... hi." Not sure why she's in the bathroom.

"Axel asked me to talk to you about a few things."

Ah, okay, that makes sense.

I turn off the faucet, and a fluffy white towel surprises me through the shower curtain. "Thanks," I say timidly, quickly wrapping the towel around me. I pull back the curtain, and the perky blonde is standing before me. She's dressed in a black silk nightdress that shows off her generous cleavage, killer black heels that show off her long legs, and her blonde hair is pulled up into a high, tight ponytail. I notice a beautiful collar around her neck, the jewels catching under the bathroom light. She's beautiful. All of Vanessa's friends are, and it can be a tad overwhelming being around all of them. Stacey gives me a warm smile, her blue eyes sparkling with mischief as she looks at me.

"So, you and Axel, hey?"

I'm blushing, I know I am. I can feel the heat rising over my skin.

"He's just helping me," I squeak.

Stacey's eyes take me in. "Maybe, but—"

"But what?" Panic rises through me.

"Nothing bad, just from what he has told us, he hasn't stuck to his normal rules, that's all." I still. "No, no, it's a good thing." She tries to reassure me, but I'm not sure.

"Here." She hands me an identical slip like hers. "Axel requested no underwear." She smiles as I take the silky material from her hands. I turn my back to her, slipping the material over my head, then letting the towel fall so I can pull it over the rest of me.

"Liv, don't be shy now that I'm here. Axel wanted me to

explain things because I have requested the same style of fantasy that you have."

Her confession grabs my attention. "Which one?"

She smiles. "The multiple men and women." I take a shaky breath.

"And?"

"They were fun. Oscar organized Axel to play with us. He wanted someone we both trusted."

I freeze, my stomach twisting in knots, knowing Stacey has been with Axel.

"Hey." She notices my reaction. "I'm not interested in him, he just helped with my experience, that's all." I nod, trying to process everything. "Plus, Axel has asked Oscar to help repay the favor."

Now, panic seeps in. "What?"

Stacey giggles. "You'll like it, trust me on this. They'll both give you what you want."

"And you're okay with this? Sharing your boyfriend?"

"What? No, Oscar isn't my boyfriend. We just like playing together at the club, that's all. Outside of these walls, we're free to do what we like with whomever we like."

Wow, that sounds kind of progressive. Not sure if my Englishness is quite up to that level of sexuality yet.

"He has also asked me if I mind being the woman as well."

I can feel the red-hot heat of embarrassment from my request seeping into my skin. Stacey is beautiful, but could I do something with her? I'm not sure, maybe, I mean, I'm not into women, but I can most definitely appreciate one.

"Do you like women?"

She smiles. "I like playing with women now and again, but I'm mostly straight." I nod, feeling a little awkward in this situation.

"And you would want to do something with me?" I don't think she should be forced to do something if she isn't into it.

"Olivia, you're stunning, plus your body is all kinds of insane, but if you don't want to do this, then that's okay. If you think it will change the way we hang out, then don't do this. Things are different when you're at the club, but once you step out of those front doors and back into normal society, most of our desires stay hidden. Well, mine do anyway. I don't shout what I like from the rooftops. It's no one's business, and that's why I'm so happy I found The Paradise Club. I can explore my newfound liberation without fear or worry from the world."

Wow, that makes total sense.

"So, if you want to try anything, and I mean anything, being behind these walls is the best and safest place to experience everything your heart desires. And when you step out of those front doors, know that no one, and I mean no one, will ever talk about it."

The tension in my body relaxes. I didn't know that was exactly what I needed to hear. "I was worried that you know… people can't know I'm here, my family, they would…" Stacey puts a hand on my shoulder and gives it a squeeze, her touch sending tingles over my body, a feeling I'm not used to from a woman.

"You're safe here, okay." I nod in agreement. "So tonight, Axel and Oscar have agreed not to be their normal domineering selves. Tonight, things will happen a little more organically, just until you feel comfortable with these new experiences." She's saying everything I need to hear, and she is calming every fear running through my head.

"Just remember to have fun. I know we spoke about the life you're returning to in England a little at Ness' place. If this is the only weekend in your life that you can be free, then do it. I promise you won't regret it."

Before Stacey realizes it, I wrap my arms around her and hug her. "Thank you. Thank you so much." I pull away from her but notice her cheeks are a little flushed. "I'm glad it's you here with me."

She smiles. "Come on, let's rock these boys' world."

I take in a deep breath and soak up Stacey's confidence.

I *can* do this.

"Ladies?" Axel questions.

Axel is standing before me in just his tuxedo trousers and bare feet, and I can really take him all in. The tattoos that cover his body are blue Japanese-style patterns and incredibly interesting. His body is lean yet muscular with the standard six-pack that all hot men have. I don't think I have been with a man with a six-pack before. Then, I notice the other people in the room. Oscar, his bandmate, is standing there dressed in just his tuxedo trousers as well. The man looks like a damn Viking—he's huge, all muscle and brawn, plus he towers over everyone in the room and is quite intimidating. His blond hair is pulled back in a man bun. I notice the tattoos that decorate his body as well, which I'm guessing is standard rocker attire. I see his ice-blue eyes looking over me hungrily, and he licks his lips. A shiver courses over my body. Does he find me attractive?

I can feel Stacey beside me. She takes my hand and laces it with hers. There's a knock at the door, Axel turns and opens it, muffled conversation happens, and Jackson, their head of security and Finn's brother, enters the room still dressed in his tuxedo. He turns, looks at me, and a small smile laces his face as his bright green eyes rove over my body.

"Liv," Axel calls my name. "This is all who will be present in the room." His words are slow and articulate. "I thought it might relax you to know who was here first, and then we could work up to your top fantasy." The look Axel gives me is asking me if that's the right thing to do, so I smile at him.

"Good. Are you okay with who I have chosen?" I look over at Oscar and Jackson. Who the hell would say no to those two men? They are stunning, hot, and male, and I've run out of words, but there are too many rushing through my head to describe them. "And are you okay with Stacey?" Axel asks. I nod, not daring to look at her just yet.

"I think we should start with this... for nerves." Oscar produces a bottle of tequila, a welcome sight. He walks toward me slowly, his eyes never leaving mine. Stacey has moved behind me, and my heart begins to race.

"Open up," Oscar instructs, the slightest German lilt to his accent coming through. I obey, and the cool, acrid liquid hits my mouth. I swallow it down, the heat warming my belly. "It will help you relax." Oscar smiles at me as he takes a sip from the same bottle.

My eyes flick behind Oscar's large frame to see Axel standing there, his whiskey eyes focused on me. I feel Stacey move behind me, the tips of her fingers running up my arms, making me shiver, and it makes Oscar smile at her.

"Open," he commands, pressing the glass bottle to my lips again. I feel the warmth from the tequila run through my body, but then I feel the softest lips on my neck, lightly kissing me. Oscar licks his lips at the display in front of him. Stacey's hands move along my body, over the curve of my bottom, along my hips, and across my breast making me squeak. Axel has moved forward now and takes a swig from the tequila bottle, his eyes never leaving mine. My body feels like it's on fire, and my mind is blank from so much stimuli.

Jackson now moves to the other side of Oscar and takes a sip from the bottle of tequila. "Would you like one more?" Jackson asks, shaking the bottle in front of me.

I nod. Of course, I do. A woman is touching me, and I think I'm kind of turned on. There are three of the world's most stunning men looking at me like they are ready to devour me—me, little old me—so, yeah, I damn well need the tequila to give me the confidence to keep going with this fantasy because I kind of don't want to stop.

"Yes, please."

Jackson grins and moves closer, placing the bottle against my mouth once again, the liquid not burning so much. Jackson places the bottle on the table beside him, and now I have three men's undivided attention.

What do I do next? Maybe it's the three shots of tequila or the fact that three men are looking at me with hunger in their eyes that I do what I do. Turning my back to them, I grab Stacey's face and plant a kiss on her lips, and she lets out a little surprised yelp. I touch her soft lips—it's different to kissing a man but yet, still the same. The men let out a groan as we continue kissing each other. Stacey is an extremely good kisser, and all I can think about is that damn Katy Perry song, "I Kissed A Girl." The thought makes me giggle, and I break our kiss.

"You okay?" Stacey asks, her pink lips plump from our kiss.

"Tequila makes me giggly."

Stacey smiles. "Follow me," she says, taking my hand, leading me toward the large four-poster bed. My heart is thumping. What's going to happen next? She touches a panel on the wall, and I watch as the bed disappears into the wall. Wow, that's kind of cool. She then pulls down what looks like a padded table from underneath the bed. Slight panic fills me.

"Do you trust me?" she asks. I nod because I do. I trust them all to give me the experience that I'm asking for. She leans in and retakes my lips while her fingers find the thin straps of the black slip I am wearing and starts pulling it down. I hesitate, and she stops. "Are you okay?"

"Sorry, just surprised, that's all."

Stacey smiles, then looks behind me. "Axel, maybe you would like to do the honors?" Her fingers trail down over my peaked nipples as she walks away.

"You okay?" Axel whispers behind me, his hard body pressed against my back.

"Yes," I reply breathlessly.

"Good. I promise you, Liv, nothing bad will happen to you. I'll make sure of it." I relax again, his words soothing me.

"Now, put your hands on the table." I follow his instruction, placing my hands on the soft leather of the table. He kicks my legs wider apart, and the slip rides up and exposes my bottom.

"Perfect." I hear Jackson mumble behind me.

"That ass would look amazing with a shade of pink to it," Oscar adds.

"Don't move, Liv," Axel commands. "No matter what, do not move. Nothing but pleasure is about to happen, even if there's a tiny bit of pain with it." I flinch at the word 'pain.' A hand rests on my back, and I can only assume it's Axel's as I dare not move.

"Stacey," Axel calls out. "She'll need this." I hear Stacey's heels coming toward me. I tilt my head as she stands beside me, and I notice she has a black sash in her hands.

"What's that?"

"A blindfold," she replies.

"Oh," is all I can muster. Blimey, I'm about to be blindfolded. It's what I asked for, but now I don't know.

"Shh, relax, Liv. I promise being blindfolded will heighten the experience... you won't know who's touching you. It could be Stacey, it could be Oscar, or it could be Jackson, and it most certainly will be me," he whispers into my ear. "I promise to make your fantasy all that you have ever dreamed about."

8

AXEL

Holy shit, she looks so beautiful standing there all pink and wet. Oscar started out lightly on her perfect, creamy ass. Light hits with the riding crop, picking the perfect spots for maximum pleasure. He worked his way toward her pussy, and each hit against it made Liv moan, but she never moved a muscle. She's such a good girl.

Watching her and Stacey kiss, fuck me, that's going to keep recurring in my spank bank. I know Stacey was going easy on her, which was good, just a little taste of her desires because she's succumbing to a lot tonight, especially someone with limited experience.

I called upon my friends to help out with Olivia. For starters, I can trust them. Secondly, I know there will be no feelings involved, and lastly, I know they understand how The Paradise Club works.

Oscar and Stacey are pretty tight in the club, and Jackson, well, he's a lone wolf and keeps to himself most of the time, but he has played with Oscar and Stacey before, so he understands the rules. I have shared plenty of girls before while at The Paradise Club, but never one who has affected me so quickly.

I watch as Oscar murmurs things to Liv as he spanks her. Her teeth have been firmly planted into her bottom lip since he started. I wonder what she's thinking. Does she like it? I know her body does. I can see her arousal glistening underneath the lights, but is it something she would like to do again?

That stabbing pain of thinking about her leaving here and experiencing these things with another is back. Maybe I need an antacid—must be all that French food I ate tonight. I turn and notice that Stacey is on her knees, sucking Jackson off. Maybe we need to be moving this along a little more as everyone is turned on. I place my hand onto Oscar's shoulder, letting him know that Olivia has had enough. He takes a step back, and I can see he's turned on too—the tenting in his trousers tells me everything I need to know.

I let my hand run over Liv's pink ass, she flinches at the sudden touch, but I see her relax again. Slowly, I soothe the heat that's radiating off her with my hand. I get closer to her glistening pussy and let my finger slip between her folds. She lets out a heavenly groan. She has no idea whose finger it is inside of her, and I'm not going to let her know either. I pull my fingers away and unzip my trousers, my dick ready to burst. I kick them to the side, along with my briefs.

I touch Liv's back and silently move her to stand. I turn her in my arms, and notice her chest moving quickly with the unknown. She still has the black slip on, so I pull the straps down her creamy shoulders, and the flimsy material falls to the floor. She's naked in front of me, and her beauty floors me. I can't help myself, taking a step forward, I kiss her. Her soft lips open for me, her tongue tastes like tequila, and it dances with mine. She's practically purring with excitement.

I pick her up under her arms, making her squeal, and place her back onto the padded table. Her chest is heaving with excitement and probably uncertainty. I let my fingers run over her naked body, and she shivers at my touch. I pull out arm and leg restraints from the sides of the table. Olivia flinches at the sound. I soothe her skin and whisper to let her know it's going to be okay, that her arms will not be restrained, but her legs will be. I ask her if that's okay.

The room is quiet, waiting for her answer.

"Yes," Olivia whispers.

"Good. I promise you'll like everything that's about to happen to you."

Her head nods as she lets her body relax.

I pull her legs apart, making her gasp, and place her ankles in the restraints. I don't tie them too tight, just enough that she can move.

"Test them." I watch as she tries to lift her feet, and they move an inch. She smiles but stays quiet. I step away from her. Oscar is in the process of kicking off his trousers and briefs while Jackson is undressing as Stacey keeps his dick occupied. Once naked, Oscar turns to me, inclines his head, asking if it's okay to sample Olivia. I give him the go-ahead and just hope this unease in my stomach disappears.

Oscar steps between Olivia's legs, his thick fingers trailing over her skin. I watch as she arches a little against his touch. Stacey has moved away from Jackson and joins Oscar at his side, and her fingers link with Olivia's for support. Jackson moves to the other side of Olivia, his wet dick standing at attention. He takes Olivia's other hand and wraps it around him.

Olivia lets out a startled gasp at the first touch of another naked man. I move now and take my position at Olivia's head. Stacey is moving Olivia's hand all over her body while her other hand jerks off Jackson. Oscar is taking his time, getting her ready. I know when he hits the spot with his fingers as Olivia screams out a moan. I watch as Oscar's fingers move in and out of her wetness, coating his finger in her desire, and the unease I was feeling is passing. I don't need to be jealous of my friends, not when Olivia is making the most beautiful purrs of ecstasy below me. Tonight, we're just enjoying a night of wicked fantasies coming to life.

Fuck, I need to get out of my fucking head. It's not Olivia's fault I'm going through some sort of existential crisis. She has come to me asking for help, and instead, I'm lost in my own thoughts. Shaking my head, I flick the switch in my mind and push down the swirling thoughts I have, reminding myself tonight isn't about me but Olivia, and I'm going to give her what she wants and needs. Tomorrow, when I am alone in my bed, perfectly sated from an amazing night, I can worry about whatever is troubling me, but until then, I will enjoy life.

And so, I do.

Placing my dick against her lips, she flinches for a moment but opens wide—such a good girl. Her creamy fingers are still wrapped tightly around Jackson's cock, his hand tweaking her perky nipples. Stacey is beginning to moan as I notice Olivia's fingers have dipped between her thighs. I reach out, catching her attention. I tell her to take off her black slip, I want to see Olivia's fingers inside her. All of a sudden, Olivia arches her back as Oscar's thumb flicks over her clit.

"Yes, oh God, yes," Olivia mumbles around my dick as she orgasms. Oscar slips his fingers out of her, then offers them to Stacey to lick clean, which she does while his face is buried between Olivia's thighs. This makes Olivia hum against my dick. Shit, that feels amazing.

Moments later, Stacey is coming around Olivia's fingers. It's so fucking hot that I could blow my load down her throat. Jackson grabs Olivia's fingers and sucks Stacey off of them. Olivia starts wriggling again, her back arching off the table, her moans humming against my cock until she screams, this time letting go of my dick in the process.

Oscar lifts from between her legs, his beard wet with Olivia. Stacey looks over at Oscar, the desire for him is written all over her face. She slowly walks toward him, grabs his face, and kisses him. Oscar growls in appreciation. The room smells of sex, and it's the biggest fucking turn-on.

Olivia is panting.

I lean down and whisper in her ear, "How are you doing, darlin'?"

She moans a little, licking her lips. "I want the blindfold off."

The room stills at her request.

"But I thought…"

Olivia chews on her lip for a couple of moments. "I want to watch. I want to watch all of us." That bottom lip is dipping between her teeth, and yet she remains motionless.

I lean down and slowly take off the blindfold.

She blinks a couple of times, her eyes adjusting to the light. The foggy haze of lust slips from her eyes, and she quickly tries to hide her naked self.

My hand comes out to stop her. "No, no, no. There's no hiding, you wanted the blindfold off." She takes in a deep breath and nods. "Good girl, now let me unbuckle you." I walk down to her ankles and start to set her free. I'm impressed that she's willing to try so many things. Maybe she isn't as inexperienced as she has led us to believe, or maybe she needed to meet the right people. Once she's free, I help her sit up and move her off the bench.

"Maybe we should make it a little more comfortable, then." Jackson smirks as I realize Stacey is jerking Oscar off while he surveys the room.

"Good idea," I reply as Jackson lifts the bench, securing it back underneath the bed. We move back, he presses the button again, and the bed comes back down. Once in place, I tap the duvet for Olivia to get on. I join her, pulling her back against my front, her plush little ass nestled against my raging cock. My hand runs down over her goose-pimpled skin, down her legs, and back up between her thighs. I skim the edge of her pussy which makes her gasp. "Sweetheart, concentrate and watch the show."

Jackson joins the other two. Stacey is now bent in half, legs wide open for us to see her gorgeous, wet pussy as she sucks on Oscar. Jackson drops to his knees and buries his face between her legs. She lets out a moan on contact.

Olivia squirms in my arms.

"Do you like watching?" My lips touch her earlobe.

"Yes," she replies breathlessly.

"Do you wish two men were worshiping you like that?"

"Yes," she replies again with the faintest of whispers. My hand moves from her thigh to her cunt, my fingers finding her soaked. I tease her throbbing slit as my fingers push in and out of her tight little pussy.

Oscar has Stacey's hair wrapped around his hand as he fucks her face, and saliva drips down Stacey's chin.

Jackson moves from between her legs and walks over to one of the drawers, pulling out a condom. I know Olivia is watching him as her breathing has increased. Jackson rips open the wrapper and sheaths himself. Returning his hands to Stacey's hips, he turns his face, and his eyes lock with Olivia's as he thrusts into Stacey. She lets out a feral moan at his intrusion. His grip tightens as he continues fucking her.

"Do you like that, darlin'? The way Jackson is looking at you while he's fucking Stacey? Watching the way my fingers work inside of you while his cock works inside of her? The way his thrusts are in time with my fingers. Do you like that?" Olivia is panting now.

"Look at her, I bet you're fucking jealous of her, aren't you?" She nods in agreement. "Being sandwiched between two men, her body filled with two hot cocks. You want to be filled like her, don't you?" Olivia moans again, her body starting to tremble—another orgasm is coming.

"Look at the way she's sucking Oscar's dick. She loves it. Do you love sucking cock?" My fingers continue working inside of her, my movements easy with the slickness. She's so close, so very close. Jackson continues his steady thrusts into Stacey.

"Shit, Stace, you know... I can't last when you do that," Jackson moans. I know exactly what she's doing—kegeling his dick, making her pussy fucking tighter—it sends a man wild. "Fuck, Stace," Jackson curses as he comes. His moans set off Olivia as she comes all over my fingers.

"Such a good girl. Now I think it's your turn." I reach over to the drawer beside the bed and pull out a condom.

"Get up," I tell Olivia. She slowly moves off the bed, and I can see the confusion on her face. I give her a reassuring smile as I quickly sheath myself and pull her back against me.

"Bend over," I command her, and she does what she's told, placing her hands on the bed. I pull her perfect little pussy back against my dick and slowly sink into heaven. Oscar moves forward and offers his dick to Olivia, and she takes it willingly. Movement catches my attention behind him. Stacey has straddled Jackson's face as he finishes what he started. My hand comes out and slaps her ass which makes her choke on Oscar's dick. Oscar laughs, so I do it again, and he groans in appreciation. Stacey is making a lot of noise behind him, and I can tell Liv is trying to watch them while trying to handle Oscar's dick.

My fingers dig into her porcelain skin. I'm probably going to leave bruises tomorrow, but that doesn't matter. She'll remember exactly what happened tonight when she feels them.

"Fuck, Liv. You feel so fucking good." My mind is going hazy as my legs turn to jelly. This woman has worked some kind of voodoo magic over me because I'm so ready to come. If I do, it's going to be embarrassing since I don't ever come this quickly. Olivia does that thing that Stacey does, the kegeling, and that's it. Just like Jackson before me, my balls start to tingle.

"Yes," I scream out.

Oscar has wrapped his hand in her hair and is fucking her face just like he did to Stacey earlier. "Your mouth is so fucking hot, Liv. Fuck," Oscar moans. "I'm about to come." He taps her on the shoulder. "If you don't want to swallow, then you better let me go." Oscar's dick falls with a pop from Olivia's mouth, and he comes in his hand as I continue to fuck her, and just like Oscar, I come seconds later.

My entire body is twitching, aching, liquefied, and my breaths are heavy.

Oscar has disappeared into the bathroom to clean up.

Slowly, Olivia moves away from me, but instead of going to the bathroom, she turns around and pushes me onto the bed while my hand keeps hold of my sheathed dick. She straddles me, my chest still heaving rapidly as she leans down and ever so gently kisses my lips. "Thank you," she says repeatedly. Her feather-light kisses rain all over my face, and those hazel eyes stare at me in wonderment as if I were the sun.

"I'll never forget this night." A small tear falls down her cheek.

"Hey," I soothe as I capture it with my thumb. "Tonight doesn't have to be over." If I'm being honest, I kind of want to get out of here and take her back to a hotel room and continue fucking her.

It's too early to let her go.

I don't want to let her go.

I still have so much I want to do with her.

The sound of doors closing pulls me from my thoughts. I look around, and the room is empty.

Olivia takes in a deep breath, the spell of the night is slowly wearing off. "I'd better go," she says as she crawls off of me. She grabs her clothes and hastily gets dressed.

I quickly go and clean myself up and also get dressed.

We're both dressed but maybe a little more disheveled than we were at the start of the night.

I pull her into my arms. "I don't want tonight to end," I confess.

Olivia frowns but stays wrapped against me. "You want more of The Paradise Club?"

"No, just you and me."

She smiles. "Just me?" she questions, looking like she doesn't believe me.

"Yep, just you. There's so much left to explore with your body."

She smiles at me. "Just for tonight?" she questions me again.

"Probably not. I'm pretty sure I am not going to be able to think about anything else other than you and your perfect pussy."

She gives me a nervous giggle. "So, you want to continue over the weekend?"

I still in her arms. *Do I want all weekend?*

She looks worried, so I grab her face between my palms. "Yes, all weekend. I want you in a bed. I don't care whose bed, preferably yours or mine, but either way, I want to be able to taste you whenever I want. I want to be able to touch you, fuck you, make you scream at any moment."

Her hazel eyes widen at my honesty. "Just the weekend?"

"Yes."

"Okay, I can manage that."

"And if I want more than one weekend?" I ask, not sure why I'm asking, but for the first time in my life, I forgot to think about what was coming out of my mouth. Shit, I better not be turning into Christian as that's something he does.

She gives me a look that answers my question. "One weekend, and that's all," she states.

My usual motto is 'hell, yeah, limited time with a woman, no strings,' but this time I kind of don't want it to end after only forty-eight hours.

She lives in England, I live in America, and nothing can ever happen.

"Deal," I agree and kiss her, sealing it.

9

OLIVIA

"How are you this morning, my dirty little princess?" Derrick coos beside me. We're relaxing in Vanessa's penthouse suite having brunch.

"Good," I answer, not really wanting to go into any more detail with Derrick because his mouth is as big as his personality.

"Mm-hmm." He stares at me. "Something is different about you." He waves his hands in front of me.

"No, I'm still the same old Liv." I hope to put him off the scent because Axel is asleep as we speak. I thought he'd have bolted at first light, but no, he's still there, naked as the day he was born, sprawled out on my bed.

"So did you and Axel, you know… bump uglies?" The question silences the room. I catch Stacey's eye across the room, and she slyly smiles. I thought it would've been awkward this morning seeing her again, especially after everything, but she acted as if last night never happened. It was exactly what I wanted. I most definitely don't regret last night at all. It was the most amazing sexual experience I have ever had, and the memories alone will keep me warm at night.

"Derrick!" Camryn warns him.

"You heard Liv last night, she wanted to try things, naughty things, and I just wanted to know if Axel delivered on his promise."

I know Derrick is trying to help, but he's also an awful gossip, so I better give him something. Otherwise, he'll keep digging.

Taking a deep breath, I speak, "Axel was amazing. It was one of the most amazing nights of my life." My cheeks blush at the memories. After having fun with his friends, they all left, and we continued exploring the club. We stood and watched the cube again. This time it was me falling to my knees and sucking him off between the crowd. He took me into another room and explored some things I had read about in a book. He tied me up like a starfish and brought me to the brink so many times but never enough to let me fall over the edge. He tickled me with a feather, dripped wax over my nipples, and used various vibrators on me. Axel even tried some light flogging, and my ass is still a little sore from it.

"Oh, do tell Uncle Derrick *all* about it." He rubs his hands together with glee.

"Sorry, can't kiss and tell. All I'll say is I did things that I will probably never do again, I tried things that I'll never get a chance to do again, and I experienced things so far from what I have ever done before. But it's over now, and reality is fast approaching."

"Very well, princess. I'll let the details go for the moment, but one day, mark my words, you're going to spill them."

* * *

"Hey, how was brunch?" Axel asks as I walk into my hotel room, his presence making me jump.

"You're still here?"

Axel frowns at me. "Of course, I am. We spoke about it last night. I thought we agreed to hang out this weekend."

I nod because this is what we agreed to when we got home

last night, and I was snuggled against his bare chest. I honestly thought that maybe he was just caught up in the moment. "Um... yeah, I just didn't think you wanted to?"

Axel takes a couple of steps toward me, his large palms holding my face between them. "I had fun, and I want to do it again." His soft lips meet mine in a tender kiss. I let myself get taken away before he pulls away.

"But what about the bachelor party weekend with the rest of the boys?"

"Well, Christian is meeting up with Ness." He rolls his eyes, making me laugh. "Finn, Oscar, and Jackson are off to the casino. Evan is with Sienna. Nate is working, and I think the others are still asleep or partying on Nate's yacht."

"And you would rather hang out with me?" I hate feeling vulnerable, but I just want to check.

"Yeah, I kind of do. I've organized for a car, and I thought we might go exploring."

"What... like a date?"

Axel freezes.

I quickly try and backtrack over my words. "Sorry, I mean..."

Axel laughs. "Liv, yeah, like a date."

"But you don't date." *Why the hell am I not shutting up?*

"And yet here I am, planning an amazing date with a beautiful woman."

My stomach does a happy somersault—this playfulness is an interesting side to him.

"Okay then, what do you have in mind?"

Axel lets out a slight growl. "You don't want to know the things I have on my mind." His hand moves from my face to my ass, squeezing it. "And I can assure you, Liv, I'll make today worth your while." I gulp my nervousness down. "Make sure you wear a dress or a skirt, I want to be able to touch you." His hand cups me between my thighs. *Oh my God.* He lets me go, and I scurry away to find a dress.

We wind our way along the rugged coastline, through tiny French villages and lavender fields. Axel has hired a little red convertible car. It's a beautiful day, blue skies, not too hot and not too cold. Every once in a while, he rests his hand on my leg, his long fingers running along my inner thigh, sending shivers over my body, making my nipples and sex clench. He has kept me on a sexual high the entire drive. Even when he was pointing out things as we passed them by, all my mind was concentrating on were those fingers moving just a little bit further up.

"Okay, we're here," Axel says, pulling up to a little cottage. He jumps out and opens the door for me, taking my hand and helping me out of the car like a gentleman. "Follow me," he says as he links his fingers with mine. Axel walks around the side of the cottage, down the stone path, past the vegetable patch and the little rose garden, turning when we arrive at the back of the house. Axel turns the handle on the little red wooden door, and it opens.

"Axel, what are you doing?" I whisper yell, but he ignores me, pulling me behind him as if he has committed a crime. Well, we didn't break anything, so we're just illegally entering. We walk into a gorgeous small country kitchen, and sitting on the counter is a large picnic basket with a folded rug on top of it. He lets go of my hand and opens the refrigerator, pulls out a bottle of champagne, some meats and cheeses, and pops them into the basket.

"Come on, let's go." Before I know it, he's whisking me back out the way we just came.

"Axel." I tug on his hand, and he turns as we walk along another rocky path. "How did…"

"Liv, I'm a rock star, I can get anything I want." He gives me a cocky grin and takes me toward an open field. We walk for a couple of minutes through the long grass, nothing but sunshine, blue skies, birds chirping away, and butterflies scattering as we walk through the grass. It's idyllic. Moments later, he's stopping and placing the basket on the grass. He pulls out a rug from the top of the basket and shakes it out.

"Sit down." I'm still in shock at what we're doing here, and it's kind of a little romantic. Axel doesn't do romantic or dating kind of stuff from what Derrick has told me. I sit on the soft, red rug and kick off my heels. Axel busies himself, pulling out the meats and cheeses I saw him grab from the refrigerator, then two champagne glasses and hands one to me. He pulls out the chilled bottle of champagne and pops it, the cork flying high into the air and fills our glasses. Then he sits back beside me.

"Cheers, to a nice day." We clink our glasses, and I take a nervous sip.

We enjoy the late autumn sun as we chat about things. He tells me crazy stories about his touring days, and I tell him about the gossip of the royal circles. We fill our faces with food and champagne, the bubbles most definitely going to my head.

"Have you had enough to eat?"

"If I have one more macaroon, I'm going to explode." I giggle but am tempted to grab another latte-flavored one. It's calling my name, I know it.

"I like a woman who isn't afraid of food." Axel pops my latte macaroon in his mouth. I scowl at him, but there's no anger behind it.

"Look at me, of course, I like my food." I rub my belly. Before I know it, Axel has my wrists pinned behind my head and his hard body hovering over me.

"You're one of the most beautiful women I have had the pleasure of being with. Never underestimate how beautiful you are, Olivia." Axel's serious, his whiskey eyes glowing with desire as he looks me over.

"I like my women with curves." One of his hands trails down over my curves, over my breasts, lightly teasing my nipple through the sheer material, down over my stomach, along my hip bone, and then he squeezes my generous ass.

"Feel me, feel how much I think you're perfect." He grabs my hand and holds it against his dark denim jeans. My hand caresses his hardening length, and my fingers press against the material as he lets out a strained groan. He rubs himself against my hand.

"You feel it, Liv?" he asks.

I nod as I'm lost in his eyes as they have turned an almost honey color. I want him, I want him so much. My fingers pop the top button of his jeans, but it's a little hard to do as he still has my other hand pinned into the rug above my head.

"My greedy little lady. Are you hungry for my cock?"

"Yes."

"Then show me." He lets go of my wrist and falls back against the rug. I scamper up onto my knees, pure lust clouding my mind, and everything around me is nothing but white noise. All I can think about is unzipping his jeans and taking him into my mouth, tasting his saltiness, and feeling his veins throb against his velvety skin. I want to hear his groans of pleasure as I, little Olivia Pearce, give Axel Taylor, world-famous womanizer, a blow job and an amazing one at that.

"It's not going to magically pop out by itself." Axel chuckles, catching me in my daydream as I scramble to my knees. My shaking hands unbutton him from his jeans, his underwear straining, my hand dipping underneath the elastic, meeting with his hard length.

"Yes," Axel hisses. "Suck me, Liv. Let me come down your tight little throat."

I madly pull his jeans down a fraction, then his briefs, and his cock springs free, slapping his toned stomach. I move between his legs, grabbing his thick length again, then I place my mouth around the eager tip.

"God, I love your mouth," Axel hisses again. "Take your hair out," he commands. One of my hands pulls out the hair tie while I try to take him into my mouth. My brown hair falls out around my shoulders, covering my face. Axel's hands scoop it up as he wraps the silky strands around his fists, the slight pain of him pulling on the strands adds to the excitement.

"Suck me harder, Olivia," he growls. "I want to feel the back of your throat." He pulls tighter on my hair, pressing my mouth further down his length, his thickness hitting my throat. I gag a little, but I calm myself down. I take a little more as he starts to put pressure on my head, increasing his thrusts into my mouth. My hand slips beneath his thighs, touching his balls. Curiously, I squeeze them, and Axel almost bucks me off him.

"Shit, keep doing that," he moans. I continue rolling his balls around in my hands, sucking as hard as I can. "Yes, yes, that's it. Yes," he screams as I feel the first salty bursts hit the back of my throat. I'm not a swallower at all, and I gag a couple of times, but I keep going and give it a good old go at swallowing him down. Axel's dick falls from my mouth with a pop, and I quickly grab the bottle of champagne, taking a swig to get the taste out of my mouth. I'm sure that isn't good etiquette. He lets out a chuckle as he watches me drink.

"Not much of a swallower, hey?" I can feel my cheeks turn pink with embarrassment. I'm sure he's used to a million groupies happily swallowing him.

"Not sure yet," I reply.

He sits up, his dick slowly softening against him. "Thank you for trying, but next time, do what you feel comfortable with, okay?" His hand reaches out and touches my cheek. "Never feel afraid with me to speak your mind."

"No one has ever wanted to know about what I like or want before," I confess.

A frown forms on his brow. "I hate that you have been with men who are so selfish. I have to admit, though, I'm also so thankful. Otherwise, I'd never have gotten this time with you." His confession makes my heart bounce in my chest.

"Now, lady's turn. Lie back, Liv, and let me repay the favor." I don't even hesitate. I simply lay back and watch as Axel nestles himself between my legs. I watch the way he takes his time rolling down my underwear, the way he pushes my thighs apart, his eyes turning molten as my pussy is laid bare before him. I like the way he licks his lips just before he dives in between my legs. And I most certainly love the way his expert tongue moves against my aching core, the slow, long, frustrating licks, the ones that keep missing the target. The target that's throbbing so much now that all I feel is my entire body aching.

"Please, Axel." My hands dig into his hair, pulling him in closer, hoping I can press him in the spots that I need him in. But somehow, he still misses it as he sinks in a finger, then another easily glides into me. My back arches off the soft rug, and yet, he still isn't touching my bud.

"Please," I beg again, but he just chuckles against me, sending shivers over my body. When I think my body can't take anymore, he finds my bud and sucks hard on it. I come so hard around his fingers that I can feel liquid between my legs. My vision has gone hazy. *Shit, did I pee myself?* Then my entire body turns rigid, and I push Axel away.

"Liv, are you okay?" Concern falls across his face.

"Um, I have to go." I quickly jump up and frantically look around. Is there somewhere I can run to? I have to get away from him. I'm sure Axel didn't think he would get a golden shower when he planned this picnic.

"Liv." Axel grabs my arm, spinning me into him. I bounce off his hard chest. "What happened? Tell me, did I hurt you?" I shake my head in horror because he thinks he did something wrong, but it's me who should be apologizing.

"No, it's me, not you."

"Are you breaking up with me? Because that kind of sounds like the excuse I used in high school."

I bury my face in my hands, this man is wonderful, and he's cracking jokes when I just did something so embarrassing. "No, um… we're not dating for one and two, I just… this is so embarrassing, but um… I'm so sorry I peed all over you." There I said it, it's out in the open.

Axel frowns at me, and then he starts laughing. His entire body shakes, but when he sees me looking mortified, he just takes my face between his palms and kisses me. He showers kisses all over my face. I'm so confused.

"Liv, you just squirted, you didn't pee on me at all."

I still in his arms. "Squirted?"

"Yes, it happens when you play with a women's G-spot. I found yours, and well, you know the rest."

"And this is… was… okay for you?"

"Fuck, Liv, it was so fucking hot, you taste so fucking sweet. I could stay between your thighs all day."

My body relaxes a little. "You sure I didn't pee?" I question him again.

"No, I can assure you that you didn't pee. Want me to make you do it again?" he asks, giving me a cheeky smile.

We spent the rest of the afternoon in the field, lost in each other.

10

AXEL

"Can I grab your number?" I ask Olivia, not sure why I'm asking because we live on opposite sides of the world. I don't know, it seems like the right thing to do, and I kind of want to stay in touch.

"Um... sure." She sounds a little uneasy about my request, maybe because it was supposed to be a weekend-only fling. She types her number into my phone before giving me a quick peck on the cheek.

"Sorry, I have to go," she says as she grabs her bags from her room. "Thanks for this weekend, it's been fun." Her cheeks turn pink.

I frown, a little taken aback that she's so eager to get away from me.

"Well, I guess I'll see you at the wedding, then?"

Why was I excited about seeing her again?

"Yes, I guess so." Why is she pushing me away? I grab her face and press my lips against hers. She eventually relents and opens for me, and I kiss her, letting her know that I'm going to want more next time I see her. She pulls me against her, and it calms me.

We pull away.

"Until next time," she says, giving me a weak smile as she walks out the door.

"Dammit." I thump my fist on the desk. "I thought she was interested." I look at my phone and the text message flashing back at me.

Sorry, I think you have the wrong number.

I can't believe Olivia gave me the wrong number.

Did she not want to see me again?

Why the fuck do I care?

Why the hell do I want to see her again?

"Everything all right?" Jackson asks, popping his head into my office.

I let out a long sigh. "Can I ask you something?" He nods. "Close the door on your way in." He does and sits in the chair opposite my desk. "Has a girl ever given you a fake number?"

Jackson blinks at me a couple of times and then bursts out laughing.

Yeah, thanks, asshole.

"Oh my God, Olivia gave you the wrong number, didn't she?"

I glare at him. "What makes you think it's Olivia?"

This makes him laugh even more. "Dude, you were smitten from the start with her. Don't forget it's my job to look after you guys and make sure no one is a threat. I saw the way you looked at her."

Shaking my head, I growl. "If I was so into her, then why the hell did I share her with my friends?" I cross my arms in annoyance.

Jackson raises his eyebrow as he stares at me. "Because you loved it. You love being in control, and even though you let her call the shots, you still had the power to stop it all. She looked for you at every chance to make sure you were okay with what she was doing. You loved that she automatically desired your approval. She's naturally submissive, but you also liked that with each new experience, she was becoming more confident."

My eyes squint at him. I hate that he's right. "She was just a fling."

He laughs again. "Then why did you ask for her number? Why are you pissed off that she gave you a fake one?" I glare at him again as he holds his hands up in the air.

"Hey, you asked for my advice, man. Just trying to help."

"Whatever, she was just a fling."

Jackson gets up out of his chair and keeps laughing to himself. "You keep telling yourself that, Ax, but don't forget you'll be seeing her again soon." And with that, he walks out the door, leaving me even more pissed off and confused.

This is what happens when you give control to a woman—they walk all over you. Fuck it, there are plenty of women who want me. I don't have to wait around for some stuck-up princess from the mountains.

"Welcome back to The Paradise Club, Mr. Taylor," the receptionist greets me, handing over my wristbands. Taking them, I walk through the doors, and instantly, the anxiety I'm feeling leaves me. This is my safe place. I walk past the bar area and head toward the stairs, security allowing me to pass easily.

I take the stairs two at a time, eager to get started and put this woman out of my mind. There's a crowd hanging around the cube, and a massive free-for-all orgy is happening in there, but for the first time, my dick doesn't twitch. What's going on? I love watching, and the cube never fails to get me going. I make myself stand there and watch it, rubbing my hand over my crotch, begging for it to come to life. Watching two women enjoying each other is an automatic dick twitch. Right now, all I'm getting is a pathetic limp of a twitch. What the hell is happening, dude?

"May I help you?" A beautiful blonde stands before me, watching my hand trying desperately to get my dick started. An eager mouth will always get me going.

"Of course." I smile at her. She instantly drops to her knees, her long, tanned fingers start to unzip my jeans, her cold hands pull down my briefs, and she pulls out my flaccid dick. She licks her red, glossy lips and eagerly takes me in her mouth. The scene is all wrong, my dick isn't playing along, and it stays limp in her mouth even though she's using every trick in the book to get me going. She's sucking my balls, a tight grip around my shaft, her ruby red lips sucking sweetly on my tip, but nothing.

Did Olivia break my dick? Just thinking about her makes him twitch, and the blonde smiles, thinking she's the one to make it come to life. But it's not, it is Olivia. Again, my cock twitches in her mouth. I look down, and he starts to deflate again.

I close my eyes and remember the way Olivia's lips felt wrapped around my dick. *Twitch.*

The way her warm hands tentatively touched my skin, her soft grip around my cock that slowly started to become tighter, the more uninhibited she became. *Twitch.*

The tiny mews of pleasure as I wrapped her hair around my palm and pulled it tight, taking control of her suck. *Twitch.*

I loved hearing the way she gagged on my cock while I pushed it down her throat. *Twitch, twitch, twitch.*

All I can think about are those pink cheeks and her ass after Oscar spanked her. *Shit. Fuck, I'm coming.*

The blonde looks pleased with herself, but I just zip up, turn, and walk out of the club.

What the fuck is happening to me?

"Are you okay?" Christian asks as we head toward the Dirty Texas jet, our families not far behind us. We're on our way to England for Christmas, and, of course, my brother's wedding.

"Yeah, all good. I should be asking you that question. No second thoughts?"

My brother stops and punches me in the arm. "Dick. Ness is it for me, you know that. Years I have been waiting for this day. There's no way in hell I'd ever back out, especially now that she's knocked up."

My brother finally has what he has always dreamed of. He has Ness, he is becoming a husband, and finally he's going to be a dad. I don't mean to rain on his parade, I'm just peeved about Olivia. It makes me so angry because she totally ghosted me. "I know, man, sorry, just not myself at the moment."

Christian frowns at me. "What's going on?"

"Nothing for you to worry about." I put my arm around his shoulders. "My little brother is getting married," I say, changing the subject, then pulling him into a headlock and giving him a noogie just like I did when we were younger.

"Fuck off, man." He punches me in the gut.

Shit, it hurts. I forget that my little brother has become stronger. Maybe I need to be working out more at the gym to keep up with him.

"Come on, let's get going."

11

OLIVIA

"Hey, Liv." Camryn's voice sounds strained through the telephone.

"Are you okay?"

There's silence on the end of the phone, then the distinct sound of a sniffle. "Cam, are you okay?" Worry starts to set in. Cam is usually extremely focused when we have our weekly phone calls about Vanessa's wedding.

"It's Harris," she sniffles again.

Oh shit, did they break up?

"He's marrying someone else." She bursts out crying.

Holy shit!

"Oh my God, Cam. How? When? I don't understand, you guys are together."

"I know. Last night I organized a last-minute party. It was shrouded in secrecy which I'm used to, and when I met the couple who were getting engaged, it was Harris and another woman." She bursts out crying again—this isn't the Camryn I know.

"Babe, I'm so sorry. I don't understand. How is he marrying another woman? You two looked so happy, so in love." All over

Cam's social media are pictures of them loved up. When we spoke on the phone, she gushed about him. Even in Monaco, they were constantly talking. I really don't understand. Blimey, if I don't understand, how does poor Cam feel?

"He says he doesn't love her, but he has no choice."

My stomach churns. I know exactly what Harris is saying, it sounds like he has a duty to his family. But the difference is I don't have a boyfriend that I have started a life with or have been leading on for the past six months. *Except you spent a wild weekend with a rock star.* But I gave him a fake number. I knew it would be wrong if we continued communicating. I mean I'm marrying someone else, so there's no future between Axel and me.

What am I saying? As if there would've ever been a future between us. I'm some woman who lives in a castle in the middle of the English countryside, and he's this hot, famous rock star. I hate that he is the last thing I think of every night, I hate that his image is what I need to orgasm, and I hate that he has gotten under my skin.

You're so pathetic, Olivia. The first man to give you mind-blowing sex, and you lose your mind over him. Just shows how inexperienced you are.

"I'm sorry, babe. He's an asshole. You're a bloody good catch, and he's stupid to want anyone else."

More sniffles. "You know what's worse, his fucking engagement party is the talk of the town, and their smiling faces are plastered everywhere. All I see is his betrayal."

That would have to suck, never being able to get away from it. I know what the tabloids are like with my sister, let alone an ex. "Why don't you come here. I can give Ivy a call, and we can have girl time." Ivy is Camryn's younger sister and my best friend. She's a well-known interior designer for the rich and famous in London. I had her renovate the castle for me to entice rich clients to rent it out for functions. Of course, she did an amazing job, so much so that she won a design award for her work.

"You can get away from New York and everything to do with Harris, and no one would ever find you here. You can help me finish off all the things for Ness' wedding, and you get to hang out with your sister. I'm sure you could probably use her at the moment." The line goes quiet, I look at my phone, thinking she's hung up, but no, she is still there.

"I'm jumping onto the next plane. Fuck Harris and fuck Isabelle and their smiling fucking faces."

"I promise to raid the cellar when you arrive."

"You've sold me."

"Okay, just text me the details, and I can come get you."

"No worries, will do." And with that, she's gone.

I better call Ivy.

Cam needs her more than ever.

We're all drunk and sitting around the fire in my little cottage. The temperature has dropped considerably, and we may even get a dusting of snow.

"Men fucking suck." Camryn takes another swig from her glass.

"Tell me about it," Ivy concurs.

"Who needs them?" I add, and they both look at me. "What?"

"I'm not going to use my vibrator for the rest of my life, Liv. I need a fucking man. I need dick, cock, balls even. I need strong arms and whiskers." The tears start streaming down Camryn's cheeks again, but she pulls it together.

"I could've cheated on Harris when we were in Monaco, but I said no."

Ivy and I look at her.

"Who?" My gut twists, hoping it wasn't Axel.

"Nate."

Phew, I can relax a little.

"Who's Nate?" Ivy asks.

"Nate owns The Paradise Club, these exclusive sex clubs." Camryn opens another bottle.

"Sex club," Ivy squeals.

Camryn smiles at her younger sister. "Oh yes, and it's so fucking hot. Isn't it, Liv?"

"You went to a sex club?" Ivy questions me. She's as clueless about men as I am and one of the many reasons we get on so well.

"Um… yeah, they took us there."

"Who?" Ivy questions.

"Dirty Texas," Camryn adds like it's no big deal. Ivy's eyes widen. "And Liv here most definitely had some fun, didn't you?" Camryn winks at me, and I roll my eyes at her. I feel bad because I didn't spill my guts to Ivy about what happened at The Paradise Club, not because I was ashamed but because it was my little secret.

"Um…"

"She totally banged Axel Taylor," Camryn adds.

"What? The Axel Taylor?" Ivy looks at me.

Camryn is giggling in the corner.

"Um… so Camryn, what happened with Nate?" I try to change the subject. Ivy looks at me, her eyes wide. "I'll tell you later," I mouth to her, and she gives me a glare telling me I most certainly will.

"Nate's my new client…" Camryn hiccups. "And he's so hot, like *GQ* model hot, Christian Grey sexy, kinky, billionaire hot." She giggles to herself again—she's pretty wasted.

"He likes to flirt, but I loved Harris and told him I had a partner. He respected that, but he also told me all the things that he'd have done to me had I been single. I wanted to come right there and then." Ivy and I are silent, our eyes wide as Camryn rambles on.

"He wants me to host exclusive parties for him, and he also has a launch of a sex resort he wants me to organize. Fuck, that man is so bloody fine. I bet he knows how to fuck. I mean, you don't own a sex club if you don't know how to fuck, right?" Ivy and I shrug because we have no clue.

"Hmm… maybe I need to tell him I'm single now, so he can do all those dirty things to me like he promised."

"Don't you think that's a little soon?" Ivy questions her.

"Fuck you, Ivy. Harris is engaged to someone else. You don't think that's too soon?" She glares at her sister.

"Fine, you're right. But you never screw around with a client."

Camryn huffs. "I know, I know, I just want someone to take the pain away. I want to feel normal again." A single tear falls down her cheek. "Anyway, I'm off to bed, damn jet lag. Night," she mumbles as she slowly and unsteadily makes her way upstairs to her bedroom.

"Is she going to be okay?" I ask Ivy.

"I think this one is going to take a little longer to get over, but she will be, she always is. I thought he was different, but I guess you can't always trust the ones who look too good to be true."

I nod in agreement, hoping poor Camryn's heart mends well and isn't left with jagged bits.

"Now, Olivia, you have some secrets to spill. What the hell happened at this sex club?"

I take a sip of my champagne. I'm going to need it to tell my best friend all about my weekend of adult fun.

Ivy gasps as I finally finish telling her about my dirty weekend. "I can't believe it."

"I know, it feels like it happened to another person. It's so crazy."

"I can't believe you have been with two of the Dirty Texas guys, plus their head of security and a woman." I can feel the embarrassment run up my neck.

"Liv, hey, it's nothing to be embarrassed about," Ivy tells me. "I think you're kind of awesome for doing it."

"You do?"

"Yeah, I'd never have the guts to do something like that, and well…"

"Well, what?"

"Far out, Liv, I'd love to try something so crazy. All the men I have been with screw like dead fish."

This makes me giggle. "I totally get it, but I don't think I'd do something like that again, not now that I'm marrying Eddie." The thought makes my stomach burn with anxiety.

"Well, I guess now you have some tricks up your sleeves." She gives me a weak smile.

"Yeah, I guess. But I know he isn't going to stay faithful to me. He likes partying too much. Am I really going to put up with that for the rest of my life?"

Ivy is quiet for a couple of moments. "If he isn't going to stay faithful, then I don't think you should either."

"Really?"

"It's not fair that he can go and screw whoever he wants, but you can't." Yeah, I guess she's right. But who the hell am I going to meet up a mountain when Eddie is probably going to stay partying in London or Edinburgh? "Maybe you can keep Axel on the side." Ivy wiggles her eyebrows at me, and I throw a cushion at her head.

"Axel is a famous rock star. I hardly doubt that he needs a piece on the side stuck in the middle of nowhere." I hate thinking about Axel, so much so that I may have stalked his Instagram account. There was nothing much to see except photos of him with other hot celebrities or working out in the studio and hanging out with the other Dirty Texas boys. I hate that I looked.

I also hated when I accidentally liked a photo when I was supposed to be stealth stalking.

"But you're going to see him again at the wedding."

"Yeah."

"So, are you going to hook up again?"

"Probably not. I gave him a fake phone number."

"What did you say?" Ivy looks at me, shocked.

"He asked me for my number, and well, I panicked because you know... I'm kind of supposed to be engaged, and that little hook-up was only supposed to be for the weekend."

"Seriously?" my friend questions me.

"Yes."

"And what do you think he's going to do when he sees you again after giving him a fake number?"

I still. I hadn't thought that far in my plan. "Um... probably nothing. He probably already has a date for the wedding. Anyway, I'm going to be busy, so..."

Ivy bursts out laughing. "You're so screwed, Olivia Pearce."

I think she might be right.

12

OLIVIA

Everyone is here for Vanessa and Christian's wedding, and I'm hiding away in my office. Seeing Axel again is too much, way too much. Axel had a deep scowl on his face when he arrived, and his tone was short toward me. How dare he question me about my sister? I know I told him about her when we were in France, but that was because he had given me multiple orgasms, and I was tipsy on champagne.

Note to self—*don't drink champagne around Axel Taylor and most definitely no more orgasms.*

Knock, knock, knock.

"Come in."

Ivy stands in the doorway. "Just wanted to check in on you. I heard they are here." She takes a seat in front of my desk.

"Axel is a little grumpy, which I shouldn't be shocked about, but other than that, everything is all good."

"So why are you hiding out in your office when your guests have just arrived?"

"Sebastien is kind of hot, don't you think?" I try to change the subject.

Ivy rolls her eyes at me. "Yes, I did notice that, but you still haven't answered my question."

"You know he's single," I continue.

"Oh, that's nice, you know who else is single? Axel."

Well played, Ivy, well played.

"Ivy, I can't, okay? Please, I just can't." Panic clutches at my heart.

"Hey, hey, I'm sorry. I didn't realize you were so stressed out about him being here."

"We can't be together, nothing can happen. It was a great weekend in Monaco, that's it. Even if he wanted more, I can't. I have no choice, I have to marry Eddie. Father needs me to, and my legacy needs me to." A single tear falls down my cheek and lands on some paperwork.

Ivy rushes toward me and pulls me into a hug. "When do you get to be happy, Liv? You have sacrificed so much in your life. Why do you have to sacrifice love as well?"

"I could learn to love Eddie."

Ivy laughs. "Yeah, the same way people learn to love Brussels sprouts." This makes me laugh. "You're my best friend, Liv, and I want what makes you happy."

"And you think a kinky, famous rock star would make me happy?"

Ivy giggles. "That sounds pretty damn good at the moment." She elbows me in the ribs.

"Also, a hot, Spanish, single chef is in the castle. Maybe you should do something to make yourself happy as well?"

Ivy smiles at me. "That man is seriously delicious, but I've heard of his reputation."

"Well, the Sons of Brooklyn and The California Bros. are coming as well. From what I've seen, they look hot as well."

Ivy giggles. "I may have stalked their social media profiles when Cammie mentioned it."

Now it's my turn to laugh. "Oh my God, stalker alert. Do I

have to mention something to Jackson's staff and let them know to keep an eye on you? If someone's underwear goes missing, you're the number one suspect."

"Ha-ha, you're such a comedian. I'm sick of being single. I need to get laid, it's been a very long time. Not all of us can have their fantasies fulfilled in a sex club."

I flip her off as she laughs her way out the door.

"Princess?" Derrick knocks on the door of my cottage.

"Hey." I kiss him on the cheek. "What are you doing over here? Am I late for dinner?" I look at the clock to confirm the time. No, it's still early.

"No, no. I just wanted to come over and check out what you're wearing for dinner." I can see the mischievous look in his eyes.

"Why?"

He rolls his eyes. "Because I know something happened between you and Axel."

"It's called sex, Derrick."

He sighs. "Believe me, princess, I know all about that. But what I mean is… I think maybe there was something a little more."

I put my hand up. "I'm going to stop you right there. Nothing will happen between Axel and me, so if you're here to try and matchmake, then turn around and walk back over to the castle. Derrick, I can't afford to like Axel any more than I already do. There's no future between us, nothing. I'm already betrothed to someone else. One weekend of fun was all I was allowed, and I can't keep doing this behind Eddie's back."

Derrick scoffs. "You have seen the tabloids, haven't you? You've seen who your fiancé is hanging out with?"

I have, and it makes me sick. He's running around London

with my sister. As if I'd expect anything less from her.

"I know, D," I whisper.

"Hey, I'm not trying to make you upset. I haven't even met your sister yet, and I already know I hate her. What I am saying is he doesn't give a shit about you or your marriage. So why are you giving up a week of mind-blowing orgasms for some douchebag?"

He's right, but I don't know. "Why would Axel want anything to do with me? I blew him off, Derrick. He looked angry with me."

Derrick gives me a big smile. "Axel has never in his life ever been told no by a woman. He always gets what he wants. I mean, look at the man, he's spectacular, especially naked." I raise my eyebrows.

"It was my birthday present, and he gave me a lap dance. Best moment of my life, but anyway…" He tries to shake the thoughts of Axel naked from his mind. "I haven't seen him at The Paradise Club since Monaco."

"So, he's probably busy." Not sure what that has to do with me.

"That boy practically lives there. I know this because I'm there most nights." Derrick sounds a little sad. I'm not sure why because he's a famous stylist to the stars, who's mega hot and has amazing friends.

"I'm just saying that he hasn't been there, and when I asked him why, he just said he needed a break. That boy never takes a break from sex. I wonder why he needs a break after a weekend of hot sex with a princess." He gives me a pointed look. "He just all of a sudden stops going to his favorite place?"

"Derrick, maybe he needs a break. Maybe he's busy or stressed? I don't know, maybe he's met someone." That thought makes my stomach sink.

"Or maybe his lethal weapon got a taste of royal pussy, and now it doesn't want anything else."

I laugh at him. "Derrick, please, you're living in a fantasy." He rolls his eyes at me. "Okay, fine, even if this is true, it doesn't matter. I'm still getting married to someone else."

"But you don't have to. Axel is richer than God, he can save your castle."

"Derrick, I love you, I really do, but please, I know my marriage isn't based on love. I know I'm marrying a playboy, but I am doing it because it will make my dying father happy."

Derrick's face slumps. "Babe, I know. You're just so fucking perfect that I want to squish you." He pulls me into a bear hug. "Eddie won't make you happy."

"Neither will Axel."

Derrick stills. "Maybe, maybe not, but don't you think you could give it a chance? Your parents want you to be happy. They want you to find the man of your dreams, don't they?"

I look up at him. "They think Eddie is the man of my dreams." Derrick frowns. "Please, D, it's a hard enough decision as it is, I don't need my friends not supporting me as well."

"Babe, I'll support you, I promise. Fine, this will be the last you hear of Axel from my lips." He pretends to shut them and throw away the key.

"So, Sebastien's hot?" Derrick wiggles his eyebrows at me.

"D, enough."

"Okay, okay, no more matchmaking. How about I style you, though? That I can do."

"You don't like what I'm wearing?" I look down at my simple black dress.

Derrick's eyebrows rise in disapproval. "It's boring, princess. Now, I have left a bag outside full of things I think will look gorgeous on you. Please let me do this… you know I live for this."

I roll my eyes at him. "Fine, but please don't dress me like a hooker."

He bursts out laughing. "I promise it will be fit for a lady."

13

AXEL

Four days, Olivia has been avoiding me for four days! I know the castle is big, but still, we're the only people in it. I bet there are secret passages somewhere like they have in the movies. That has to be the only way she has been getting around this castle without me running into her.

Why the hell am I pining over a woman who clearly isn't interested in me? I haven't been laid in a while, and I'm sick of jerking off in my hand. How the hell has Olivia voodooed me when hundreds of girls before her haven't even come close?

Why the hell her? She lives in a fucking castle, for God's sake, in the middle of the English countryside, and I live in LA. My life is there, and her life is here. How would we ever work?

Why the hell am I even thinking about a relationship? It has to be wedding fever messing with my brain. Watching my twin pledge himself to one woman for the rest of his life must be making me crazy. It's not like she's going out of her way to jump me while I've been here. I mean, I've hardly even seen her.

I know she has been busy with the girls organizing this wedding, but still, we just had Christmas together. Apparently, her parents are in the Caribbean on the island of Mustique for

Christmas this year, along with her sister, so she's alone this Christmas. Of course, Mom fell in love with Olivia, especially when she took her horseback riding to look at the gardens on the estate. Mom is a keen gardener and horse rider, so the fact that Olivia took time out to show her around really meant something to me, yet she still ignores me.

Olivia hardly even looks in my direction. I rub my face with my hands, feeling like some mooning high schooler with a crush on the pretty cheerleader who doesn't even know I exist. That isn't me! I am the one that women moon over, and I'm the one who has women chasing me.

But why is it that the one woman who has fascinated me for the first time in forever doesn't want me?

Knock, knock, knock.

Thank God, saved by the bell. I shouldn't be alone right now, my mind is sending me crazy. I open the door, it's my brother, and he has the most pained expression on his face. "Hey, what's the matter with you?" I ask as he falls on the second bed in my room. He looks as if he has the weight of the world on his shoulders.

"Just don't like being away from Ness, that's all."

I laugh. "Such a pussy."

Christian glares at me. "Whatever, your time will come, and I can't wait to call you a pussy."

Little does he know I'm halfway there to being a pussy. I straighten myself up, hiding my true feelings. "That's going to be a long time in hell before that happens."

Christian raises his brow to me. "Really?" he questions like he knows something I don't. He's so easy to read. I have been doing it all my life, and I know the signs.

"If you know something, spit it out."

He grins. "What I have heard is you're getting pretty close with one Lady Olivia Pearce. Are you getting ready to become Lord of the Manor?"

Shit, maybe he does know something. Obviously, the girls have been talking.

"She's just a bit of fun, nothing more," I deflect. But he's not buying it.

"You sure?"

I sit on the bed opposite him. Maybe I need to talk to someone about what happened between Olivia and me. Christian knows me best, he's all loved up, and maybe he does know something about women. "If you tell anyone, I'll fucking kill you. None of this gossiping shit that we do, okay?" He nods in agreement, smirking a little.

"Fine, yes, I like Olivia, a little more than I should. It's complicated. I'm not sure what the girls have told you about it."

"Nothing much. Ness just said that you and Olivia had hooked up in Monaco, and that was about it."

I scrub my face feeling very uncomfortable talking about this. "Yeah, it's true." I pause for a moment before I continue, "They asked me to teach her things."

Now it's Christian's turn to look uncomfortable. "What do you mean, teach?"

"Sex stuff that she wasn't very experienced in because she's stuck up on a mountain here in the middle of nowhere. Derrick thought I'd be a good candidate for her."

Christian nods. "They'd be right. You have made it clear time and time again that you just want sex and nothing more."

"Yeah…"

"But?"

"After you and Ness went home together, which I might add sucked because when it's your bachelor party, you should be partying." Christian just looks at me. "Yeah, yeah, I get it. Anyway, Nate took us to The Paradise Club, and the two parties kind of mingled together. That's where Derrick approached me. He didn't need to, though, as I already had my sights on her."

"And?"

"She's my type in every way," I tell him, hoping he can read between the lines because this conversation is becoming awkward.

"But I thought she was inexperienced," he states.

"Kind of, I think she's just more cautious around men, except me. I don't know what happened, but it was kind of intense."

"So have you kept in touch, or was it just a holiday fling?"

He's going to laugh when he finds out.

"You've been texting her?" he pushes again.

"Fuck, I wish… she won't talk to me. After that weekend in Monaco, she disappeared, gave me a fake number."

Christian laughs like a hold-your-belly-and-roll-around-the-floor kind of laugh. "She must have known she would see you again. I mean, hello… the wedding."

I just shrug my shoulders. I really don't get it. Women don't normally confuse me.

"Guess there's a first time for everything, brother. A chick that just isn't into you."

"Asshole, I know you're enjoying this." I glare at him.

"Okay, I'm not going to lie, I am laughing on the inside, but I can see you don't know what to do about her. Have you tried to talk to her since you arrived?"

"Yes, but she keeps ignoring me, telling me she's busy."

"Well, technically, that's true. She's running this estate by herself, and she is helping Cammie and Kim with the wedding details." These are all things that I already know and tell myself. "So, maybe just wait until after the wedding. It's only one more day, and perhaps then the stress of hosting it at her home will be gone. We still have New Year's here, don't forget."

"Yeah, maybe you're right," I mumble.

"I'm sorry, what did you say? I didn't quite hear it."

"I said maybe you're right, asshole." I chuckle. He's such a dick sometimes.

"Yeah, that's what I thought you said. I just wanted you to repeat it because I think pigs have flown over or something."

"Asshole," I grumble and flip him off.

"Yeah, yeah, I know. But can I ask you something? Do you like her? I mean really like her, or are you just pissed because someone turned you down?"

I'm silent for a moment. I don't think that's the reason. I mean, yes there's a small bit of me that's pissed, and I want to prove that I still have it, but that isn't why I'm pissed. "I like her, and she's the first girl in forever that I like. Now don't go calling me a pussy, all right, because it's not like that, so don't get ahead of yourself. We clicked, especially sexually." My brother looks shocked at my confession. "I know, shocking… the innocent girl clicking with the manwhore rock star. I showed her some of the things I'm into, and well…"

"Do I really need to hear this?" he asks.

"No, probably not. But, anyway, she shocked me, and in a good way. In a way that I want to keep doing."

"Aww, you've got a crush."

"Yeah, I guess I do, but she wants nothing to do with me. Is this like karma for all the years that I have done this to girls?"

"Probably."

"Well, it sucks."

"Maybe it was just a holiday fling. I mean really, how would you work together? Would you become Lord of the Manor? Would you want to live here away from everything you built in LA?"

"Chris, I just want more sex, and we aren't talking about anything more." Christian frowns at me. "I know we would never work, but…"

"You want to see if it was just a one-off kind of thing between the two of you?"

"Yeah, was it just holiday Olivia?"

"Well, just wait, you still have plenty of time before we have to leave. I mean, you could always extend your stay after we have all gone."

I shrug. I don't see that happening. "Come on, let's go catch up with the others. I need a drink," I suggest. I've had enough of talking about feelings and shit.

I can't believe my brother is married!

I watched him pledge his life to the woman he loves, and even I, who likes to keep my emotions tucked away in a nice little box deep down inside of me, became emotional. When my brother saw his bride walking down the aisle and the first string of tears fell, I'm not going to lie, it choked me up. Stupidly, I looked at my parents, and Mom was bawling her eyes out, making it even harder to hold back my feelings.

The day has flown by so quickly. Ness and Chris are lost in their little love bubble, and Evan and Sienna are just as loved up as the newlyweds. Stacey and Oscar are being a little more public with their connection, dancing together.

I have noticed Finn is being quite frosty with Isla, but that might be because Isla announced that she was moving to Europe to work with Sebastien. I'm going to be sad to see Isla go, but she needs to find her way. I don't think being our assistant was what she wanted to do with her life. Why not move to Europe? The job might be a little easier than looking after the five of us, and there's only one of him.

Sienna suggested Stacey should take over for Isla as she's leaving on short notice. We need a super experienced assistant, and Stacey already knows everyone, plus she's incredibly good at her job.

I guess big changes are happening with the Dirty Texas family. I mean, Sienna and Vanessa are knocked up, Derrick and Sienna's business is expanding rapidly, and we have to look at hiring a new PR person for the label when Ness goes on maternity leave. Isla will no longer be the sixth member of our band. Our record label is taking off, the Sons of Brooklyn boys are killing it, and after tonight's duet with the Gypsy Sisters, I think we might need to explore that more.

It's funny how in the space of a year, life can change. This time last year, we were in Australia celebrating Sienna and Evan's wedding. The year before that, we were all single and partying up in Mexico for Evan's thirtieth, being wild as ever. And here I am, still in the same place I was last year and the year before that and the year before that. It feels like damn Groundhog Day.

A flash of blue, brown curls, and porcelain skin catches my attention. *Olivia.* Damn, she looks beautiful tonight in a strapless, midnight blue evening dress. Her chocolate curls are cascading around her creamy shoulders, and stunning sapphire jewels are hanging along her collarbone. I wonder if they are family heirlooms. I follow her as she winds her way through the crowd. I get stopped by a couple of well-wishers, so by the time I catch up to where I had last seen her, she's gone. Why is she in such a hurry?

14

OLIVIA

My sister just can't help herself. Texting me pictures of Eddie kissing some girls while he was in London. I knew he wouldn't be faithful to me, he told me to my face that he wouldn't, but it doesn't mean I want to see it. I'm sure Penny is reveling in this news, hence, the millions of texts and images from her. It shouldn't bother me as this is probably going to be the norm in our marriage—him partying it up with a heap of beautiful women while I'm stuck on a mountain.

"Fuck," I groan audibly.

"Are you okay?"

That voice, the one I have been trying to put out of my mind for the last couple of days, the one that I have been trying to avoid. I pop my head around the corner, and there's Axel, looking like a real-life book boyfriend. He's dressed in a tuxedo, the designer suit cut perfectly to his long, lean body. His shaggy, light caramel brown hair is pulled back in a styled man bun. He's clean-shaven as well, his square jaw and perfect cheekbones proudly on display. Those whiskey eyes are staring at me like he's either going to grab hold and press me up against this stone wall, or he's going to flip me over and spank me. Both scenarios sound pretty enticing right about now.

Screw Penny, screw Eddie, I am so sick of being the good girl. I'm sick of being the one who has to give up everything all the time. Why can't I just take what I want for once? Why can't I let loose and screw around? Screw it.

I drop my bag on the floor and take a couple of steps toward him. Axel must sense the shift in me because he starts toward me also, his long legs eating up the distance. Before I know it, I'm in his arms again, our mouths are crashing against each other, teeth clashing, large hands pressing me closer, and my hands grabbing chunks of his perfect ass.

"Fuck, Liv," Axel groans as he walks me backward, my back hitting the cold stone wall.

"Please, Axel. I need you, please," I beg. I don't care that I do because the lust feels like it's crawling out of my skin. I want him so badly. Why have I denied myself this man?

"Fuck, Liv," he repeats again, his sizable erection grinding against me. I need him inside of me as urgently as I need air to breathe.

"Follow me," I say, disentangling myself from him. I grab his warm hand and pull him down the hallway to where there's a hidden door behind a large grandfather clock. I pull the lever, and the clock moves to the side.

"No way." Axel looks impressed. "That's awesome." I smile at him as I pull him into the darkness. It's cool once you leave the warmth of the castle. I flick the light switch on, and it lights up the narrow passage. "Liv, do you know where you're going?" Axel questions me.

I stop, and he barrels into me. "Do you trust me?" I ask him, those whiskey eyes sparkling in the dim fluorescent light.

"Yes, I do."

I give him a small smile and pull him along the corridor. If anyone found these hidden passages, they would most certainly get lost, but I have been running around these halls all my life. When my uncle showed me these secret passages, I loved it, especially because he only told me about it and not Penny. I could disappear at any moment to get away from her. She never did find them, so they are my little secret. I pull him further and deeper into the castle, and we can hear the music through the stone walls.

"These secret passages were built so that my family could hide if there were an attack, especially from the Scots." I love telling people about my family history.

"If these walls could talk…" Axel muses to himself as we continue down some tiny stairs. We aren't far, but he doesn't know it yet. We rush along another long, narrow corridor until we're where we need to be. I open the door, and we have arrived at my cottage.

"Where are we?" Axel blinks, his eyes adjusting to the bright light.

"My cottage." My nerves are coming back because now what do I do with him?

"Your cottage is linked to the castle?" I nod. "That's interesting." He gives me a mischievous grin.

"I doubt you'll be able to find your way back," I nervously laugh.

Axel is walking, no, prowling toward me slowly. Inch by inch, I'm backing up. "I have a great sense of direction. I think I could manage."

"I'm pretty sure someone would find you if you disappeared."

He just shrugs casually. "I like that at any moment, I could sneak into your bedroom, tie you to the bed, and have my way with you." I gulp as that image makes me feel giddy. That's a fantasy of mine to be surprised by some hot stranger who ties me up and has his wicked way with me. Maybe that's what I get for reading my grandmother's old romance books.

"I see you like that idea, darlin'." Axel trails his thumb along my jaw, and his touch sends shivers over my body.

"Would you like me to do that one night?" Holding my chin between his fingers, he lifts my head to look at him. "Would you, Olivia?" he demands.

I swallow my nerves and respond, "Yes." My chest rises with each heartbeat.

"Do you want me to take you, use you, fuck you?" I nod in agreement, my body trembling with need. "Tie you up, blindfold you, and fuck you anyway I want?" His eyes are burning with desire with each dirty thought.

"Yes."

"Fuck, Liv." He lets out a strangled moan then closes his eyes for a moment before opening them again.

"Why did you run from me?" He surprises me with his serious question rendering me speechless. "Answer me, Olivia," he commands. "Why did you give me a fake number?" I stay silent because I can't tell him I have a fiancé. "Stubborn little one, aren't you?"

Before I know it, he's turning me around and pushes me onto the bed. I bounce once, but he's on me in an instant, his weight pushing me into my fluffy duvet. The sound of the zip on my evening dress being undone filters through the quiet room.

"I'm not happy with you, little one," Axel's voice is cool and calm as he whispers into my ear. I try and move a little, testing my limits. "Oh no, you're not going anywhere. You and I need to sort some things out first, okay?"

I'm still silent. He moves off of me, and I turn my head to see he's facing away from me, looking out the window. I turn over onto my back, the back of my dress is gaping wide, so I have to hold it as I get off the bed.

"Don't zip up your dress," Axel states. I stop where I am and wait. "Take it off." He still hasn't turned around. I do as I'm told and let the designer frock fall to the floor. And there I stand in nothing but a skimpy, navy G-string and heels.

"Don't cover yourself." He catches me trying to hide. "Get on your knees," he commands. I do as I'm told and kneel on my dress that has puddled around my feet.

Finally, he turns around, takes off his tuxedo jacket, and places it on the chair beside him. He undoes his tie, the silky material sliding through his fingers as he plays with it.

"You're beautiful." He stares at me. "But I want answers, and if you answer correctly, then I'm going to reward you. Do you understand the rules?"

He looks at me, his eyes staying on mine, never dipping to my breasts where I know my nipples are standing at attention directed at him. He walks closer to me, playfully playing with his tie, then he stops and looks down at me, smiling.

"Do you understand, Olivia?"

"Yes." I look up at him.

"Good, now tell me… why did you gave me a fake number?"

My heart begins to race, but I need to tell him the truth, just not the whole truth. "It was supposed to have been one weekend." I look up at him, his face is hiding any emotion he might be having about me.

"This is true, but you knew you would see me again at Vanessa and Christian's wedding."

"Honestly, I hadn't thought that far through."

Axel gives me a nod at my answer. He's quiet for a moment, then he pulls his white tuxedo shirt out of his pants and starts unbuttoning it. My heart thumps wildly as each button exposes his hard, decorated skin once it's hanging open. I take in all his tattoos. His shirt falls to the floor, and he smiles.

"I enjoyed our weekend together in Monaco. I wanted to stay in touch," he confesses.

This kind of shocks me.

After all, this is Axel Taylor, and he wanted to stay in touch with me after a wild weekend of sex?

"But…" I start, then stop, shaking my head.

"What?"

"You could have any woman in the world. Why would you want to stay in touch with me?" There, I said it.

His hand comes up and touches my cheek. "You have no idea how amazing you are, do you?" His words touch my heart, and butterflies take flight in my stomach. No, no, no, this isn't good. I shake my head.

"Liv, you're so different than the women I usually meet."

I huff. "Yeah, me and all my awkward inexperience."

"Honestly, that's a major turn-on." I look up at him, confused. "Yes, little one, watching you experience everything sex has to offer for the first time was one of the biggest aphrodisiacs I have ever experienced."

There are those butterflies again.

"Your trust, your willingness, your enthusiasm, I know all of us involved enjoyed that night very much." I can feel my blush creeping over my skin. "Hey, don't be embarrassed. It's rare for us all to play like that, even rarer for us to want to do it again."

"Again?" I squeak.

"Only if you want to, but if I'm honest, I want you all to myself." I nod in agreement. "Good, so next question. Why have you been hiding from me since I arrived?"

I take a deep breath. "Honestly, because I gave you the wrong number, I was embarrassed that I couldn't be the girl I was in Monaco with you. Because I'm here in my home, I have to be…"

"Lady Olivia Pearce," Axel answers.

"Yes, Monaco was my one and only time when I could be someone else, and I loved it. But that time is over now."

Axel stares at me for a moment, and then he fiddles with his belt buckle. He unclips it, and I watch as he slowly pulls it through the loops of his tuxedo pants, then drops it on the floor away from him. He toes off his black, shiny dress shoes, then his socks, and kicks them to the side.

"And now?"

I'm so mesmerized by him. "And now what?" I ask.

"And now I have you on your knees before me, in your home as Lady Olivia Pearce, not Liv from Monaco who had one night of freedom." I lick my lips because he's right. I'm supposed to be enjoying my friend's wedding, and here I am running through secret passages in the castle with a man I can never have, no matter how much I want him. I'm here naked before him doing the opposite of everything I should be doing, and I don't care.

"You do this to me," I confess.

His hand comes out and tips up my chin, so I look at him. "And you like it, don't you?"

I nod.

"You want more?"

I nod again.

"Let's make a deal." He quirks an eyebrow at me. "Be with me until I have to leave." I freeze at his words. "We can sneak around, no one has to know… but please, Liv, let me spend the next couple of days feasting on you."

I take a deep breath and slowly let it out. "Yes."

Axel smirks at me. "Right answer, little one. Now open wide, I have your reward." He unzips his pants and pulls out his cock. The tip is already glistening with need. I do as I'm told and open wide for him.

"Good girl." He slowly places himself on my tongue, my lips wrap around his girth, and a hiss falls from his lips. "That's it, take it all." He presses his velvety length further past my lips. I take him all the way even though I gag a couple of times which seems to turn him on even more.

"Fuck, how I have missed your perfect little mouth." Saliva is dripping down my chin which is gross, but I don't dare move from my spot even though my knees have become numb. All I can feel at this moment is my blinding need to please this man.

"That's it, take it." His hands move to my head as he literally fucks my face. "Shit. Yes. Fuck! I'm going to come," he tells me on a groan. I keep sucking and sucking, feeling the saltiness hit the back of my throat. I'm most definitely not a swallower, and as he slowly slips out of my mouth, I grab an old T-shirt that's on the floor and spit the contents of my mouth into it.

Axel chuckles. "Maybe one day you'll get used to swallowing." He touches my cheek with his thumb, and I smile. "Now, I think the lady needs an orgasm." Axel picks me up under my arms and throws me onto the bed, and I squeal at the sudden movement. He opens my legs and dives in, moving the tiny scrap of material to the side. Once his tongue hits its target, I fall back, and my eyes roll to the back of my head.

"Morning," a gravelly voice murmurs beside me.

Who the hell is in my bed? I quickly sit up in alarm, then a husky chuckle brings my attention to the occupant next to me. *Axel.* Last night's shenanigans all come flooding back—me on my knees taking him into my mouth and me being tied to my bed and being pleased repeatedly. My bottom is a little sore from the delicious spankings he gave me, and my body aches in places it's never ached before from the wild sex we had. Every time I'm with him, I feel like a different person—I feel freer. The sheet is hardly covering his naked body, and I let my eyes roam over all that glistening flesh.

"Keep looking at me like that, darlin', and I'm going to do somethin' about it," he says with a smirk.

I pull the sheet up around my body, covering myself.

"Hey." His hand catches the sheet and tries to pull it away. "I licked and kissed every inch of your body last night, so don't feel ashamed of it now." He tugs the sheet more, and I let it fall, exposing my naked breasts. I shiver as the cool air hits my skin.

"That's better." He puts his hands behind his head, his muscular biceps bulging at the movement. "I like waking up with you. It's been too long."

My stomach does a somersault. I shouldn't be feeling something for Axel because nothing can happen between us, but it's hard when he's staring at me the way he is, telling me things I have longed to hear from a man.

"I like you, Liv." Axel shocks me with his confession. My eyes meet his again, gold flecks swirling through whiskey-colored eyes.

"Axel." I pull the sheet up again, covering myself. I'm too exposed.

"Liv, don't." He sits up and pulls me onto his lap, so I'm straddling him. "I know you and I come from different worlds. God, we live on the opposite sides of the world, but you're the first girl in a long time who…"

I shake my head. "I can't be that girl for you, Axel." I'm trying to keep the tears back—he isn't supposed to like me. He's supposed to want hot sex and then be on his merry way back to LA. He's not meant to change the goalposts.

Axel reaches out and touches my face ever so gently. "But what happens if I want you to be that girl?" he confesses.

Shit!

He's supposed to be a good time and not any more than that. I squirm and try to move away from him.

"Liv, please." He has a frown on his face. "Are you not interested?" The tiniest sliver of vulnerability crosses his face.

"Of course, I'm interested. It's just…" I let the words trail off.

"You wouldn't want to do a long-distance relationship?"

I look at him in surprise. "Relationship?"

He grins at me. "Yeah, for you, I want to try."

Oh my God! Axel Taylor wants to be in a relationship with me. Bugger, bugger, bugger. This can't be happening.

"I don't think we would work." My answer hits him hard, and he tenses for a moment. "You could have any woman in the world, why me?"

He grabs me and pulls me closer. "You make me feel good, Olivia. When you're around, I can relax, be myself, not Axel Taylor from Dirty Texas. For some reason, I feel like I can trust you. It's hard when you're a celebrity because everyone wants something from you. But you don't, you aren't caught up in the hype around who I am."

Guilt is eating at me.

I can never be yours, Axel.

Never.

I look away because I can't look at him anymore.

"You don't have to say anything now, I just…" There's that vulnerability again, and it looks good on him. "Just think about it, okay?" I nod. "We still have some time here together before I have to get back to LA, and I'd like to spend it with you. Would that be okay?"

My heart is beating furiously. I can't lead this man on. I'm not that kind of girl, but I also don't want to let him go. "Can I think about it?" Axel's face falls at my answer. My hand traces the hard plains of his chest. "If I keep waking up with you in my bed, Axel, I don't know if I can let you go." My eyes meet his, a single tear falls down my cheek.

"Hey, hey, I didn't mean to upset you." He presses feather-light kisses against my face. "I just want to be honest with you. I like you. I want you. If all you can give me of yourself is this until I leave, then I'll take it. I'd rather have you for a short time than not have you at all."

This man is killing me. I nod because who the hell can say no to those declarations. "Until you leave, that's all I can give you." I lean forward and press my lips against his in a soft kiss and rest my forehead against his. "I wish our lives were different, but they're not. I'm going to be selfish for the first time in my life. I want to spend the rest of your time here with you." I pull myself away from him. "I don't want the other guests to know about us. Is that okay?"

"Of course. No one needs to know about us unless you want them to know."

"Thank you." I snuggle back into his chest, absorbing his heat around me. I take it all because I know it's the only male affection I'm ever going to receive for a very long time.

"Oh, Liv," Ivy sighs.

"I know, I know… I'm weak. The man was naked in my bed. What the hell was I meant to say?"

"I don't blame you, but you need to be careful, especially if he's declaring feelings."

My stomach sinks. "I know, it's so wrong, but… I mean, he's leaving, and I'll never see him again. It can't hurt, can it?"

"Maybe not, but…" Ivy shrugs.

"I know. I just have to make sure not to fall for him."

Ivy gives me a look.

"Fine… any more than I already have."

"Just be careful, you know if Penny or Eddie find out about this, they are going to make your life a living hell."

I shudder at the thought. God, if Penny knew Dirty Texas was up here, she would be on the next plane from London.

15

AXEL

The last couple of days, I have been sneaking into Olivia's room at night once everyone else has gone to bed. After spending the night loving every inch of her body, I take the secret passages back to my bedroom in the morning and meet everyone for breakfast. Olivia always joins us and gives me a knowing smile as I take a seat near her.

I know it was stupid of me to declare my feelings for her, but I thought I wanted to take a chance on a woman for the first time in my life. Her reaction wasn't exactly what I was expecting, but I get her reservations about the two of us. I have no idea how a relationship between us would ever work. But I do know that eventually, I don't want a long-distance relationship. I want to be able to wake up next to her and turn over and have my way with her whenever I desire. The other thing is I don't see myself leaving LA, either. My family is there, my friends, my business, everything I am is there, but everything that's Olivia is here. I just need to enjoy our time together, as limited as it is.

"Happy birthday, brother," I cheer, slapping Evan on his back as I enter the game room.

"Thanks, man." Evan starts racking up the billiard balls.

"I just remembered your thirtieth the other day." Evan grins. "And now look at you... married, wife, baby, and another baby on the way."

Evan laughs. "Yeah, if you had told me that two years ago, I'd have thought you were mad. But as cliché as it sounds, the love of a good woman changes everything." I now understand those words a little better, not that I'm in love with Olivia or anything, just that I've met a girl that has made me think of wanting different things for my life.

"You got lucky with Sienna, man," I say as I take a shot and split the colored balls across the table.

"Yeah, I did." He gives me a stupid grin. "You thinking that you might want to settle down?"

I stop what I'm doing and straighten up from the table. "I'm not sure." And that's the truth.

"I am not meant to break the marriage code, but... I've heard you and Olivia have been hanging out."

Has Olivia been talking to the girls? I thought she didn't want anyone to know about us. "What have you heard?" I ask, not wanting to say too much.

Evan bends over and takes his shot, sinking a couple of balls. "You know, I heard about Monaco." He raises his eyebrows at me.

"That was just fun."

"So magical dates in the French countryside, were they just fun as well?" he questions me as he takes another shot, sinking a ball. He moves around the table to take another.

"They were fun..."

He chuckles. "I'm sure they were. I also heard that you took her to The Paradise Club." He misses his next shot.

"Again, fun," I state as I line up and take my shot, sinking another ball.

"Interesting, that's all."

"Don't suppose you heard she gave me a fake number by any chance?"

He bursts out laughing. "She didn't?" I nod. "No wonder you're chasing after her. I think that might be the first time anyone has said no to you." He twirls his cue in his hands.

"Ha-ha," I say, taking my shot but missing. "She's a good girl."

"Then why the hell is she interested in you?" Evan laughs.

"I forgot how much of an ass you are."

He misses his next shot. He straightens up and has a serious look on his face. "This business is a lonely place, mate." Sienna's Australian words have started creeping into Evan's vocabulary. "And I'm guessing seeing Christian settle down is making you think." He flicks me on the forehead with his finger.

"Ouch, fucker." I rub my forehead.

"I'm just making sure you're listening. If you think Olivia might be the right girl for you, don't be a dick like me and be scared of your feelings. I messed up with Sienna, and I very nearly lost her for good. My life would honestly suck right now if I didn't have her." Wow, Evan's going all relationship guru on me. I frown at him.

"Look, I know we don't always share what's going on with our feelings and shit, but you're my best mate. If you need to talk, I'm here. Sometimes I might even have some good advice."

I chuckle as he slaps me on the back.

"I told her I liked her," I confess.

"And?"

"And, she told me she couldn't give me more after I left."

"Hey, at least she's honest." I nod in agreement. "But you might want more?"

"She's different to the girls we normally pick up or the girls I have fun with at The Paradise Club. She's honest, open, and she doesn't care how much money I have or what material things I may own."

"She does own a fucking castle," Evan points out.

"Yeah, exactly. But when we're alone together, we can talk. She's super intelligent, especially when it comes to business. And the sex..." my words trail off as I usually don't talk about my sex life with the guys.

"Sounds like you might have met your match." Evan smiles at me, handing me a beer.

"Yeah, I think so. It sucks that it can't go any further. My life is in LA, and hers is here in a fucking castle in the middle of nowhere."

"We could always open a London office," Evan jokes.

I stop to think, and the wheels in my head start to turn.

"Oh shit!" Evan laughs, taking a sip of his beer.

"Well, why shouldn't we expand? I know we're talking about opening a New York office, and I know you were wondering about an Australian one, seeing as you guys spend so much time down there. Why can't we open one in London? There are so many talented artists here in the UK, and don't forget Duo is from Sweden." Duo is a DJ act on our label that has exploded onto the scene over the past six months, especially during the European summer circuit.

"You that serious about the girl?" Evan questions me, which makes me stop to think, really think. *Am I seriously thinking about expanding our business just so I can be closer to Olivia?*

"Um... no... just might be a great business idea."

Evan scoffs.

"It would be," I argue.

"Okay, let's go with that."

I haven't seen Olivia all day, but I know she's busy getting everything set up for tonight.

"Hey, sweetheart," Mom hollers when I stick my head into the library. "Come sit down beside this fire and warm up." I do as I'm told and sink into the old leather chair.

"This place is magical." She closes the book she was reading and looks outside. The tiniest dusting of snow has landed on the gardens.

"Could you imagine if these walls could talk, what they would say? They are hundreds of years old. Imagine all the things they have seen over the centuries." Mom is a bit of a fan of historical romance stories.

"Yeah, it's amazing that it's still standing after all the wars and things that have happened around it." Olivia filled me in on her family history one night as we snuggled by the fireplace. It was cool being able to trace her ancestors back hundreds of years.

"Olivia is lovely, isn't she?" Mom looks up at me, and I can see the mischief in her eyes.

"Mom," I say sternly.

"Oh hush, you. I see the way you two exchange sneaky glances at each other, you're both not very subtle. I also notice that you disappear together when you think no one is watching."

Shit, I thought we were being a little more covert than that.

"A mother knows her sons. I knew it the first time Christian brought Vanessa home, she was the right woman for him, but neither were ready for what they have now."

"Mom, it's not like that."

"I know all about your groupies. I know that you have one-night stands or friends with benefits and things. Do I wish that both of my boys can find love? Of course, I want them to be happy. But I also know that you're more guarded than your brother with your feelings. I worry that you have buried them so far down that there's no chance you could ever find them again."

Mom reaches out and takes my hand in hers. "I love you, Axel, I want you to be happy. You deserve to be happy. I know what happened when you were younger changed you, and I wish I could've taken your place. I wish I could take away your pain. It kills me." Tears slip down my mom's cheeks.

"Mom, please, I've moved past what happened to me."

She nods and sniffles. "I know, baby, you have. You're such a strong boy, and I know counseling helped you, but you don't let people in, Ax. You keep most people at arm's length, especially women, and I understand it, I do." Those tears fall again. "I love you. You are still my baby even though you're thirty years old. You deserve happiness, just as much as your brother. I want that for you." She squeezes my hand.

"I know, Mom, I know."

She shakes her head, trying to get the terrible thoughts of what happened to me all those years ago from her mind.

"Olivia is a beautiful woman. She's also smart, funny, and polite. The way she looks at you, Axel… it's like you're something she has been waiting for all her life, and she doesn't quite believe you're there." My heart skips a beat, and I shake my head in disagreement. "No, Axel, she does. I can see you're looking at her the same way, wondering where the hell this woman came from. She challenges you, and she doesn't care that you're a rock star. She isn't after fame or fortune. She owns a castle, she's royalty, and doesn't need you for anything other than to be her partner."

"Mom," I say sternly.

She puts her hands in the air and smiles. "Just calling it as I see it, sweetheart."

"I'm not going to lie to you and say there's nothing happening between Olivia and me. Your eagle eyes have somehow noticed it, but we both agreed that we would have fun until I leave."

Her smile sinks a little. "I understand, sweetheart. You do both live on the opposite sides of the world. But I wouldn't be sad if you know... we had to visit you here at a castle. Just saying."

I roll my eyes at my mom. She doesn't give up.

16

OLIVIA

I stare out of my office window, looking over the snowy gardens. The end of the year is upon me, and I'm thinking about what a crazy one it has ended up being. I wonder what the new year will bring. Actually, I know what it will bring. It will bring heartbreak as I say goodbye to a man I like but can never have more of. A wedding to a man I don't love or will ever love, and a life I'm dreading. There's nothing to look forward to. *Gee, could it get more depressing?*

"Hey." I squeal as Axel wraps himself around me, my heart racing from the surprise.

"Bloody hell, you scared me." I try to get my heart rate down from heart attack level to normal.

"Sorry, I thought you heard me. You must have been deep in thought. Wanna talk about it?" He turns me in his arms, so my back is against the cold window, prickling my skin with goosebumps.

"No, not really." I give him a small smile.

"Hey," he says, taking my face in his palms. "Honestly, I'm not happy about leaving either."

My heart skips a beat as his lips touch mine. He's gentle at first, soft, sweet, telling me he understands there's some sort of crazy chemistry between each other. A small moan falls from my lips as he lightly nibbles my bottom lip, my hands finding his taut ass, and I squeeze it. Now it's his turn to let out a groan. He deepens the kiss. His hands move from my face and over my body. My nipples are pressed achingly hard against my sweater, and I can feel him hardening against me. How does this man make my body come alive with just the barest of touches?

"What's going on here?"

I push Axel away from me. *I know that voice.*

"Penny," I squeak out.

She's standing in the doorway with a shocked expression on her face. Well, I'm assuming it's shock, but she has had a lot of Botox. Her two best friends, Arabella and Isadora, her minions who happily follow her around like she's a queen, are standing by her side.

"What the hell are you doing here?"

Her eyes look Axel over hungrily, stopping at the considerable bulge in his jeans. She slips over to where he's standing beside me. "Hi, I'm Penelope, Olivia's younger sister," she introduces herself as she gives her hand to Axel. He takes it, but she grabs it and turns it over.

"Oh, your hands are so large," she purrs. "They look like they have been well worked." She gives him a flirty smile, admiring his calloused fingers. "I bet you know what to do with them."

Axel removes his hands from her. "And you'll never find out," he tells her. His blatant refusal stuns her for a moment. Not everyone is fooled by her advances, and Axel's little comment makes me happy.

She narrows her eyes at him and then focuses on me. "Well, well, well, Livy, never knew you had it in you."

"What are you doing here, Penny?"

"What, can't a sister come and spend New Year's with her family?" Penny puts on her cutesy mask.

"First time in what…" I tap my lip with my finger, "… ten years."

She silently fumes at me, but our upbringing has trained her not to make a scene. "Something has changed about you, Liv." Her eyes drift over to where Axel is standing. "Guess someone's been working their magic on you. I'm sure people will be impressed with this new Olivia."

My heart is racing.

Please don't mention Eddie, please don't say anything.

I don't respond.

"I'll catch up with you later, Axel." I break the silence, and he frowns. He doesn't want to leave me with my sister. Another little bit of information I shared while in bed with him—Penny and all the havoc she likes to bring to my family.

"Are you sure?" He steps toward me.

I step back away from him, making the frown on his face deepen. This little bubble we had created here has finally burst, and our time together is now over. We knew it couldn't last forever.

"Yes." I straighten myself up. I know the fight I'm going to have with Penny as soon as Axel leaves. He nods and walks out of the room.

Penny gives me a couple of moments before she starts laying into me. "Well, well, well… I'm sure Mother and Father would love to hear about how their precious Olivia has been slumming it with a dirty rock star."

"At least he isn't a D-grade celebrity like the ones you slum with."

Penny's jaw drops to the floor. I never fight back. I'm always the good girl. I don't want to stress my father out, and Penny does enough of it for both of us.

"Wow, he obviously has a magic dick because whatever he

has been doing to you has most certainly loosened up that giant stick up your ass. Oh wait, you did anal, didn't you? That's why the stick has gone." She lets out a cackle, and her bloody minions follow.

"What the hell are you doing here, Penny? Why are you not in the Caribbean with Mother and Father?"

"Because New Year's in London is so much better than some low-rent island. And I read the gossip on the social scene that some of the hottest rock stars were partying at my home, and I had no idea."

"That's because this is a private function I have been working."

"Working? Gee, maybe I should've helped out more if it meant I could screw around with my clients. Especially if fucking a 'Lady' was on the menu, they could've had two for the price of one."

My hand comes out and connects with my sister's cheek, the slap reverberating through my office. Everyone stills, all in shock at my reaction.

"Hurt a nerve there, sister, have I?" she snarls, rubbing her reddening cheek. I just glare at her, my chest heaving with anger. "I'm sure Eddie would love to hear about how his fiancée has been screwing around behind his back."

"Really? After everything he has done. Like he cares." I cross my arms in front of me defensively.

"Probably not, his bed has hardly been cold. But I'm sure Mother and Father would, especially when Eddie calls them in tears about the news that his lady love has been cheating on him. I'm sure the *Daily Star* would love that information. This time it will be your name splashed across the pages of a tabloid paper instead of mine, ruining your holier-than-thou reputation."

My stomach sinks. "What do you want?"

"Lucky you're smart. Let us stay and party with some rock

stars. I'll even promise not to touch Axel unless he wants me to." She smiles wickedly.

"And what do I get in return?"

"My silence." She smiles sweetly.

I take a deep breath. "Fine, stay, but you better be gone by lunchtime."

They all nod in agreement. "And you're staying in this cottage."

Penny shrugs. "Yeah, that's fine, I won't be coming home." I seriously want to slap her again.

"There are many single men here, so only go for them," I warn her. Penny likes a challenge, and married men are very much a challenge she likes to take on.

"So, Axel's single, right?" she asks, getting under my skin. I don't reply.

"That's okay, I'm not interested in your sloppy seconds, anyway."

"Well, that's a first," I mumble. She chooses to ignore me as she and her minions leave to work out what to wear tonight.

"What the hell is Penny and her evil minions doing here?" Ivy asks.

"They found out through the media that Dirty Texas is here, so they wanted to come and bag a rock star."

Ivy groans. "Of course, so let me guess, Axel is in her sights."

The thought makes me sick, but I'm hoping he'll be the first guy to say no to her advances.

"He told her she would never find out how good his fingers are when she flirted with him, so I'm kind of hoping that lasts."

"Oh, to be a fly on the wall for that reaction."

"It was pretty awesome. She didn't know what to do with herself. I also slapped her."

Ivy chokes on her champagne. "I'm sorry, what did you say?"

"She riled me up so much with her venom that I snapped. I've never done that before."

"I kind of love this new Olivia. She's so sassy." We both giggle.

"Sorry, do you mind if I butt in?" Axel asks.

"No, please, I need a refill." Ivy walks to the bar leaving us alone.

Axel looks devastatingly handsome tonight, dressed in jeans and a white button-down shirt, the sleeves rolled up showing off his blue tattoos. He grabs my hand and leads me away from the party out into the hallway. He looks both ways to see if anyone is around. With the hallway being clear, he pulls me toward the library. He opens the door, ducks his head in, then back out again, and pulls me in behind him. Axel presses me up against the wall, his lips descending on mine in an instant.

"It's been too long," he growls, pushing the material of my cocktail dress up. His hand slips into my underwear, finding me wet with want. "I just need to be inside of you, okay?" His forehead presses against mine. I mumble something that sounds like a yes, and he rips my panties right off.

"Axel," I gasp at his reaction, but if I'm honest, it's kind of hot.

Then before I know it, he's unzipping, sheathing himself, and is pressing inside of me. His hand covers my mouth. "Shh, there's someone outside."

I tense, hearing the click-clacking of heels along the stone floor and some giggling. My eyes glance down to the doorknob, it's locked, so I can relax a little. He pushes up inside of me, knocking a couple of books off the shelf, probably limited-edition books, but at the moment, I don't care because I can feel my orgasm begin to take shape. Axel is animalistic with his frantic thrusts. I grip him harder, urging him on. His name falls from my lips and vibrates against his hand as my orgasm shudders through my body. Axel isn't far behind me, his teeth sinking into my shoulder as he comes. Those whiskey eyes are flecked with gold.

"Sorry, I needed that." He seems a little shy confessing that to me.

"Please, no need to apologize for something that fantastic."

He kisses me quickly and pulls himself from me then he disposes of the condom and hands me my shredded underwear to clean myself up with.

"Um... yeah, sorry about those." His grin tells another story.

"You're incorrigible." I laugh, throwing my underwear in the bin. He ushers me to one of the velvet chairs, making me straddle him.

"How are you?" He wraps his arms around me, pulling me tight against him.

"I've been better." I give him a weak smile.

"She's a piece of work, your sister." He chuckles.

"That's putting it mildly."

"I'm sorry, I wish I were able to stay and support you." That's sweet of him, but he doesn't need to know how crazy the Pearce sisters are.

"Just be careful, she... um... might have you in her sights just to piss me off."

Axel smiles at me. "Why would I want anyone else but you?"

"Many have said those very same lines, and moments later, I have found them in bed with her."

Anger bubbles across Axel's face. "I may be a lot go things, but I'm not that much of a bastard." I rest my hand on his wildly beating heart.

"I know, but now she's here, I just can't let my guard down." I give him a weak smile.

"I understand. It's hard to trust people." He looks over my shoulder and out the window, becoming quiet for a moment. "I know first-hand that you can't always trust people you're supposed to be able to trust."

That seems very cryptic but true. His eyes have gone a little darker, and his body has tensed. I lean forward and press my lips to his forehead, hoping that I can give him some moral support.

"When the one person you thought you could trust is the one who betrays you, it's hard to come back from that."

"I'm so sorry someone betrayed you. It makes me angry that someone did that to you." The words fall quietly from my lips. Axel looks up at me, and I can see the pain etched into his face. My hand is still on his heart, and it's beating even wilder than before.

"My parents sent me to after-school music lessons when I was twelve." He pauses for a moment before he continues, "I always wanted to be a rock star." He gives me a goofy grin. "I loved going to my lessons until one day when what I thought was encouraging touches became something more."

Oh no, no, no. I shake my head, then drop kisses all over his rigid face.

"You don't have to tell me."

He's quiet for a moment, but he looks at me. "I trust you, Liv. I've never told anyone before other than my parents, even Christian doesn't really know the extent of what happened." My heart is breaking for him. "I was only twelve years old, for God's sake, and she was my teacher." I stop breathing. *She, I was assuming it was a male teacher.* "It went on for a year until I finally told my parents why I didn't want to go back to music class." There's that vulnerability again, that piece of him he hides.

"Is that why you like control in the bedroom?" I ask. Many things start to make sense.

"Yeah, I've been to counseling, and this was the only way for me to enjoy a healthy sex life. Until… you." I freeze. *What does that mean?* "Until you, I was so regimented with sex, I wanted things a certain way. But with you, I have broken all my rules, and I don't need to be in control."

I press my lips against his. "I like you being in control most of the time."

He chuckles. "I know. You're almost dripping wet from it." I bite my lip and try not to rub myself against him. "I trust you, Olivia." Those four little words make my stomach sink, the guilt over being engaged to someone else is sitting like a lead balloon in my stomach. I jump off his lap and fix myself up. "Liv?" Axel looks at me.

"I think I heard someone calling our names," I lie. He frowns, but he starts to follow me. Before I open the library door, I swing around and wrap my arms around his waist. "Thank you, thank you for sharing your secret with me. I'll never tell another soul."

He strokes my hair tenderly. "I know, Liv, I know."

I look up at him through tear-soaked lashes.

I need to tell him.

I need to tell him everything.

"Just know that I have fallen for you, Axel, and I wasn't supposed to."

He looks down at me with a huge smile on his face. He's happy, but my secret is killing me inside.

"I could fall for you as well, Olivia." The look he gives me is disarming. I quickly disentangle myself from him, but he pulls me back to him. "Are you okay?"

I take a deep breath. "Later, I have to tell you something, but let's get back to the party before we're missed." I plaster on my biggest smile, but he doesn't look convinced. I open the door and step out into the hallway.

Oh shit!

17

AXEL

It all happens in slow motion. A guy I have never seen before strolls up to Olivia, grabs her by the face, and kisses her right in front of me. I'm about to put my fist in his face until I hear Olivia's voice.

"Eddie, what the hell are you doing here?"

She knows this guy?

"I wanted to spend New Year's Eve with my fiancée."

What the fuck did he just say?

Olivia freezes at the man's words. The guy is oblivious to the tension surrounding us and decides it's a good time to introduce himself to me.

"Hi, I'm Marquees Edmund Lumley, but I'm known around here as Eddie." He holds out his hand, and I stare at him. I don't take his hand, and he eventually drops it. "I have to say, I'm surprised that you, of all people, would choose Liv here to hook up with."

I glare at him. He's dressed in a tailored, navy blue, three-piece suit, his brown hair slicked back, and his blue eyes are dull and lifeless. He's tanned and I assume he spends most of his days lazing on a yacht—he looks like a douche.

"Unless old Liv here has been hiding some kind of magic pussy that I don't know about." He chuckles arrogantly. I ball my fists, ready to knock this man out. But what I can't get over is how small Olivia has made herself. She has retreated into some kind of shell around him.

"Oh great, now my night is about to get better." Olivia's sister walks in from outside, fixing herself up, and Johnny from Sons of Brooklyn walks in moments later with a smirk on his face.

"What's up, Ax." He waves as he walks back into the party.

"So, Liv, have you made the introductions yet?" Her sister chuckles. Unlike what I saw earlier today where Liv fought back, now she just stands there taking her sister's vicious barbs. I want to shake and throttle her all at the same time.

"Eddie, have you met Liv's new boyfriend?" Her sister turns her attention to the guy.

"Boyfriend? Gee, you really must be a freak in bed. Have you been holding out on me, sweetheart?" Eddie lets his hand run down over her skin, and I can see her recoiling in disgust. "Thanks, Axel, man, for breaking her in for me. At least now I know the wedding night won't be a bust." He laughs again.

My fist lands in his stomach with a big oomph making him double over in pain. Her sister shrieks and comes right over, trying to look after him.

"Show some respect," are the last words I say as I turn on my heel and walk away from the carnage.

My mind is racing.

Olivia has a fiancée?

What the fuck is going on?

I don't get it.

She lied to me, she fucking lied to me. I kick over a bin in my rage. I push open the outside doors, the freezing air hits my hot skin, and I bolt. I need to clear my head.

So I run.

Images cloud my mind—us together in Monaco, lazing in bed, our picnic date, then these past few days of perfect bliss, her confession of falling for me, my childhood confession to her. I thought I could trust her because I thought she was different.

I run and run and run.

An hour later, and I can't feel anything on my body. My mind is clear as I walk back into the castle. I head straight up to my room to get changed. After a long hot shower, I get dressed again.

"Axel?" Olivia peaks in through the secret door.

God, she's beautiful, but she is a fucking liar.

"You have a fiancé?" My hands are actually shaking, I'm so angry.

She nods in agreement. "I'm sorry, Axel… but it's not what you think."

Is she serious? "Do you or do you not have a fiancé?"

She stands there silently, her brown eyes can't meet mine, they are glued firmly to the floor. "Yes, yes, I do have a fiancé."

I never expected something like this from her. She was different, she was supposed to have been different.

"I know I should've told you, it's just that…"

"There are no fucking buts, Olivia. You have a fiancé. You chose to continue whatever was happening between us, knowing full well that you were engaged to another. I can't stand to look at you. Was I just a convenient fuck? Or are you really a Dirty Texas groupie? Ha, groupie is too good a word for you. At least those women are honest when they fuck me."

I can see my words are hitting their mark.

"Go back to your fiancé. I never want to see you again." Turning my back on her, I walk out of the room while shaking my head.

"Happy New Year, Axel," Derrick says, grabbing me into a man hug.

"Happy New Year," I mumble back.

He stops what he's doing and looks at me. "What's the matter, and where's the sexy princess? Shouldn't she be trying to make your sad face happy again, if you know what I mean," he says as he wiggles his eyebrows at me.

"I don't fucking care where she is as long as it's far, far away from me." Derrick stops his dancing and looks at me, his once tipsy face now perfectly sober.

"Excuse me, what the hell did you say?" Derrick is very protective of his girls, but this time one of them doesn't deserve his protection.

"She's a fucking liar, D. She played me and played me good." I shake my head, the anger still pumping through my veins.

"What the fuck is going on?" His voice is tense.

"She has a fucking fiancé, D. A fiancé," I scream back at him.

He glares at me, grabs my arm, and hauls me off the dance floor and back out into the corridor.

"No shit! The dude is a douchebag. He's spent all holiday screwing his way around London. He's been on holiday with her sister, *her fucking sister,* and we all know what probably happened there, don't we?"

"You knew?"

Derrick freezes, and his eyes widen. "Yes, we all did."

"How long?" My fists ball again.

"Since Monaco."

"That's been over a month." I can't believe my friends have lied to me as well.

"You weren't supposed to fall for her," Derrick adds.

"Yeah, no fucking shit, D." I turn on my heel and stalk away from him. I can't believe he's been lying to me as well.

"Ax," he screams after me, but I ignore him. I don't want to be around these people anymore. He catches up to me and grabs my arm. I almost swing at him, but he stops me.

"You wanna have a fucking go, mate." His full Australian accent is coming out at me.

"No, I want you to leave me the fuck alone." I push Derrick in the chest, making him take a couple of steps back. "I can't believe you fucking lied to me, D. *You* lied to *me*." I poke myself in the chest, and his face sinks.

"I'm sorry, Ax. I am so sorry," he says.

"I have never in my life felt so betrayed." Derrick can't look at me. He stands there shuffling his feet from side to side.

"I made him promise to keep my secret," Olivia's voice cuts the tension between us.

"Don't you have some fiancé to go and keep happy," I snarl at her.

"I'm so sorry, Axel. I never meant to hurt you, that's why I gave you a fake number so nothing could happen."

"Ah, so it's my fault. My fault that I got sucked into your... what did your fiancé call it? Oh, that's right, your magic pussy."

SLAP. Olivia slaps me.

Derrick and Olivia both look shocked.

"Fuck you," I scream at her.

"Hey," Derrick yells back. "Calm the fuck down. She had her reasons to keep that from you."

"Oh, she had her reasons," I snarl.

"Fuck you, Ax. You're being a dick." Derrick pushes me, I push him back, and we end up in a scuffle.

Olivia tries jumping between us but just ends up with me elbowing her in the nose, and it starts bleeding.

Fucking great!

"Fuck, Liv, are you okay?" Derrick asks.

"Um… yeah, I'll be okay." She grabs a tissue from her bra and pushes it against her nose.

"Don't you ever fucking touch her again, you hear me," Derrick yells at me.

"It was a fucking accident, D. I'm sorry, Liv, but you shouldn't put yourself into the middle of a scuffle."

"Get the fuck away from us," Derrick screams at me.

I flip him off and walk outside again. I'm not in the mood to see anyone. Moments later, Christian and Evan are outside and have me pushed up against the stone wall.

"Tell me you didn't fucking touch her," my brother screams in my face.

"Fuck no, bro. Come on, I'd never hit a woman."

"Then why the fuck does she have a bleeding nose?" Evan questions.

"Because Derrick and I got into a scuffle, and she tried to break us up. I elbowed her in her nose while she was in between us. I said I was sorry," I explain, trying my best to smile at them.

"You're a fucking cocksucker sometimes," Christian yells at me.

"She has a fucking fiancé."

The boys stop dead in their movements.

"Excuse me, what did you say?" Evan asks me to repeat myself, and so I do.

"She's engaged to someone else, and apparently Derrick has known since Monaco."

The boys look at me in shock.

"Man, didn't see that coming," Evan adds.

"Me neither. Fucking happy New Year to me. I get to start the new year being totally fucked over."

Christian frowns at me. "Why did she do it? I don't understand."

"Because she has no choice, she has to marry him. Her father is dying, and this is like his last wish to see the two of them married," Vanessa adds, joining us outside with Sienna.

"You, too? You knew?" I ask.

"Yes, and we're the ones who encouraged her to explore herself in Monaco. None of us realized you would fall for her." She gives me a weak smile.

"I didn't fall for her." My argument doesn't even sound convincing to my ears.

"She never wanted to hurt you. I know it sounds bad, but, Ax, we thought you would be up for a little holiday fun and then move on. We never expected this," Sienna adds.

"You must think this is all funny, don't you? Look at Axel, finally getting a taste of his own medicine after all these years. So, thank you all. I never thought that the people I was the closest to would keep secrets from me."

"She has no choice, Axel," Vanessa implores.

"She had a choice to stop what was happening between us, and she chose not to."

"She should've told you, yes, but honestly, she didn't think she would see you again." Vanessa is still advocating for her friend. "That's why she gave you a fake number."

"So, this is my fault, is it?"

"No, of course not. But everything isn't black and white either," Vanessa argues back.

"I don't date liars, Ness, and she's the biggest fucking liar I have ever met."

And with that, I walk away.

I can't be here anymore.

18

OLIVIA

"Sucks to be you," Penny laughs, walking into my cottage. "Guess your rock star isn't that interested, after all." She gives me a sneer. "He's probably ripe for the picking. Little innocent Olivia has been hiding a dirty secret from him. I bet he needs a shoulder to cry on. No, actually, he probably needs someone to make him feel better and forget all about you."

I pick up my tumbler of whiskey and throw it at her. She ducks at the last moment, and the crystal glass shatters into bits against the stone wall.

"You fucking bitch," Penny screams at me, her minions holding her back.

"You're the fucking bitch, Penny. You have been your entire life," Ivy screams at my sister from the door. She pushes past Penny and stands by my side. "I just heard. I'm so sorry."

I give her a weak smile. "I hurt him, Ivy."

"I know, I know."

"You two are so pathetic. I'm going back to the party." Penny and her minions storm out of my home.

"God, I hate your sister." Ivy sighs.

"Welcome to my world."

"What are you going to do?" I grab another glass and pour myself a whiskey.

"Nothing, absolutely nothing."

Ivy looks at me.

"Ivy, I fucked up majorly, and he wants nothing to do with me. I hurt him, and now he hates me. Plus, I'm still marrying Eddie. I can't change that, so what does it even matter?"

Ivy frowns at me. "But you love him."

I roll my eyes. "It's a little too soon for love…"

"Really?" she questions me.

"I have feelings for him, of course. Could those feelings turn into love? Yes, so very easily."

"Why are you going through with this wedding? Eddie is a bloody pig. He's going to cheat on you for the rest of your life. Why… why do you think you don't deserve better?"

"Of course, I deserve better, Ivy. But my father… if I cancel the wedding, it will kill him. I can't destroy my father that way, and be the cause his death." Tears run down my cheeks.

"Livy…" Ivy pulls me into a hug as I sob my heart out.

"He's sick, really sick. I can't risk it. I can't risk decreasing what time he has left."

"You're leaving?" Derrick questions me. Everyone has come over to check on me as soon as they all woke up.

"I think it's for the best. This is your holiday, and me being here is only going to cause strain."

"But you're my friend as well," Vanessa adds.

"And he's your family, and family comes first. That's why I'm in this mess." I smile sadly.

"But can't you two work it out?" Stacey asks.

"There's nothing to work out. I have to marry Eddie, so there is no future between Axel and me."

"Eddie is a douche," Camryn adds. "He tried to pick me up even when I told him I was your best friend. He said that hasn't stopped your friends in the past."

A lead weight drops into my stomach. *He's been screwing around with my friends as well. What the hell am I doing?* I collapse onto my bed and start sobbing. My friends all gather around me.

"I'm sorry, Liv, I didn't mean to upset you," Camryn adds.

"No, no, I don't care, really I don't. I hate that this is what I'm going to have to put up with for the rest of my life. My soon-to-be husband will be screwing around with my friends behind my back."

"Why the hell are you putting up with this," Derrick demands.

"My father is dying, D. This is his last wish. How can I deny him that?"

Everyone is quiet.

"But your dad wants you to be happy, doesn't he?" Sienna asks.

"Yes, of course, but only with the right person, and he deems Eddie to be the right person."

"God, I wanted to punch his smug-ass face last night. He thought he was king of the castle," Derrick explains. "I was this…" he puts his fingers almost together, "… close to punching him."

"Axel did… in the stomach."

Everyone bursts out laughing.

"Even though Axel was mad, when Eddie started insulting me, he hit him."

Everyone nods their head in agreement.

"Axel has feelings for you, strong feelings," Vanessa tells me.

I can't look at anyone. "I know. And I know you all don't

understand my decision when it comes to Eddie, but I love my father more." They all nod quietly, understanding my meaning.

"Well, it sucks that you're leaving," Isla pipes up.

"Yeah, we have so much more stuff to do together," Vanessa adds.

"I know, but it's your special time, and me being here is going to make Axel uncomfortable. He doesn't deserve that."

"See, you care for him." Sienna smiles.

"Of course, I do. I'll never forget Axel. He has my heart, but that's all I can give him, the rest of me will belong to another."

I say my goodbyes to everyone and promise to stay in touch.

Beep. Beep. Beep.

My phone wakes me up from my deep sleep. I've been holed up in London at Ivy's place for the past couple of days licking my wounds. The glowing screen hurts my sleep-deprived eyes.

It's a message from Penny.

I open it up, and my world shifts.

There's her smiling face taking up the screen, a sheet wrapped around her naked body, and just to her left, the tattooed arm catches my attention. That's when I notice the artwork—all blue, Japanese origami-style ink—Axel's. She's in Axel's bed. He fucking lied when he said he'd never touch my sister. Bloody fucking, fuck face, douchebag!

My heart is racing as I zoom into the picture. Yep, that's him. My heart breaks all over again. I hate him. I hate him so fucking much. He told me he never lets girls sleep over. He's never had them in his bed until me, but there's Penny staring smugly back at me.

Her text reads: **So exhausted, oh what a night!**

Her bloody emojis are making my eye twitch. I have never wanted to murder someone so much as I do my sister right now. I hate her just as much as I hate Axel right at this moment. I have to get out of London. I don't want to be anywhere near her ever again. She's gone too far now in her quest to hurt me. We can never come back from this. I start packing my bags again, stomping around angrily.

"Hey, what are you doing up so early?" Ivy walks into my room half asleep.

"Axel slept with Penny."

"What? No way. I wouldn't believe anything your sister says, she's a pathological liar."

I hand my phone over to Ivy. She looks at the screen, and her face drops. "Oh, Liv. I'm so sorry. Your sister is a class-A bitch. I've seen her do some low things, but this one takes the cake. And him, how fucking dare he! I was team Axel until this." She shakes the cell phone in her hand. "Screw him, screw her, you deserve so much better than all these fuckheads, Liv."

"I know, that's why I'm getting out of London. I'm heading to Mustique, where my parents are. Want to come for a girls' trip? We can sit on the beach sipping cocktails. I need to get out of here, I can't see Penny, not after this."

"Okay, why not. Screw London. Let's get out of here. A change of scenery will be good."

"Hey, ladies. Having fun in the Caribbean?" Camryn asks during our FaceTime call. We've been away from London for a week now. The Dirty Texas gang have left and gone back to their lives on the other side of the world.

"Yes, it's exactly what the doctor ordered." I love how the Caribbean sun is kissing my skin, it's exactly what my soul needed. Thankfully, Mother and Father didn't ask questions as to why Ivy and I had decided to join them for their annual holiday.

Ivy said she was complaining about the weather, and that prompted us to have a holiday.

"You both look relaxed. I'm freezing my butt off here in New York," she moans.

"We'll have a cocktail for you," Ivy teases.

"You're such a giver, sis. Actually, I was thinking we could have a cocktail together in a couple of days."

"You want to come and stay with us?" I ask, taking a sip of my cocktail.

"Um… that's sweet, but actually no. I was thinking that you ladies could come and stay with me."

Ivy and I both looked at each other. *What on earth is Camryn going on about?*

"I'm organizing the soft launch of The Paradise Club Resorts with Nate… and well, I thought maybe you two lovely ladies would like to test out the facilities. When I say facilities, I mean have hot, wild sex." Ivy and I are stunned into silence. "Hello, guys, I can't hear anything? Did we lose the connection?"

"Um… no we're here, Cam. We are just a little stunned by your request," Ivy responds.

"What, you don't want to come to a sex resort?" she questions her sister.

"Of course, we do. We just weren't expecting that," Ivy answers.

"Um… so who's going?" I know exactly who likes The Paradise Club.

"Don't worry, he declined the invite. He won't be there, neither will the rest of the crew. Something about expanding into New York, so they are here looking at office spaces."

That's good to hear. I definitely don't want to run into him, especially alone at a sex resort.

"Come on, it will be fun and wicked. The resort looks amazing. We're talking about a seven-star luxury resort on an island.

What Nate has built is spectacular. Plus, you both need some hot, wild sex as well."

"Cammie," Ivy squeals at her sister.

"Ivy, please. I know for a fact that it has been too bloody long since you got your cage rattled." Ivy groans at her sister's words.

"Come on, Liv, I know you had fun at the club. I know things are shit right now. You don't have to do anything you don't want to do, but I'd really appreciate two of my best friends helping me on this big project."

Ivy and I look at each other.

"Fine, we'll come," I answer, and Camryn squeals on the other end of the line.

"Thank you both so much. I promise you won't regret it at all."

Famous last words.

19

AXEL

"You made it," Nate greets me at the private heliport on his island, the warm tropical breeze hitting my skin. This is exactly what I need, a week of nonstop sex on a tropical island to forget about Olivia.

"You're a persuasive man."

He chuckles. "Hey, you're doing me a favor, man. I trust your thoughts on the resort." He's probably helping me out way more than I'll be helping him. It's been over a week since leaving England, my brother is sunning himself in Tahiti, and Isla is training Stacey on her new role at the record label before she flies out to Europe to start working with Sebastien. Oscar and Finn are in New York looking at offices, and Evan is helping Sienna and Derrick with the renovations of their new office.

So that leaves me sitting in my office all alone, trying not to think about Olivia. And when I'm not thinking about Olivia, my dick is remembering how it used to be wrapped in her sweetness, and then that leads me to thinking about her again, and the vicious cycle continues.

I'm sick or crazy, probably crazier because when you're trying to get over someone, the best way is to probably forget about them, not stalk their social media pages. There was nothing on any of her pages, which was kind of good. But to add to my stalkerish ways, I might have looked up her douchebag fiancé's pages too. Photo after photo of him with random women, pictures of him in exotic places, of him cruising in luxury cars—it all screamed douche, douche, douche.

What I didn't like were the pictures of him and Penny together. They seemed awfully close. I'm sure they have already slept together behind Olivia's back. I wouldn't put it past them. I mean, Penny tried to put the moves on me after Olivia left. Every corner I turned she was there trying to seduce me. There was no way in hell I'd ever sleep with her, even if I didn't know she was Olivia's sister. I know women like her—gold diggers. You can smell the desperation a mile away, and I'm not interested in that. Plus, she has nothing on Olivia's natural beauty with her silicon-enhanced breasts, Botox face, and over-plumped lips.

"So, how are you holding up?" Nate questions me. "I heard what happened."

"That's why I've come here… to forget all my troubles."

"Well, this is paradise. Everything you have ever desired can be fulfilled," he states as he hops into a golf cart.

"How's Camryn working out?" I ask, making conversation as we pass the millionth palm tree.

"Yeah, she's a pretty cool chick. She's also kind of scary." He chuckles.

"You should've seen her organizing the wedding, she treated it like a military operation."

"It's kind of hot." He smirks.

"Really?"

"I'm her client, so nothing can happen. I don't mix business and pleasure."

I cough at his statement.

"Ha-ha. You know what I mean. She's a beautiful woman,

super smart, driven, and a workaholic. All the things I find sexy."

"But you don't mix business and pleasure," I tease him.

"Screw you, man. I can turn this cart around, and you can hop on the next helicopter off the island."

"Hey, don't be a dick. I need to get laid. That's why I'm here."

"Fine, only because you're a friend. Now, here is your humble abode." He stops outside of a grand two-story villa. Nate jumps out of the cart and opens the door for me. I step into the villa, and all I see before me is pure white sand and the azure waters of the Caribbean.

"Man, this really is paradise."

Nate chuckles. "Glad you approve. I have so much more to show you, but that can wait if you want to hang out here for a while to chill. I can come and get you for dinner in a couple of hours." I can't take my eyes off the large pool that's pressed up against the back deck of my villa.

"Yeah, that should be fine, just text when you're ready." Then he's gone. I take a couple of steps through the living room and straight out onto my back deck. I kick off my shoes, toe off my jeans, and take off my T-shirt, then jump into the pool. I do a couple of breaststrokes as it's not that large for me to do laps in, but enough to wake me up from my long journey. I sit back and look out over the empty beach to the beautiful ocean. This is certainly paradise.

There's a button beside the pool that says *Butler*, so I press it. I could definitely use something to eat and drink. Moments later, a beautiful woman is walking through my villa.

"Yes, Mr. Taylor. How may I help you?" The woman smiles at me. She's wearing tight-fitted navy shorts that cup her pert ass, a white polo that's cut very low against her large breasts, giving me an eyeful of her impressive cleavage and blonde hair that's pulled up in a high ponytail—perfect to be wrapped around my fist as she sucks my dick. My stare falls to her wrist, where multi-colored bracelets adorn it just like they do at The Paradise Club, letting me know what she's up for. It looks like everything except intercourse.

"What's your name?" I ask.

"I'm Layla, and I'll be your personal butler for your stay. I am here to serve you." She licks her ruby red lips.

"Lovely to meet you, Layla. At the moment, I'd love something to eat and some beer."

"Of course, what do you desire?"

"Anything is fine. I'm not fussy."

She gives me a smile and nods. "Anything else, sir?"

"That's all, thanks." As beautiful as she is, my cock remains deflated. I stare out toward the ocean because I need to get my head together. I'm acting like a damn pussy.

There's a knock at the door.

"Hey, man, are you ready for the tour of the resort?" Nate smiles, handing me a beer.

"Damn right I am. If this place is as awesome as your clubs are, I can't wait to test it all out." We jump into the cart and tear off into the rainforest.

"The island has been split off into sections, just like the levels of the clubs. There's a beginner, intermediate, and expert area. We have sections just for couples and just for singles and, of course, areas where people can all mingle. All beaches are clothing optional. Well, the entire resort is clothing optional except for eating areas or bars… no one wants to eat with a bunch of naked people." This makes me laugh.

"We have rainforest villas which are like luxurious treehouses set up high in the trees overlooking the resort. This is for people who like their space. There are also overwater bungalows with see-through floors so you can watch the ocean below. All guests get their own golf cart to cruise around the resort to cater to all of their needs. This includes possibly being the third person in their bed or just bringing them food and drinks to replenish. So, did you enjoy Layla?" Nate asks me.

"She fed me and brought me a beer, but that was as far as we took it."

Nate gives me a look but leaves it.

"Now over here, set away from the beach, is a large glass room. This is made for the voyeurs and exhibitionists. They can come straight off the beach to the open showers. As you can see, there's enough space for more than a couple of people."

Yeah, it most certainly rivals the glass cube at the clubs—I can see many people having fun in there. We travel further, and Nate shows me a hidden waterfall that has a grotto inside that people can enjoy. There's a whole section of the resort set up for kinks with playrooms tucked away between the rainforest where you would have no idea they existed. Each one is set up for whatever you could desire with high-tech facilities and equipment.

"I had my best Doms and Dommes at my clubs consult me on their wish-list rooms, and that's what we have." So many ideas are running through my head of what I could do to Olivia if she were here, but I need to shut that down real quick.

"We have a dedicated spa area for massages... the sexual and non-sexual kind. People here are also on holidays, and not everyone wants sex twenty-four seven." He makes a face, and I laugh. "That's why we have so many activities, day tours, the best restaurants, bars, and everything you would expect from a luxury resort."

We continue around the island. It's huge, and I'm totally lost, so I'm glad he's navigating. "As this is a resort, most of the play areas are set far and wide which might be hard for people to find, so I have also built a smaller version of The Paradise Club here at the resort. The only catch here is most of the rooms are open for everyone to see, no closed doors. If you want closed doors, we have hundreds of closed-door playrooms scattered around the island. One of our staff will happily drive anyone to a free one if they want."

Nate has thought of everything. I can see myself holidaying here quite often.

"I'm starved. Let's grab something to eat, and then we can sample the delights the resort has to offer." He presses the accelerator on the golf cart and has us hurtling down the sandy path toward the restaurant and bar area of the resort. He parks outside of a large jetty and gestures for me to follow him. As I walk behind him, I look around and notice all these villas jutting out into the ocean.

"Pretty cool, aren't they? You might want to try them out later in the week. These are further away from everything going on at the resort, so that's why I started you off at the beachfront villa." The sun is starting to set slowly, casting orange and pink shimmers all over the crystal-clear water. *Now, this is paradise.* I look over the edge and see tropical fish darting around, a lazy stingray gliding over the sand, and a pod of dolphins is off in the distance playing around in the calm waters.

"There's a restaurant and bar right on the point here, where the sunset view is pretty spectacular."

"Aren't you a romantic, Nate. Is this a date?" I joke, and he flips me off.

We finally reach the end of the jetty, the maître d ushers us into the empty restaurant, and that's when I notice three beautiful women sitting outside on the large oversized sofas taking in the sunset, cocktails in their hands. My feet start to slow because I don't believe what I'm seeing. Nate's slow as well.

"Shit, man. I had no idea," Nate curses once he realizes who's sitting there. "Camryn asked if she could invite two friends to the resort to test it out, but I had no idea one of them was her."

I shake my head.

I can do this.

We'll just go over and say hi but leave them to their cocktails.

"It's okay, I knew I'd run into her again at some stage. She's friends with Ness, so how could I not? I just thought I would have more time." Two weeks hasn't been enough time. I'm angry with her and still hurt. I trusted her, and she betrayed me.

"You sure? They haven't spotted us yet, and I have another six restaurants."

I power on, my legs feeling like lead. It's probably better seeing her here instead of being a willing participant in some orgy. Nate pushes on ahead. I see Camryn stand and smile when she sees Nate walk outside. He gives her a quick, professional peck on the cheek and says hello to the other two girls. Then it's my turn to walk outside, and that's when Camryn spots me.

"Shit, what are you doing here?" Never one to mince her words.

I smile at her, but my attention is on the beautiful brunette dressed in an off-the-shoulder, white lace, 50s style cocktail dress. Even at a sex resort, she dresses like a lady. I hate how my body is reacting to seeing her again, her creamy legs crossed and her delicate hand holding the silver martini glass. Those doe eyes refusing to look at me, but I can see a nice shade of pink crawling up her neck. She's either embarrassed or angry.

"Evening, Olivia."

Finally, she looks up at me, fire blazing behind those hazel eyes, her grip on her glass tightening, but years of training has her manners in check.

"Evening, what a surprise." She takes a shaky sip of her cocktail—I like that I affect her.

"Certainly is, I'm surprised your fiancé would let you come to such a corrupt place."

Those hazel eyes flash daggers at me at the mention of him.

"He assumes I'm with my family in Mustique."

"Oh, that's right, I forgot how much of a skillful liar you are." Anger creeps through my veins now at her ice-princess reaction to me. The pink on her neck has increased, flaming all over her décolletage and cheeks.

She puts down her cocktail, uncrosses her legs, picks up her purse, and stands. "It wasn't the only thing I learned from you then." She turns to Nate. "I'm sorry I won't be staying for dinner. I've lost my appetite." Ivy stands with her, and they both turn their backs on us and walk away.

"You're such a dick, Axel." Camryn gets up as well, quickly polishing off her cocktail, and with a perfect hair flick, she struts away.

"Wow, not sure what you have done, but they are three pissed-off women." He chuckles.

"Not sure why they're angry at me. I don't have a fiancée stuffed away somewhere."

20

AXEL

Later that night, after one too many beers, Nate and I head out to explore paradise. We got a lift on a golf cart by a staff member heading toward The Paradise Club. We're currently sitting on the first level watching the action unfolding in the cube, but my dick isn't rejoicing at all. He's firmly tucked away, not wanting to come out to play.

"Fellas," a tall man with a British accent interrupts us.

"Bro." Nate lights up seeing his younger brother. "What are you doing here?" He looks genuinely shocked.

"I needed to check in on my investment." He chuckles.

"Silent partner, remember?" Nate laughs, and Alex rolls his eyes at him. "Hey, you remember Axel Taylor from Dirty Texas, don't you?"

His brother's face forms a smile. "Yeah, man. Long time, no see." He shakes my hand. I have met Alex on and off over the years I've known Nate. He looks after the family's property development business. Nate wasn't interested in taking over the family business as he had his own ideas for success.

"Yeah, good to see you again. I'll tell you something, this resort is pretty amazing."

"I just flew in, so I haven't seen much, but I'm sure my night has just gotten better." He looks at something off in the distance. We both follow what has caught his attention, and in the corner watching the cube is none other than Camryn, Ivy, and Olivia. Now my dick decides it wants to come out and play.

"They are nothing but trouble," I mumble.

"Ignore him. He has history with one of them," Nate tells his brother.

"Hopefully, not the one in the pink dress?" Looking again, I notice Ivy is in pink.

"Nope, lady in white," Nate answers for me.

"Good choice." Alex chuckles.

"Your brother has a thing for his new event planner, the one in red." I throw Nate under the bus.

Alex whistles. "What about your motto? Never mix business and pleasure together, only make business out of pleasure."

Nate groans. "Yeah, well, that one is biting me in the ass at the moment. When we first met, she had a boyfriend and now… now she's single and trying to get over the douchebag who fucked her over. It's so hard because she is curious about everything."

"Stay strong, brother, stay strong." Alex slaps his brother on the back.

"I'm practically a fucking saint," Nate groans, which makes us all laugh.

"Why don't we join them?" Alex asks. We both give him a look. *Are you serious?* "Guys, come on. I want to meet the beauty in pink," he groans. And just like good wingmen, we finally falter and follow Alex toward the girls.

"Evening, ladies," Alex starts, using his fancy British accent on them.

"And who are you?" Camryn asks, looking him over.

"My brother." Nate glares at her.

"Well, it's nice to meet you, Nate's brother." Camryn smiles at him.

"It's Alex, my name's Alex." He introduces himself to all three ladies but pays special attention to Ivy.

I look over at Olivia, and she's looking everywhere but at me.

"If you'll excuse us, I might show Camryn around. I haven't had a chance to give her much of a tour yet." Camryn smiles and follows Nate out into the crowd and then off down a secret passage.

Now, this is awkward.

"So, ladies, are you both single?" Alex asks the loaded question.

"Yes, we are," Olivia answers for Ivy, and I turn to look at her.

"Really? I'm pretty sure your fiancé back in England might say something different, don't you?" I bite back.

"I'm pretty sure he's screwing every single woman in London as we speak, so I don't think he has grounds to stand on to be upset."

Ivy and Alex look on as we throw barb after barb at each other.

"Yet, you still continue with this farce of an engagement. I don't know if I should admire your loyalty or your stupidity for the cause."

Olivia is fuming. Even in the semi-darkness, I can see the redness creeping up her neck again. She's so easy to read. If she's so easy to read, then how the hell did I not know she was lying to me?

"I was pretty stupid to think that you were any different than all the other men I have been with. In the end, you're all the same, you think with your dicks." She's shaking with anger.

"Maybe we should leave them alone for a moment." I hear Alex talking to Ivy.

"Yeah, I think so."

"Of course, I was thinking with my dick. It was hypnotized by your magic pussy."

SLAP.

Olivia slaps me across the face, and I'm stunned into silence for a couple of moments. "Is that why you're here tonight, to mesmerize some poor guy with your damsel-in-distress routine?"

"Screw you, Axel."

"You wish, darlin', you wish," I bite back.

"You think that I can't get anyone else?" she questions me.

"Oh, darlin', I know no one else out there is going to be able to compete with me. I'm the best you've ever had. I remember the way you screamed my name as I fucked you like no one has before."

If steam could come out of her ears, I think it would at this moment.

"Fuck you."

Hearing Olivia swear makes me laugh. It sounds so foreign coming out of her mouth. It's kind of cute.

"I'll show you, Axel Taylor. You aren't as special as you think you are." And with that, she turns on her heel and makes her way through the crowd. She stumbles past half-naked people, people in the throes of ecstasy while they watch the orgy going on in the cube. I follow her, winding through the crowd. I notice she starts to unzip her dress.

What's she doing?

She doesn't take her dress off but lets it hang open then she steps out of her high heels and places them in her hand. Then with her other hand, she opens the door to the cube and disappears inside.

What the fuck is she doing?

My heart is racing.

What's she playing at?

I watch on as she throws her heels into one corner then shimmies her dress off, kicking it to the side with her shoes.

One of the young men notices the latest addition to their show. He's well-built, good-looking, and well-hung, not that I'm looking, but it's kind of there in front of me. He's making his way over to her. I can see the feral hunger in his eyes, the knowing smirk that he knows he has hit the jackpot with Olivia joining them. The others are still playing around, but eyes are glancing every now and again, looking at the new situation developing.

The guy is saying something to her, making her blush. He reaches out and touches her skin. I want to be sick. Why is she not telling him to fuck off? He says something again, and she turns away, blushing, her eyes locking on mine. She gives me a *fuck you* kind of smirk and drops to her knees, and that's it, I see red. I push my way through the crowd. I don't care who I'm pissing off, but there's no way in hell I'm going to witness Olivia's perfect lips on another man's fucking cock. I yank open the door, the guy is whispering dirty things to her, and his fingers are twisted in her hair.

"Don't you fucking touch her," I scream at him.

Everyone in the cube stops what they are doing. I stalk over to where Olivia is on her knees. I pick her up and throw her over my shoulder.

"Axel," she screams.

"Shut the fuck up, Olivia, just shut the fuck up," I growl. "Please carry on, just not with my girl." I slam the glass door, making the cube vibrate behind me, and I push my way through the shocked crowd. Thankfully, Olivia isn't making any more of a scene than it is. I see one of the rooms is free by the green light above it, and I walk toward it. Opening the door, I slam it shut again and lock it.

The first thing I see is a black leather table with straps. I throw Olivia off my shoulder, turn her around, and place her face down on the table, her bottom half bends as her feet land on the floor, and she lets out a startled yelp. She's still wearing her flesh-colored lace underwear. I grab her wrist and shackle one to the bench.

"Axel," she screams, but I ignore her. I'm so angry with her little stunt. Did she seriously think I'd stand there and watch her give some fucker a blow job?

"What are you doing?" She squirms on the table, and I grab her other wrist and tie her down with some effort as she fights me on it. Her legs are still loose. She looks perfectly curved around the table like that. "Axel, you're scaring me," she whimpers, and I can hear it in her voice. I move to where she's lying and let my hand touch her head.

"Do you have any idea how jealous you just made me, little one?"

Those hazel eyes focus on me. "That was the point."

"I know, darlin', but I couldn't let you go through with it." I stroke her cheek.

She closes her eyes. "I didn't want to go through with it either," she confesses. *Thank fuck!* Hearing that makes my heart beat normal again.

"Then why did you do it?" I question her, letting my fingers run down her exposed back, her body goose pimples under my touch.

"Because I wanted to make you hurt as much as I do." Another confession.

"Do you think I didn't hurt over what happened between us?" I let my hand trace the curves of her body, the ones I have missed these last couple of weeks.

"I know so," she says defiantly.

I stop moving. I hear the anger and hurt in her voice. "No, you don't. You have no idea what I have been thinking." Moving around her again, this time I let my fingers slide down her legs. There's an ankle restraint at the bottom, and I tie it around one, then I move to the other and do the same. She doesn't fight me.

"I know because you did the one thing you promised you would never do to me. You promised me you weren't like all the other men before you, you made me believe you were different." I watch as tears fall from her eyes.

"I am. I trusted you, I trusted you with all my heart, and you betrayed me." I thump my hand against my chest, over my heart, the one that's a little bit chipped from her.

"I know..." She lets out a sigh. "I should've told you. I should have been honest. But I was scared, confused, all those things, but in hindsight, I know I should've maybe done things differently, but..." Tears fall rapidly against her cheek. "I'd never change the time we had together because for the rest of my life, I'll remember that as the first time in my life a man cherished me, worshiped me, and made me believe I was beautiful. No matter what you did to me after you found out about my lie, I'll never forget those moments."

"You're all those things to me, Olivia," I whisper, my hand stroking her silky brown hair.

"But I can never forgive you for what you did, Axel." I freeze. "I'll never forgive you for sleeping with Penny." The words catch in her throat.

What's she talking about?"

"I never slept with your sister."

"I have proof. She texted me a picture of you two in bed together."

What's she talking about?

I quickly release her feet, then her wrists.

"Why the hell would I sleep with your sister?" I can't believe she would think that.

"I have the photo, Axel. There's no denying what happened. I know I hurt you, I know I abused your trust, but never did I think you hated me so much that you would do that to me."

Then she drops to the floor, fainting.

21

OLIVIA

Where am I? I watch as palm trees zoom by, my eyes blinking and trying to adjust. Strong arms are wrapped around me protectively. I squint in the darkness, but nothing looks familiar.

"It's going to be okay, little one. I have you." I hear that voice I'm so familiar with.

"Axel," I whisper, wondering why he's here.

"Shh, babe. We're almost there." Moments later, the movements stop, and I'm picked up as if I weigh nothing more than a feather. I burrow into Axel's chest as he carries me to wherever he needs to go. I hear the creak of a door opening, then closing again, and the only sound I hear after that is of Axel's footsteps across the wooden floor. I'm placed very gently onto the soft duvet, and he disappears again. I can hear the ocean waves now just outside of the room. I have a headache, but I don't remember drinking.

"Here, take these for your head." He hands me two white pills and a glass of water. I knock them both back and finish my water. I sit up in bed and look at Axel's worried face. "Are you okay?" he asks me.

"I have a headache. Thanks for helping me."

"I'm so sorry. I watched you faint right before me, and I couldn't reach you in time… you hit your head. I should've caught you." I can see the pain on Axel's face.

"Hey, it's okay. I'm okay," I reassure him.

"Liv, do you remember anything that happened before you fainted?"

I frown for a moment, trying to remember, then it all comes rushing back to me. *Shit!*

"Are you okay? You've gone pale." Axel asks.

"Yeah, I'm okay. I think you should go now." I pull the duvet up around me.

"I'm not leaving you. We have stuff to sort out."

"No, we don't."

"I didn't sleep with your sister, Liv." He raises his voice.

"You can deny it all you want, but I have proof."

"Show me this proof," he demands.

I look around the room for my clutch, but it's not here. "It's in my bag. The bag I had tonight, where is it?" Axel jumps up and walks out of the room, and within a few minutes, he's back again.

"Here." He hands me my clutch. I take it, open it up, and find my phone. I unlock it and bring up the message and shove the picture in his face. He's quiet, studying the photo. "I'll text it to you if you want to reminisce about the magical night you had together."

"I didn't sleep with her," Axel argues.

"I call bullshit." I shake the phone in my hand.

"Your sister is fucking messed up… that's what she is." He stands up and starts pacing the room.

"Screw you, don't blame her when all you could think about was getting your rocks off." I want to throw my phone at him, but I hold myself back.

"Of course, you would think the worst of me."

"I don't have to think, Axel, I can see it."

"You're looking at something she wants you to see. Am I awake? Do I have my arms wrapped around her? Am I giving the camera a big thumbs up?"

"You were so exhausted from screwing her all night, you fell asleep."

"Yeah, I was exhausted all right, but not from fucking your sister. I drank myself into oblivion most nights because I couldn't get you out of my mind. Every single time I opened my eyes, I saw you. You were the last fucking thing I thought of when I went to sleep. I drank myself to the point I couldn't stand up because that was the only way to wipe you from my mind."

The butterflies in my stomach wake up with each of his words, but I still can't forget the picture I saw of them together.

"Why would she do it?"

Axel gives me an are-you-serious stare.

"She's my sister."

"And you should know how far she would go to fuck with you."

I know he's right, but this, this seems way too harsh even for her.

"She's in your bed, Axel."

He starts pacing again. "I know. I know it looks bad, and I can't explain it, but all I know is I didn't do it. No matter how much I hated you right at that moment, I could never hurt you like that." I can see the anguish on his face.

"Call her."

Axel gives some a strange look.

"Call her and find out what happened that night. Here's her number." I give him the phone.

"You want me to call your sister right now?" He looks at me like I have gone crazy.

"Please," I whisper, shaking my phone at him. He huffs and takes the phone from me, takes his out from his back pocket, and dials the number. He hits call and puts it on speaker. The room is filled with silence and tension as we listen to the phone ring.

"Hello…" A groggy male voice answers the phone.

"Who's this?" Axel asks.

"It's Eddie."

I know that voice, that's my fiancé. My stomach sinks. Penny's gotten her claws into him.

"Baby, who's on the phone." My sister's voice comes through loud and clear, and I think I'm going to be sick. Axel reaches out and takes my hand in his, giving me an encouraging squeeze.

"It's Axel, Axel Taylor."

There's rustling and mumblings as Penny grabs the phone. "Oh, Axel, hi. How are you? What a pleasant surprise." Her voice is thick with flirtation.

"Hope I wasn't interrupting," Axel continues.

"No, no. Just my friend playing a trick." She giggles.

"Was that Eddie… Olivia's Eddie?"

Penny is silent.

"Penny, I don't care if you're sleeping with him, she probably deserves it."

Axel's tone shocks me. I try and shake my hand free from his, but he holds it tighter.

Penny bursts out laughing. "Phew, thought I was busted for a moment." She giggles. I hate her, I hate her so much.

"So, what's going on between the two of you?" Axel asks.

"Oh, nothing much. We have been hooking up for years. My sister's engagement wasn't going to get in the way of a really good friends-with-benefits relationship, if you know what I mean," she purrs into the phone.

"Yeah, darlin', I know exactly what you mean," Axel plays along.

"Eddie doesn't want to marry her, but he has no choice. His

family is in a huge amount of debt, and they need our family to get them out of it. Plus, you can't tame my Eddie."

"That's right, babe," Eddie calls from the background.

I don't think I can listen much longer. I knew my sister hated me, but I didn't realize the extent.

"Well, I was just calling because I heard about a photo of you and me in bed together, and I swear I have no memory of that happening. I know I should remember having sex with a beautiful woman."

Penny giggles on the other end of the line. "Oh, sorry about that, Axel. I was so angry over the way Olivia treated Eddie that I wanted to get some revenge. Sorry, I looked like some creeper jumping into your bed while you were asleep, but I had to teach my sister a lesson."

Tears start running down my cheeks. I don't understand why she hates me so much.

"Sounds like you're in love with him."

Penny goes quiet for a few seconds and then says, "It doesn't matter, he has to marry Olivia."

"That must sting, the man you love having to marry someone else."

"Honestly, if it were anyone else, I could cope with it, but Olivia, anyone but her."

Penny is that jealous of me that she would stoop this low. I don't get it.

"But Axel..." Penny starts. "If... you know... you ever want to hook up, I'd like that."

Really? She's a bloody nasty piece of work. I don't know who she is anymore. Has jealousy rotted her that much?

"Darlin', not sure when the next time I'll be in London, but I'll give you a call if I am."

"Oh, yes, please, I'd love that."

"I have to go but stay in touch." And with that, Axel hangs up.

I flick off the duvet and bolt from the bedroom. I need to get out of here.

I run out through the back deck and toward the beach. My feet sink into the cool sand, and one after the other, I run, trying to erase the venom I heard in my sister's voice. I try to forget that my sister is sleeping with the man I'm about to marry and will probably keep doing it forever. She hates me so much that she made me think Axel slept with her.

What the hell is wrong with her?

Why the hell do I always defend her?

Why am I killing myself for this business, so she can reap the rewards by fucking me over every single chance she can get?

If it weren't for me, she'd have no money.

"Liv... Liv, wait." Axel pants behind me.

"Go away, Axel," I scream back at him. "I need to be alone."

"No," he yells back defiantly. I turn to look at him chasing after me, and I trip over my feet and fall to my knees. A guttural sob breaks through my defenses and fills the night air.

Axel is upon me, picking me up and cradling me in his arms. "I'm sorry, I am so sorry you had to hear that." His large hands brush my hair as he cradles me.

"What did I ever do to her?" I sob.

"Nothing, she's a jealous little girl," he reassures me.

"She hates me so much."

"Shh... it's jealousy, not hate, sweetheart. No one could hate you."

I look up at his concerned face. "You do."

"I was hurt, Liv, and I said things in anger that I didn't mean. I don't hate you. I could never hate you. My feelings for you are so far from hate it's not funny."

I lean forward and kiss his lips gently, tasting the saltiness from my tears against his lips. Axel is hesitant about the kiss, knowing the weird state I'm in. I slowly sink my teeth into his bottom lip, telling him I want more. He lets out a growl and opens for me. He lets me take control of the kiss, and this makes my heart explode even further. After everything that has happened to him in the past and after everything I have put him through, he lets me be in control. I move in his arms so that I'm straddling him, and then I realize I'm still in my underwear from the club.

"I need you, Axel. I need you inside of me."

"You have me, Liv. I'm all yours." His kiss deepens with the potency of his words. I unzip his jeans and see he has gone commando. Thank God. His perfect dick pops out for me, and he moves his jeans down further, so I have access to him. My hand wraps around his length.

"I've missed you." My palm strokes along his velvety length. "This needs to be inside of me." I moan, my body on fire with desire.

"Then do it." Axel smiles against my lips. I let go of his length and push my underwear to the side and sink down on him. We both hiss at our connection.

"Liv, we're not using protection," Axel groans out as I move myself up and down him, feeling his thickness against my walls.

I frown, he feels so good, but that was so stupid.

"There are some in the hotel," he says, and we both stop moving. "Honestly, I don't want to move. You feel so fucking perfect wrapped around me."

"Axel."

"I know. I know it's incredibly stupid, but…" he nuzzles into my neck, "… please tell me you're on birth control."

"Yes, have been for ten years, and I've never had sex without a condom."

"Me either, darlin', me either." He thrusts up ever so slowly.

"I got checked after Monaco," I quickly add, and he stops moving.

"You did?"

I nod. "I just wanted to be sure. I trusted you all that we were safe, but… you know…"

He nods in agreement. "I did as well, always do after a group session."

My stomach flutters with nerves. "And you're clean?"

"Yes. And you?"

"Yes."

"Thank fuck! Because there was no way in hell I am pulling my fucking aching cock out of you. No way in hell." He starts thrusting up into me. "I have missed your beautiful cunt so much, and feeling it bare, fuck me, I have died and gone to heaven," he groans out.

I'm lost as my entire body searches for nirvana.

22

AXEL

I think I love you. Those simple words changed my world. Olivia snuggles into my side as I stroke her hair feeling sated and content from three rounds of the best sex of my life. Then on a whisper, she utters the words that have always filled me with dread.

Usually, the women saying it don't mean it, or they want something from me. But I know with Olivia, they mean something. My mind is ready to fall asleep, but it perks up to life with swirling emotions. I know she isn't expecting me to say those words back to her, but for the first time in my life, those words are a hell of a lot closer to the tip of my tongue than they have ever been.

My heart is racing with the possibilities of what loving Olivia could bring to me, to us. I can imagine waking up to her in my arms every day and coming home from work to her smiling face. Images of her with a rounded belly float through my mind, and usually, the feeling of being bound to another freaks me out, but instead, this feels right. The only hurdle that's in our way is this damn fiancé situation. After last night, there's no way in hell I'm going to let her marry that man even if it's the last thing I do.

"Morning." Olivia stretches out beside me. I watch as her perfect breasts rise and fall, her brown hair a messy nest from our lovemaking.

"Morning, darlin'." I lean over, kissing her forehead.

"Hmm... I could get used to waking up with you on a tropical island." The sound of the ocean lapping at the shore filters in through the open windows.

"Maybe I need to buy us an island to escape to, then." I pull her in tightly. I'd buy an island if it means I don't have to give her back.

"If it means I get to stay with you, I'm sold."

My heart restricts in my chest. "Stay with me, don't go back." Olivia stills beside me, my heart beating rapidly. She's the first girl I have asked to stay, to give me more, but there's a big chance that what we have at the moment will only ever be a moment because our lives are just so different.

"You want me to stay here on the island?" she questions me nervously.

I sit up in bed and pull Olivia onto my lap. I need to look at her when I ask her what I want, so she knows I'm telling the truth. "I heard you last night as you fell asleep, the words you mumbled."

Olivia's face turns a perfect shade of pink. I know she remembers what she said. "Axel, I'm sorry... I... just..." She tries to backtrack.

"No, Olivia. You know what? I agree with you."

"You do?" She looks shocked.

"Somehow, we have moved at lightning speed with our feelings, and in the past, for me, it would've freaked me out. When I'm with you... I don't know... my world just seems right." This makes Olivia smile. "I want to settle down, Liv, and I know what I'm about to say might freak you out, it kind of freaks me out, but I am just going to let it all out. I want a future with you, Liv. I want to wake up in the morning feeling your skin against mine.

I want to build something with you. I want to introduce you to my friends and family as my girlfriend. I want to love you like you have never been loved before. I want to be the man who you talk to, the man who fixes your problems. I want to be your one." Olivia's eyes are glassy, and she wraps her arms around my neck.

"How on earth did I find you?" she whispers into my neck, not letting me go.

"I don't know. Guess we must have done something right in our life." I chuckle. She moves away from me, and I can see the wheels turning.

"I want all of that, too, all of it." She smiles. "But how will it work?"

Reality can be a bitch. "I don't know, Liv," I confess truthfully. We sit there together, both of us lost in contemplation. "Come to LA," I blurt out. "Let's leave the island today. You were supposed to have a week here, right?" She nods her head. "Then let's spend that time together at my home, just you and me, and see if we can't somehow make this work."

"What, like a trial?"

"Yeah, you might hate the way I brush my teeth or something, and that's a deal-breaker."

She giggles. "You might hate my crazy addiction to tea," she adds, which makes me smirk.

"Doubt it. Everything about you makes me crazy." I squeeze her ass as it's straddled against me.

"I think we're kind of crazy to do this." She grinds herself against me.

"And if things are still amazing after that week, then you call off your engagement." Olivia stops grinding. Maybe I have asked for too much too soon. But there's no way in hell I'm letting her leave my home to continue with another.

"Okay," she replies. I'm shocked that she agreed so easily.

"Are you serious?" I question her just to be sure.

.

"Yes, you crazy fool. I'm serious. I have fallen head over heels for you, and I know there's no way in the world I want to go back to the sham that's my engagement."

"Thank fuck." I capture her lips with my own.

I was never going to let her go, anyway.

"Wow, I'm in shock." Nate slaps me on the back as we have drinks at the bar. "But I'm happy for you, man." I sip my beer and look over to Olivia, chatting with Camryn and Ivy over some cocktails.

"I'm sorry I can't stay and hang out more at your resort, but…"

Nate laughs. "Man, I'm just glad you have sorted stuff out. You were a miserable bastard without her." I nod in agreement.

"It's going to be tough. We have lots of obstacles in our way, but she's worth it."

"Man, you sound just like Christian and Evan. Guess you're as pussy- whipped as they are."

I laugh. "Yeah, guess I am. I get it now, and I bet those two bastards are going to have a field day with this little bit of information, but I don't care. I'm happy to be a fucking pussy." I take another sip of my beer.

"Another Dirty Texas member bites the dust." And I couldn't be happier.

"Are you sure?" We sit in the first-class cabin heading back to the US.

"Yes, I'm sure. Never been surer in my life." She kisses my palm. I'm nervous about taking her back to my home. I hope she likes it, I hope that I'm enough for her, and I hope I'm enough for her to stay.

"You're the first woman I've ever brought to my home."

"Really?"

"Yeah, really. It's my sanctuary, my place to get away from the world."

"Well, I'm very honored." She squeezes my hand as the plane takes off.

Hours later, we're touching down in LAX and being escorted through the VIP area. Thankfully, we are out before any paparazzi can find us. Sam, my bodyguard, is there waiting for us and whisks us away.

"Have you been to LA before?" I ask Olivia.

"No, I haven't." Her doe eyes are wide with wonderment as we drive.

"Sammy, we need to give this lady a tour." I squeeze her hand in mine.

"No problem, boss," the big Samoan man replies.

I show her Rodeo Drive, the Hollywood Sign, Hollywood itself, the Dolby Theatre where the Oscars are held, and Grauman's Chinese Theatre. I also point out the millions of star-spotting buses. We pass by Bel Air and go down to Santa Monica. I also thought it was a good idea to drive past the label offices in West Hollywood, where Sienna and Derrick's shop is as well. We didn't get out to say hello as I want her all to myself for the first twenty-four hours before the rest of the crew find out that she's here. Because once they do, I know they'll be all over her and us.

We make our way out to the Hills, where I live. Surprisingly, we all live not far from each other. Thankfully, the lots are large, so we're not on top of one another. We make our way up the steep hills where large, gated estates are nestled behind leafy trees. It's not long before we get to mine. Sammy presses the buzzer, opening the large, wooden gate, and we enter the property. I'm lucky that groupies have not found out where I live, so there aren't any offerings sitting outside the gate. This has happened to friends of mine.

I look over to Olivia, and she's sitting silently in awe. We round the corner of the driveway until we're in the front of my home. I love my home—it's my sanctuary. I've never brought a groupie or a woman here before because this is my personal space and it's private. But this time, I'm excited to be showing my home to Olivia. I am nervous as well. I know I'm well-off, but Olivia comes from a completely different world. The SUV pulls up at my front door, and Sammy unloads our bags at the front step, then he's gone.

Earlier, I asked him not to hang around and to grab some essentials like a kettle because I didn't have one, Olivia's favorite tea, which is Earl Grey, and some English chocolate and food so that she would feel at home here. I really want her to stay. I know I'm being selfish because her entire life is back in England.

"Axel, this place is…" Olivia runs through the main living area and out to the large deck. My view is spectacular, looking out beyond the hills with downtown LA before us. "I have never seen so much…" She can't seem to continue her sentence as she takes in the view.

"A little different to your view, hey?" I rub my neck nervously.

"Oh yes, but all I can see is green grass, trees, and the damn sheep or cows on the horizon. But this, this is spectacular. I never thought I was a city girl, or maybe I never let myself dream I could be a city girl because that was never going to be an option for me, but this…" she waves her arms wide, "… I want this. I want to be able to go shopping on Rodeo Drive. I want to be able to go to a café or a bar or go dancing. I want to check out the beach and feel the sun on my skin. I want to jump in my car and just drive and see where the road takes us."

I wrap my arms around her and nuzzle her neck as she looks out over the valley. "You've made me so happy. I want to be able to do all those things, too. The only thing is… I'm not that free to go walking around as you are. People know who I am, and they get crazy."

She turns in my embrace and wraps her arms around my neck. "I can handle crazy. I've had to deal with *her* all my life."

This makes me smile. "You know once we go public, the Dirty Texas groupies are going to be pissed that you've snatched me off the market."

"You're so modest, Axel Taylor."

"Just warning you, millions will be devastated."

"Are you trying to talk me out of this?" She smiles up at me.

"Never! Don't you realize now that I have you in my lair, young lady, I'm never letting you go?" I pull her tightly against me.

"I think I like your lair, Mr. Taylor. I don't think I'm going to leave either."

My heart skips a beat at her confession.

I'm one lucky son of a gun.

23

OLIVIA

I was nervous about going to LA. When I told Ivy and Camryn that I was leaving the island to give what's happening between Axel and myself a go, they were happy but wary.

"I can't believe your sister did that to you." Camryn was shocked by the lengths Penny would go to hurt me.

"She's a sad, sad little girl," Ivy added. *"You need to do something about her. You need to tell your parents that Penny is sleeping with Eddie."*

I have been thinking about what Ivy said, and I'm worried about what the shock might do to my father. I want to give Axel and me this week to work out what's happening between us and not just move forward on the insane chemistry we have. We have fun together, and he seems more relaxed around me, almost like the character of Axel Taylor, Dirty Texas frontman, doesn't exist anymore. I'm getting to see the real man underneath the public persona, and that man is the man that I'm falling for. The one who had a basket full of English goodies waiting for me on the kitchen counter—my favorite tea, crisps, chocolates—all things that are purely British that I'm guessing you can't find here in

America. Something to make me feel at home while being halfway across the world.

Those thoughtful things make me want to throw caution to the wind, tell my parents to forget about Eddie and the engagement. Tell them that we aren't a perfect match, that we, in fact, can't stand each other, and that I want to spend the rest of my life with Axel.

My stomach sinks—the rest of my life—this man has only been in my life for a couple of months.

Am I seriously thinking of a happily ever after with Axel? It's been such a short time. Or am I still stuck in some sex haze that he keeps leaving me in?

Axel is currently passed out in his enormous bed. It was hard leaving him there sleeping so soundly, but I was restless. I came downstairs to make myself a cup of tea. I'm currently sitting on a large daybed overlooking the most inviting pool and the twinkling lights of downtown LA.

"What about England?" Ivy asked me. *"Are you just going to leave everything you know behind for a man?"*

That's the million-dollar question. Axel and I both might have strong feelings for each other, but when it comes down to it, my entire world is in England, and his is here. One of us would have to give up everything for the other, and at the moment, I don't know who it would be. I worry that if someone does make that sacrifice, they'll eventually resent the other person, and the life we build together will crumble down around us.

"Hey, what are you doing up? It's late." A sleepy Axel joins me on the daybed.

"Just thinking," I tell him honestly.

"Thinking about what?" He wraps his arms around me and looks out over the impressive view.

"If we progress, who would have to sacrifice their life for the other."

Axel is silent, and I let the silence settle between us.

"I've been thinking the same thing." *Wow, this shocks me.* "Someone told me that if you were worth it, I'd make it work. That got me thinking about maybe expanding Dirty Texas records into Europe."

My heart stops, and I turn to look at him. "Are you serious?"

"Yeah, I mean, I couldn't be there year-round, but I could spend a fair chunk of it there. We have one amazing group from Sweden on our label, and I wouldn't mind trying to add to it." This gives me hope and settles my nerves. I place my mug on the ground and push Axel onto his back against the plush daybed and straddle him. He's wearing loose-fitting pajama pants which definitely leave nothing to the imagination by the impression sticking to my stomach. I'm only wearing one of Axel's T-shirts, nothing else.

"I could maybe look at moving to London. I can do a lot of my work on my computer and maybe hire a manager to run the castle full-time instead of me."

"Yeah, darlin'. You'd do that?" He smiles as he looks up at me.

"If you're looking at starting an office in London, then yeah, I think I can manage that. If me working remotely works for the business, then I can't see why I can't work some of the time here in LA."

Axel sits up quickly, his abs scrunching up as he holds my face between his palms. "You think we can do this, you and me?"

I nod. "Honestly, it's going to be complicated in the beginning until we get things set up, but as long as we communicate, then yeah, I think we can make us work."

"Thank fuck, baby, because you make me feel too good to let go now." His lips press against mine, and I open them willingly. We probably have a million things working against us at the moment, but as long as we can stay as a united front, then that's all that matters. I pull down his pajamas as he kisses me, his expert tongue dueling with my own. As soon as I sink down on his length, his teeth bite into my lip, the pain adding to the extreme pleasure of us together.

"Ride me, Liv, fucking ride me," Axel begs as he lays against the soft material of the daybed. I pull off the T-shirt and throw it to the floor. "Your tits are perfect, so fucking perfect." His large hands squeeze them as I grind myself against him. His calloused thumbs tweak my nipples, and my teeth sink into my bottom lip just the way he had done earlier.

"That's it, Liv, show me the wild girl beneath the lady." My cheeks turn pink, but he's right. He makes me wild and makes me want to break out of this prim and proper lady shell I live behind. "That's it, take your pleasure from me. Take what you need, baby. I'll always make sure you get what you need, always."

I love Axel's dirty talking. Before him, if any man said those words, I'd have run for the hills, but coming from him, it adds to the pleasure that's already swirling around me. A large slap echoes through the early morning stillness, and my ass vibrates from the sting of it.

"Fuck, you just clenched down on me when I slapped you. Again, Liv, again." He slaps my other cheek, and Axel moans in delirious pleasure. "You're so wet, keep going, please keep going," Axel begs, and I ride him as hard as I can. His length hits the spot that has never been touched before, making my entire body tingle. I'm so wet that the friction of my clit against his skin is making me shake.

"You're so close, babe, so close," he pants. I am, my body is on that perfect precipice, and I know I'm about to fall over the edge, but I need more, so much more. It's as if Axel can read my thoughts because, at that moment, he thrusts up hard into me, his penis hitting the detonate button in me, and I scream out his name. The sound echoes down the valley, but I don't care because I'm in ecstasy. The world around me has gone black, and I think I may pass out from it all. But Axel isn't finished with me yet. He picks me and slams me onto my back, so he's hovering over me.

"You look so beautiful when you come." His strokes are slow as they set off waves of mini orgasms. I can't speak. No words will come out of my mouth, making him chuckle. "I love fucking you speechless." I nod, and even that's too much for me, but then Axel increases his strokes inside of me. "I'm going to take my time, babe. I'm going to make love to you."

I look up into his whiskey eyes and know that I love him. I know that no matter what happens in the future, this man will always be the love of my life. And as the sun rises on a new day in LA, Axel slowly makes love to me, whispering promises to me of a life we both want together.

24

OLIVIA

"I knew it. I knew he was the one for you," Derrick squeals, pulling me into the foyer of Evan and Sienna's stunning home. He wraps his muscular arms around my body and squeezes the life out of me.

"Derrick, let the girl go, you're going to squeeze her to death," Axel jokes.

"Sorry, sorry," Derrick apologizes. "I'm just so freaking happy." He jumps up and down.

"Stop hogging our guests of honor." Sienna comes walking out looking like a damn supermodel. Her blonde hair is like strands of gold as it catches in the late afternoon light. I am instantly jealous, and if I'm honest, I kind of want to be her. She has baby Ryder on her hip, looking effortlessly like some earth mother. The strapless, yellow-fitted dress shows off her perfect little baby bump, and she's not wearing any shoes but still looks like a million dollars. Like I said, jealous. She hands off Ryder to Derrick and gives me a big hug.

"Welcome to the family." She smiles at me then greets Axel warmly. "Come, let me show you around." She loops her arm through mine and takes me on a tour of her home. I turn around, and Axel smiles at us from where he stands, playing with Ryder, who has his arms out to be picked up by him.

Ovaries exploding.

The back garden is filled with all of Axel's friends, most of whom I recognize and know except for the tall, gorgeous, tanned, and bald-headed guy who Sienna introduces as Evan's brother, Jake. My goodness, they are a good-looking family. Charlotte, Evan's sister, pops over and says hi. She introduces her boyfriend, Blake, from Sons of Brooklyn as well. I remember most from the wedding, where I met them all briefly. Then Sienna introduces me to Parker, Finn's youngest brother, who's in LA for a modeling assignment. Again, what the hell is in the water in Texas? These men are fine. Apparently, there's another brother, Hudson, who's in Syria working as a freelance war photojournalist. Wow, that's a scary job.

"The newlyweds are here," Christian yells from the deck. They are swamped by well wishes, and I catch Axel hugging his brother, a huge smile on his face. I look around at the large congregation of Axel's friends and notice how happy he is here. How can I take him away from all this? He'd know no one if he moved to London, only me. Would he resent me if we moved so far away from what looks to be a super-tight bunch of friends?

"Hey, there she is," Christian calls out as he heads toward me. I'm a little nervous. God, they look so alike but so different in so many ways.

"Come here," he says to me as he opens his arms. I'm a little confused and look to see where Axel is. He happens to have a big grin on his face, so I step into Christian's embrace.

"Thank you, thank you so much for finding him," he whispers in my ear before letting me go. He turns to his brother. "I think we need to drink to Axel joining the pussy club. Never thought I'd see the day, but I couldn't be happier." Christian gives Axel another big man hug.

"Go to the man cave, then," Sienna suggests, and all the men head off.

Vanessa comes running up to me and pulls me into a hug. "We're so going to be sisters." She lets me go, and I blink a couple of times.

"Don't scare the shit out of her," Derrick chastises Ness. "We know you're still stuck in your honeymoon love bubble, just don't push your love agenda onto unsuspecting women."

"So, give us the details. What have I missed?" Vanessa ignores Derrick and pulls me down to sit beside her on the outside sofa.

"Um… well, it's kind of a long story, but we're still trying to work things out," I start.

"You still engaged to that douchebag?" Derrick asks.

My heart starts racing because these are Axel's friends, and they're going to have his back if things head south for us. "We're sorting things out… it's all happened kind of fast."

"Axel is very safe when it comes to his decisions, and he isn't known for his spontaneity," Vanessa adds.

"Well, neither am I." I chuckle, feeling a little uncomfortable.

"Hey, ignore her. She doesn't know when she's prying too much," Sienna adds. "Honestly, Evan and I happened quickly. When these guys fall, they fall fast. No mucking around."

"I've known Axel most of my life, and you're the first woman we have ever met," Isla adds.

"And he stopped going to The Paradise Club," Stacey adds.

I turn and look at her. "Really?"

"Yep, he told Oscar that he wasn't interested in one-night stands anymore." Those butterflies start taking flight in my stomach.

"Fuck me dead, my princess has pussy-whipped Axel. The staunchest *I'm staying a single man* there ever was," Derrick announces.

I frown. It sounds like I'm changing him into someone he doesn't want to be.

"Hey, don't think like that," Stacey pulls me from my thoughts. "Axel is bloody stubborn and strong-willed. There's no way in the world you would be able to make him do something he didn't want to do." I smile at Stacey. That was exactly what I wanted to hear.

"I know we have heaps of hurdles to overcome."

"I heard about what your sister did," Vanessa pipes in. I turn and look at her and raise an eyebrow. "Yeah, Axel called Christian and told him all about it."

"Really?" He never told me this.

"Yeah, he was upset, pissed off. He told him all about the conversation, about how Eddie and Penny have been carrying on an affair together."

The group falls to a hush over this little bit of news.

"No fucking way. That fucking slut," Derrick pipes up. "How the hell you two came from the same vagina, I'll never know. You don't deserve a sister like her, Liv. You don't deserve people like that in your life. You're the kindest, most thoughtful, beautiful, and hardworking person I know, and these fuck faces fuck around behind your back. Do they have any idea what an amazing gift they have just by knowing you?"

I stand and rush over to Derrick and wrap my arms around him, tears running down my face because no one in my family has ever supported me like that, ever. I hug him something fierce, both of us crying.

"You're special, Olivia, and if she doesn't want you for a sister, I do. As you know, I don't have any family, and when I see people being treated unfairly by theirs, I have to reach out to them." He's looking at me through tear-soaked lashes. "Just know that if you decide that Axel is the man for you, that you aren't losing your family, you're gaining one, and one that's there for you no matter what."

I hug him tightly again. He's right, if I decide to stay here in LA, I know that my parents will shun me. They'll probably take me out of their will, and maybe months ago that thought would've made me rethink my decision, but now I know that I have the potential to gain so much more, more than family history, more than money, and more than a duty. I'll gain a family who's loving and accepting of me, and to me, that means more than anything else in the world.

"Family isn't always linked by blood, Liv." Derrick kisses me on the cheek. "Just think about that."

"Hey, why is my girl crying?" Axel steps out of the man cave and gives Derrick a death stare. He starts walking toward us, but I move from where I'm embracing Derrick and run into Axel's arms. I hit him hard, making him chuckle. I tip my lips up and kiss him forcefully, pouring everything I feel into that kiss.

"I love you, Axel Taylor." The look he gives me is one of wonderment like he can't believe someone would say that to him.

"I don't know what Derrick said to you, but I'll thank him later." Axel smiles, but a small part of me sinks because he didn't say those words back to me. I know that he does because of how he is around me, and I can feel that he has fallen for me too. I just have to be patient because when the time is right, he's going to say those words to me, and they are going to mean so much more than they would now.

25

AXEL

The boys pull me away from the girls toward the man cave, and I know exactly what's happening next—they are going to want to find out the gossip going on between Olivia and me. They are such a bunch of teenage girls.

"Okay, men. What's your poison... beers, champagne, or spirits?" Evan calls out from behind his bar. He has a pretty sick set up in his backyard. He's turned his pool house into the ultimate man cave with a fully stocked bar, big-screen television to watch football, arcade games, pool table, and anything else men could possibly need. We all call out our orders to Evan as he works behind the bar.

"How was the honeymoon?" I ask my brother, hoping to distract them from the topic of Olivia.

"Man, that place is amazing, bungalows over the crystal-clear water, and no one around. It was sheer paradise." I nod in agreement because it sounds like the paradise I just left.

"I'm happy for you." I slap my brother on the back.

"Yeah, well, I'm happy for you, too." He gives me a big smile. "So, are you fully pussy-whipped yet?" he goads me.

"Fuck you, it's been pretty awesome with you gone. Maybe you should've stayed there."

Christian flips me off as Evan hands us our beers.

"So, Olivia, hey?" Finn questions me.

"Yeah, and…" I reply, not liking his tone.

"Just never thought I'd see the day, that's all." He takes a sip of his drink.

Oscar punches him in the arm. "Ignore him, he's been a little bitch since the wedding. I think Finn's a little jealous of everyone's happy endings."

We all burst out laughing at Oscar's choice of words.

"You know what I mean." He grumpily takes a sip of his beer.

"So, you really taking a chance on her?" Christian asks.

"Yeah, man, I am."

He holds up his beer to clink against mine in acceptance. "She's a cool girl," he adds. The fact my brother approves means a lot to me. I won't ever tell him that, though. He'd gloat about it, and I'd never hear the end of it.

"So what happened with her fiancé?" Evan asks, looking concerned.

"That's over…" I start and launch into the long-winded story about the phone call to Penny and how Eddie was there and all the stuff that she spilled about them, all while Olivia was there with me on the phone.

"Fuck, what a bitch," Blake adds.

"That's all kinds of messed up," Parker agrees.

"Yeah, it is. She's given up everything for her family, and they repay her like this." I feel the anger bubble to the surface every time I think about Olivia's family.

"You see a future with her?" Christian asks.

"Yeah, I do. We need to work out where to live and stuff seeing as we live on the opposite sides of the world, but I think we'll work it out."

"So, you starting up that London office, then?" Evan questions me as he reminds me of the talk we had together.

"Maybe," I say, giving him a knowing smile. My eyes travel outside to see how Olivia is doing with her integrating, and I see her in tears, hugging Derrick. *What the hell is going on?* "Excuse me, guys." I put my beer down and rush out the door.

"Hey, why is my girl crying?" I call out to them. Olivia looks up at me through her tears and quickly lets go of Derrick who I notice has been crying as well. *What the hell is going on here?* Then she starts for me, her feet moving quickly through the grass, my body automatically gravitating toward her, my legs moving fast. She doesn't stop and runs straight into me, knocking the air out of me, making me laugh. I love her enthusiasm. She kisses me passionately, stunning me for a moment with her public display of affection.

"I love you, Axel Taylor."

I'm in shock, so I just stare at this beautiful creature before me as she looks at me as if I am her world. I'm too stunned to answer. Those three little words are on the tip of my tongue, but again, I can't get them to come out.

"I don't know what Derrick said to you, but I'll thank him later," is the only thing I can think of in reply. I can see her disappointment at me not returning those words to her, but she quickly hides it.

"Aww, you guys are so cute," Derrick coos from behind us.

"Ugh, come on, stop with all this love fest. I'm starved," Christian calls out from behind me, nudging me with his shoulder as he passes, giving me a secret smile.

"Yep, the food won't grill itself," Evan adds as the boys join the ladies again.

I love having Olivia here. We're laughing and chatting with my friends as we hang around the fire pit, all full from the amazing barbecue we just had. Her hand is resting on my thigh as she talks about something, our connection never apart, even for a moment. Now I get what Christian and Evan went through when they finally fell for their women. I know I have fallen for her—I just need to tell her.

I've already lost her twice now, I won't let it happen a third time.

"Where are we going?" Olivia asks me as we make our way along the coast, following the road's curves. I decided to take out my vintage mustang in hopes that it would impress Olivia. It did. Especially the way her small hands moved over my crotch as we made our way along the coast. My dick has been in a permanent state of arousal. The naughty temptress knows exactly what she's doing even though she is feigning innocence.

I've booked us into a beach house in Carmel, where we'll stay for a couple of nights to get out of the city. This week is going by so quickly that I need to have her all to myself without our friends dropping in on us every two seconds. Vanessa always wants to hang out, Derrick wants to go shopping, and Sienna is popping over with the baby. This is all good for any other normal time, but not when our time is limited. I'm hoping that after this little getaway, she doesn't go back to England, but I know that's wishful thinking. Her business and life are all there, and, at some point, she has to go back.

"This is so beautiful." She's repeated that same statement pretty much every couple of miles, but I love it. She's so excited about everything. For someone who's cultured and well-traveled, she really hasn't experienced much. I guess she's more sheltered than I thought. "Do you know how to surf?" she asks me.

"Um… no. I leave that stuff to Evan's brother." Jake has tried to teach us a couple of times while we visited him in Malibu, but we all sucked. I think we're better rock stars than surfers.

"He was hot," she mentions in passing.

"Um… excuse me." I turn and look at her.

"Oh, sorry. Was I not supposed to say that?" She slightly smiles at me. "Are you jealous of Evan's brother?" She squeezes my leg playfully.

"Um… no." I try and fail at pulling off not being jealous.

"Oh my God, you are." She bursts out laughing at me. I pout and keep my eyes on the road.

"Axel, really? After everything?" I can feel her looking at me, and I know my little tantrum is over with. "I don't care if you say a woman is hot as long as you remember which side your bread is best buttered." She squeezes my thigh again, and this time, it makes me laugh.

"You're a slice of bread now?"

"What, you don't use that expression?"

"Nope."

"Well, then, look but don't touch." She points at me.

"I promise, I promise. Same goes for you. Remember, I'm your slice of bread," I tease.

AXEL

We continue for a couple more hours. We did stop off for some lunch at a cute little village. The conversation flowed easily. I guess being stuck in a car for nearly five hours will do that. Subconsciously, I think I must have thought it would be a great way to test if we're compatible. We talked about our favorite music, and even though she has awful taste in music, she's hot, so that equals it all out.

"Here we are." I pull the car in front of the house.

"Oh, my goodness, this place is beautiful." Her statement amuses me. I grab her hand and enter the code at the front door. The house hangs over the cliffs, and as far as you can see, there's nothing but the Pacific Ocean. "This is heaven, Axel." She looks in awe at the natural beauty before her.

"I think heaven is right here." I nuzzle her neck. Yeah, it's kind of corny, but that's the kind of guy I've become. Olivia is wearing a white and black spotted sundress, and after the way she has mercilessly teased me for hours, I need to relieve this ache inside of my pants.

"Hands on the railing, Liv," I command her. Her body stops moving, but she does what I tell her. "You didn't think I was going to let you get away with teasing me all day, did you?" My hands pull off her jacket, throwing it to the floor.

"Axel," she says my name breathlessly, turning to look over her shoulder.

"Liv, eyes on the ocean, sweetheart." I turn her head to look forward. "You aren't allowed to move, do you hear me?" Olivia nods in agreement, her face still looking ahead. "Good girl."

I kneel and let my hands stroke up her legs. An audible gasp falls from her lips as my fingers climb against her soft thighs and pull down her panties. I bring them to my nose and smell her sweetness and stand again. "Don't turn around, hands behind your back." She removes them from the edge and places them behind her back. "Perfect." I tie her wrists together with her underwear.

"Remember, face forward." I notice her head turning to see what I'm doing, then she quickly turns it forward again. I lift her dress and expose her naked bottom. She tenses for a moment but relaxes as my hand runs over her soft ass. I tightly squeeze it, making her whimper.

"Now, I'm going to need you to move for me." Olivia nods. As soon as we walk into the living room, the huge sofa that dominates the room catches my eye. "I want you to walk to the sofa, but before you do, hold your dress up for me, darlin'."

I give Olivia the hem of her dress to hold between her fingers and watch as she walks before me, half-naked. Her creamy, white ass is mesmerizing me as she struts across the room. I thought this might push her, but I never expected her to push back. I watch the swing in her steps as she slowly and seductively walks toward the sofa. Her hips moving side to side, my teeth wanting to dig into that glorious flesh. She makes it to the sofa, those doe eyes turn to me, and she raises her eyebrow as if to say, *what now, sir?*

"Bend over that sofa, Olivia, and wait for me."

She slightly frowns but does what she's told, folding her

tiny body over the curve of the arm of the sofa and waits there for me. Now it's my turn to take my time. I shed my jacket onto the floor, I kick off my boots and socks as I move hungrily closer to her, and I even throw off my T-shirt, discarding it to the floor like some kind of sexy breadcrumbs. I move to where our bags are and open the one that has some toys packed inside. I pull out the riding crop, which I noticed she liked when Oscar used it on her. I slap the leather against my palm, the crack echoes through the room, and I notice Olivia shiver. I do it again, and she clenches her thighs together.

"Legs apart, sweetheart. No matter how turned on you are, legs apart." She moves slowly, opening her legs for me. I inspect her to make sure she's how I want her, and then I bring the leather down on her delicate ass.

"One," I start to count. "That's for teasing me in the car, my dick was rock-hard for five hours." A small whimper falls from her lips.

"Two." I don't hit her hard, just enough to put the perfect pink stain on her ass. "That's for touching yourself while I was driving." Another whimper.

"Three. That was for your bad taste in music. The Spice Girls isn't acceptable music to be played in my Mustang." She giggles, so I put a little bit more bite into my swing, and this makes her moan.

"And four..." I pause, thinking about what I'm going to say, but decide to go with it, "... and four, four is for making me fall in love with you."

Olivia's head turns as the crop comes down on her ass, making her hiss. "What the hell did you say?" Those hazel eyes glare at me.

"Turn around, Olivia, and let me love you." She begrudgingly turns around in a huff. I drop the crop on the floor because I've had enough of the games, I simply need to be inside of her.

My hands soothe her pink ass, and my fingers dip between her wet folds.

"I think someone enjoyed the crop a little too much." My fingers slide easily through her wetness.

"I think it was your declaration that made me wet," she mumbles back at me. I unzip my fly and pull down my jeans and underwear and kick them to the side. Then I line myself up, my hands gripping her hips, and I let my aching dick slide between her ready folds, back and forth, making her hiss with each stroke.

"What did you say?"

"I said, your declaration... Made. Me. Wet." She annunciates each word, and I thrust in hard on the last word, making her scream out at the sudden intrusion.

"What?" Thrust.

"That I..." Thrust.

"Have fallen..." Thrust.

"In love..." Thrust.

"With you." Thrust.

"Yes, yes, yes," Olivia screams at my punctuated thrusts.

"That's because it's true." Thrust.

"Yes, oh, yes," Olivia moans as her screams are muffled by the sofa.

"I'm crazy about you." I hold onto her cuffed hands as I press into her, the sofa squeaking with each hard thrust along the tiled floor.

"I'm... oh, yes, there..." Olivia moans. "I'm crazy... please don't stop," she pants. "I'm crazy about you... too... oh my God." Olivia groans as I continue my pounding. We're slowly moving the sofa around the room. "Yes, that's it, yes, yes, yes..." She lets out a guttural moan as her pussy clamps tight around me, squeezing my dick. The tingling starts up my legs, through my balls, and before I know it, I'm coming right behind her.

She's slumped underneath me, panting, while my legs are about to crumple underneath me from the force of my orgasm. I slowly pull out of her and grab my T-shirt. She doesn't move, and I gently wipe myself from between her legs and untie her wrists from her panties. I take a step back as she gets up off the sofa.

"You bastard, how dare you, how dare you tell me you love me while you're spanking me." She slaps my bare chest playfully.

I grab her two wrists and smirk at her. "Because I felt it at that moment." I let go of her hands. "Looking at you so vulnerable, so willing, so trusting. I knew it. I know that I'm crazy about you."

She glares at me before launching herself into my arms, nearly bowling us over.

"You're lucky I'm crazy about you. Otherwise, I'd be pissed about how you told me." She's clinging to me like a koala, my dick is still semi-hard and getting harder being pushed up against her stomach.

"I know I'm a lucky man," I say, kissing her.

She wraps her arms higher around my neck. "As long as you know that." She giggles.

"Yes, ma'am, I do. And I'm never letting you go, as long as you know that."

"Yeah, I guess that would be okay." She giggles again, kissing my cheek.

"Hey, don't be cheeky. I have a bag full of toys I want to use on you."

She shivers. "I can't wait."

27

OLIVIA

There's a faint ringing in my ears which keeps stopping and starting. I open my eyes and see Axel is passed out beside me. The moonlight is streaming through the bedroom window, and I take a moment to enjoy his naked body. He's lying on his stomach, and my eyes roam over the muscular plains of his back until I reach his perfect ass. Why the hell do men have the best asses in the world? It's so unfair. It looks like two perfect round globes. If he wasn't asleep, I'd totally squeeze them, they look so glorious. I can hear the ringing again, and I look around and see one of our cells is lit up, the green illumination lighting the room. I shimmy over to the bedside table and see who's calling.

Penny.

And there are ten missed calls from her. *Why the hell is she calling?*

Then the phone lights up again, and it's her. *What's going on?* I answer it.

"Fucking finally. Dragged yourself away from your rock star long enough to answer your phone," she screams down the line.

"What the hell do you want, Penny?" I'm not in the mood to

listen to her shit. I actually never want to hear from her ever again.

"Oh, are you too good for us now that you have a famous lover boy," she sneers down the phone.

"Your jealousy knows no bounds, Penny."

"I wonder if he compares us. I wonder who he thinks the better shag is," she goads me. "Not like you're any competition."

"Oh, I know he didn't touch you because guess what? I was on the other end of the phone during his late-night phone call to you. Who do you think gave him your number?"

Penny is silent for a moment. I can practically hear her seething through the phone. "Fuck you! You think you're so good, bagging Axel Taylor. Your picture is all over the tabloids here, pictures of you arriving into LA together, pictures of you and him shopping on Rodeo Drive, pictures of you hanging out at Wyld Jones with the rest of the Dirty Texas gang. Never thought I'd see the day my sister went to Hollywood. You're such a fucking try hard, Liv. You don't belong in that world."

"And what, you do?"

"Of course, I do… look at me and look at you. It's pretty easy to see which one looks better in the papers."

"Babe, are you okay?" Axel groans beside me. I cup my hand over the phone so Penny doesn't hear him and then go back to the call. "Is that the only reason for your call? To tell me you look better in the tabloids than me?"

"Oh no. I called to tell you that your little stunt has put Father in the hospital. They're not sure if he's going to make it."

My world stops.

I feel Axel jump up beside me, and he starts moving around the room.

"What did you say?"

No, I don't believe anything she says.

"*You* put Father *in the hospital*," she screams down the

phone. "If he dies, it's on your conscience." Then she hangs up on me. The bitch! She bloody just hung up on me.

"I'm grabbing our stuff. We can be out of here in half an hour. Let me make a call and find out where the jet is." I can hear Axel talking, but it's not registering. "Babe…" He kneels before me, trying to gain my attention. "It's going to be okay. He's going to be okay."

"What if I've killed him?"

"No, your sister is being a bitch. There's no way in the world you have killed him."

"But… but apparently we're in the tabloids."

"Don't worry about that. We can deal with that later. Let's get you dressed and ready to be on a plane back to England."

I look up at him, and Axel is being my rock at this very moment. "Okay," I say, because that's all I can gather, everything has shut down.

I think I'm in shock.

A couple of hours later, we're sitting on a helicopter heading back to LA where Axel's jet is hangered. He's going to fly me there straightaway. The first commercial flight is still hours away. As we make it to the heliport, Sammy is there waiting for us with all our bags packed and breakfast. We make our way to the private plane section of LAX. There are paparazzi lurking around, and some have managed to take our photo, but we're ushered quite quickly onto the luxurious jet. I'm not in the right frame of mind to be able to take it all in, but I find a seat and sink into it. Axel talks to the flight attendant, and she brings over a pot of Earl Grey tea. Axel pours me a cup.

"Here, drink this, it will help." He holds the piping hot mug to me. I take a sip and instantly feel like I'm back home. I have sent a message to Ivy and Camryn, who are still at The Paradise

Club Resort. I've told Ivy not to rush home because I have Axel with me. I told her to enjoy her time, and I'll see her in a couple of days, anyway. She can't do much for me right now.

Before I know it, we have taken off, and I fall away into oblivion.

Not the best of flights, not because of turbulence or anything but because it took so bloody long. We finally make it to Edinburgh, where Father is in the hospital, and there's a car waiting to take us directly to him. Mother has texted me the details of which room he's in. We arrive at the hospital, and there are paparazzi everywhere waiting for us. Such vultures. The driver takes us around to a back entrance. Axel jumps out of the car and opens my door.

"Axel..." I look up at him. He has been my rock, but I don't think it would be good for my father's heart for me to arrive with him on my arm. "I think... um... it might be best if you head to the hotel."

Axel's body tenses, and I'm expecting him to argue with me, but he doesn't. "I understand, but just know that I'm here for you. Just say the word, and I'll be by your side no matter what, okay?"

He leans down and kisses me. *My God, this man is bloody perfect.* "Thank you," I say, moving away from his embrace. I take a couple of steps before Axel is pulling me into another kiss. It's desperate and full of knowing that this changes everything. This bubble that we're living in has burst, and reality has now hit us smack in the face.

"Liv, just remember..." he presses our foreheads together, "... I love you."

My heart skips a beat as I pull myself away from him and head into the hospital.

"Olivia." Mother sees me first, and I run toward her and wrap her in a hug. I can tell she hates it by the stiff body that's pressed against mine, but I don't care. "Thank you for coming so quickly."

"No, of course. How is he?"

"He's okay, it was touch and go, but your father is as strong as an ox."

Mother likes to put on a façade that everything is okay when in reality, it isn't. "This whole matter could've been avoided if you weren't gallivanting all around town with some rock star." I can hear the disdain in her voice.

"That rock star is the reason why I'm here so quickly. He dropped everything to fly me halfway across the world to be with my sick father. And that rock star isn't some person I'm gallivanting around town with, I am not Penny. He's the man I love, and I want to spend the rest of my life with."

My mother recoils at my words. "Do you want to kill your father?"

Her words strike me. "Of course not."

"Then you'll not ever speak of this rock star again, and you most definitely will not speak about loving him. We just got your father back. He'll not have another episode because *you're* having some kind of episode."

"Episode?" I squeal.

"Keep your voice down, there are people around," she scolds me. "Yes, you're having an episode. That has to be the only reason you're acting like this. I think we should take you to see a doctor. I knew running the estate would be too much for you. I told your father you would have a breakdown one day."

I'm shocked at the way my mother is speaking to me. *Really, Olivia, are you that shocked?*

"I've come here to support Father. Where is he?"

"In his room, darling." She points to his open door. I make my way toward it, but I hear laughing and chatting from familiar voices. I enter the room and see Penny and Eddie sitting on either side of my father, chatting away as if they don't have a care in the world.

"Olivia," my father murmurs, noticing me first.

"Sweetheart." Eddie smiles brightly, coming over and kissing me on the cheek. Penny gives me a death stare but stays quiet.

"Father, are you okay?" I walk over and sit beside him on the bed.

"I am now that you're here," he croaks.

"What happened?" I hold his cold hand in mine.

"The golden child defied expectations, that's what happened," Penny mumbles beside me. I throw daggers at her. "Goodbye, Father. Eddie and I have to go. We'll see you later, okay?" They both say their goodbyes.

"Oh, it was so lovely for Eddie to come and see me in the hospital, wasn't it?"

I ignore my father's statement. The last thing I want to do is stress my father out. Talking about Eddie is going to do that.

"What did the doctor say?" I change the subject.

"Just a small heart attack. He says one of my valves is clogged, and I'm going to have to have bypass surgery to clean it out."

My stomach sinks. *No, no, no, this is not good.*

"Hey, I'm going to be okay. It was just a little scare. I promise I'm going to stay here to walk you down that aisle. It's the only thing keeping me going, sweetheart. Seeing you marrying Eddie is my one and only wish from my life."

A lead balloon is stuck inside of me. My father is only hanging on because he thinks Eddie and I are going to get married. I've already given him one heart attack with all this tabloid gossip about Axel and me.

"Thank you for coming so quickly, I'm so happy you're here. Family means the world to me." *God, I feel like the biggest asshole.*

"I know, Father. I'd never leave you, you know that." I kiss his hand.

"You're such a wonderful child. We're so blessed to have you." He smiles at me, then he lets out a yawn.

"I'll let you get some rest. I'm going to go home and get changed. I'll be back later." I lean down and kiss his cheek.

"You make me so proud," he whispers. I have to catch my tears because he doesn't need to see them. I wave him goodbye, and as soon as I'm out of the hospital, I burst into tears.

I need to get out of here.

28

AXEL

The door to the hotel clicks open, and I jump off the bed. Olivia has only been gone a couple of hours—I thought she would've stayed there all day. When I see how little and fragile she looks, my heart hurts for her. I rush toward her, pick her up in my arms, and cradle her against my chest. Olivia lets out loud, sorrowful sobs, clings to me like I'm her anchor, and buries her face as close as she can get to me. I walk her over to our bed, lay down with her, and just let her sob. She cries for a good ten minutes or so until she's out of tears. She looks up at me with red, puffy eyes and a pink nose. Her makeup has run a little, but I still think she's the most beautiful woman on the planet.

"Thank you, thank you for being here for me."

"Anytime, darlin', anytime." This sets her off again, and a few minutes later, she settles down again.

"I think we need to talk."

Those words—those words don't sound good, especially as she moves from my arms and walks into the bathroom to wash her face. She comes back into the room, and I'm sitting up, not sure what's going on. "I appreciate everything you have done for me, Axel."

Why does this sound like a kiss-off?

"I don't know how long I'm going to be here for, and you're a busy man and…"

"Stop right there." I put my hand up, jumping off the bed, moving to where she's standing. "Cut the bullshit, stop buttering me up just to fuck me over."

Those hazel eyes are red-rimmed as she looks at me. "Axel, I'm… it's just…"

"Spit it out, Olivia, you have no problem telling me where to stick my dick, this shouldn't be so hard." I'm so angry with her because what she's going to say is written all over her face.

"I think you should go back to LA."

There, she's said it.

"Why? What happened? We were so happy. I don't get it." I grab her hands in mine, but she rips them away and stalks across the room.

"It's for the best, Axel."

"For who? You? Your family? Because it's certainly not the best for me."

"We would never work. My life is here, and your life is in America."

"We spoke about this. I can set up an office in London, and you would try and work remotely."

"I think we were kidding ourselves."

"Are you fucking serious right now?" I don't mean to make her jump with the tone of my voice, but I'm fucking angry.

"We are too different," she whispers.

"No, we aren't. Who told you that? Was it your parents? Was it your sister? Was that fuck face Eddie there at the hospital?" She doesn't look at me, which is telling. "I was proud of your family loyalty, but now it's fucking pathetic. Your family uses you, Olivia.

They use you for their own gain, and you're so fucking blind to it that you will give up on us because of it." I thump my chest. "You are so far under my skin, and you're buried deep inside my heart. But none of that matters to you, does it? Because I'll never be enough for you. I will never be enough to risk everything for."

"My father is dying, Axel. Don't you get that? He's dying, he has heart failure. He has to have an operation which might keep him going for a little bit longer, but..." The tears fall down her cheeks. "He's asking one thing from me... one small, insignificant thing."

"Marriage? You think marriage is insignificant?"

Olivia blanches at me.

"You're sacrificing your life for what? Some old bastard's fucked-up sense of legacy." I know that's a low blow about her father, but I'm furious. I'm pissed that she's prepared to throw away the time we have had together, the connection, the love, everything to make every other person in her life happy.

"He's my father, Axel."

"And yet, he doesn't want you to be happy, he puts his own selfishness before yours. That's not love, Liv." I walk out of the room and start packing up the bits that I had unpacked and throw them into my bag. She follows me quietly.

"I would have made you happy. I would have loved you until our final days. I would have given you everything you have ever wanted in the world. I would have been faithful." I can't look at her, especially not when she's crying.

I can't deal with it.

We were never going to happen.

It was all a goddamn fantasy.

I grab my bags and walk out. Sammy is waiting downstairs for me and gives me a concerned look, his eyes taking in my bag.

"To the airport, thanks."

He nods but hesitates. "Are you sure, boss?" He never second-guesses anything I ask.

"Yeah, man, I am. Sometimes some obstacles are just too big to get over."

He nods once and takes me back to the jet.

It's been a week, and I haven't heard anything from Olivia, and I hate it.

I needed to get away, so I asked Christian if I could go to his house in Big Bear. I hate my house in LA at the moment because all I can see are images of Olivia spread out on my bed or perched on the outside terrace with a cup of tea in her hand. Thankfully, the cabin is a long way away from LA, and I can just sit and wallow without anyone knowing or interfering. I will say, heartbreak has given me great ideas for some songs, so I guess I should thank Olivia for that, for being my muse for all these depressing musical pieces.

There's a knock on the door, and when I open it, I'm surprised to see my bandmates. "What the hell are y'all doin' here?" I look at them. They all have overnight bags and bottles of beer under their arms.

"Thought we needed bro time, seeing as the girls are always going away together, we never get to just hang out," Evan replies.

"Plus, I haven't used my awesome home much yet, so why not start with bro week," Christian adds.

"Bro week?" Confused, I look at them.

"Yes, a week full of testosterone-fueled bro stuff," Derrick adds. "And before you say anything, Mr. Taylor, I know how to be a bro." This makes me laugh.

They push their way past me into Christian's home.

"Looks like you have been writing," Oscar states, touching my scattered papers on the coffee table.

"You know, got nothing else to do." I shrug.

"Well, it's good." He smiles and continues into the kitchen with the other men.

"You know I came up here to get away from it all?"

"Yeah, and so have we," Christian adds.

"Why the hell are you running away from your new wife?"

"Evan and I are sick to death of planning nurseries and shit," my brother complains. "I don't want to know how much it's costing me. I mean for the love of God, I have two, and they are already costing me a small fortune, and they aren't even born yet."

"Now Sienna has Vanessa to talk baby stuff with… it's like, you know, baby shit has exploded everywhere. Plus, Ryder's first birthday is about to happen, and they are going crazy over themes and shit, especially now Camryn is in town," Evan groans out.

"Hey, I'm missing valuable party planning time to hang with you boys," Derrick adds. "So stop the moaning because we all know in the end, you love it, and you wouldn't change anything no matter how much you both moan about it. These women are pushing out babies the size of watermelons from their sacred place, and the least you can do is hand over your credit cards."

Derrick makes me burst out laughing, something I haven't done in a long time.

"You're right, D. You are absolutely right." Christian claps him on the back.

"Good, now just remember that feeling, especially when you have teenage girls who are addicted to shopping. Just remember how much you love them," Derrick chuckles, and Christian flips him off.

"Come on, enough about women. Let's drink some beers, jump on some snowmobiles, and go crazy. What's the point of all this land and all this snow if we sit around gossiping like a bunch of women?" Finn adds.

"Isla leaves next week. I think someone's not dealing with it," Derrick whispers to me as the others walk back into the kitchen to grab supplies before we head off on some crazy guy adventure.

"Women make you crazy," I reply.

"So still nothing from Olivia?" Derrick asks, and I shake my head.

"I know she loves you, but she has some crazy ass loyalty to her family, which I don't understand. But I guess she's just scared that if she doesn't do what her father wants, and he dies, she's going to feel responsible."

"I wish she had that kind of loyalty to me."

"Honestly, Axel, I don't think she's going to go ahead with the wedding."

"To be honest, Derrick, I don't know if I have the energy to care anymore. This is something Olivia needs to work out for herself."

"Are you still going to be here if she finally comes to her senses?"

I look up at him. "Yeah, but I won't wait forever."

"Fair enough, just please don't give up on her. I know she's hurt you, and I honestly don't blame you for being angry. I'm pissed at her, and I'm not in love with her... well, I am, but only as my princess. I think deep down, she's scared and just wants extra time with her father, and she thinks this is the only way to do it."

"Yeah, I know, but it still sucks." He slaps me on the back, and we head outside to where the rest of the boys are. I'm going to enjoy this time with my boys, and maybe for the first time in a week, I can get her out of my head, even if it's for a couple of hours.

29

OLIVIA

"You look beautiful," my mother coos as I stand on the step in the middle of the wedding dress shop, twirling around like I'm her toy doll. My sister and Ivy are standing in front of me, both of them looking at me with scowls on their faces, but for two very different reasons. Father is still in the hospital, and I thought this might cheer Mother up. It has but has depressed me even more.

"Honey, smile, you're getting married to the man of your dreams."

I don't plaster on the fake smile that I normally would. Instead, I show her how I really feel.

"What do you think of the dress, sweetheart?" She changes tactics.

"Yeah, it's nice." It looks like a million other white dresses. In all honesty, I don't care. I want this over and done with, so we can go about our normal lives again.

"I don't know what's wrong with you." She glares at me.

"Olivia's just pining after some rock star like a love-sick groupie, that's all, Mother," Penny replies.

Mother glares at Penny. "There will be no talk about that,

especially not in public, do you hear me?" She hisses at Penny, who zips her lips on the matter.

"I think this dress looks beautiful, it's very traditional and is similar to my wedding dress, actually. I think Eddie is going to have tears in his eyes when he sees you walking down the aisle." My mother smiles at me.

I look at Penny, and she looks like she's ready to rip the stupid dress off me and burn it at the stake.

"We'll take it," Mother tells the boutique owner.

I shuffle back to the dressing room and change back into my clothes.

"Can I leave now?" Penny asks.

"Of course, dear, see you later." Mother kisses her on each cheek, and then she's gone.

"I'm off to the hospital, I'll see you later, sweetheart." My mother does the same to me, kissing me on each cheek. "Lovely to see you again, Ivy." She nods at my best friend before getting into a town car.

"I need a drink," I blurt out.

"So do I," Ivy agrees.

We make our way down the street and find the nearest pub. We order two champagnes at the bar, and once we get them, we sit down and look over the lunch menu.

"I'd say cheers to a great day wedding dress shopping, but I'd be lying."

My best friend's honesty hurts. "I know you don't understand why I'm doing this."

"No, Olivia, that's the thing. I do get why you're doing it, I just don't agree with it." That stings. Ivy and I never fight, but this wedding is putting a wedge between us. I haven't seen her since she got back from The Paradise Club Resort.

"So, how was your holiday?" I try to change the subject.

"I had so much fun at the resort, it was amazing." I notice her cheeks are pink.

"And?" I push.

"I did things that I never thought I'd ever do," she quickly confesses.

"Which was?" Come on, Ivy, spill the beans.

"I was spanked, I walked around naked on the beach, I was tied up. I…" Her cheeks are now red.

"Yes, go on. Come on, let me live vicariously through you."

Ivy takes a gulp. "I had a threesome."

I gasp loudly before reigning it in. "No way," I whisper. "Tell me more."

She shakes her head. "It's nothing, but it was fun. Two men." She giggles.

"I'm so excited for you."

"I want to go to the club in London. I think I want to become a member."

"Really?" Ivy is about as adventurous as I am, but that was before Axel.

"Yes, I get why you changed when you came back from Monaco."

"What do you mean?"

"You were more confident in yourself as a woman. There's something about being with two men who desire you… they make you feel like you can take on the world." This makes me smile because I'm so happy for my friend, but I know why I felt different, it was because of Axel and the way he was with me. He showed me that I was beautiful and desirable. He was gentle with me, took control of the situation, and made me trust him. I know I'm a fool to have chosen Eddie over Axel, but I feel trapped trying to please everyone.

"Hot sex will do that." I giggle.

"Also, the love of the right man will as well." Yep, she gets right to the point.

"I messed up, I get it. You're upset with me. I sent invitations to Vanessa and everyone, and they all declined. I guess they are all firmly on team Axel."

Ivy takes my hand. "Vanessa is now Axel's sister-in-law, and he's her family." I know she's right, but it stings. "And Camryn, well, you know she never keeps her opinions to herself. She's upset because she wants to see you happy, and you know Eddie is never going to make you happy."

I let out a heavy sigh. "I'm going to divorce Eddie when my father…" I can't finish the words, and tears start to stream down my cheeks.

"Oh, Liv." She pulls me in beside her.

"I know he won't make me happy. I hate him, and I hate my sister, but I love my father, and this is his dying wish. He's hanging onto life waiting to watch me walk down the aisle."

"I know, Liv, I know, and it's noble what you're doing. People can't judge unless they have walked in your shoes, but you can't ask people to support something they are against, either."

I sniffle, knowing she's right.

The weeks have dragged on since I broke up with Axel. My father's health has improved significantly. He had his double bypass and is now at home recovering. Penny is gallivanting around London with Eddie. Thankfully, the tabloids aren't reporting on it, but it's still all over their social media pages. I checked Axel's Instagram account, and there are pictures of him at Ryder's first birthday party. Looking at all my friends having fun, the pang of regret hits me like a ton of bricks. I should be there beside him. I should be in these photos. We should be planning a life together, except he's moving on, and I'm stuck in some messed-up soap opera scenario marrying a man who's screwing my sister and everyone else around town.

I sent a text to Sienna, wishing Ryder a happy birthday, and she replied, thanking me for the present. I got him a life-size Paddington Bear. The pictures of him hugging it and trying to eat it made my ovaries burst as did my heart.

At least Stacey has been chatting with me. She told me Axel doesn't frequent The Paradise Club anymore. If I'm honest, this makes me happy. The thought of him moving on is too much for me. She's also told me that he walks around the label like a bear with a sore head, he's pretty grumpy, and people tend to stay out of his way. Stacey loves working at the label, especially now that Oscar likes to call her into his office and do wicked things to her. This makes me laugh.

Isla left last week for her new life in Europe with hot chef Sebastien.

Finn has decided to stay in the New York office instead of LA, so she doesn't see him much anymore. She told me how Sienna's new children's boutique is really coming along, and the grand opening should be happening in the next couple of weeks. They have also moved Wyld Jones Boutique next door into the two-story space. The boutique is on the bottom floor, and Derrick's styling space is on the second floor. They've even hired staff.

I also sent Derrick a message congratulating him on his new space, and he replied by telling me that he misses me and wants his sister back. This, of course, makes me cry because I miss all of them. In such a short time, they became my friends and family, something I don't have here. Sitting in my office, I look out of the window over the forest, the rain pouring down, and the countryside looking miserable—it matches me perfectly. *How the hell have I gotten myself into such a mess?* I grab a bottle of wine and drink it straight from the bottle. Fuck it.

A couple of hours later, after I have watched maybe one too many episodes of Dirty Texas live on Netflix, my finger hovers over the call button. The large amount of wine is flowing through my veins, giving me courage, and I just need to hear his voice. That's all it takes for me to call him, just once. It rings and rings and rings. I have no idea what time it is in LA. He's probably asleep.

"Olivia," his gravelly voice answers the phone.

I freak out and hang up.

30

AXEL

I've been up late writing most nights. This break-up with Olivia has been great for my writing, and I have been putting my heart and soul into new songs. I've given some to the Sons of Brooklyn boys and the Gypsy Sisters to play around with. They are about to go on a small tour together. After seeing them play at Christian's wedding, we knew that a national small-venue tour might be a great way to get new fans to come and see them together.

The label has been keeping me busy. Finn's setting up the New York office, and Ness is there as well, training Harper, Camryn's friend, on all PR responsibilities for the label. Her company is going to take over when Vanessa goes on maternity leave, which isn't for a few months, but she likes to be prepared. Carrying twins can be dangerous, and they could come at any time, so she wants to make sure work is covered. Like we would care if it wasn't—her and the babies' health are the first priority.

I'm not going to lie, seeing the ultrasound of my nieces really got to me. I envisioned images of Olivia maybe pregnant with twins, showing our family and friends photos of our babies. I'm such a fucking pussy. I hate that meeting Olivia has made me want more than I'm able to have. It was nice that Olivia sent Ryder a present. The Paddington Bear was pretty damn cute, and Ryder loved it. Why wouldn't he? It was a big fluff ball that was double his size that he could crash tackle all the time.

Christian told me he and Vanessa received wedding invites in the mail for Olivia's wedding. So did a couple of the other guys. I was pretty pissed off that she had invited my friends, but Vanessa reminded me that she had known Olivia a long time, and that it was only natural for her to invite her. But she then told me she declined. One reason being the babies, another being she didn't agree with the wedding, and lastly because I was family.

Derrick told me he declined the invite as well. He said he was having a protest vote, but he'd send a kick-ass wedding present because he's not that much of a bitch. All my friends and family's support over her wedding made me feel good, but a small portion of me also felt bad that Liv wasn't going to have any friends there. Well, except Ivy. Even Camryn declined organizing the event. Olivia probably feels terribly alone with all her friends not supporting her decision. I'm not saying I support it at all because, fuck no, but I get why she's doing it. However, it still stings.

I'm working late, not sure what time it is, but it's nearly sunrise. I think the first rays of the morning sun are breaking through the night sky. My phone starts ringing. I didn't realize I'd fallen asleep at my writing desk. My face is glued to bits and pieces of paper as I fumble around on my desk looking for my phone. When I glance down at the screen, I can't believe my eyes as the word **Olivia** is flashing across it. I answer the phone, wondering what on earth she has to say after all this time. But when she hears my voice, she hangs up. I guess it's just a pocket dial, and she doesn't really want to talk to me.

"Hey, Ax," Derrick calls me. It's late on a Friday night.

"Hey, D, what's up."

"We can still stop the wedding."

This makes me laugh. "Why would I do that?"

"Because you love her," Derrick huffs out.

"Love sometimes doesn't conquer all, D. This is the real world, not some fairy tale."

"You're so goddamn stubborn. The both of you are. That stubbornness is letting the woman you love marry Marquees de Dick Face."

"Yeah, well, that's her choice."

"So, you're totally fine with her taking that royal douche to bed tomorrow night and letting him touch her, fuck her, impregnate her."

My fists ball up. "Of course, I'm not, D," I yell at him. He's such a meddler. "But she chose him. What do you not understand about this situation? Tomorrow she's marrying someone else. That someone is *not* me."

"But you never fought for her."

"I flew to fucking Scotland to be by her side, then she told me to take a hike."

"She was hurting, her father almost died, and she wasn't thinking straight." Derrick tries to reason on behalf of his friend.

"She never contacted me. It's been months."

"I know…" Derrick concedes. "I just… I wanted you two to make it."

"I know, D, so did I. It just wasn't our time… right girl, wrong time."

"Yeah, I guess you're right. Well, I'm here for you tomorrow if you need me."

"Thanks, D, but I have heaps of work to do. Tomorrow is simply another day." I know I am kidding myself, but I have no choice.

"Okay, well, I'm here anyway, anytime."

"Thanks, D."

I will not look, I will not look, I will not look. I repeat that mantra over and over, determined not to check any social media or the internet until Christian calls me.

"Hey," I say, picking up the phone.

"Holy shit, the wedding," he splutters down the phone.

My heart is racing.

What the hell has happened?

Is Olivia okay?

"I can't believe it," he continues in shock.

"What? What's happened?"

31

OLIVIA

It's been a month since my stupid drunk call to Axel. He never called me back after that fateful call, and it infuriated me, but I understood why. I had fucked up—this was all on me. He didn't owe me anything. I just hope that he's okay, happy even. Oh, who am I kidding? I don't want him to move on. I'm not ready for him to move on.

"Hey, how are you doing?" Ivy pops her head into my dressing room.

Today is my wedding day.

Yes, I know! How did I make it to this point?

In a couple of hours, I'll be walking down the aisle with my father by my side to a man I loathe and despise, and I'll be wishing that the man greeting me at the end of the aisle was someone else. I can't think of him today. Otherwise, I'll burst into tears. The gravity of the day has hit me hard, and I'm barely functioning and only hanging on by a thread.

"You okay? You're looking pale." Ivy glances at me with concern in her eyes. I rush to the toilet and proceed to throw up my breakfast into the bowl, over and over again until there's nothing left. I slump on the floor knocking over the wastebasket, but I don't care.

"Um, Liv. Do you have something to tell me?" She points to the mess on the floor, and that's when I see it—a pregnancy test.

"That's not mine." I point to it.

"But you just threw up," Ivy states.

"Yeah, because I am about to make the biggest mistake of my life, that's why I'm throwing up. Not because I am pregnant."

"Then how the hell did that test get into your trash basket?"

This morning Mother made Ivy, Penny, and me have breakfast together in my suite, all for the photos, of course. Penny excused herself to go to the bathroom after breakfast. *Did she leave it there?*

I jump up from the cool, tiled floor and throw some water on my face. "Someone needs to answer some questions, and I'm going to find out exactly what's going on."

"Liv, wait... wait for me." Ivy runs after me as I walk out of the hotel room. I'm dressed in my bathrobe and bare feet. I knock on Penny's door, but there's no answer, so I continue down to my parents' door and knock on it.

"Sweetheart," Father greets me warmly, pulling me in for a hug. "I'm so proud of my little girl, it's her wedding day. I never thought I'd get to see this day, but it's here." I feel sick to my stomach.

"Where's Penny?"

Mother pops in. "She's just gone down to Eddie's room to grab your wedding present from him."

I'm sure she is. "I think you better follow me to Eddie's room then, I have some questions to ask my sister, and I think you might want to hear the answers to them," I tell my parents.

"It's bad luck to see the groom before the wedding," Mother squeals.

"If you don't come with me right now, there will be no wedding," I hiss at her.

My parents look at me in shock, but they do as they're told and follow me down the hallway. There's a maid about to knock on the door with fresh towels, and her eyes widen as she sees us barreling toward the door.

"Hi, it's my wedding day, and this is my fiancé's room. I have a surprise for him, so would you mind if I take those towels?" She hands them over to me silently. "Oh, would you be so kind as to let me in, please?" She looks over my shoulder and does what she's asked unlocking the door.

"Olivia, what are you doing?" Mother whisper yells at me.

"Just wait and see, Mother. All will be revealed." I push open the doors, and everything is definitely revealed.

"What the hell?" Eddie screams, his naked body hovering over Penny's, who's screaming for him to get off her.

"Oh my God," my mother screams at finding Eddie and Penny naked together.

"What the hell is going on here?" my father yells.

"It's not what it looks like, sir." Eddie pulls the sheet up around him while Penny is hiding under the duvet, refusing to show her face.

"It looks like you're in bed with the wrong daughter, son," my father says between clenched teeth.

"It... not..." Eddie stutters.

"If you tell me again, it's not what it looks like, then I'll bloody well clobber you with one of these vases over here. Tell me, what are you doing in bed with Penny?" he commands.

"This is all so unsavory," my mother pants, fanning herself.

"Maybe you should ask Penny," I comment, folding my arms in front of me, feeling like I'm on the set of *Cheaters* or something.

"Penelope, what the hell do you think you're doing?" My father moves his attention to my sister. She slowly reveals herself from behind the duvet.

"I love him, Father." She bursts out crying, and I can see my father softening.

"Penny, no, it was just supposed to be fun," Eddie comments.

God, he's an idiot.

"A bit of fun? She was supposed to be a bit of fun? You thought sleeping with one sister while being engaged to the other sister was a bit of fun?" Father roars.

I place my hand on his arm. "Calm down, Father. You just had heart surgery."

He takes a couple of deep breaths.

"Sorry, sir, that's not what I meant." Eddie is trying to scramble for the right words.

"You told me you loved me," Penny cries.

"I like you..." Eddie says, rubbing his neck uncomfortably.

"You obviously like her enough to knock her up," I add.

The room falls silent, and Penny's face goes pale.

"What did you say?" Eddie questions me.

"I found a pregnancy test in my trash can, and I know it's not mine, definitely not Ivy's, and I'm pretty sure it wasn't my mother's. That only leaves Penny, who was there this morning for breakfast."

"You're pregnant?" Father questions her.

Penny bursts out crying, and my mother runs to her side. There's a knock at the door, and I rush to open it. I'm surprised to see Eddie's parents standing at the door.

"Olivia, what are you doing here? It's bad luck to see Eddie before the wedding," his mother says.

"I think you need to come in. I don't think there's going to be a wedding today." They both look at me strangely but enter the room. That's when they see Eddie and Penny in bed together.

"No, no, say you didn't, son. Not her sister?" his father asks him.

"I'm sorry, Father," Eddie croaks.

"Why? Why would you do that to her?" his mother questions him.

"Because I don't love her, and I never wanted to marry her. I felt pressured into it. You told me I had no choice."

His parents straighten themselves up and glare at their son.

"But that isn't all that has happened, is it Eddie?" I glare at him.

"Apparently, Penny is pregnant. I don't even know if it's my baby, she sleeps around a lot, and I use a condom with her."

My father is ready to launch at him, except Penny beats him to the punch, so to speak, and slaps him across the face.

"I have been sleeping with you and only you for months. You're the one who has been screwing every single lady in London. I love you, I wanted it to be me marrying you today. Instead, I'm now knocked up with your bastard baby."

"You're pregnant?" His parents look at her.

"Yes, and it's his. I never slept with anyone else? Unless the condom broke on all your other whores, then there might be a litter of bastard children coming along."

"Penny, don't be so vulgar," Mother chastises her.

"Whatever, I don't care. I'm now going to be a single parent, and my sister is going to marry my baby's daddy. My life is messed up." She bursts out crying.

I can't believe she's playing the victim here—she needs an Oscar—this performance is top shelf. "Actually, no... I won't be marrying anyone today. I think this is enough *Jerry Springer* for me. I have put this family first all my life, I gave up on the man that I love to be here today to honor some misguided sense of family loyalty, and what do I get in return, nothing but people who are all about themselves. I wanted to make you happy, Father. I thought by marrying Eddie today, I could make you happy. But I can't marry him. I don't love him. I don't even like him. I can't even stand to be in the same room as him, but I was willing to do that for you because I wanted to give you this one thing you wanted… to see me walk down the aisle."

My father moves away from the bed. "I thought you liked him?"

I shake my head, and tears litter my cheeks. "He told me the night we became engaged that he was never going to stay faithful to me, that he was never going to try. He was just doing his duty."

My father turns to where Eddie is sitting, looking very sheepish. "I don't know who you are anymore," he says, shaking his head. "I'm sorry, Olivia, I thought I was doing the right thing. I knew you were lonely, and I wanted to help. I wanted to fix things before I ran out of time. I just wanted you to be happy." He looks ashamed of himself. "But I see I guilted you into something you were not comfortable with."

I weakly smile at him.

"I failed you, sweetheart."

"No, you didn't." I wrap my arms around him, hugging him.

"I should've trusted you. I should have let you find your way. You have transformed the estate around, and I should've trusted you enough to find your own happiness."

I hug him tighter.

"Did you really meet someone?" he questions me.

I nod. "He's probably not at all who you thought I should be with, but he loves me, Father, with all his heart, and I broke it. I told him there was no future for us… that I had to marry Eddie." I burst out crying.

"Oh my, sweetheart, I seem to have ruined things for you. I thought I was doing the right thing, but it looks like I just messed up everything."

My father has a pained expression on his face.

"I should've stood up for myself more, I should have told you. I was scared, and then you had your turn, and I didn't want to lose you."

He hugs me tighter.

"So where's this young man, then?" He smiles at me.

"Um... LA."

"The rock star?" He frowns.

"Yes, the rock star, but he's a good man, Father."

He looks down at me and smiles. "I trust you, sweetheart."

"But what about the wedding?" my mother asks, her arm wrapped around a sobbing Penny.

"Oh, there will definitely be a wedding. No grandchild of mine is going to be born out of wedlock, wouldn't you agree, William?" My father turns to Eddie's father.

"Most certainly do agree on that."

"What?" Eddie exclaims. "You want me to swap brides?"

"You had no problem jumping into her bed every chance you got, and I'm sure you would've continued if I hadn't have found out," I add.

"Olivia, watch your mouth."

"How can you defend her after everything she has done to me?" I question my mother. I knew Penny was her favorite, but this, this is too much—sticking up for her when irrefutable evidence is laid out before her.

"She's carrying my grandbaby."

"How do I know it's mine? I want a paternity test," Eddie adds.

"I think you have done enough here, son. Sit down and shut up. I'm pretty sure after the way you have behaved, the last thing Penelope wants to own up to is you being the father to her unborn baby," Eddie's father chastises him. "You will be marrying that young lady today. You will no longer be allowed to cavort in London, and you will no longer have an allowance. You will have to work for a living. I think we have been way too soft on you."

"I'm a thirty-year-old man, you can't ground me," Eddie argues.

"But I can certainly take you out of the will, and I can certainly take away all your privileges," his father argues, which shuts him up.

"Maybe Richard here might take pity on you and offer you a job to support your upcoming family commitments."

"Olivia's the boss of the estate. It's up to her." My father turns to me.

"I'm sure I can find work for him to do on the estate." I give Eddie a smirk. "As long as he knows who the boss is, then there shouldn't be a problem."

Eddie nods, looking like a scolded child.

"I'm sure the same goes for your sister as well." My father looks at my mother, who appears shocked but keeps her mouth shut.

"It's probably about time she takes pride in the family, seeing as she's producing the next generation." I smirk at Penny.

"Glad that's all settled." Father claps his hands together. "Now, Olivia, I think there's a plane for you to catch." My father smiles. "And we have a wedding to rearrange." He pushes me out the door, Ivy following right behind me.

"What the hell just happened?" Ivy asks me.

"I think I might be in the twilight zone."

"Well, don't knock it. You have a rock star's heart to win back."

"Yes, that I do."

32

AXEL

"What? What's happened?" I yell down the phone at my brother.

"Olivia never married Eddie." Everything stops around me.

"What did you say?"

"She never married him. In fact, the tabloids say she wasn't even at the wedding."

"Where the hell is she?" My heart is racing.

"I don't know, they don't say."

"Shit, has something happened to her?" I rake my hands through my hair and pace around my living room. "How long ago was the wedding?"

"It happened while we were sleeping. It's late evening there now. I'm not even sure if the reception is finished or not."

"Who got married then?" I'm confused about why there was still a wedding.

"Penny married Eddie."

"What?"

"Yeah, that's what the internet says. Says that they have been long-time sweethearts and didn't realize they loved each other until his parents arranged his marriage to Olivia."

"Such fucking bullshit."

"Well, at least Olivia isn't married to him."

Yeah, Christian was right, but where the hell is she?

"Ask Ness to call Ivy and find out where she is? She's been missing all day. I need to find her."

"On it, brother. Hang tight, we're going to find your woman." Then he hangs up.

I pick up my phone and call Derrick because he's close to Olivia, but it just rings out. Come on, D, pick up the phone? I scroll through my phone and try Stacey.

She picks up after a couple of rings. "Axel?"

"Where's Olivia?" I question.

"She's in Scotland getting married. Are you okay?" she asks.

"She didn't marry him, her sister did. But no one has heard from her. I need to find her, Stace."

"Shit, okay. I'll make some calls and let you know."

I hang up and pace.

Where would she go?

Maybe I should get the jet ready and fly over there and search for her? No, it takes half a day to get there.

What happens if she's somewhere else? I can't go on some cross-continent search for her. Yes, I can. I love her, and I'll fly to the ends of the earth to find her.

I rush around and pack some stuff into an overnight bag. I'm heading out the door when I see movement on the security camera. The bottom gate is opening, and one of our SUVs is driving through. It must be someone I know. They must have news. I drop the bag and swing open the door, but the last person I thought I'd see steps out.

"Axel."

Fuck, she looks beautiful. I don't care why she's here, I'm just so relieved that she isn't lost, that nothing happened to her.

So much so that I launch myself at her, grabbing her face and kissing her. She lets out a tiny, surprised squeal, but then her hands are on me. I barely register Sammy dropping off a bag and then the car driving away. I'm so absorbed in kissing Olivia, feeling her soft lips against mine, her warm hands on my skin, those tiny little whimpers that she does when she's excited. My heart is racing a million miles a minute, but everything feels right. Having her here in my arms feels right, and I never ever want to let her go—*never* again. Like Derrick said, our stubbornness kept us apart, and I'm never going to allow that to happen again.

"I need you, Liv. Fuck, I need you. We can talk later, okay?" I say, holding her face in my palms.

"Okay." She smiles at me.

I pick her up and throw her over my shoulder like a damn caveman. I feel like a caveman who has finally found his woman. This caveman is taking her back to his cave.

I rush through my house and run up the stairs, kicking over various things on my way as I go, making her giggle. *God, that laugh, how I have missed it.* I make it up the stairs, kick open my bedroom door, and throw her onto the bed. I kick off my jeans, briefs, and T-shirt as I stalk toward her on the bed. She's dressed in leggings, a long gray top, and she lost her flip-flops at some point during our journey to the bedroom.

The hunger in her eyes matches mine, and she quickly takes her top off and throws it to the side, followed by her bra. I watch as she shimmies her leggings off along with her underwear. She lays back against my bed and crooks her finger for me to come closer, which I do. Her eyes watch me as I stalk her, my dick bobbing against my stomach, he's so hard and desperate for her. She smirks as I reach the bed, opens her legs for me, and fuck, there's that perfect pussy.

I place one knee on the bed and then another, kneeling before her, taking her in, and she licks her lips in anticipation. I lean forward, placing my hands on either side of her creamy thighs, my head dipping down between her legs. I'm home. I let her intoxicating scent surround me before I taste her. It's been too long, way too long. I let my tongue come out and lick her sweetness.

"Yes," she hisses, her fingers burying themselves into my hair. I do it again, those fingers tightening against my roots. God, I have missed her. I lap at her sweetness over and over again, my tongue swirling around her bud, teasing her, loving the way she whimpers beneath me. I suck her clit into my mouth, and she arches her back with a purr.

"I've missed your tongue," she murmurs breathlessly, wriggling underneath me as I increase the suction. I could stay between her legs all night, but I know my dick would revolt if I did. My tongue continues tasting her, licking her, sucking her until she arches her back, those fingers dig into my scalp again, and her thighs begin to shudder.

"Axel," she calls my name as she comes on my tongue. I lick until she can't take it anymore. I wipe my face on the bedsheet and move up between her legs, sucking on a nipple as I pass. She looks exhausted but sated. Her cheeks are pink, her eyes are wide, and her brown hair is a disheveled mess.

She looks beautiful.

I take a moment to admire her—the moments after her orgasms when she's relaxed and free are when she's perfect. She catches me staring, which I know embarrasses her, but I don't care. It has been too long.

"I've missed you, Axel." Her fingers brush over my prickly skin.

"I never thought you were coming back," I confess, moving my body against hers, my aching cock pressing against her belly. One of her hands moves down her body and finds my shaft. She wraps her tiny hand around its girth and starts sliding along it. It feels so good, I can hardly concentrate.

"I'm so sorry, Axel. So very sorry," she apologizes while jerking me off. I shake my head, the words unable to form in my mind due to the sheer delight of her touching me. Then she moves me so that my dick is sliding between her, over her sensitive clit, through her wet folds, hypnotizing it, back and forth.

"I should've stayed and tried harder," I tell her.

Back and forth, back and forth, I slide.

"No, this is all on me. This was my fault, and I plan on making it up to you." And on the word, 'you,' she slides my dick into her, and I swear I see stars, or maybe it's heaven. Fuck, it feels like heaven. Sinking deep into Olivia is heaven, and if I die now, I'd be happy. Because what a way to go!

"I plan on…" Her fingers dig into my ass, urging me deeper. "I… plan on… never letting you go." Fuck me, I'm so deep, so connected to her, I don't know if I can possibly move. I might come right now just from being inside of her bare. Nothing between us, not anymore, not ever again. Just her and me loving each other the way it should've always been.

We spend the rest of the night in bed together, catching up on huge amounts of sex we have been missing since splitting up and finally falling asleep sated and happy for the first time in months.

I roll over in the morning, her side is empty, and mild panic grips me. I jump up out of my bed and grab my briefs from the floor and run out the door. The smell of bacon cooking stops me. I look down from the upper level, and there she is, dressed in my T-shirt, cooking me breakfast. There's bacon cooking on the grill, and eggs and hash browns are in the frying pan with tomatoes, mushrooms, and spinach leaves. She's squeezing fresh orange juice into a cup and is humming away to herself. That moment transports me to years from now, the image slightly different, maybe a couple of kids running around, a belly swollen with a baby inside, still looking as beautiful as the moment I met her.

"Hey," she calls from below. "I was going to surprise you with breakfast in bed." She smiles up at me. I make my way down the stairs toward her, my heart ready to explode with joy, but we have some things to sort out before I start declaring things like I want to marry you and knock you up.

"Sit down at the table and let me serve you." I do as I'm told and take my seat. She puts down a full breakfast in front of me. "You didn't have any black or white pudding, pork sausages, or baked beans in your kitchen for me to cook you a proper fry up, but this is close enough. She lays a kiss on my head as she saunters away, bringing back the glass of orange juice. I slap her ass the second time she walks away, making her giggle.

I dig in because I'm starved from last night, but after a couple of mouthfuls, I stop. "You know, we need to talk about things."

She puts her knife and fork down and takes a sip of her juice. "Yeah, I owe you an apology."

"No, you gave that to me last night. We're both to blame for what happened, but I don't want to dwell on that. I want us to look forward. You came back, you didn't marry another man, and everything else doesn't matter." It is the truth. The blame game, well, we were both to blame, and it doesn't matter now. She never married Eddie, and she flew halfway across the world to me. I think that's the line in the sand, but now we need to work out how our future is going to work.

"Penny is pregnant by Eddie."

I drop my cutlery onto the table. "Pregnant?"

"Yes, I found the test in the bathroom. That was the straw that broke the camel's back. I knew Penny was with Eddie while I was getting ready, especially after finding the test. It probably wasn't the right thing to do, but I wasn't thinking."

I let her continue.

"I surprised Penny and Eddie in bed together, with my parents at my side."

"What?"

Olivia giggles. "Yeah, I should maybe be a little sorrier about what I did, but I'm not."

I high-five her from across the table.

"Pretty much everything turned into chaos because not long after that, his parents turned up to help him get ready, and they found out about the baby, and well, they made Eddie marry Penny."

"How was your father? How is his heart?" I'm pretty sure finding your daughter in bed with your other daughter's fiancé on their wedding day is up there as heart-attack material.

"He actually took it really well. He had double bypass surgery, and I'm guessing that's given him a new lease on life."

I reach out and squeeze her hand, and she smiles at me.

"Then I told him that I was actually in love with someone else. He questioned me if it was the rock star they saw in the papers, and I said yes."

"Bet he's not so happy about that." I take a sip of juice.

"He struggled, I could see it, but he apologized for pushing Eddie and me together. He's the one who told me to come after you."

I raise my brows in shock. "Really?"

"Yeah, I know, crazy, hey, but I think he realized how much of a mess the wedding became, plus there was no way in the world he was going to have a grandchild out of wedlock. I guess me running off to find my rock star was the least of his worries at that point."

"Lucky me." I smile.

"Yeah, lucky me."

"So, you staying then?" I ask.

"If you'll have me?" She looks at me nervously.

"If you cook me breakfast every morning, I could kind of get used to you being around," I joke, and she throws a slice of toast at me. "But you have to go back at some point, don't you?"

Olivia takes a deep breath. "Yeah, I do. I just left, and I've been gone on and off for a while now." I nod, understanding she runs her own business. "But I can try to work from here for a while and see how it goes."

"Yeah?" She nods enthusiastically.

"I'll have to go back and find a replacement for me, but maybe… you could come, too." She looks at me nervously.

"I'd love to. I might even have a look at office space in London while I'm there."

"Yeah, you'd do that?" She looks at me excitedly.

"Come here." I gesture to her, pushing my chair out from the table and asking her to sit on my lap. "Yes, I want to make us work. Our lives are spread across two continents, and we're just going to have to get a little creative with them."

Her smile is wide. "I don't know how I got so lucky with you, Axel Taylor." She gives me a lingering kiss. "But I plan on never letting you go, even if that means I have to tie you to something."

"I think I can handle being bound to you for the rest of my life."

And I couldn't wait to start.

THE END

Continue for more Olivia and Axel

BOOK 3.5
IN THE DIRTY TEXAS SERIES

33

OLIVIA

"Are you sure about this?" Axel asks me, concern written all over his face.

"Yes, you know we have kept them away for as long as possible. They are all happy for us."

Axel rolls his eyes. "But I kind of like having you to myself. I've only just got you back. I don't want to share you with everyone yet." I know what he's saying. We have stayed in our love bubble for the past week, but our friends have constantly been calling and texting, wanting to catch up.

"Come on, the sooner we get this over with, the sooner I can get you home and do naughty things to you."

Axel slaps my ass as we walk out his front door. "Damn right, you will."

Sammy, Axel's bodyguard, opens the SUV's door for us, and we hop in.

Christian and Vanessa wanted to put on a celebratory dinner for us at their home, officially welcoming me into the group. I'm so excited to see everyone again, even if I have a grumbling rock star on my arm.

It's funny how life works out sometimes. I have been lonely

for so long, thinking that I had missed my chance at love and there was no hope of finding someone. And now, I finally have it with the world's hottest rock star, someone I never envisioned would be my one.

It's not a long drive to Vanessa and Christian's home. We haven't even made it out of the car, and Derrick and the girls are greeting us.

"You're finally here." Vanessa tries to wrap herself around me, but her adorable belly is in the way.

"Princess, you finally made the right choice," Derrick adds, giving me a big hug and a kiss.

"I know, it took me a while."

"Glad to see you again," Sienna says, throwing me an air kiss.

"I'm so happy to see you." Stacey pulls me into a big hug.

"Hey, move out of the way, I want to see my soon-to-be sister-in-law," Christian calls out. Pushing through the mass of people, he picks me up in his arms and twirls me around. "I've always wanted a sister." He smiles at me with kindness in his eyes.

"Thank you." I'm not sure how to respond to it all, it's a little overwhelming. I know Axel and I are heading down that forever path, but it's still all a bit too soon to be planning anything.

"Hey, I just got her back, Chris. I don't need you scaring her away, man," Axel chastises his brother.

Christian holds up his hands in self-defense. "I'm just happy, that's all," Christian states as he puts his arm around Vanessa and happily rubs her belly.

"Come on inside, grab some drinks and food. I'm starving," Vanessa adds, patting her ever-expanding belly.

We walk into their home, and it's stunning. The large foyer opens into the living room and then through to the back pool area, where it's lit up with fairy lights. It has a similar city view to Axel's home.

"Hey, man." Oscar claps Axel on his back, then kisses me on the cheek, making me blush. "Good to see you guys together."

Axel pulls me in under his arm. "I couldn't be happier." His whiskey eyes look down at me, making my stomach flutter.

"Finn still in New York?" he asks Oscar as he turns his attention back to him.

"Yeah, he's with one of Nate's friends, Sam. Some hotelier guy who knows New York real estate. He's helping him find and narrow down some prospects," Oscar explains.

"Great. Do you think he wants to be based out of that office?" Axel asks.

Oscar shrugs. "Not sure, he's in a weird place at the moment. I know Isla leaving has hit him hard. They were close."

Both Axel and I stay mute on that point. We believe Oscar is oblivious to Finn and Isla's real relationship as he has never mentioned it to anyone.

"How's Isla doing? I didn't get a chance to see her before she left." I regret missing her. Maybe we need a girls' catch-up next time I'm in London.

"She sounds happy, relaxed… I think it was the best thing for her, honestly. But she's my baby sister, and I miss her." The big Viking looks sad thinking about her, but his face soon lights up when Stacey joins us, even though he keeps his distance from her publicly.

"I'm so happy for you two." Stacey gives us a big smile. "I'm glad it worked out in the end… you two were meant to be."

"Me, too. I still feel bad for putting Axel through everything." And it's the truth. He has the patience of a saint—not many men would've stuck around. Axel squeezes my hand, and the look he gives me tells me that I don't need to apologize anymore.

"I'm happy you came to your senses," Axel jokes, kissing my forehead. I give him a light swat on the arm with my hand.

"So, are you two planning on going to The Paradise Club

anytime soon?" Stacey asks, with a look of mischief in her eyes as she takes a sip from her champagne glass.

"Maybe, we haven't had time to think about it," I answer for us.

"Oh, okay. Well… Liv, if you ever want to… you know…" Stacey gives me a flirty wink, and my cheeks turn an instant shade of pink, realizing what she's suggesting. It was fun last time we were all together at The Paradise Club.

"Interesting." Axel smirks.

"Yes, it is, isn't it," Oscar adds, looking at Stacey with lust-filled eyes. I know I'm turning redder by the thought of what's being implied.

Axel leans into our little circle after checking no one is nearby. He lowers his voice, "Do you think that's something that might interest you, Olivia?" he says in a seductive tone.

I take a quick sip of my champagne and feel like there's a giant spotlight on me. "Um… what… with Oscar and Stacey?" I ask nervously.

"Maybe, or just you and Stacey, something for Oscar and me to enjoy."

I gulp down another hasty mouthful of champagne. *Is it hot in here?* I start fanning myself. I swear someone has turned the heat on.

"I think that sounds fun," Stacey smiles.

"Maybe…" I let my answer hang as sexual tension swirls between us.

Axel whispers into my ear, "If it's something you feel comfortable with, I wouldn't mind watching." He presses his lips against my cheek, and my body feels like it's on fire with lust.

"Something to talk about another day," Oscar says, breaking the tension within the circle.

"We'll leave you to it." He winks at me as he walks away with Stacey.

"You look flustered." Axel laughs.

"That's because I am." I swallow the rest of my champagne, trying to steady my nerves.

"No need to be flustered, darlin'."

"Not all of us are as sexually liberated as you." I smile up at him as he wraps his arms around me, pulling me against his hard body.

"I know… that's what I love about you. The fact that Stacey is asking for round two, and it has you so worked up, it's turning me on." I can feel his semi-hard length pushing against his jeans.

"I'm just shocked that you would want to share me with another man."

Axel tenses for a moment. "Oh no, darlin'. I'm not sharing you with another man, don't think I could handle that. But with another woman, hmm… I think that would be hot."

"Maybe we should talk about this later?" I look around the room filled with Axel's friends.

"Good Idea." He leans down and kisses me softly. "I want to explore so many new experiences with you, Olivia. We have all the time in the world."

His words make me happy.

34

AXEL

"Hey, y'all," a voice calls from the foyer.

"Mom?" I look up to see my parents walking into Christian and Vanessa's home. I jump up from where I'm sitting at the dinner table and head straight over to them, pulling them both into my arms. "It's so good to see you both. What are you doing here?"

"We heard the good news, and we just had to come and celebrate." Mom smiles as she looks over my shoulder.

"Mr. and Mrs. Taylor, so nice to see you again," Olivia greets them from behind me.

"Her accent is just so adorable, it's like talking to the Queen." Mom pushes me out of the way and cuddles Olivia. "You need to call me Viv, and that hunk over there is Frank. You're family now." Tears well in Olivia's eyes as she's strangled to death by Mom.

"Good to see everything worked out, son." Dad slaps me on the back. "Now, I need a beer," he states, walking off to where everyone else is currently seated.

"I'm so happy you two found each other again." Mom squishes us together. "Just so happy. Now, where are my grandbabies? Ness, show me your belly. I want to feel them moving," she hollers through the house.

"Wow, that was pretty amazing." Olivia smiles at me.

"Yeah, I know. They told me they couldn't come. But they are known for just showing up unannounced, so be prepared," I warn her.

"Poor Christian and Vanessa got a fright when my parents surprised them in their home after they got married in Vegas. They were half-naked when they noticed my parents sitting on the couch." She giggles at the image I have described.

"I'd have died," Olivia laughs. "But I like it, they are so much warmer than my parents," she says, sounding a little sad.

"I'm sure we can smooth things over with your parents. I know you have to go back soon to sort things out with the estate."

She sighs. "Guess reality is hitting. You and I stretched between two continents... I hate the sound of that."

"Hey," I soothe her fears, grabbing her face. "You and me, no matter what, we'll work it out. We just need to communicate with each other." She smiles at me.

"We're going to have growing pains adjusting to a new normal, but I have faith we can do this." Honestly, we are lucky that we have the money to travel back and forth between the UK and America. Otherwise, it would make our relationship much more difficult.

"I'll need to get back soon since I left so abruptly. I have nothing with me."

"I know, darlin'. We can leave whenever you want. I probably need to meet your parents as well." She makes a face at that comment. "They'll love me. Look at me, I'm so pretty."

She laughs loudly. "True, I'm sure you have had many mothers falling at your feet."

"Well, I'm the lead singer in a band, and it's only right that everyone swoons over me." There's that giggle again. I'll do pretty much anything to hear it.

"Okay, well, I guess a couple more days, and we should head back."

"Not a problem. I'll organize everything." Giving her another kiss, I want to make sure she's happy.

"I'm so happy for you." Mom kisses me on the cheek.

Olivia is sitting chatting with the girls, touching Sienna and Vanessa's stomachs as the babies kick. My heart is expanding at the thought that I want Olivia to be in the same situation as them sooner rather than later.

"Thanks, it's so good to see you," I reply, taking a sip from my beer.

"I knew she would be the one." Mom smiles at me, and I roll my eyes.

"We weren't in that place, then, except I knew she was different than all the other women I have been with."

"I'm glad she finally came around." Mom squeezes my knee.

"You aren't going to hold what happened against her, are you?" Mom was upset when it was revealed Olivia had a fiancé, but she had faith that deep down, Olivia would work it out and realize I was the better man for her.

"Of course not, sweetheart, she was in a tough position. Olivia thought she was doing the right thing. I can't fault the girl's loyalty to her family even if it was misplaced a little. It means she's going to be loyal to you and your family when the time comes."

"I'm going to propose to her, just don't know when." Mom gives me a big, squishy hug and showers kisses all over my face.

"All I want is for my boys to be happy, and they are. I'm one happy momma."

"Might be a while before we have kids."

"There's no rush, sweetheart. You and Olivia have so much to work out regarding your living situation, adding kids into the mix at the moment might be a little much." I raise my brows at her—she's been begging for grandkids for years.

"You're off the hook for a while as Christian is giving me those little girls, so I'll be fine for a year or so, and then you need to get on it." She laughs.

"You and Dad thought about our offer?" Christian wanted to buy our parents a home near us. He and Vanessa are going to need their help with twin girls arriving in the next couple of months.

"We love our home, but…" pausing, she smiles, "… now that you're settling down as well and will probably have kids soon, I'm thinking we just might." Christian is going to be ecstatic over this news. I know he's been worried about being a dad to twins.

"Christian will be happy. They are going to need the help."

"Oh boy, will they! Two little girls… I'm sure the lungs on them are going to be very good."

"Liv needs to go back to England in a couple of days." Mom nods, listening. "I'm worried that her family is going to hate me." We have been through so much that we don't need any more obstacles.

"Sweetheart, don't worry about it. They need to ignore the outside." She points to my tattoos. "They need to look on the inside, and they'll soon see that their daughter has found a man who treats her right, adores her, and will look after her."

I look out to Liv and hope that they'll be accepting because I know as much as they have hurt her, Olivia's family means the world to her. She's already chosen me once over them, and I don't want her to have to do it a second time.

35

AXEL

Olivia is really nervous about flying back to the UK. Even though it hasn't been long since everything went down, it honestly feels like a lifetime ago. I really want to make sure that Olivia is comfortable. I know she's worried about what her parents think of me. I know I'm not at all who they saw for her, but I'll love her way more than that douche Eddie ever would have. Hopefully, that's enough.

"Hey." I touch her knee, the same one that hasn't stopped bouncing since we left Los Angeles. "It's going to be okay," I try to reassure her as we sit in the town car.

"Maybe we should've stayed in a hotel." She chews her nails nervously. Olivia's parents insisted we stay with them at their home in Edinburgh instead of going to Liv's cottage on the castle's grounds near the border in England.

"Darlin', it's going to be okay, and even if it isn't, I'm not going to love you any less," I try to reassure her. I lean in to give her a quick kiss on the lips, hoping to put her at ease, but she's wound up tight. If we didn't have a driver, I'd be pulling over on the side of the road and fucking the tension from her.

"My parents aren't as relaxed as yours." She lets out a deep breath. "They are set in their ways." *No shit! Forcing their daughter to marry some guy because he came from the right family and had the right connections was kind of a big giveaway that her parents were not like mine, but I keep that to myself.*

"They like things a certain way, the way people have done things for hundreds of years." I know the world Olivia grew up in is completely different from the one I did, but still, it can't be that bad.

"Liv, it's okay. I promise not to do anything that might embarrass you."

"What? No, Axel… I didn't mean it like that." Liv looks horrified that she might have offended me, but it's pretty cute. I put my arm around her and pull her close. Feeling her burrow into my side, my lips kiss the top of her head.

"I love you, and I'll make sure that I'm on my best behavior." I let my hand roam and then cup her boob, giving it a little squeeze. She squirms a little in her seat, especially as my fingers start to twist her nipple. She lets out a sigh.

"This is going to be different than a normal family dinner. My parents have staff and people to look after them. Dinner is always formal, so we dress up in gowns and suits, etcetera. It isn't like what we had at Christian and Vanessa's place, it's not that laid back. We have crystal, fine bone china, a million forks and spoons, and…" she continues to ramble.

"Sounds horrible. Why are we going again?" I joke, hoping to lighten the mood. She gives me a giggle and then a sigh as I keep massaging her breast with my hand.

"I am just trying to warn you."

"I've watched *Downton Abbey*. Is it going to be like that?"

Olivia lets out a groan. "Yes, it's kind of like that."

Now, it's my turn to laugh because I was kind of joking. I guess I don't really understand the world she comes from, then. Panic starts to bubble beneath the surface. I'm not up with etiquette classes. Maybe I'll just take my cues from Olivia and watch what she does so I don't embarrass her.

We turn off from the main street and start down what looks to be a long driveway. I can't even see a house at the end of it. Finally, we arrive in front of what looks to me like another castle, but apparently, this is her parents' manor house and it's massive. If this is what they call downgrading, I'd hate to see what a huge home is to them. I'm used to wealth. By most people's standards, I am wealthy, but this old-money wealth is something I think I'm going to have to get used to. Olivia's parents aren't waiting for us at the front door.

"Are your parents not home?" I ask, wondering why they aren't there.

"Yes, they're home. They don't greet people at the front entrance, you have to wait to be introduced."

I raise an eyebrow as the car slows to a stop and a man dressed in a black suit opens the car door.

"Lady Pearce, Mr. Taylor, welcome to Firth Manor," the butler says with a crisp accent. He helps her out of the car, and the driver is now holding open the door for me. I reach into my pocket and hand him a fifty-pound note, which he declines.

"We don't tip here." He smiles at me.

Oh, right. Putting the money back into my pocket, I make a note to myself—*do not tip*. I join Olivia and hold her hand as the butler leads us through the entrance. We walk into the large foyer, which looks like we have stepped into a museum with antiques, tapestries, and old paintings lining the walls. We're greeted by a grand gold staircase that leads upstairs to who knows where. We continue down the spacious hall, past numerous doors that lead to places I have no idea of because I'm not sure why you need that many rooms.

Finally, we stop. The butler knocks on the door, and I hear a male's voice reply, "Enter." He opens the door for us, and Olivia walks straight through.

"Olivia, my darling." An elegant woman, dressed like the Queen, kisses Olivia's cheeks, but I notice she doesn't hug her.

"Oh my, sweetheart, it's so good to see you." An elegant gentleman gives her a quick hug.

"Mother, Father, this is Axel," Olivia introduces me to her parents.

I give them my hand, and they both take it, giving it a firm shake.

"So, this is the young man." Her father sits down on a brown leather chair while her mother sits on a cream one. There's a tea set between them with fancy cups.

"It's a pleasure to meet you, sir."

His hazel eyes give me the once over. I can see he's not sure yet if I'm worthy enough for his daughter.

"Excuse me, sir. May I get anyone anything to drink?" a maid addresses Olivia's father.

"Oh yes, please, Julie. Some sparkling mineral water for both of us," Olivia responds, and then the maid is dismissed.

"So, Axel, you're a singer?" Olivia's mom asks me, sipping on her cup of tea.

"Yes, ma'am, I was."

She nods in agreement, sipping from her china teacup.

"Was? What do you do now?" her father asks.

"We started Dirty Texas Records. We wanted to mentor young bands coming through. We didn't want them to be taken advantage of like we were at the beginning of our career. We want them to be able to be creative, not just commercial." I give Olivia a small smile, feeling extremely nervous.

"Axel is looking at opening up an office down in London," Olivia adds. "So we can split our time between here and America."

Olivia's parents still, and the room goes quiet.

"Are you planning on moving to America?" her father asks.

"Of course, I am, if I want to be with Axel."

My stomach sinks. Here we go, this is where they decide Olivia isn't moving anywhere.

"And what do you plan on doing in America?" her father continues calmly.

"I'd still be working with the estate. I'm looking at hiring a full-time manager to oversee our holdings. I can concentrate on building business avenues in America. Axel lives in Los Angeles, not far from Hollywood. This might be a great opportunity to entice movie producers to use some of our homes in their productions."

Her father rubs his smooth chin. "There's a lot of money in that, especially as *Downton Abbey* and *Harry Potter* were big over there."

Wow, he might actually be okay with it.

"And where will you be living when you're in America?" her mom asks.

"She would be living with me. I'm one hundred percent committed to a long-term future with Olivia."

"How long term?" She looks at me, her eyes narrowing.

"The forever kind," I reply.

Olivia gasps beside me.

"We would have to ask for a prenuptial agreement, Axel. You understand, being the businessman you are?"

"Daddy," Olivia scolds him.

"Sweetheart, you're the heir to this estate. I just want to protect it for future generations." Olivia glares at her father.

"It's okay, I most definitely would've asked for one for Olivia. When we get married and if something unforeseeable happens, I don't want a piece of your family's heritage." Her father nods, but I can feel Olivia is a little skirmish with the talk of a prenuptial and divorce.

"As long as my daughter is taken care of, that's all I want." And I understand the double meaning of his statement.

"Olivia will always be my priority." Olivia puts her hand in mine, and I bring it to my lips and kiss the back, making her cheeks turn pink.

"I know I may not be the person you wanted for your daughter, but I promise you I'm the right person for her. I promise I'll make her happy until my dying breath." Olivia's eyes are glassy as she looks at me in awe.

Her father clears his throat. "That's all I want for my little girl. I can see she's happy with you, and I believe that you'll put her first."

I nod in agreement at him.

"I have to admit, I'm upset that she'll be living so far away from us."

"I can understand that, sir. Living on two different continents isn't how I wanted things, but we'll make sure that our time is spent equally in both as I think that's fair. That's why I want to look at opening a London office, not only is it good business practice, but it would also mean that Olivia doesn't have to give up her home for me."

He nods again in agreement and clears his throat. "Thank you."

Olivia looks at me in shock, her eyes wide at her father's reply.

"You'll be happy for me, won't you?" she asks her parents.

Her mother looks to her father for the correct answer.

"Yes, sweetheart, we will. I have never traveled to America before. I'm sure your mother would love to go shopping along Rodeo Drive. Wouldn't you, dear?" He turns playfully to his wife.

"Of course, my love. I am a woman, after all." She smiles back, and this makes her father burst out laughing.

"Okay, then, we shall let you both retire. You must be tired from your long journey," her father suggests.

"Yes, that would be great. Thank you. What time for dinner?" Olivia asks.

"Seven sharp," he replies.

Olivia nods and grabs my hand.

The butler is waiting for us on the other side of the door. "Follow me, please." His crisp accent echoes through the empty halls. We're escorted up the grand stairs, and finally, I get to see where they lead. I was sorely disappointed when all there was were more doors and even more doors. We follow the butler down the hall to the far end, where he opens one of the doors for us. Then with a quick nod, he disappears again.

Olivia falls dramatically on the bed. "Thank God that's over." She giggles.

I kick off my shoes and jump on the bed beside her. "See, told you it would be okay." Nuzzling into her neck, she lets out a big sigh.

"Yeah, it went pretty well... and thank you for saying all those things to my father. I know you don't have to defend yourself to them, but thank you," she says as she lays a kiss on my cheek.

"I needed them to know I am serious, that we're serious. I'm sure your parents have fears about you living halfway across the world. I just wanted them to know it will be okay, that I'll look after you." I look up into her hazel eyes.

"I think I got pretty lucky meeting you." Olivia leans down, her soft lips meeting mine in a gentle kiss.

"Yeah, you did," I say with a smirk, kissing her lips.

"You're so full of yourself." She laughs as she gives me a light swat on the arm.

I grab her and pull her on top of me. "I'd rather fill you up instead."

Olivia groans. "That was bad."

"Yeah, it was, but so true." I rub my palms against her ass.

"We can't, we're at my parents' house. It doesn't feel right."

I stop. "Babe, we're here for a couple of days..." I let those words hang in the air.

"I know, I know. I promise as soon as we're away from here, I'll make it up to you."

I groan. *Dammit! I'm going to have a serious case of blue balls.*

"Not even a blow job?" I ask, hoping and praying that I get something.

She gives me a look. "You seriously think you could stop at a blow job?"

She's right because as soon as those soft lips touch me, I'll probably flip her over and plow into her.

"Can I at least jack off in front of you?" I'm clutching at straws now.

Olivia's hazel eyes widen. "I'd love to watch you," she purrs.

Fuck, yes!

OLIVIA

I never thought watching a man jerk off would be hot, but it is. Axel's large hand wraps tightly around his penis, his strokes much harder than mine. The deep guttural grunts that fall from his lips feed my inner sex goddess and make her purr with delight. It's such a rush slowly undressing for your man as his whiskey eyes gaze upon you like you're the most beautiful creature he has ever seen. His body appreciates you in an entirely different way. The filthy words falling from his lips turning me on, making me feel empowered.

I let my hands roam over my heated skin, touching myself in ways I had never done before, especially not in front of another human being. I'm fully exposed, not just in the flesh but with my emotions. I let my fingers fall between my legs, and I watch as Axel's hand increases in speed each time I dip a finger inside of me, repeatedly, my eyes never leaving his.

The sexual tension between us anchors each of us in our places. It is an intense experience, one I have with utter faith and trust in my partner. My fingers work in time with his strokes over and over my sensitive bud until I explode. I swear I see stars. When I finally open my eyes and look at Axel, he's moments away from coming. His grunts and moans are increasing with every stroke until he comes on a guttural growl into his hand. Pump after pump after pump until he's sated.

"I know what you're thinking," Axel whispers against my ear. "It's written all over your face." I look up into the mirror and see my cheeks are a perfect rosy color.

"You're just so hot," I say as I turn and wrap my arms around his neck.

"If I'd known you would get so turned on by my jerking off, I'd do it more often for you."

"Please," I whisper against his lips, making him groan.

"How many more days until I can be inside of you?" His large palm squeezes my ass, pressing his semi-hard penis into me.

"Not long, I promise. Not long." I rub myself against him.

"If you keep teasing me like that, Olivia, I'll not be held responsible for my actions."

I take a step back and put my hands up. "I promise, no more teasing."

Axel is looking suave, dressed up in a suit, his tattoos completely covered. You can't tell he has them underneath all that designer cotton.

"We better go, it's almost seven, and Daddy doesn't like to wait." Grabbing his hand, I pull him out the door.

"Do I look okay?" he asks.

"You're so hot. It's driving me insane," I confess, making him chuckle as we head off quickly for dinner.

"Lady Pearce and Mr. Taylor," one of the butlers announce us as we enter the dining room. My parents have gone all out. Our best china dinnerware and crystal glasses are all on show, as well as the gold cutlery. The table is covered in rich red and gold cloths. Axel greets my parents warmly as do I. A server offers me champagne and Axel a whiskey.

"Who else is joining us?" I look down at the extra two place settings.

"We are."

Turning around, I see Penny standing there, her arm linked with Eddie's, and they look sun-kissed. Axel stiffens beside me, his whiskey eyes glaring at them both.

"I'm so happy to see you both." My mother embraces each of them. "Isn't it exciting, the newlyweds are back home from their exotic honeymoon," my mother announces enthusiastically.

A wedding that was supposed to be mine to a groom who was supposed to marry me, and my stomach sinks at that thought. I take another sip of champagne. Actually, I guzzle it all down. I'm going to need it if I have to sit through dinner with these two idiots.

"Olivia, looking gorgeous as always." Eddie reaches out to greet me, I take a step back and find Axel's arm tightly wrapped around me. Eddie looks taken aback by my lack of greeting, but I don't care. They are a bunch of dumb-asses as far as I'm concerned, and being stuck at dinner with them is the last thing I want to be doing.

"Come, sit down, so we can start dinner," my father interrupts the tension.

Axel pulls out a chair for me and takes his seat opposite Penny, and mine is opposite Eddie. My parents have taken a chair at each end of the table.

Servers come in and top off our water glasses and then our wine glasses. I watch as Penny takes a sip of red wine.

"Do you think you should be doing that?" I ask. She is pregnant after all, and I'm sure having a glass of red wine isn't good for the baby.

"Yes, dear. You can't have that." Eddie takes her glass away, and Penny glares at me.

"Yes, sweetheart, you know alcohol isn't good for the baby," my mother adds.

"So, how was the honeymoon?" my father asks, trying to lighten the mood.

"Oh, the Seychelles are magnificent," Penny starts. "We stayed in a villa on the beach, and we had our own butler who brought us anything we wanted twenty-four hours a day. It was heavenly. I bet you haven't been anywhere as beautiful as that, have you, Olivia?"

I can see what my sister is doing, trying to rub her marriage to Eddie in my face.

"Actually, Olivia and I caught up in the Caribbean a while ago at this luxurious hotel where it's invitation only. A friend of mine had an exclusive launch of his new hotel, and we were both invited to test it out before it opened to the guests. It was stunning," Axel replies, then takes a sip of his whiskey.

I can't hide my smile.

"That's when I knew she was the woman for me." He reaches for my hand and brings it to his lips, kissing my knuckles in front of the table. Penny's mouth is wide open with jealousy, and Eddie is too busy texting under the table to care.

"Oh, that sounds wonderful. Do you think we could go there?" my mother asks Axel.

"I could always try, but the waitlist is four years long." He gives her a blinding smile.

"Put my name down as well, see if you can get our names bumped to the top, seeing as we're family and all," Eddie adds, his arrogance radiating off him.

"Not a problem, anything for family." Axel smiles, playing along with the charade. Pretty sure there's no way in hell my parents are going to The Paradise Club, and if Eddie ever found out about it, he'd probably live there. Thankfully, dinner is served, cutting off that line of questions.

"So, Liv," Penny starts, putting her cutlery down. "How is it going to work with you both living on the opposite sides of the world? I mean, Axel's a rock star, and I'm sure he has women throwing themselves at him all the time. That kind of temptation would make it hard to have a long-distance relationship. Don't you think?" She gives me a sly smile.

Axel's hand rests on my leg, feeling the tension running through me. She just can't help herself. Even after everything, she's still trying to get in between Axel and me.

"Actually, Penny, I'm looking at opening a London office for our label so that we can be together. I am one hundred percent committed to Olivia. There has never been, and will never be, a woman who takes my breath away like she does. No woman can ever compare to her." He presses a kiss on my cheek.

Penny's smile fades as Axel declares his feelings for me.

"I'm going to be looking at hiring a manager to run the estate while I'm living in Los Angeles."

"You're moving to LA?" Eddie asks.

"Of course, she is. She's moving in with me," Axel replies.

"Daddy, are you seriously letting Olivia walk out on her job?" Penny questions our father.

He slowly puts down his cutlery and turns to Penny. "Olivia has built our estate back into a flourishing business. She has given up years and years of her life to make it so. If Olivia believes she can handle splitting her time between the two continents, then I believe she'll be able to do it. She has a bright head on her shoulders. Olivia believes she can chase new avenues while she's in America, and I believe her. She has nothing but our best interests at heart."

Penny's jaw grows wider by the minute at my father's comments. Even I'm a little bit shocked.

"Olivia, I have never given you enough credit for the way you have helped this family out of a bad situation. We wouldn't have the luxuries we have today if it weren't for you." He glares at Penny, who refuses to look at anyone. "So, I have been thinking, maybe it's time that Penny starts taking an interest in the family business, especially if she wants to reap the rewards from it."

"What?" she exclaims. "Daddy, I'm pregnant. You can't expect me to work while I'm pregnant."

"Darling, she's pregnant," my mother adds from across the table.

"I'm sure there are plenty of things for Penny to do that won't be too strenuous. What else is she going to do for the next seven months? I'm pretty sure she isn't going to be sunning herself on some luxury yacht, is she?" my father adds.

"But I'm a wife now."

"Yes, one who will have staff, so you won't have to lift a finger."

Eddie is suspiciously quiet through all of this.

"But what about Eddie? I have to stay with him, and he lives in London. You can't expect us to live apart?" Penny whines.

"Actually, I have spoken to Edmund's parents about this."

Now it's Eddie's turn to look worried.

"He's going to take over his family's estate here in Scotland, but his father doesn't think he is ready for that responsibility right now."

Eddie sits up taller, about to argue back with my father, but he refrains.

"He would like Edmund to be shown how we were able to turn our business around, and seeing as we're now joined through marriage, our estates are joined as well."

"I can assure you I don't need any training in how to run my family's estate," Eddie argues.

"I'd have to disagree as does your father." My father turns to me. "Olivia, I know you don't owe Edmund any favors, but I would appreciate it if you could look over their estate books and see where they can improve."

Wow, I'm in shock.

"Of course, I'll have a look."

"Good, this makes me happy. I'd like Edmund and Penelope to move into your cottage as that's the main hub of the estate."

"Oh, I was planning on offering the cottage to the manager as part of their employment package."

My father clears his throat. "Of course, of course, you are correct."

"We have a cottage in the village, it's only fifteen minutes from the castle's estate."

"You expect me to live in the village? What about one of our homes in France? What about something in London? I'll not be banished to some tiny village in the middle of nowhere while she skips off to London and LA," Penny throws a tantrum.

"Enough, Penelope. You are about to become a mother, and you're a wife. You need to grow up. If you are so unhappy about the village life, then I'm more than happy to let you find something on your own and pay for it out of your own pocket."

"But I don't have a job." She just doesn't know when to quit.

"Exactly, so complaining about receiving a luxurious free home sounds quite spoilt."

"Richard," my mother scolds him.

"I've had enough, Agnes. You baby her too much. She's now married with a child on the way, and she has no idea how to function in life. She gets away with too much, and the way she has treated Olivia makes me ashamed. I didn't raise my daughter to be like that."

Axel and I continue eating our dinner, shocked by the family drama playing out in front of us.

"I'm sorry, Axel, for discussing such sensitive family matters in front of you like this. But I'm sure you'll be family very soon, so it doesn't matter."

Axel nods at my father.

"Oh my God, I'm so sorry about all that," I whisper yell as I close the door to our bedroom.

"Babe, it's okay. It was awesome that your father was sticking up for you." Axel starts undressing, laying his suit jacket on the chair, slowly undoing his cufflinks, and his tie falls onto a side table. I watch in fascination as his fingers slowly unbutton his white button-down shirt then he places it on the chair.

"If you keep looking at me like that, darlin', I'm going to have to do something about it."

I shake my head out of my lustful Axel thoughts. "Sorry, it's your fault you're so good-looking."

He smiles as he walks toward me, then he turns me around and unzips my cocktail dress, his lips touching my neck ever so softly. His fingers pull down the straps of my dress over my shoulders, giving me goosebumps where his fingers touch—my dress pools on the floor.

"I love you," he whispers as his lips trail down my spine. I close my eyes and enjoy the sensation of them against me. His rough fingers trace over my body, the prickles of his stubble tickle as he kisses his way back up my spine and along my neck.

"You're the most beautiful woman in the world, Olivia. And I'm in awe of just how lucky I am to have found you."

My breath hitches at his declaration. I spin around, and I can see the love burning behind those whiskey eyes.

"I'm the lucky one. If I hadn't met you…" I wrap my arms around his neck, "… I could've been married to that moron downstairs."

Axel stiffens.

"I'd have been stuck in a dull, loveless marriage, putting on a fake front, so people didn't know exactly how unhappy I really was, just like my sister is doing." I press my lips against his, he opens for me, and I kiss him ever so lightly. "So, for as long as I live, I'm going to show you exactly how grateful I am for finding you."

Moving away from him, I fall to my knees. Axel's eyes widen in surprise. My hands start to make quick work of his belt, then his zipper. Axel is motionless, watching my every move. I push his dress pants down, and I can already see a distinct bulge in his boxer briefs. I rub my hand over it, feeling it thicken with each touch.

"So grateful," I whisper, pulling down the elastic of his Calvin's, watching his magnificent cock spring free. "So very grateful." My lips wrap themselves over the tip of his dick, a low groan falling from Axel's throat.

37

OLIVIA

Axel and my father disappeared together after breakfast, which is odd, but it is nice that they're getting along. Mother and Penny have gone into town to do some baby shopping, something that I wasn't invited to. So, I decide to catch up on some work until Axel returns. I set myself up in my father's library and open and scan through hundreds of unread emails. Bugger, I really have let the business slide. As I flag the urgent ones, and slowly make my way through them, there's a light knock against the wooden door.

"Come in," I call out, lost in my work. My eyes widen when I notice Eddie standing before me. He gives me a small smile.

"Can we talk?" The look he gives me is genuine. I nod, and he enters the room, sitting down opposite me at the table. "Firstly, I'm here to apologize to you, Olivia." Eddie being humble, this is a first. "The way I treated you was unacceptable, and for that I am truly sorry."

I'm not sure what his motives are for being so nice to me, so I say with a smile, "It all worked out in the end."

"For you, yes. I'm glad that you're happy, Olivia. Honestly, I am. Axel adores you, and what you two have is real."

I blush at his compliment. "Unlike you and Penny?" I question.

Eddie lets out a heavy sigh. "Your sister is a lot to take on full-time."

"I guess the novelty of hooking up behind my back is wearing off."

Was that harsh? Probably, but I think he deserved it.

"Yes, I suppose it has. But Penny and I were never more than a fling, a way to pass the time." I cringe a little.

"She was sleeping with other people when we were together."

Okay, so what does that have to do with me?

"I've asked for a paternity test."

Ah, I see now.

"That's fair enough, I wouldn't trust my sister either, but you're married now. Do you seriously think our parents are going to let you divorce, if by some mistake, that child isn't yours?"

Another heavy sigh. "If the baby is truly mine, then I'll give this marriage my all."

"So, no hooking up with other people?"

He rolls his eyes. "Penny and I have agreed that we'd have an open marriage."

Well, this shocks me. "Really?"

He chuckles. "Your sister is a great actress. She isn't in love with me. I was a challenge to her because I was yours."

"You were never mine, Eddie," I quickly add.

He waves his hand in the air. "You know what I mean."

Yes, I do. I have lived with it all my life.

"Anyway, catching your wife in a compromising position with your best man on your wedding day makes you question things a little more."

Okay, now I'm really shocked.

"No way."

He laughs. "Oh, yes, it happened. Not that I care. I should've cared, though, right? You should care if your wife is screwing your best man during the reception, but I didn't. I know this sounds bad, but I hope that the baby isn't mine, so I can get out of this marriage." Eddie's shoulders relax as if he has been waiting to get that weight off his chest for a while now.

What the hell am I meant to do with this information?

"Sounds like you're in a pickle."

He laughs again. "That I am. I guess it's karma teaching me a lesson."

"What happens if the baby is yours, though?"

"I'll love that baby with all my heart and give it the best life it could ever have." This makes me smile, and it sounds like Eddie might make a good dad.

"Guess the child will need one parent to look after it."

He roars with laughter. "So true." Then he composes himself before saying, "Are you really going to move to LA?"

"Of course, I love Axel."

Eddie nods and is quiet for a moment. "What does love feel like?"

What a strange question to ask and it does shock me.

"Love makes you feel secure. No matter what happens, that person has your back. It makes you a better version of yourself, it gives you the confidence to do things you didn't think you could do on your own. They are your best friend. Being in love just makes my world better because he's in it."

Eddie looks at me with wide eyes. "I hope one day I get to experience it."

My heart aches for Eddie and the fact that he might not get to experience being happy with a life partner. Maybe, over time, he and Penny could be happy. *Who am I kidding? No one would be happy living with Penny.*

I hear a throat clear and look up to see Axel standing in the doorway, his heavily tattooed arms crossed and a scowl covering his face. "You're back." I smile at him, but his whiskey eyes are staring daggers at Eddie.

"Axel," Eddie greets him coolly.

"Eddie," Axel growls back before he strides across the room to where I'm sitting. He stops before me, bends down, grabs my face between his large palms, and kisses me, claiming me in front of Eddie. He pulls away, and I can see the triumphant smile on his face as he turns to Eddie and takes a seat beside me.

"So, what did I miss?" he asks.

"Olivia was so kind to listen to me apologize for the way I treated her."

Axel raises his eyebrow at Eddie's honesty.

"It was the least I could do."

Axel nods.

"I told her I was happy that I did mess up so she could find someone who deserved her." Axel sits straighter in his seat. "I never deserved her, and I'd never have made her happy. She's too special to have wasted her life on a person like me." Wow, Eddie was going all out on self-deprecation. "I see the way you two look at each other, and I envy it."

I think Axel is going to fall over in shock.

"I'm one lucky son of a gun." Axel pulls my hand into his and kisses my knuckles.

"That you are," Eddie says sadly. "Anyway, I'll leave you both to it." Eddie holds his hand out to Axel, who shakes it and then makes his way to the door.

"Oh, and Liv..." he stops and looks at me, "... the test is happening today, that's why you were not invited to go shopping. I should have the results by the end of the week. I think we should hold off on teaching me the business until then." And with that, he's gone.

"What test?" Axel questions me.

"Paternity... he's asked Penny for a test."

Axel whistles. "He doesn't think he's the father?" I shake my head. "Holy shit."

"I know, and he also told me Penny was shagging his best man during the reception."

Axel slaps his hand on the desk, making me jump. "No way." He shakes his head. "Seriously, this is like an episode of *The Bold and the Beautiful*."

Because it kind of is, I giggle.

"How was your morning with my father?"

Axel smiles. "We went clay pigeon shooting. A boy from Texas getting to shoot things is right up my alley. I impressed him so that's a start. He wants to take me trout fishing next. Somewhere up in Scotland."

This makes me smile. "Yeah, we have a house up in the highlands."

Axel rolls his eyes. "Of course, you do." I slap his arm. "Sorry, I forgot my girlfriend is a fucking princess." I slap him again, then I start tickling him, knowing how much he hates it. "Oh, you want to start that now, do you?"

His large hands grab my wrists, so I can't touch him. The look he gives me is pure desire. "What I wouldn't give to wipe everything off this desk right now, bend you over, and fuck your sweet, hot pussy until we both come."

My chest rises and falls quickly at the thought. It's been days since he has been inside me, and I think I'm having the female equivalent of blue balls. "Maybe you should," I whisper and watch as Axel's nostrils flare and his eyes widen.

"Don't tease me, darlin'. I'm holding on by the tiniest of threads."

"My mother and Penny are out. I'm assuming my father has gone for a rest." Axel nods. "Eddie has disappeared to lick his wounds."

I watch as Axel drops my wrists and stands up, walks calmly over to the door, and flips the lock. The click echoes through the quiet room. My heart is pounding with excitement, the adrenaline pumping through my veins as I realize I'm going to do something naughty in my parents' home.

"Hands on the desk and legs apart, Olivia," Axel says my name slowly, every syllable popping against his lips. I stand up quickly and do as I'm told, and praise myself for putting on a dress this morning. Axel pulls the chair away from me and stands behind me. I can feel his heat against me.

"You think you can be quiet?" I nod quickly. It's been too long since he has been inside of me.

His hands run up my spine. "Thank God, you're wearing this dress." A hand lifts its hem while the other wraps around my neck. "And you are wearing a tiny scrap of fabric for panties as well."

It was another last-minute decision from my normal cotton underwear to a sexy, midnight blue, lacy thong that I packed in my bag in a frenzy when traveling to America. Axel's large fingers move from my hip to the front of my thong, one finger moving the tiny bit of fabric to the side, so the other one can sink inside of me. A small hiss leaves my mouth as he drags his fingers through my slickness.

"You're already wet for me, aren't you, sweetheart?" I moan quietly against my lips as his skillful fingers play with me.

"I don't think we have much time, sweetheart, which kills me, so as much as I'd love to prolong this foreplay, we might have to quicken things up." His fingers disappear from me, my body aching at the loss, but moments later, I hear the sound of his zipper coming down, and his hands are back on my hips as he steadies me. He moves my thong to the side, and I can feel his blunt tip pressing against me. Inch by glorious inch, he pushes inside of me. We both hiss with pleasure.

"God, I've missed your pussy," Axel whispers against me.

"I've missed you, too." He slowly starts moving.

Oh, how I have missed the feeling of him stretching me. I had no idea that you could ache for a man's penis until now. Never again am I going to deny myself every little bit of Axel. We are better when we're together in all ways.

"God, Liv, I've missed you so much." Axel groans as he continues to move inside of me.

"I'm sorry for making you wait. Never again." He hits me in that sweet spot that makes my body quiver. A hand moves forward and slips down the front of my underwear. Thick, calloused fingers start circling my bud, over and over again as he takes me, and I feel myself begin to quake. I clench down against Axel, making him moan. His thumb flicks over my bud at just the right angle and sends me hurtling over the edge. I bite down on my lip, trying to stifle my scream. The sound of smacking flesh filters through the room, and moments later, I feel Axel's teeth sink into my shoulder as he tries to stifle his release.

A giggle escapes me.

"What's so funny, sweetheart?"

I turn my face toward Axel as he's still inside of me. "I can't believe I just did that in my father's office."

"You look so beautiful letting go for me." Axel leans over and kisses my lips ever so lightly. "Thank you, I needed that. It's been hard not being able to love you like that for the past couple of days." Pushing my messy hair away from my face, he looks at me adoringly.

"I'm sorry…"

Axel shakes his head. "You have nothing to be sorry about, this is your parents' home, and I love that you want to be respectful." I smile at him. I know I can be quirky sometimes, but I love that he understands that part of me.

"But we should probably clean ourselves up first. The room

smells like sex." He slowly pulls himself from me and pushes my underwear back in place.

"Come on, my little rule breaker, maybe we can have a quickie in the shower as well, seeing as I have already dirtied you up ."

I like the sound of that.

OLIVIA

"Oh my God, I have missed you so much." Ivy wraps her arms around me, greeting me enthusiastically as I arrive at her front door. Ivy's home is a gorgeous Mews house situated over three levels. Of course, it's masterfully decorated in her girly luxe style. Her interior design office is just around the corner on the fashionable Chelsea High Street.

"I've missed you, too." I hug her tightly.

"Come, come, I have canapés and champagne. We have so much to catch up on." As she guides me toward her living room, the doorbell rings.

"Coming," Ivy calls as she heads toward it. Moments later, Isla is standing before me.

"Isla!" We rush over toward each other, hugging tightly.

"I am so happy to see you. I'm so sorry I missed you leaving."

Isla waves her hand. "Please, you had a lot going on. But I am incredibly happy that you and Axel are together."

"Thank you, took me a while to work it out, but I'm so glad I did."

Ivy ushers us back into the living room, where a beautiful

array of tiny canapés is set out before us. Ivy pops the cork on the champagne bottle and pours us all a glass.

"Just water for me today." Isla states. Ivy and I give her a strange look. "Hangover," she declares.

"Cheers to Liv and love," Ivy says, smiling at me. We all clink our glasses and settle back into the soft sofas.

"So, how did things go with the parents?" Ivy asks.

I roll my eyes. "Penny and Eddie were there."

Ivy chokes on her champagne. "No way, really? Gosh, how did that go?" she asks.

"As you could imagine, swimmingly." Isla and Ivy chuckle. "But Axel stood up for me and basically told Penny off for one of her snide comments about me."

"He's a good guy, Axel," Isla adds.

"That he is. But surprisingly, my father had my back as well."

"Really?" Ivy looks shocked. She's been around my parents and my family for years now and knows them all well. "It's about time."

"He told Penny that she needed to join the family business." Ivy chokes again. "Yes, that went down like a lead balloon. Of course, mother took Penny's side, but Father wouldn't hear of it. He told her that she would be moving into the village down from the estate. He also asked me to teach Eddie about the business side of running an estate as he'd be taking over his own family's estate one day soon, but his father believes he's not ready."

"Wow, things are changing, then."

"I think they are. Axel and my father went shooting the other morning and had a great time. They get on really well, which is amazing. While he was away, Eddie found me and apologized."

"No, he didn't," Ivy gasps.

"Yes, he sure did. He also told me that Penny and my mother were not out shopping for the baby as they led me to believe. She was having a paternity test done." Both girls gasp.

"Eddie doesn't think the baby is his?" Ivy questions.

I shake my head. "No, he doesn't. He knows she was sleeping with someone else while they were together, but so was he. He also told me that he found her screwing the best man during their reception."

"No fucking way," Isla exclaims.

"Seriously, this is like a soap opera," Ivy adds.

"I know, right? He says that if it's his baby, then he'll stay married, but if it isn't, then he's going to demand a divorce or something."

The girls nod in agreement.

"What do you think?" Ivy asks.

"Honestly, I have no idea. Eddie seemed genuinely shocked when she announced she was pregnant." Ivy nods. "But who knows. I guess we'll find out over the next couple of days."

"If it's not Eddie's baby, I wonder whose it is," Isla contemplates.

We all go quiet for a moment, thinking it over. It could be anyone's, judging from the tabloid gossip.

"Who cares about her. How are you and Axel?" Ivy asks.

"We're perfect. I couldn't be happier. We just have to sort out the living arrangements, that's why he's checking out real estate for a London office."

"And will you spend time in LA?" Isla asks.

"Yeah, not sure how it will all work, but I need to find a manager for the estate. Ever since Christian and Vanessa's wedding, we have been inundated with wedding requests from the general public and celebrities."

"Sounds like you need a full-time wedding planner now," Ivy adds.

"Yeah, I think I might. I should probably ask Camryn. She might know some people."

"I know Cam's friend, Harper, has an exclusive PR firm. Maybe you could talk to her about how best to capture this media attention from Vanessa's wedding and turn it into dollars," Ivy suggests.

"That's an awesome idea. See, I have so much to do. I don't know how I'm going to be able to make everything happen."

"I know Penny is a bitch, but... she's pretty good at organizing parties," Ivy says quietly. "Maybe, you know, she could be the event organizer. I mean she does have all those celebrity contacts."

I frown for a moment, anything to do with Penny makes me squirm, but Ivy could be right. I'm not sure what else she would be capable of in the business.

"Anyway, what has been going on with you two?" I ask, turning the attention back onto them.

"Nothing much, just the same old things," Ivy adds.

My eyes narrow. "What happened with Alex?" Ivy met Alex when we were at The Paradise Club Resort. He's the owner, Nate's younger brother. He's also some real estate tycoon or something, and he's helping Axel out with finding a new office today.

"It was just some holiday fun, nothing more," she states.

I nod, then turn my attention to Isla. "And you? How's everything going working with that hot chef, Sebastien?"

Isla sighs. "He's wonderful, I'm having the best time. I have been jet-setting all over Europe. I got to catch up with Yvette in Paris." Yvette is this amazingly talented designer who's friends with the Dirty Texas girls. She designed Vanessa's wedding dress, which was stunning, plus she's a really fun girl to hang out with.

"So, you know, has anything happened?" Ivy asks.

Another sigh from Isla. "Stupidly, once."

We both raise our eyebrows.

"I was lonely, a little drunk and horny, and one thing led to another, and we slept together."

"Please tell me that man was amazing," Ivy pries.

Isla giggles. "Of course, but..." We both hang on the edge of our seats. "We're just friends. After it happened and we both woke up, we knew it was a mistake. He's hot and everything, but we're more friends than anything else."

"So, what about Finn?" I ask.

Isla tenses. "Finn... he's one big complication. I don't know. He was my first love... we have been together through so much. He's my best friend, and I miss him, but..."

"Why have you two always hidden what has happened between you both?" I ask.

"I didn't want it to affect his friendship with Oscar. Plus, we were so young when we started hooking up. Oscar was protective of me growing up. I think we just got used to the fact that was how our relationship was." Isla takes a sip of her water before continuing, "Once Finn became famous, everything between us stopped. I guess you grow up, and that teenage love dies out."

"But haven't you been hooking up recently?" I ask her.

"Yeah, it started a couple of years ago. I broke up with my long-term boyfriend. He was a dick and jealous of me hanging out with rock stars all day. Touring with them, etcetera, even though he was an actor, and his days were spent kissing other women. Of course, I didn't know, at the time, he was also screwing them in his trailer. You know the story... you surprise your supposedly loving boyfriend, and you end up being the one surprised. Five years I wasted on him."

"Bugger, Isla. I'm sorry," Ivy adds.

"Yeah, me, too. I was only dating him because I was sick of watching Finn screw around with groupies all the time." Ivy and I both make faces. "Yeah, exactly." Isla laughs. "I jumped into my car and drove straight to Finn's house, and thankfully it was skank-free. I knew if I saw Oscar, he'd charge down to the studios and kick my ex's ass. I just needed a friend. And, well... after some tears, one thing led to another, and that's how we started sleeping with each other again." Isla shrugs.

"And now?" I ask.

"Now, I don't know. What I do know is things have become complicated."

"How so?" Ivy asks.

Isla shakes her head. "Ugh, that's a story for another day. We're here to celebrate Axel and Olivia," she says, changing the subject, and we both let her, knowing she was getting upset.

I've been thinking about what Ivy said about Penny maybe taking over the events side of the estate. She's pregnant, so it would only be temporary. I don't think I can see Penny being a stay-at-home mother.

"Hey, you okay? You have a big frown line right here." Axel presses the deep line between my brows.

"Sorry, just thinking about Penny."

He chuckles. "Well, that will do it."

I smile at him.

We're currently chilling in the hotel room. Axel has just returned from looking at real estate. He has narrowed it down to a couple of places that Alex owns and said he'd give him a good deal. Just has to pick which location will suit the label.

"Ivy suggested that I should hire Penny to work in our events team, seeing as that's pretty much all she has done is plan parties all her life."

Axel is quiet for a moment. "Can you trust her?" he asks.

"I hope so. I'm not sure what else she would be interested in, and I know my father is going to want her to do something." Axel nods. "I think she might actually like it, and it would give her some independence."

"You're too good, do you know that?" He kisses my lips.

"Even after everything that sister has put you through, you still want to help her."

I sigh. "Does that make me a sucker?"

"No, not at all. That makes you a wonderful human being." Kissing my lips again, he adds, "One who I'm madly in love with." Another soft kiss follows.

OLIVIA

I'm back at the castle in England and have spent the last week sorting out all the work I dropped while I was with Axel. Luckily, it hasn't been too bad, but I think I'm going to need more staff—the publicity from Christian and Vanessa's wedding, as well as Penny and Eddie's at another one of our properties, has propelled us into the spotlight.

I called Camryn's friend, Harper, and hired her services for PR for our holdings. She wants to capture the momentum from the last couple of well-known weddings held at our properties. I spoke to Camryn about helping me put together a special events team for all our properties, and she came up with the perfect solution.

Starr & Skye Events will be looking after the events side of our holdings. Having someone as experienced in high-end events like Camryn and her company, takes a huge amount of stress off me, plus I trust Camryn's company as well. It's the best in the world. She already has high-end clients who would love to hold an event at one of our English, Scottish, or French castles. There's even interest in events at our manor homes and little rustic villages. They could even holiday at our villa in Mustique in the Caribbean—a great honeymoon destination.

"You wanted to see me," Penny snarls as she enters my office.

I plaster a smile on my face trying to block out her attitude. "How are you feeling?" I ask as I motion for her to sit in front of me.

She eyes me suspiciously. "Sick, morning sickness is a bitch."

I give her a small smile. "Oh dear, hopefully, that passes soon."

Well, this is awkward.

"Did you call me down here to just ask me about my morning sickness or is there another reason?" I guess being pregnant hasn't mellowed out her bitchiness.

"Actually, I wanted to talk to you about something." She raises her eyebrows at me but stays mute. "I know Father is pretty adamant about you working in the family business…" Penny crosses her arms and huffs, "… and I was thinking about what you could do."

"If you're going to make me the cleaner to seek some kind of revenge on me, I'm not doing it. I'd rather be cut off than clean up other people's shit."

I roll my eyes. "I would never be that petty, Penny. I'm not like you." Penny gasps at my bitchy retort. "But you do have a certain skill set that I think would be a good asset to the business."

Penny narrows her eyes at me, trying to work out if I'm teasing her or not.

"Starr & Skye Events, Camryn's event company, will be taking over the events side of our business. I have decided that they have the knowledge and the contacts to help raise our profile in conjunction with the PR company I have hired. They'll help expand on the media attention attached to yours and Vanessa's wedding."

She sits up a little. "My wedding?" she questions.

"Yes, I'm sure you're aware that your wedding was the talk of the town and not because of the change of brides." She rolls her eyes at me. "You have a high profile, Penny, and I think we can use that profile to create more business."

Penny looks at me genuinely shocked. "Me? You think I could help the business?" Penny questions me.

"Yes, I do. I was wondering if you would like to join the events team. There will be lots of planning with the up-and-coming celebrity weddings, film shoots, magazine articles, all those sorts of things. I mean you have all the contacts already."

Penny is staring at me in bewilderment before she says, "You seriously think I could do this?"

"Yes, I really do. I know we don't get on, but I do know one thing… you know how to throw a party."

She gives me a genuine smile. "Well, yes, that's true."

"And you know all the right people," I add.

"Yes, this is also true."

"So, why not combine them together and use those contacts? I know it would make our parents proud, plus I thought you might genuinely like to do it. I'm guessing you'll be pretty bored stuck in the village instead of London."

Penny stays quiet for a moment. "Why are you doing this for me?" She looks up at me, her eyes are watery.

"We're family. It's just what we do."

Penny frowns. "But after everything I have done to you, you still want to help me?"

"I can't do this on my own, Penny, and I need your help. I never wanted to be enemies and never understood why you hated me so much."

"Because you're so fucking perfect," she confesses.

I burst out laughing. "Seriously, I'm so far from perfect, Penny."

"Daddy adores you… you're his favorite."

"And you are Mummy's favorite, but you don't see me acting out over it."

Penny frowns again. "I guess… I guess I need to grow up." She surprises me with her comment. "I'm having this baby, and there's a chance I am going to be doing it on my own." Her honesty surprises me.

"Eddie isn't the father?" I ask.

Penny shrugs. "Honestly, I'm not sure." She shifts in her seat uncomfortably. "I know that makes me sounds like a slut, but… um… okay, I was a slut, and I guess this is my karma." A small tear falls down her cheek.

"I'm sorry, Pen."

"This is my mess, and I am going to fix it." She straightens up in the seat. "I see how happy you are with Axel, and I want that." It's my turn to stiffen.

"No, I don't want Axel," she adds. I raise a brow at her, making her laugh. "Yeah, I wouldn't trust me either after everything. But honestly, no, I don't want him. He's so in love with you, it's disgusting. I'll never have that with Eddie… ever. If this baby isn't his, then he's going to leave me, and if it is…"

"He told me that he'd make it work." This surprises her.

"He spoke to you?"

"Yes, the other day. He apologized and told me about your little… um… indiscretion at the wedding reception." Penny looks surprisingly embarrassed.

"Oh, that… yeah… well… um… I'm an idiot. I wanted to hurt Eddie. I'm sure he didn't tell you about his indiscretion at the reception either." I'm sure I look a little shocked because my mouth pops open automatically. "Yeah, I didn't think he did. So, I needed to pee, and all the toilets were full, so I went up to one of the bedrooms on the second floor. I also needed a moment after the surprise wedding I just had. So, after I finished my business, I heard voices in the room. I stuck my head out, and what do I see? Eddie getting a blow job from one of my friends." I shake my head. "Yep, never going to guess who?"

"Who?" I ask, and Penny chuckles.

"Karma… I think you told me one day that karma would get me, and well, it did, in the form of Arabella on her knees sucking off my brand-new husband on my wedding day."

"I'm sorry, Pen."

She waves her hands at me. "Don't be, I deserved it. I was horrible to Arabella and Isadora, treating my two best friends as my minions, not as my friends. I shouldn't be shocked that this happened to me at all."

I know I shouldn't feel bad for my sister, not after everything she has done to me, but for some strange reason I do.

"So, you see, our wedding day wasn't the happiest." She shrugs her shoulders nonchalantly.

"Are you worried that you might end up being a single mother?"

"Yes and no. I mean, I know our parents will help me, but I know that my friends will look at me differently. The stigma is still there. I'm sure Eddie will be relieved if he isn't the father."

Eddie is such a douche.

"Look, Liv, thank you." *I'm genuinely shocked by her thanks.* "I know I have been a bitch to you." I guess she's growing up. "Eddie demanding this paternity test has really made me see things differently. I've made some stupid decisions in my life, and now I need to stop doing that because I'll have a little person involved." Wow, who knew getting knocked up would mature my sister. "Do you want to see a picture?" she asks quietly.

"Of course, that's my niece or nephew in there." I smile as she hands over her phone. The black and white image of a little bean, the image of her baby, makes me all emotional.

"I'm so happy for you," I say through my tears. I look up, and she's crying as well.

"I'm sorry, Liv. I am sorry for everything. I know we'll never be close because of the things I have done. I was so horrible to you for as long as I can remember. The things I did to you, I'll never forgive me for them. But what you have done for me today, giving me this chance in the company, you're truly a better person than me. I honestly don't know how I can ever repay you for this opportunity."

Now I'm bawling. All of my life, my sister has been a bitch, but this side, this new mature side I have never seen before, and it's what I have always wanted.

"I know it's going to take time to repair what I have done to you, but I'd like to try."

Honestly, I believe her, so I jump up out of my seat and make my way over to her, bending I give her a tight hug. Penny stiffens but eventually hugs me back.

"I would like that. It's going to take time for me to trust you again, but I'd like to have my sister back."

"Is everything okay?" Axel asks from the doorway, looking at the two of us crying.

"Just me doing some groveling," Penny responds as she stands and straightens herself.

"I'm sorry, Axel, for the stunt I pulled with the photo." She puts out her hand for him, which he takes and shakes. He's looking at me a little bewildered.

"I better go. I have to meet Mother down in the village to pick out which house to live in." And with that statement, she walks out of the room.

"Seriously, did I walk into the twilight zone?"

I walk over to Axel and throw my arms around his neck. "No, but apparently, Penny is growing up." I kiss him passionately because I'm so happy I found him. He lets out a groan as he picks me up, and my legs wrap around his waist. He places my bottom on my desk.

"Well, that's good." He smiles, pushing up the hem of my skirt, his calloused fingers rubbing along my inner thigh, his stubble tickling me as he nuzzles my neck.

"Can you trust her?" he mumbles against my skin.

"I think so. She genuinely seemed happy about the job."

Axel moves away and looks at me with surprise in his eyes. "I guess she's maturing."

"She showed me a picture of the baby. It's a tiny jelly bean." Axel smiles at me. "I think seeing her baby for the first time has kind of hit her that her actions now have consequences. She's worried the baby isn't Eddie's…" Axel doesn't say anything, "…and she might end up being a single mother."

"Maybe that's a good thing. The child won't grow up in a home where his or her parents don't like each other." *Maybe Axel is right.*

"It's all a bit of a mess, isn't it?"

Axel pushes himself between my legs. "Can we stop talking about your sister and fuck?" Axel's words jolt me and hit my core with desire.

"I think I can arrange that, Mr. Taylor," I purr, giving him a seductive smirk.

"Good, now take off your clothes so I can feast on you."

I quickly follow his orders, throwing my dress to the floor.

40

AXEL

I'm whisking Olivia away for a holiday to France; she has a country estate in the Loire Valley. Somewhere we can spend some time together before I have to go back to LA. I spoke to the boys about the two locations for the London office and we agreed on the office in Peckham, in south-east London. The area has a cool artistic vibe about it. Alex assures us that it's one of the up and coming trendier neighborhoods, hence why he has purchased and developed in the area. I also asked him to find me a house near the office that we could use as a place for bands or staff to stay at as we will be commuting between LA and London. Alex did find this cool warehouse apartment in an old piano factory. If that wasn't fate telling me that I had made the right decision, then I don't know what would be.

    I am also looking for an apartment in London where Olivia and I could live. We need somewhere secure. I may not be touring or releasing music anymore, but that doesn't mean our fans have died down either. I know when they find out how serious I am about Olivia there is going to be some backlash on social media about it. All the other boys have been through it. I want her to be safe; a penthouse apartment somewhere with twenty-four-hour security is exactly what I am looking for. Somewhere near Ivy would be perfect as they are pretty tight.

"I haven't been to our place in Amboise for years," Olivia says excitedly as we take a chauffeured car from Paris. "I am excited to show you this place. I remember so many summers spent running around the country side, riding my horse and picking berries. It was divine." Apparently, Olivia's mother's family is equally as rich as her father's side, and this is some of what she inherited from them. They also own a vineyard in the Champagne region, a chalet in the Alps and an apartment in Paris as well as some more properties scattered throughout Europe and other exotic locations. Olivia is richer than I ever thought she was. It's safe to say she isn't a gold digger.

A couple of hours later and we are pulling up through the large gates of Olivia's home. There is a long, rocky driveway with large oak trees sprawling on either side.

"This home has been in my mother's family since before the revolution," Olivia tells me excitedly. Damn, history wasn't my strongest subject, but I do know that was a long time ago. I might have to brush up on it if I am going to spend the rest of my life with this woman. We pull up to a large chateau and the driver gets out and opens Olivia's door. I follow behind her.

"Bonjour, Mademoiselle Olivia," A small, older woman greets her, they quickly start conversing in French. I had no idea Olivia spoke French, another little bit of information I am learning about her. Shit, that accent is hot. I stare at my beautiful girlfriend in amazement.

"Sorry, this is Frieda, the housekeeper. She was just telling me everything is set up for our stay." The older lady starts talking again, something she says makes Olivia laugh and blush then she gives her a double cheeked kiss and is gone.

"What did she say?"

Olivia hooks her arm with mine. "She said that you are sex on legs and that she will disappear so I can ravage you." My eyes widen in shock.

"No way she said that." Olivia just giggles, pulling me into the extravagant house.

"Oh yes she did." Olivia gives my ass a slap; she's in a playful mood. She lets go of my arm and runs away from me.

"Does the Lady want to play a game?" I see a flash of her brunette hair disappear around a corner. I follow after her as she runs up the stairs. My legs are longer than hers as I take the stone stairs two at a time. I reach out to grab her which makes her squeal, but she slips through my fingers. Olivia runs down the long corridor and skids on the polished concert floors. She opens a door and slams it shut. I follow after her and thankfully the door isn't locked. I pull it open and stop when I see the room. My eyes widen at the four poster bed. It's a dark, chestnut color, but the thing hanging from the bed is what truly has my attention. Are they restraints? What has my little minx been up to?

"Olivia?" My voice is low; my chest is pounding from the exertion of chasing her. "What...what is this?" Olivia moves from her hiding spot behind the ornate curtains, her cheeks are pink from running, her chest is moving rapidly. As she moves toward me I watch in utter fascination as she slowly starts undressing. Her thin fingers unbuttoning the pearl buttons of her blouse, the silky material falling to the floor and only her white lacy bra is left. I am in awe of what is happening before me. Her shoes have been kicked off at some point, I'm not sure when, but it doesn't matter. I watch as her hips sway with each seductive step toward me, hypnotizing me. I am ready to fall to my knees and worship at the altar that is Olivia Pearce. She is breathtaking. I try to speak but my mouth is dry, my throat is tight, it's not the only place that is tight. Her fingers find the zipper of her jeans. She slowly unzips them; the sound of the metal teeth fills the quiet room. My heart is beating inside my chest and I swear she can hear it. I am so used to being the one in control, but since meeting Olivia, all that has changed. However, this is the first time she has taken charge. I watch in appreciation as she shimmies out of her jeans and kicks them to one side, leaving her in nothing but her innocent, white lace underwear. My God, she is a vision and she is all mine. I try to reach for her but she stops me and moves away from me. She moves toward the bed and I watch as she jumps onto the soft mattress. Olivia positions herself in the middle of the bed, she looks up and pulls one of the furry covered wrist restraints down and secures it around one wrist. She then tries to secure the other but she is unable to move, a little frown surfaces on her face.

"This worked out differently in my mind," she pouts. Her statement makes me laugh.

"Do you need some help, princess?" I kick off my shoes and toe off my socks.

"Yes please," she answers, giving me a flirtatious smile.

"So, you have something planned for me, hey, sweetheart?" I pull off my shirt and take my phone and wallet out of my jeans and place them on one of the bedside tables.

"Yes, I wanted to seduce you." She gives me a slightly defeated smile.

"Oh, sweetheart, you most certainly have done that." My comment perks her up and I make my way to her. I step up onto the bed, my feet sinking into the soft mattress. She hands me her wrist as I take the other restraint and secure her.

"There are foot restraints as well," she whispers and I raise my brows at her.

"And how did this little set up come about?" I ask, because I am truly curious about why my girlfriend's bedroom is set up like a mini sex dungeon.

She lets out a heavy sigh. "I asked Frieda to set it up for me. I bought it online..." Her teeth catch her bottom lip.

"Frieda, the old lady that we just met?"

She nods her head. "She was my nanny; she knows everything about me. Plus, she's French, she is pretty sexually explorative." I shake my head of the mental images of Frieda in a sex swing.

"Babe, seriously, are you trying to get my dick to retract on itself?" Olivia giggles. "Okay, enough about your kinky housekeeper, back to my beautiful girlfriend and the sexy surprise she has set up for me." I stare down at her. I am so much taller, especially without her heels on and her sinking into the mattress. Her brown colored eyes look up at me, her cheeks glowing pink with lust. "You set this up for me?" She nods. "Have I corrupted the Lady?" She gives me a wicked smile. "Hmm, so many things I want to do to you." Rubbing my thumb across the apple of her cheek, I notice the rise and fall of her chest. My eyes travel over her milky skin, over her not so innocent white lace underwear. Where to start first? I just stare at the goddess before me. "You forgot something though." Olivia raises her brows at me. I jump off the bed and head toward the curtains, I grab what I need and return. Olivia's eyes widen as she watches me pull the curtain sash from my hand. "Trust me?" I ask. She nods furiously which makes me smile. I tie the gold, silk sash over her eyes, taking away her sight, knowing that her other senses will heighten. "Remember the last time I blindfolded you?"

"Yes," she says breathlessly as she remembers her fantasy at The Paradise Club that first night I met her. She was so naive and inexperienced. It was all about this one night, her one and only night of freedom, and I gave it to her, along with some extra pair of hands.

I kneel before her and secure the ankle restraints around each one of her petite ankles. My lips caressing each one as I secure them. She is spread out before me like a beautiful star. "Do you remember the things we did to you?" She nods, moving against her restraints. God, she is beautiful and she is mine. I move around the bed to her back, her head moving around trying to follow my movements. I lean in and whisper into her ear, "Do you remember Stacey's lips on you?" I ask her. Olivia sucks in a heavy breath. "Seeing her lips on you was so fucking hot, Liv." Olivia's breath quickens. "Would you like to do it again?" I ask, knowing we had a conversation a couple of weeks ago with Stacey and Oscar.

"I think so," she whispers. My hands travel over her body, her skin prickling with goosebumps as I touch her. Over her shoulder, down over her breast before traveling further along her slim stomach until I reach the edge of her lace panties. "I remember the way you brought her to orgasm with your fingers, the pure ecstasy on Stacey's face made my dick hard. Two beautiful women pleasuring each other." My fingers slip beneath the lace and dip between her legs which are soaked. Hmm, seems like my Olivia also likes that scene from the club. I'm not sure if I could watch her fuck another man, but maybe I could handle her lips wrapped around another cock, *of someone I trusted,* as I licked her pussy. My dick twitches achingly at the thought. *Interesting.* Dipping further between her legs, I swirl my fingers around her slickness and feel her heated breath against my cheek. "God, you are so beautiful, Olivia." I continue to play with her clit. "You are the most beautiful woman in the world." Olivia lets out a breathy moan. "I am the luckiest son of a bitch to call you mine."

"Yes." Olivia pulls against her restraints as my fingers bring her to the edge.

"You're mine, Olivia."

"Yes," she moans again as her body arches against my fingers.

"Mine," I growl into her ear as she shatters against my fingers. Her body shaking as she finds her release. The tiny sparks of her orgasm make her body quake as she slowly comes back down to earth. I pull my fingers from her soaking panties and suck on them. Fuck, she tastes so sweet. "Your pussy tastes like heaven," I murmur against her milky skin. Olivia just mumbles something incoherently. I pull myself away from her; my dick aching to be inside. She still has on her cute, little, white lace panties. My fingers find a hole in the lace and I start to rip the material.

"Axel," she squeals.

"Babe, I'm not uncuffing you to pull these off." There is a large hole exposing her ripe little ass. My fingers dip between her ass cheeks, her body tenses. Tonight is not the night that I take her virgin hole, but one night I will. "Don't tense, sweetheart. Your hole is safe…for the moment." She relaxes ever so slightly. I unzip my aching cock; it springs free from my jeans. I pull them down enough so that I have movement and I line myself up to her entrance. I rub my cock through her juices making her hum. Slowly, devastatingly slowly, I sink inside her.

"Axel," she moans as I fill her up. God, I hope these restraints hold her because I can't hold back, I don't want to hold back. I pull myself nearly all the way out as my hands slip to her hips and I drive myself into her again. "Yes," she calls out over and over. I thrust into her, the sound of the straining restraints mixes with our moans. My fingers dig into her milky skin as I hold her in place. I love that she has given herself over to me like this. It's been a while since I have felt the need for control. Since meeting her, for the first time in my life I didn't need to control every single sexual situation. "Yes, Axel. Harder, harder…" The words falling from her lips on a moan. I do as the woman asks and continue to drive into her. My balls begin to ache, the tingling rises up my spine, her pussy tightening around me as she comes again. My cock can't take much more as she clamps down on my dick and I come. Hard. Holding her delicious ass in place as I empty myself into her.

Mine. She is mine. Olivia sags against the restraints, my legs are like jelly and I lean myself against her. One moment we are upright; the next we are falling. Olivia lets out a squeal and I follow suit. Luckily, my dick falls from her and I roll to the side. I don't really want to end up in the news headlines. *Axel Taylor, front man for Dirty Texas, in hospital with a broken dick.*

"Babe, are you okay?" Olivia is spread eagle, face down against the duvet. I notice her shoulders start shaking. Shit, is she crying? "Babe." I move her to the side so I can comfort her, but she isn't crying she's laughing. Tears are rolling down her cheeks.

"I can't believe we broke it," she giggles.

"Damn right we did. That's how we roll." I smile at her, my heart bursting when she gives me a shy one back. "You're not hurt, are you?" I ask, double checking because she is not in the most comfortable position.

"No, but could you uncuff me please, I need to go pee." I jump up and quickly undo her ankle restraints. She rolls over and quickly jumps off the bed and rushes to the bathroom like she is on a mission. I follow behind her and watch as she sits on the toilet to relieve herself.

"Hey, get out," she squeals as I walk through the door. I ignore her and start up the shower. "Axel, get out, you can't see me pee."

I turn and look at her. "Seriously?" Still looking at her, my hand tests the water temperature of the shower.

"Yes!" she squeals.

I frown. "But babe, it's natural."

She rolls her eyes at me. "We haven't been dating that long, this is the honeymoon phase, we are just not there yet." Her comments immobilize me.

"I love you, Olivia. Even when you are peeing, nothing is ever going to change that." She looks at me with her mouth open. I step into the shower closing the door. A couple of moments later she joins me in the shower.

"I'm sorry. It's just, I don't know…" I grab her face and look in her eyes.

"There is nothing to be embarrassed about, okay? I love you." I kiss her showing her I am all in, warts and all.

41

AXEL

We have been having a great time in the beautiful Loire Valley in France. Olivia has loved showing me all the old chateaus the area is famous for. We've discovered little vineyards that dot the countryside and spend the days sampling wine and stuffing our faces with the most delicious cheeses and crusty pieces of bread. Listening to Olivia converse in French is so fucking hot. It was hard to keep my hands off her, which is no different than any other day, I guess.

Today we're going on a horseback ride around her property. We are currently at the stables getting the horses ready. Olivia will be on her old horse, a beautiful gray mare named Lottie, and I, of course, will be on a stallion called Sarge. He's a stunning chestnut-colored horse that used to be her father's, but he stopped riding when his health took a turn. I haven't been horseback riding much, and I hope this steed doesn't knock me off. I watch as Olivia tightens the saddle around the beast's large belly —no hesitation, no fear, and here I am, standing away from it like a pussy.

"You ready?" She looks up at me with a smile on her face.

She looks so beautiful dressed in a white shirt and those fucking super tight riding pants that mold to her perfect ass with knee-high riding boots. I walk to her, grab her face, and kiss her, which takes her breath away. Not a long kiss as I'm nudged quite hard by her horse.

"Hey, buddy, she's mine," I reply to the horse, who just shakes her head at me and flares her nostrils. "I think your horse is jealous," I say to her.

Olivia laughs. "No, she's just raring to go riding." She pats the beast's nose lovingly. And if I'm honest, it makes me jealous.

"Come on, let's go." She points to my horse, and I tentatively move toward him. We both look each other up and down, and I'm not sure if I passed his muster.

"I'll hold him while you get on." Olivia grabs Sarge and holds his reins, and he nuzzles her. Goddammit, I want to nuzzle her too.

Okay, you can do this. You have played in front of hundreds of thousands of people and have never been nervous. This is just a horse. There's no need to be afraid. I try to pump myself up.

I grab hold of the saddle, put one foot into the stirrup, and hoist myself over the large beast's frame until I'm settled against the soft leather. Shit, I am high up. I look around the forest where the stables are set.

"Here, hold onto your reins. Now, remember to show him who's the boss."

Olivia winks at me and expertly jumps up onto her horse, looking like some sort of horseback-riding sex kitten. So hot. I asked Frieda a couple of days ago if I could set up a romantic picnic somewhere. She mentioned that there are some old stables deep in the grounds where Olivia used to go whenever she needed a break from Penny. It was her secret, special place, and I thought it would be perfect for a romantic picnic. My horse starts to follow Olivia's, and I hang on for dear life as we trot away.

A couple of hours later, my ass is numb, and my balls hurt,

but Olivia looks so happy letting herself go. Her hair is blowing in the wind as she takes off on her horse, mine deciding he wants to join them and follows with a quick gallop. I literally thought I was going to die and probably screamed like a little bitch as he took off. I'm pretty sure Sarge was walking me into low-hanging branches just to be a dick. Now, I have a couple of scratches on my face to add to all the other aches and pains happening all over my body.

"Axel," Olivia gasps as she turns the corner and sees the old stables for the first time. I, too, am taken aback. Frieda has set up a luxurious picnic area. A large daybed with a white canopy sits in the middle of the doorway. To its right is an old wooden table with wooden bench seats, and it's set for two. There are crystal glasses, bone china crockery, and a huge vase of pink peonies—*a bit of an overkill for a picnic, Frieda.* I turn and look at Olivia, who has tears in her eyes, and maybe, just maybe, the old girl knows what she's doing.

Olivia jumps off her horse and quickly ties her up outside. I follow suit and feel like my legs don't work and stumble a bit. Eventually, I get my shit together and tie Sarge up beside Lottie.

"You did this?" Olivia asks.

"Well, technically, Frieda did. I asked for a picnic, but instead, it looks like I got a three-course Michelin dinner."

"I love it," she says. Jumping into my arms, she kisses me. I'll take that reaction any day.

"I'm glad, I wanted to do something special for you." Letting my arms fall, I rest them on her pert ass and squeeze it before picking her up, and Olivia wraps her legs around my waist. I take a couple of steps and lay her down on the bed, nestling myself between her legs. She looks up at me, and all I can see is adoration across her beautiful face. I'm not sure how the fuck I got so lucky. I look down at her, and my heart literally aches from the love that's flowing through it. Never in my wildest dreams did I ever think I'd find someone, let alone want to settle down with them. But there's no one else I want in this world, this life, except her.

"I love you, Olivia," I say seriously.

"I love you, too, Axel," she says in return, holding onto the connection we have between us.

"Marry me?" The words tumble out before I even have a chance to realize what I've said.

Olivia stiffens underneath me, but I'm serious.

"I want to spend the rest of my life with you. I know we haven't been together long, and I know we're living on opposite sides of the world, but I also know that I want to marry you. I want to spend the rest of my life with you. I want to have kids with you and watch your belly grow nice and big. I want to explore this world with you." I notice a single tear fall down her cheek.

Shit, it's too soon, Axel. Way too soon.

"I'm sorry, you don't have to answer me." Feeling a little defeated, I start to move away from her, but her legs tighten around me, and her hands reach up to touch my face.

"I'd be honored to be your wife."

My heart stops.

Did she really just say what I think she said?

"Yes, Axel. Yes." Now more tears fall down her cheeks, and I'm stunned for a moment. It takes me a little while to realize what she has said, and once I do, my lips come crashing down against hers as I hold her close to me.

"You're saying yes?" I pull away and look at her. Her pink lips are swollen from our kisses.

"Yes... I'm saying yes." She smiles up at me. "I want to grow old with you, Axel. I want us to have kids. To be a family. I want it all."

"Fuck, I... shit... I don't have a ring." Now I feel like a total douche.

"Hey, we can get a ring another day, it doesn't matter. This, you and me..." she points between us, "... this is what matters."

My God, I'm a lucky son of a bitch.

I claim her mouth again with a searing kiss.

"I can't believe you asked me to marry you," Olivia states, still in shock after I spent a long time making love to my fiancée. *Shit, fiancée.* I made love to her on the bed in a stable in the middle of the woods in France.

"It wasn't exactly how I wanted to propose."

"Really?" She seems surprised.

"Yeah, I knew when you came to LA, that was it... I was going to marry you. There's no one else in this world who's made for me like you are."

Olivia lets out a happy sigh.

"But you deserve to have the most epic of proposals, and at the very least, a stunning ring." I rake my hands through my hair. I feel guilty for not giving this woman the best goddamn proposal ever.

"Axel." She grabs my attention—her chocolate-colored hair blowing in the breeze, her creamy skin on display in the sunshine, and a simple throw wrapped around her naked body. "It was perfect. Today was perfect. This place was perfect... it has such significance to me. The fact that you did it here makes it so much *more* special." My heart thumps in my chest. "It was *perfect*, so please don't feel bad about it. I'm sure what you might have had planned would have been just as beautiful and romantic as well, but this, to me, right now, this is exactly how I have always envisioned it to happen."

"Do you think Frieda knew that?"

Olivia giggles. "I think you might be onto something. I've never told her, but she knows me so well."

"Guess she knows me pretty well, too." That crafty old lady knew that seeing this all set up would put me in the mood to propose.

"As soon as we get to Paris, I'm taking you shopping wherever you want to go and buying you a ring. I need the world to know that you're mine." I look at her seriously, making her smile.

"I'm yours," she whispers, pulling me back on top of her.

After another hour of lovemaking with my fiancée—I don't think I'm going to get sick of hearing those words—we spend the rest of day wrapped in each other's arms, eating the large amounts of food Frieda organized for us. We may have also consumed a bottle of champagne and are already onto the second one.

"So, will this be a long or short engagement?" Olivia asks.

I pop a strawberry in my mouth and think this over. "I hadn't thought about it. If I'm honest, I'd love for you to be Mrs. Taylor sooner rather than later."

"Mrs. Taylor, huh?" Olivia jokes.

"I assume you'll be taking my name?"

She just smiles at me. "I think I could handle that... Olivia Taylor."

I frown. "Would you not be a Lady anymore?"

"Yes, I'd stay a Lady as it's the title I received at birth. I would be Lady Taylor instead of Lady Pearce."

"I don't get a title if I'm marrying you?" I ask, confused by how this all works.

She shakes her head. "No, unless the Queen bestows a title onto you."

"Guess that isn't going to happen."

We both burst out laughing and fall into a comfortable silence.

"Can I ask you something?" Olivia asks.

"You can ask me anything, sweetheart."

"Would we be able to get married here?"

"In the stable?"

She laughs. "No, here at this home. This place has meant so

much to me, and I always thought it would be the place where I got married."

"Of course, I'm sure my family and the gang would love to come here for a wedding."

She smiles so wide, her eyes sparkle. "How did I get so lucky?" she asks as she kisses me.

"I keep asking the same thing."

"You proposed!" Christian shouts through the computer screen, and the room erupts into shouting and screaming. Liv and I decided that we would Skype through for family dinner night in LA. One night a month the gang gets together for a big sit-down dinner with everyone. This time Vanessa and Christian are hosting, and everyone is there.

"Guys, guys, guys," I shout through the screen. I can see everyone is losing their minds over my news. "She said yes." Again, chaos ensues, and more screaming and crying come through the screen.

"Show us the ring," Vanessa booms.

"I don't have one yet," Olivia answers, and the room goes silent.

"Seriously, dickhead, you proposed with no ring," Christian chastises.

"Um... remember you skipped getting engaged and got married in Vegas instead?" I remind my brother what happened between him and Vanessa.

"Yeah, but I totally bought her one that same night. I may have been drunk, but I remembered that bit."

"It sort of happened in the moment," I confess.

The girls turn giddy over that statement, judging by their faces on the screen.

"Yvette needs to do your dress. You have to pop in when

you're in Paris. I bet Ivy and Isla could meet you there," Derrick adds.

"What? Wedding dress shopping. Um… isn't it a little early for that, I mean we haven't planned the wedding or anything yet. She doesn't even have a ring. We just got engaged."

Olivia puts a hand on my shaking thigh. "Breathe, babe, breathe." I nod as I get my emotions under control.

"Derrick, I can pop over to Paris anytime. I want to spend as much time as I can with Axel first before he has to leave," Olivia adds.

Ugh, the thought of leaving my now fiancée halfway across the world isn't sitting well with me.

"Fine, but you better call Camryn when you can to book her in. There's so much to do. So, so much," Derrick carries on.

I think I'm going to throw up.

"Is it going to be a long engagement?" Christian asks.

"We haven't gotten that far yet," I add.

"Dude, you're so slow. Seriously, you need to lock her down before someone better comes along."

Gee, thanks, brother, for your support.

Vanessa slaps him across the head.

"Hey, I was just saying he can't do better than Olivia, and before she changes her mind, he needs to put a ring on her finger."

Olivia smiles. "We have so much going on at the moment. I don't think we're in a hurry. I mean, we need to work out our living arrangements first before we can think of adding wedding stress to it," Olivia tells the group.

"She's smart, as well as beautiful. Not sure why she's with my brother," Christian adds, and I flip him off.

"We miss you. We need to have a girls' night soon. When will you be back in LA?" Vanessa asks Olivia.

"Probably in a month or two, I'm not sure. Once I have hired a manager and trained them, then I can come."

My stomach sinks that we're going to be apart for that length of time, but in the bigger scheme of things, it's just a small blip until we can sort out what we're doing.

"We are so excited for the two of you," Sienna calls out.

"We can't wait for you to be back in LA. I miss my Lady," Derrick moans.

Yeah, yeah, I get it. All my friends love my fiancée.

"Hey, Ax, when do you want a press release to go out announcing your engagement?" Vanessa asks.

"Shit. Do I have to?"

Vanessa smirks. "You know the paparazzi have been following you both." Olivia stiffens. "But you're pretty safe in France because of the strict laws there. You know once they see a massive diamond on her finger, they are going to be all over the two of you."

I turn and look at Olivia, who looks a little white with fear. "We'll talk about it and get back to you," I advise Ness. "Okay, guys, well, I need to go and be with my fiancée."

The room erupts into cheers and shouting.

"Bye," we both say, quickly shutting off the computer before they notice.

"We don't have to say anything to the public, they don't need to know. It's none of their business," I tell her.

"I know, but you're a sizzling hot rock star, one of the world's most eligible bachelors… I think I need everyone to know you're mine." Olivia smiles as she crawls into my lap.

"Is that right?"

"Yep. I want all those groupies to know your dick is out of commission. No more groupies." She gives me a steely look that is kind of adorable and cute, and I love how she says dick because it gets him going.

"I'm all yours." I smile back.

"Good, now show me."

Olivia being controlling is all kinds of hot.

42

OLIVIA

Today sucks! I spent the morning waving off my fiancé at the Edinburgh airport. I was a sniffling mess. I didn't realize that saying goodbye would hit me so hard.

Blimey, he's my fiancé!

Of course, the paparazzi were all over us, and hours later, my bloodshot eyes and snotty nose were plastered on the gossip pages. Thankfully, I had swapped my engagement ring over to my other hand and turned it around so they wouldn't see it.

The tabloids only just realized Axel and I are actually dating because some fans spotted us in France. They would lose their minds if they really knew the extent of our relationship. If they smell one little bit of news that we're engaged, all hell will break loose.

Luckily, I'll be staying at my old cottage at the castle while I search for a manager for the estate. There's no way they can find me there. It will give me a little bit of peace and quiet.

I keep staring at my stunning engagement ring—the thing is huge. I didn't want something so ostentatious, but when you're presented with the most beautiful rings in the world to choose from, what's a girl to do? I actually never thought I'd be *that girl* who wanted the huge diamond ring, but when the sparkling rock is on your hand and mesmerizes you, you have to have it. Of course, when the man who loves you decides it's definitely the one, you have no choice but to accept it.

"Still staring at your ring?" Penny startles me from my trance.

"Yeah, sorry," I reply, feeling a little embarrassed being caught out looking at it.

"It's okay, it's a beautiful ring, and you're just happy." Penny smiles at me. This newfound Penny is still taking me a little to get used to. She has moved into the village and set herself up in a gorgeous little home. Ivy is going to redecorate it for her as it hasn't been updated since the '80s, and I'm not sure Penny is into granny chic.

I'm really impressed, though. She has been coming into work every day and looking after our wedding and events section of the business. She's a quick learner and has only had a tantrum once. Okay, maybe once a day, but still, I think that's progress.

Eddie, on the other hand, is MIA until the paternity test results come in, which should be any day now. Guessing he doesn't want to stick around until he has to.

"Thank you."

"I know I've said this before, but I can't apologize enough for being a bitch to you. I know my quick personality change will take a while to get used to, but this baby..." she rubs her non-existent belly, "... this baby changes everything. I don't want this little one to grow up in a family where the members hate each other." I move my lips to speak, but she shushes me. "I did this to our family, not you. God, you put up with my jealousy all your life... you're a better person than me, Liv. I don't want my child to see me like that... a toxic human."

Wow, I seriously think Penny being knocked up is the best

thing in the world for her. It's like she's been replaced with a normal human being.

"Well, I'm pretty proud of you right now," I say, smiling at her.

"I know I have lots to do to repair the damage I have done between us, but I'm going to try. You're going to be the aunt to this child, and I'm going to need you… the baby's going to need you."

My eyes get glassy. I guess Penny's pregnancy is finally hitting me—I am going to be an aunty.

"Well, I'm here for you, no matter what."

Penny nods. "Okay, enough emotional crap, we have work to do. I'm so sick of carrying you." She laughs at her own joke.

This is the kind of relationship I have always wanted between us.

Penny and I have been going through the resumes of candidates for the estate manager job. We have had a meeting with Camryn and Kimberly, who are finalizing their bid proposal for taking over the events side of our estate. I think I'm finally getting on top of things, and I haven't thought about Axel in like two minutes.

Penny's phone starts ringing, making her jump. "Shit, it's the doctor." My stomach sinks. "Hello," she answers with hesitation in her voice. "Yes, this is Penny." She's silent, her face like stone. She would be great at poker, not giving anything away. "Okay, thank you." Then she hangs up.

"What? Is Eddie the father?"

Tears well in her eyes, and she bursts out crying. I quickly jump up from behind my desk and put my arms around her as she sobs against me.

"I lied to you, Liv." *What's she talking about?* "I lied, I'm so sorry." My stomach does somersaults as she pulls away from me. "I knew Eddie wasn't the father." I'm stunned. "I just said it was him because well…" at least Penny has the balls to look ashamed, "… I wanted to hurt you. You caught us the day of your wedding. You mentioned the pregnancy test. I was in shock finding out I was pregnant, and I was there with Eddie and then bombarded by our family, and I panicked. I said it was his because I knew that the guy who's probably the father will never be with me. He and I can never be together." Penny breaks down again in my arms. This is a lot of information to take in right now.

"So, you know who it could be?" She nods. "Why can't you be together?" I'm pretty sure any man would want to know if they are having a child.

"Because, Liv…" Penny takes a deep breath, "… because he's married."

"Penny!" I scold her, not meaning to.

"I know, I know… so fucking stupid. That's kind of why I was sleeping with Eddie. I could never be more than this man's mistress."

"Is he high profile? Would it be a scandal if it came out?" I ask.

"Yes, very much so," she confesses. *Bugger!* "A political scandal." My eyes widen.

"Pen, who the hell is it?" I question her.

"You have to promise, Liv. I mean it, please. No one, and I mean no one, knows I have been his mistress for five years."

"Five years," I squeal.

"Yes, I know it was stupid, but… I love him." I want to feel sorry for her because loving someone you can't have sucks. I'm also angry at her because the man is married, he has a wife and probably kids as well.

"I know exactly what you're thinking," Penny hisses. "But it isn't what you think."

"So, tell me then because, at the moment, I feel for you, but you're also messing up someone else's life. He's married, Pen. Married!"

"I know he is, but there's nothing I can do about that until he's out of office, and we can be together, plus his wife knows about me."

Yes, my jaw hits the floor at that statement.

"His wife knows?"

She nods. "It's socially accepted in France for a man to take a mistress. He also allows his wife to seek others." My mind is blown. "Eddie and I might have swung with them a couple of times."

"You and Eddie?" My voice raises to an unnatural squeal.

Penny takes a deep breath. "Yes, you might not understand this, or maybe you do now after being with a man like Axel." My body tenses at her mentioning his name.

"I'm part of a secret sex club." My stomach flip-flops. *Oh shit, does she know about The Paradise Club?* I stay quiet.

"See, I knew you would judge me." Penny stands and moves away from me.

"Penny, I'm not judging you. I am just listening to your story." She settles down a little.

"It's a private members' swingers club in Paris. It's only for couples." I relax a little as I know The Paradise Club is definitely open to all.

"Eddie and I'd go together as a couple." Okay, I can understand that bit. "It's for VIPs who want discrete fun. You know… celebrities, politicians, the odd royal. It's different to The Paradise Club…" My entire body stills. "Which I know you're familiar with." Penny gives me a sly smile.

"I don't know what you are talking about," I add quickly.

Penny laughs. "Liv, I know about The Paradise Club. Axel mentioned you two had been to an island together at dinner, an exclusive island. And I'd heard around London about The

Paradise Club Resort that was going to be opening in the Caribbean soon. Then I remembered seeing Nate Lewis, who owns the clubs on New Year's Eve, and I realized that if he was invited to the wedding, then the Dirty Texas guys must know him. So, I put two and two together, figuring they must go there if they are that friendly to invite Nate to the wedding. I also found out that it was Nate's boat that you all hung out on for the bachelor party."

How the hell does she know all this? I stay quiet.

Penny laughs. "I know you can't talk about the club. I understand, but just so you know, I think it's pretty cool if you have been there." I give her a small smile. "I knew it, I knew it, you little deviant."

"I'm not saying a word. This is your story."

Penny's eyes narrow. "You're going to tell me your story one day." I just shrug.

"I guess we're more alike than we thought."

This makes me chuckle. "So, what happened?"

Penny turns serious for a moment. "I can trust you, can't I, Liv?" she questions me.

"Of course, you can. I'd never spill your secrets."

She slowly nods and looks a little nervous. "Well, I met this couple at the club years before Eddie. One of my boyfriends introduced the club to me. I thought it was going to be fun, and, of course, it was. I didn't realize who he was when I met him, but he swept me off my feet. He and his wife are stunning. I mean the club was full of beautiful couples, but there was something about them. They came over to us, and we started to chat. You know I'm a sucker for a French accent. When they conversed with each other in French, not realizing I could understand, I replied to their conversation with a yes." She pours herself a glass of water and takes a sip.

"His wife had told him how beautiful she thought I was and how she would really like to watch us together."

Wow, not sure if I could handle Axel with another woman, but I can understand it.

"She very much liked the look of my partner at the time. I think he was some young footballer. They were older, maybe by about fifteen years, but they most definitely worked out. Anyway, I'll spare you what happened next, but after that weekend, we continued sleeping with each other as a foursome until I broke up with the footballer. I hadn't seen the husband for maybe six months until stumbling upon him at a social event. That night was the first night we were together without our partners."

"Is it still continuing?" I ask, and Penny nods. "He knows you married Eddie?"

"Yes, he does, but he doesn't know I'm pregnant."

"And you're going to tell him, aren't you?"

"Yes, I think so. Just not sure when I'll be in Paris again. He's a hard man to get a hold of."

"And who is he?"

"The President of France."

I clutch my chest.

I can't believe it.

"You mean Julien Soucy?" She nods. "Like the world's hottest politician, Julien Soucy?"

"Yes."

"The same one who's in the middle of campaigning for a second term as President." Penny nods her head. "Who's married to a famous French actress?"

Penny rolls her eyes. "Yes, that same couple."

"Shit, Pen. You have gotten yourself into a sticky situation."

"Oh, gee, thanks, *Captain Obvious*," she snaps back.

"Hey, sorry. I'm in shock here. I just… bugger. If this comes out, it's going to be a scandal."

"I know, Liv. I know all of this. For five years I have been living in fear of someone finding out, and now, I'm going to be a single mother, a soon-to-be divorcee, and I'm sure Eddie will tell everyone why he divorced me. I'm going to be the laughing stock of the social scene when people find out Eddie isn't the father. I mean, it was lucky that people didn't bat an eyelid when the wedding changed brides. But with this scandal, I'm going to lose all my friends, and I am going to be alone. I know this is some karmic retribution for being a raging bitch to you for the past twenty-eight years." Penny bursts out crying.

"Hey, hey." I try and comfort her. "You have me by your side. I'm not going to let anyone say anything about you."

"Even if it's true?" Penny sniffles.

"You've made bad decisions, but now you're going to have to make the right ones because you have a tiny human to take care of, and they are going to be relying on you for everything."

Penny sniffles again. "Jules' wife never wanted children. She has no desire for them. He said that it was one of the greatest disappointments in his life that he never had kids."

"You have to tell him, Pen."

"But it's not going to change anything."

"Maybe not, but he's still that child's biological father."

"I'm scared, Liv, so scared."

"I know, but you have me now, and I'll help you wherever I can. I mean I have to go to Paris to go wedding dress shopping. You would be in the same place at the same time. You could talk to him then."

Penny looks up at me. "You would do that? Help me?"

"Of course, we're family." She bursts out crying again.

"How did I get so lucky to have you as a sister? I'll never fuck this up ever again."

And I honestly hope she means it.

43

AXEL

It has been an entire month since I've seen Olivia. *One month!* My right hand is about ready to fall off from the amount of jerking-off I've been doing during our Skype sessions, which is most nights. I'm not going to lie and say that this transcontinental relationship is all sunshine and rainbows because it's not. It sucks.

I hate coming home to my place after work and not finding her here. I hate the damn time zones as well. I hate that she's so fucking busy all the time. But none of that matters now that she's here with me, wrapped in my arms and in my bed where she belongs. I'll say it was a surprise that she turned up at the airport with her sister and that she would be staying in my, or should I say, our home.

I want to trust her like Olivia does, but it's hard. I can't forget that she tried to tear us apart, and it worked for a while. But it means the world to Olivia if I give her sister a chance, and because I love that woman more than life, I'll try and be nice to her. She invited Penny because she's been having a horrible time since her annulment from Eddie went public, especially with the tabloids digging around about it. She thought bringing her to the other side of the world might help keep her mind off of the gossip back in London, and maybe a little retail therapy would keep her busy.

She's just in time for the grand opening of Sienna and Derrick's newest boutique, Wyld. I think it's pretty cool Sienna has expanded and opened up a children's boutique—Ryder is one fashionable little dude. Plus, with the way the Dirty Texas family keeps expanding with little ones, it's going to keep them in business for a long time.

"Thank you for letting me stay here." Penny surprises me in the kitchen as I make breakfast for Olivia, who's sleeping off her jet lag.

"It's not a problem at all," I say, flipping the pancakes.

"I know you don't like me, Axel." Her comment grains my attention. I start to disagree with her, but she cuts me off.

"What I did to you and Olivia, I don't expect you ever to forgive me."

I flip another pancake, not sure how to respond, and an uncomfortable silence settles between us.

"Penny, I don't not like you, but I'm protective over Olivia. I just don't want her to get hurt again. She's so happy finally having her sister in her life." I flip the pancakes again. "It's good you're trying to make amends, but I also saw how you destroyed her, and that image is hard to get rid of."

They say honesty is the best policy. Penny is silent, I'm guessing mulling over my statement.

"You're right. I wanted to destroy her and for what? Because I was jealous. I don't even know why. I just always felt that way. It probably started over something trivial when we were younger, and at the time, it felt big to me. I guess it just manifested itself over the years into something really ugly. All I can do now is hopefully show you that I'm changing. She's all I've got in the world, and after everything I put her through when I needed her the most, she was there for me." I notice the tears falling down

Penny's cheeks as she speaks. "Ugh, sorry, stupid hormones," she grumbles, wiping her face. "I want to be a better person, especially a better person than the one I was before. My child deserves a good mother. I've made a lot of mistakes in my life, and this whole Eddie situation is one big mess, but I guess it's my karma."

Last I heard, Eddie had announced that the baby isn't his and is now playing the victim all across London. On the other hand, Penny has kept her mouth quiet on the situation, which I'm guessing is incredibly hard for her to do.

"But it's probably lucky I messed up. Otherwise, Liv would now be married to Eddie." I stiffen at her comment. "In all honesty, I don't think she would've done it. I saw her during that time, and she hated it, she hated him, and she hated the whole situation. I'm glad I was able to give her an out. It's probably the least I could have done." Penny shrugs as she bites into an apple.

"What are you going to do?" I ask, piling the pancakes onto two separate plates and pushing one in front of Penny. As much as I don't trust the woman, she's pregnant and needs to eat.

"Thanks," she says, then she digs into them. "Liv is pushing me to tell the baby's father about the baby, but…" she pauses as she shovels pancake into her mouth, "… I'm scared."

"Why? Because he won't be happy?"

She finishes what's in her mouth and answers me, "No, because he's married."

I stop what I'm doing and stare at her. *Of course, he is.*

"It would be a huge scandal."

Well, fuck me, Penny sure knows how to create drama.

"Fuck… well… um…" I say awkwardly.

"I know, I know… I haven't added to the great picture you already have of me." I shrug because it's the truth. "But it's not what you think. At first, Olivia thought the same way as you, but she kind of gets it now."

"Olivia knows?"

Penny nods. "I'm guessing my sister kept her word not to share my secret." I know I shouldn't be pissed about Olivia keeping this secret from me, but I kind of am. "Hey…" Penny pulls me from my thoughts. "Please don't be upset with Liv. I asked her to keep my confidence, and she did, but I can tell you the story if you want."

What the hell am I meant to say to that?

"It might make it easier for my sister to have someone else to talk to about it. I know she would be killing herself over keeping this secret. She's a good person."

So, Penny proceeds to tell me how she got knocked up by the President of France, and for the first time in my life, I have no advice for someone.

Penny is right.

If this ever got out, it would be a major scandal.

"Hey, are you okay?" Olivia asks as I enter the bedroom with cold pancakes. I think I'm walking on instinct, my mind still processing the bombshell Penny just dropped on me.

"The President of France…" is all I can mutter.

Olivia is motionless.

"What did you say?"

"The President of France is Penny's baby's father."

"How did—"

"Penny told me. She didn't want you to keep secrets from your fiancé, but I'm not sure if I really needed to know this one." Yep, I am still in shock.

"I'm sorry, babe. I didn't mean to keep it from you, but I promised her, and she's my sister. I know you two don't get on, but she is trying to change and be a better person. I want to give her a chance," Olivia quickly states.

"Hey, it's okay." I sit on the bed and pull her against me,

kissing the top of her head. "I understand it now. Shit, Liv, this is huge. The President of France is a swinger."

"I know." She smiles. "She has to tell him, though. Then it's up to him how he wants to deal with it."

"It could get messy."

"I know, and I'm not sure if my father's heart will take the news if she's involved in another scandal so soon after Eddie. He didn't take it very well at all, especially the press and tabloids. They have gone to their home in the Caribbean to get away from all the stress it has caused."

"Good idea." I hug her tightly. "She's lucky to have you, Liv. You have a big heart, especially when it comes to Penny."

Olivia looks up at me, those big brown eyes devouring me. "She's family, and as much as I want to hate her, I just can't. She is going through something brutal at the moment, plus she's pregnant with my little niece. I can't abandon her."

I look down and bring our lips together.

"As I said, you're an extraordinary woman, and I'm so proud to call you mine." She smiles against my lips.

"Want me to give you a blow job to erase the conversation?" the saucy little minx asks.

"You never have to ask me twice."

"You made it," Sienna greets Olivia warmly, her big belly getting in the way as she tries to hug her.

"Look how big you have gotten." Olivia rubs Sienna's belly.

"I know! This kid is a bloody monster. I feel like I'm twice the size I was with Ryder."

"This is my sister, Penny." The two women shake hands, and I can see Sienna being polite to her, but it might take a while for Sienna to accept her into the group.

"Your shop is so beautiful." Penny smiles warmly.

"Thank you so much. Now, Liv tells me you just found out you're having a little girl. Come, I have to show you the most gorgeous little dresses. You're going to die when you see them. I think I might have to have a third, so I can have a little girl to dress up." And with that, the girls disappear through the crowd.

"Hey, brother." Christian slaps me on the back.

"Hey, how are you doing?"

Christian grumbles, "Sienna better give us a family discount because Ness is going crazy. Why the hell do my kids need bedazzled pacifiers? Can't we get one for like five dollars from Target?" Christian's seriously confused face makes me laugh.

"Man, you're so screwed. Those girls are going to want bedazzled everything."

"Fuck you, man. I can't wait until Olivia's knocked up and you're in my place. I bet you won't be laughing then." Yeah, probably not, but in all honesty, I can't wait to be in his place.

"Ha-ha. I can see those wheels turning, brother. You're thinking about knocking her up, aren't you?" Twin stuff sucks sometimes.

"It's going to be a while before any of that happens. I mean, we need to get married first."

"And live in the same country," he adds.

"Yeah, that, too."

"So, when's the wedding? If you're in a hurry to knock her up, you need to lock her down. I'm pretty sure Olivia is the kind of girl who needs to be married before she pops out any babies."

"All I know is she wants to get married in France. That's as far as we have gotten."

"Well, maybe you need a quick trip to Vegas before she goes back." I frown at my brother, but the idea doesn't sound that crazy anymore.

He bursts out laughing. "Dude, I was joking. Seriously, don't do it. Mom will kill you. You're supposed to be the responsible one."

44

OLIVIA

"I'm kind of nervous," Penny whispers to me as we get out of the car. We're celebrating the opening of Wyld at Evan and Sienna's place, where they are hosting the after-party.

"It's going to be okay. Everyone was nice to you tonight, weren't they?"

"Yes, but you know…"

"I know, but show them the new you, and it will all be okay." Penny nods as we arrive at Evan and Sienna's home.

"Welcome," Evan says, greeting us at the door. "The girls are out the back, and the guys are in the man cave," he tells Axel. We follow behind the boys as we make our way through the stunning house.

"He's hot," Penny whispers to me.

"I know, they all are. Make sure none of the girls hear you, they are very protective of their men." Penny zips her lips and walks silently through the home to where everyone is sitting outside.

"Princess." Derrick rushes up to me. "Now, let me see this ring. I didn't get to catch up with you properly tonight." I flash him my stunning, vintage Cartier diamond. Derrick whistles. "You did good, boy," he throws out to Axel as he walks past.

"Only the best for her." He kisses my cheek before walking off to where the rest of the guys are hanging out tonight.

"Ugh, that man is just way too good-looking for his own good," Derrick mumbles. "I can only assume he and Christian have the same dick, you know twins and all."

Penny chokes beside me, catching Derrick's attention. *I probably should've warned her about Derrick.*

"Oh, sorry, have I offended the scarlet woman?"

"Derrick!" I scold, surprised at his venom toward my sister.

"D, that was rude." Sienna joins us, putting a hand on Derrick's shoulder.

"It's okay, I get it. He's your friend, and he is looking out for you. But, sweetheart, you could only dream about all the dicks I've seen."

Derrick looks stunned. *I think that's a first—Derrick is shocked silent.*

Within seconds, he bursts out laughing. "Oh, I think we're going to get along just fine. Color me intrigued. If I say a name, can you tell me size, length, girth… you know, all the juicy details?" He puts his arm around my sister's shoulder and guides her toward the fire pit.

The night has been fantastic. Penny is getting along with everyone, especially Derrick, after sharing some dick pics of some footballers she has on her phone. I have never seen him so excited. I mean not like that, but as in, ugh, now I have mental images that won't leave my head. Axel kept popping out and checking on me, which is sweet. I told him we're doing okay, that we're all getting on great which calmed him down a little.

"Okay. Now, princess, when are you getting married?

Because this is going to be another epic Dirty Texas wedding, and we all need enough time to plan so we can look fabulous."

"I don't know. We haven't really had time to discuss it. Maybe next year." I shrug.

"Next year?" Derrick shrieks. "Oh, honey, no. That boy isn't going to wait until next year to marry you. You should've seen him tonight looking at the children's clothes! That boy has a desire to knock you up, and it's written all over his face."

"What? No. Kids are a long way away."

Sienna and Vanessa burst out laughing.

"Look at us," Ness says, pointing at her stomach that looks like it's about to burst. "If Axel is anything like his brother, be careful. He'll want to multiply with you as soon as possible."

"Exactly, look at me, I'm popping out my second baby in two years, and Evan wants more. *More!*" Sienna raises her voice.

Okay, mild panic starts settling over me. "We haven't discussed it yet. I want kids but… Axel and I are still so new. We don't even live in the same country. That's going to make it hard to knock me up."

"True, that part of the plan sucks. So, why don't you just move here?" Derrick asks.

"I want to, I really do. I've found someone to take over the general manager duties of the entire estate. Camryn's company has taken over the events side of our business. Penny is working closely with Kimberly as they set up their office. I guess this week away will be a test for the new manager to see how they go with things."

"Plus, the boys have settled on a location for the studio in London. So, Axel could be there soon," Vanessa adds.

"Yeah, but I know it's going to kill him to be apart from his new nieces."

"But he'd rather be with you," Vanessa adds, giving me a weak smile.

This commuting sucks.

"Hey, sorry, I didn't mean to get you down," Derrick quickly adds when he sees me deflated.

"I know, it just sucks being apart from him." I'm trying to keep my tears from falling.

"Did you seriously make my fiancée cry again, Derrick?" Axel's gravelly voice surprises me. "Are you okay, babe?" he asks, sitting beside me.

"Yeah, I was just explaining to them all about how much I hate living apart." Axel pushes my hair from my face and looks at me with those whiskey eyes that I get so easily lost in.

"It sucks, but I have been thinking…" He lets the rest of his sentence fall away.

"What?" My heart starts to kick into overdrive.

"Thinking about our wedding."

Oh no, has he changed his mind?

"Hey, hey, I can see that frown on your face, it isn't anything bad," he quickly says. "I just thought maybe we could do it sooner."

"Yes, yes, yes," Derrick squeals.

"You want to get married sooner?"

"I'd marry you tonight if you wanted to." My eyes widen, and I hear a couple of sighs.

"Vegas… let's go to Vegas," Derrick chants.

"No. No way are they going to Vegas," Vanessa adds. "Seriously, don't do it. Plus, your mom will kill you."

"That's what Chris said." Axel laughs.

"It's true, I mean if you want to get married in Vegas, I could technically see if I could distract your mom by going into labor."

"What?" I reply, confused by this conversation. "No, no, there will be no Vegas wedding and definitely no early labor distraction techniques."

"Look, you'd be doing me a favor. These babies need to get out of me. Seriously, they are squashing me to death from the inside," Ness moans.

I turn and look at Axel. "You want to get married sooner? Like how soon?"

"After our babies, please, because I want to go to the wedding," Sienna adds.

"Yeah, me, too," Vanessa seconds her.

"I guess in a couple of months, then?" Axel asks.

"What? A couple of months. You think I can organize a wedding, my dream wedding, in a couple of months?" I think I'm having a heart attack.

"Hello, that's what we are here for," Derrick states.

"You have all of us, plus Camryn at your disposal," Stacey suggests.

"You're my closest friends, you're supposed to be on my side," I tell Stacey.

"But I want to see you guys get married."

I roll my eyes.

"Come on, you have enough homes to choose from for the venue, and Yvette lives in Paris, so she can do your dress. We could even hire Sebastien again and catch up with Isla." Derrick is just full of ideas.

"See, babe, the wedding is practically organized." Axel laughs.

Yep, I'm most definitely having a heart attack. Getting married in a couple of months.

"Plus, Daddy's health isn't good," Penny whispers.

My eyes widen—I hadn't even thought about that.

"Daddy got to walk me down the aisle, yes, to Eddie, and well, we all know how that worked out… but I know he'd love to walk you down the aisle, Liv. I know he's still not a hundred percent and will never be, but he'll want that… to walk you down the aisle." A small tear falls down my cheek, and Penny grabs my hand, giving it a sympathetic squeeze.

"Maybe you're right, Pen. In a year's time, who knows if he'll be able to travel, he possibly could even have another heart attack. I'd never forgive myself if something happened to him, and if he..." tears fall rapidly down my cheeks, "... if he didn't get the chance to walk me down the aisle."

"Do it, Liv. The man loves you. You have waited too long to get married. You turn thirty in August. Why not kill two birds with one stone?" Penny suggests.

"Oh my God. Yes, yes, yes." Derrick is screaming. "We know how to celebrate thirtieth birthdays in style."

"What do you think?" Axel asks me. "August, around your birthday?" I blink a couple of times. It's a crazy idea, but why not? Why wait? I want to spend the rest of my life with Axel. So why not just do it?

"Yes." Axel stares at me for a moment, my answer not sinking in.

"Yes, as in... *yes*?" he asks to double-check.

"Yes, as in *yes*, I'll marry you in a couple of months." I wrap my arms around his neck and kiss him. The kiss turns a little more heated than I intended, and our friends' catcalls pull me away from Axel.

"What's going on here?" Christian asks.

"We're planning their wedding," Vanessa answers him, but he looks confused.

"We're getting married in a couple of months," Axel replies.

"No way, man, no way!" His brother excitedly pulls him into a hug and then grabs me. "Where, when?"

"France. August for my thirtieth birthday," I reply.

Christian whistles. "Wow, that's close, but I'm pretty sure these guys have it already planned." Pointing to his friends, they all give him a thumbs up.

I can't believe this.

I'm getting married in a couple of months.

45

AXEL

One month! I have been an uncle for one month, and I love it. Those two little perfect princesses, Ruby and Sadie, have made me totally envious of my brother. Maybe not the changing diapers and the exploding poo part—that was definitely a horrifying experience—or even when both of them are crying or screaming at the same time. Who knew babies could scream that loudly for long periods of time?

Also, Christian looking like a zombie from getting up with the girls at all hours of the night. Yeah, that bit looks painful, but all the other stuff seems awesome. I just need to put a wedding ring on her finger, and then we can talk about babies. I know she's just as broody as I am. I see the way she looks at the babies. Watching Olivia hold the twins, I know she's a natural. I know she wants to wait at least a year before we have kids, but I don't know if I can. When you know it's right, you just know.

Now it's Sienna's turn. She's just given birth to a healthy baby boy, little Levi, and I'm off to the hospital with the rest of the crew to see her. Liv is upset that she's missed the birth, but she had to get back to England to work, even though Penny has been stepping up to the plate. I have a bouquet of flowers for Sienna and a little rock-star teddy bear for Levi.

When I arrive at the hospital room, everyone is there cooing over the baby.

"Congratulations, man." I see Evan first. He looks exhausted but elated.

"Thanks, mate, another boy." He smiles proudly.

I hand him the bear and make my way over to Sienna, placing the flowers on the table. She looks amazing just hours after giving birth. I kiss her on both cheeks and congratulate her. I look over into the blue crib and see the perfect little baby. God, he's cute. Shit, seriously, can someone catch baby fever because I feel like you can, and it's happening to me. Moving away from the little bundle, I notice Finn standing in the corner.

"Finn, it's been a while, man." I've missed the big guy since he's been in New York.

"I know. I've missed y'all, too." Those pearly whites smile at me.

"How's New York been treating you?"

"The New York office has been busy, man. There's so much talent coming through the doors." I nod in agreement. I've listened to some of the bands he's sent through to us, and he's right, there's a great deal of untapped talent.

"We need to catch up for a beer while you're in town. Maybe one night down at The California Bros. or something."

"Yeah, that would be great to get the boys together again. I can't remember the last time we were all together."

I want to say that we're all together all the time, and it's only him missing, but I keep my mouth shut.

"What the fuck?" Finn curses beside me. His face has turned pale as his attention is drawn over my shoulder. I turn around and see Sebastien and Isla arm in arm. She's dressed in some weird muumuu type dress, the total opposite to the stylish Isla that left us all those months ago, but she does look glowing, radiant even.

"Holy shit, you're pregnant," Derrick calls out, silencing the room.

Isla looks like she's about to throw up, and Finn looks like he's going to join her.

"You're pregnant?" Oscar yells, adding extra tension to the room as he strolls in. Isla looks like a deer caught in headlights.

"You seriously thought you could disguise yourself in that hideous outfit?" Derrick adds, oblivious to everyone else.

"Sienna, Evan, congratulations," Sebastien says loudly, handing over a large bouquet of flowers. Evan and Sienna distract themselves, showing off Levi to Sebastien.

Isla, Finn, and Oscar are in a silent stare-off with each other.

"Issy, are you pregnant?" Oscar asks calmly.

"Yes," she whispers, a single tear falls down her cheek, her eyes darting between Finn and Oscar.

"Excuse me." Finn bolts from the room.

Shit. I should really go after him, but my feet are rooted to the floor.

"Why didn't you tell me?" Oscar sounds hurt and confused.

"Because…" Isla pauses for a moment to catch her breath. "Because I was ashamed. It was a one-night stand… a mistake."

"But I'm still your brother," Oscar adds.

"I know, I just…"

"Do Mom and Dad know?" Isla shakes her head. "So, you have kept this from all of us for what… the past four or five months?" He sounds pissed.

"It was just easier."

"Easier for who?" You can hear the hurt in his voice and the silence in the room.

"It was a shock. It wasn't planned… I just…"

"Were you ever going to tell us? Or would you have just

turned up one day saying, 'Oh, by the way, Oscar, here is your niece or nephew?'"

"Nephew, it's a boy," Isla quickly adds. Oscar looks stunned. You can see the heartache across his face.

"You're having a boy?" Isla nods, and tears are pouring down her cheeks. "Shit, Issy." Oscar pulls her against him, and she wraps herself as far as she can around the hulking Viking.

"I'm sorry, I am so sorry I didn't tell you," she mumbles into his shirt.

He brushes her hair from her face. "Shh, it's going to be okay. You're home, and it's going to be all okay."

Isla stiffens. "I'm not staying. My life is in Europe, not here."

"What? Are you seriously going back to Europe when you're about to pop out a child?"

"I've just gone five months, Oscar. I'm only halfway."

Oscar frowns at her.

"Oh shit, it was a wedding baby," Derrick adds.

Isla shoots daggers at him.

"Sorry." Derrick holds up his hands.

"Is this true?" Oscar asks.

Isla waves her hand at him. "I'm not answering that, it doesn't matter. What matters now is that we're here to celebrate Evan and Sienna, not me and my drama." She turns and looks at the new parents, walking over and hugging them both.

"Sorry about this," she whispers to them.

They both shake their heads at Isla, indicating that it's fine.

"Holy shit, Isla's pregnant," I yell down the phone to Olivia. The other end remains quiet, and I check my phone screen, and it's still connected.

"Liv, did you hear what I said?"

"Yeah, I did."

"Why are you not shocked by this news?"

Then it dawns on me. "Seriously, you knew? You knew Isla was pregnant and didn't tell me?" I don't know if I should be happy that my fiancée can keep secrets and is loyal to her friends and family, or if I should be pissed that she can so easily keep a secret from me.

"Ax, it wasn't my story to tell."

"I know, I just feel blindsided again that you've kept something from me."

"But you have to understand why I couldn't tell you. I'm sorry, I hate keeping secrets from you. I don't like not being able to tell you everything, but it's not my fault these truth bombs keep dropping in my lap."

"I know, babe, I know. I miss you and hate being apart from you. I'm just shocked that Isla is pregnant. Do you think the father is Finn? She said it was some random hook-up."

Silence fills the end of the phone.

"Okay, seeing as you know she's pregnant, I'll talk about it, but you have to promise me, babe, it's in the fiancée code of silence, yeah?"

"Of course."

Silence again as she debates what to say.

"It's Finn's."

"Shit! Oscar is going to be pissed. He's already on the warpath trying to find out who the bastard was that knocked up his sister. Derrick kind of worked out that she got knocked up during Chris and Ness' wedding."

"Oh shit. He's such a troublemaker."

"I mean, we all know that Finn and Isla have been a thing on and off for years, just not sure if Oscar knows it. Shit, he's going to lose it when he finds out his best friend knocked up his baby sister."

"What did Finn do when he saw her?"

"He ran out of the room when she confirmed she was pregnant."

"Do you think he knows it's his?" she asks.

"I think the possibility is going through his mind."

"Poor guy, that must have been a shock."

"Hell, yeah, it would be, especially when Isla came into the room hand in hand with Sebastien."

"Oh no, she didn't?" Liv gasps.

"Yeah, she sure did. I'm thinking Finn thinks the baby is Sebastien's."

"Oh no."

"I need to find him, babe."

"Yeah, I think you better. Love you and good luck. Let me know how you do."

"Will do. Love you." I hang up the phone and dial Finn. Of course, it goes directly to voice mail.

46

AXEL

Months later

"Your last night as a bachelor," my brother hollers as he enters the limousine. I didn't want a bachelor party, but the boys insisted on it. Apparently, it's Olivia-approved. I'm hoping that's true and not something they told me so they could give me a party.

We all arrived in Paris yesterday—the Dirty Texas jet completely full, especially with all the kids and the bags of crap that entails is mind-blowing. A ten-hour flight with screaming kids is kind of hellish, even if they are super cute. Sadie and Ruby have grown so much—almost three months old now, and little Levi is two months. I can't believe how quickly they are growing up. Luckily, both sets of grandparents are traveling with the group for baby duties.

"Please tell me we're not going to the strippers." I groan.

"Seriously?" Christian questions me.

"Yeah, man, seriously."

"Um… I kind of remember our birthday, and someone was very keen to sample the strippers."

"Dude, I was single then, and you weren't interested in them because of Ness."

"Okay, you got me there on a technicality, but no, we aren't going to see strippers." His smile tells me otherwise. We just had dinner at the top of the Eiffel Tower just like we did last time we were here, but this time the group looks a little different. We have now begrudgingly split up for the night. The grandparents are heading back to the apartment with all the children, letting the grown-ups have a night out. A first for poor Christian and Ness. There's this app now that lets them dial in and watch the girls sleep. I can totally see my brother being on the phone all night.

"Where are we going?" I ask.

"It's all good, don't worry," Christian tries to reassure me.

"And what are the girls doing?"

"Strippers, from what I have heard," Evan adds, and my eyes widen. The bastard bursts out laughing.

"You should've seen your face, total classic." I flip him off. "I'm actually not sure. They all remained tight-lipped."

"Could be anything with Derrick organizing it."

"Last time Derrick organized a bachelorette party, he organized strippers, and Olivia jerked one of them off."

The limousine becomes silent, and everyone looks at me.

"I'm guessing the girls didn't tell you that part of the story."

The boys shake their heads.

"I'm sure it will be okay," Evan says nervously.

See fuckers, not so nice when the shoe is on the other foot. I laugh to myself.

"Welcome to the Moulin Rouge." A small man with a thick French accent welcomes us to the VIP area of the famous Moulin Rouge.

"Congratulations, Monsieur Taylor, on your wedding. We

hope that you enjoy the show." He gives me a creepy little wink. The area is decked out in red velvet with ornate gold decorations—everything is over-the-top opulent. The VIP section is situated high up on a balcony, and the boys have hired the whole section for us. There's one long white table that overlooks the stage. It's set up with bottles of champagne and canapés.

"This is your seat." Christian pulls out the middle chair for me, giving me a front-and-center view of the stage, and the others take the seats around me. A waitress, dressed in costume, arrives with two buckets full of beer bottles. She places the buckets onto the table before picking up one champagne bottle to pop the cork and pour us all a glass before she disappears.

"I want to raise a toast to my brother. Congratulations on becoming a pussy!"

The guys all burst out laughing.

I roll my eyes.

I knew he'd need to have a go at me about my pussy comment so I simply clink his champagne glass. "Glad to be joining the pussy club."

This makes his smile widen.

"I think we need to get T-shirts made up saying *Pussy Club Member* on them," Christian jokes, making me groan because I can totally see him giving me one for Christmas or our birthday.

We watch as the room fills up with eager tourists. I hope none of them look up here and notice us. The paparazzi's attention has been intense since Olivia and I announced our engagement, something that makes her extremely uncomfortable.

The lights finally dim, and French music blasts through the sound system.

"See, told you, no strippers," Christian whispers to me. But there are most certainly just as many boobs on display. "It's art."

He elbows me when more near-naked women dance across the stage, making me laugh. It might not be a normal bachelor party that guys might have in Vegas, but my life has been one big bachelor party over the years. I don't need that anymore. I'm guessing this is a pretty good compromise for the boys.

Two hours and many drinks later, the show is finished.

"Please wait here until everyone else has left, there are photographers outside," one of the staff advises us. We wait in the darkened theater chatting to one another, mostly talking animatedly about the women dancing. A little while later, music starts through the speakers, and the dark stage is illuminated again. We watch as women dressed in Moulin Rouge outfits return to the stage.

"I may have had one too many drinks, but is that Olivia?" I punch Christian in the arm and point to the stage.

He turns and squints his eyes.

"Is that Ness?" Christian questions.

"I think that's Sienna." Evan frowns.

"Yeah, that looks like Stacey for sure." Oscar's eyes widen.

"Camryn? Ivy?" Nate adds.

"Fuck, that's not Charlotte?" Blake looks a little pissed.

"Is that Isla and Penny standing in the wings?" My eyes are widening.

"And Yvette," Evan adds.

"What the hell? Is that Derrick in drag?"

We all look at the bearded lady. Yep, that's definitely Derrick. *What the hell is going on?* The music for the can-can starts to play, and the group starts kicking their legs up with their skirts covering their faces and showing us their frilly knickers. They are then joined on stage by what looks to be proper dancers.

Finally, the song finishes, and they end it by showing us their sexy, frilly asses. The boys all stand up and wolf-whistle enthusiastically. The girls thank the dancers as they walk off stage. I can see the beaming smile on Olivia's face.

"How do we get down there?" I ask, looking for the exit.

"Follow me, Monsieur."

The small man guides us from the balcony, down the stairs, through the tables on the ground level, and to another set of stairs that lead up to the stage. I take them two at a time, making my way directly to Olivia. Her face is bright pink, and a light sheen of sweat covers her body. I grab her face and kiss her passionately. This is the hottest thing I could ever have hoped to see at my bachelor party, and she wasn't even naked.

"I'm guessing you liked it." She laughs against my mouth.

"I fucking loved it. You're crazy, do you know that?" I press my forehead against hers. "That was seriously the craziest thing."

"You can thank Derrick for that idea, but if I'm honest, I think that secretly he may have always wanted to do it. He really enjoyed it." She giggles again.

"Fuck, you look hot."

I realize what she's wearing. Her breasts are pushed up to almost spilling out of her bodice which is tight around her small waist. She looks like a fantasy brought to life, a fantasy I didn't realize I wanted until seeing her dressed like this.

"Liv, is there a chance we can... you know... go somewhere?" Her face lights up.

"I'd love to, babe, but I think we're on our way to the next destination."

"Fine, I can wait. I think. Maybe not. My dick is aching, looking at you dressed like this."

"How about I pack it for the honeymoon, and we can revisit this again?"

My eyes widen.

My naughty little fiancée, I like her thinking.

"Let me go get changed. Apparently, we're off to The Paradise Club after this."

"Really?" She nods. Olivia quickly kisses me on the cheek and disappears with the others to get changed.

"I know it's supposed to be your bachelor party, bro, but I think we all won tonight." Christian claps me on the back.

"We got lucky with those girls, man. Real lucky."

I totally agree with him.

OLIVIA

"I think the boys liked that." Derrick smiles, popping another bottle of champagne in our limousine.

"I know Christian certainly did." Ness giggles. "If I get knocked up again, I'm blaming you, D."

Tonight has been amazing—dinner at the Eiffel Tower, then a private shopping experience at Avenue Montaigne where we hit up Yves Saint Laurent, Gucci, Louis Vuitton, Chanel, etcetera. When you're on a time crunch, it's amazing how much you can buy. Thankfully, our driver took our bags back to the apartment. I'm hoping Axel doesn't notice them—if he does, I'll just distract him by getting naked.

When Derrick suggested surprising the boys with us doing the can-can, I wasn't too sure about it, but it was so much fun in the end. It was such an experience, especially doing it at the world-famous Moulin Rouge. I don't think I'll ever forget that moment.

We're all now heading off to The Paradise Club to finish the night and have a little more fun. We make our way to the club in separate limousines—I suppose it's still a bachelor and bachelorette party even though we have technically spent most of it together. It's exactly how I wanted it.

"Cheers to the beautiful bride-to-be, Olivia. She gets to wake up naked with Axel for the rest of her life." Derrick salutes me, and we all clink glasses.

We finally arrive at Nate's club, and thankfully, we have been able to slip past the paparazzi—last thing we want is for them to find out about The Paradise Club. We're ushered quickly through the secret entrance reserved for the ultra-VIPs, hiding us from curious eyes. The limousine will be taking Penny and Isla back to the apartment, both of them not feeling very well after all that dancing.

I know Penny hasn't been able to relax since arriving in Paris. She's lucky she can't just run into the President of France while she's out shopping like any other ex. It won't be long before he finds out, though, as pictures of Penny's ever-expanding stomach are frequently in the gossip magazines. Speculation about the father is making them salivate, and names of her exes are being thrown around with, many coming out publicly declaring they aren't the father, which is pretty crass, I think.

God, I feel for her. She's gotten herself into such a crazy situation. I have to admit, though, she has been working hard with Camryn and Kimberly's team regarding the events. I'd even say that she's happy working, which I never thought would ever happen. Ivy has finished renovating her cottage in the castle's village, and it's gorgeous. The nursery is just beautiful—her little princess is going to feel so loved there.

"There's my sexy fiancée." Axel surprises me as I'm lost in my thoughts. His strong, tattooed arms wrap themselves around me tightly.

"This brings back memories…" he whispers into my ear, sending shivers over my body. "Almost a year ago, we met during a bachelor party in France."

"Technically, Monaco. It is its own separate country," I tease.

Axel pinches a nipple in retaliation. "Looks like someone is being purposefully naughty. Does my fiancée want to be punished?" My legs clench together at the vivid imagery of Axel's kind of punishments.

"Maybe." I wiggle my ass against his tight crotch, teasing the beast.

"I think tonight we're going to have a lot of fun, Miss Pearce." The way he uses my name like that, I know he's feeling very dominant, so I'm in for a good time tonight. Axel unwraps himself from me and grabs my hand.

"Enjoy," he tells the rest of the party.

"Get it, girl," Derrick calls out while the others catcall and holler as we make our way across the ground floor bar area.

This club is different again than the one in Monaco. Each one seems to reflect the city it's located in. The Paris club is paying homage to Marie Antoinette and Louis XVI with the opulence and decadence of the era. I don't have time to really enjoy its beauty as Axel is on a mission tonight. He pulls me up the stairs, past the glass cube room which is prolific through all The Paradise Clubs from what Axel tells me. He walks down one of the dark corridors, ignoring the gyrating people around us. He enters the room with a green light above it and closes the door behind us. In an instant, he launches himself at me, pulling the hem of my dress up to my waist as his fingers find my wet underwear.

"You're just as turned on as I am," he hisses as he pushes the small patch of fabric out of the way so he can sink two large fingers into me.

"Yes," I moan as he fills me.

"Fuck, Liv. That little can-can dance you did for me got me hard as a rock. If we weren't in public, I'd have bent you over one of the tables and fucked you there and then. You made me so hot." Axel's fingers slide in and out of my slickness. *God, it feels so good.*

"How did I get so lucky?" he asks before his mouth descends on mine. I'm lost in the heady lust of him. He sinks his teeth into my lips, the pain and passion he generates from that action causes me to whimper. He continues with my neck as his skillful fingers glide expertly in me, bringing me closer to the edge with each flick of my clit.

"Come, Liv, I need you to come for me. I have so much planned for you tonight." His teeth sink into the fleshy skin, and that sharp bite sends me over the edge. I come around his fingers as he continues to pump them inside of me, riding my orgasm out. I sag against the wooden door, my body quivering like jelly. Axel pulls his fingers from me and licks them clean. "God, I love your taste." He savors me like a connoisseur, and it's hot.

"So, what do you have planned next? I think it's your turn to come." I smile at him.

"Oh, don't you worry, we have plenty of time for that." He kisses me again, and I can taste myself on his lips. "I need you to take off all your clothes, sweetheart."

I can see the desire behind those whiskey eyes. I slowly pull the zipper of my dress down, his eyes never leaving mine. One by one, I let the straps of my cocktail dress fall, exposing my designer bra underneath. Axel licks his lips in anticipation of touching me again. I wiggle the dress over my hips, giving him a little appreciative dance.

He kneels before me, the dress pooling around my high-heel-covered feet. A warm hand wraps around my ankle and slowly lifts my foot, letting me step out of my dress. He does the same with my other foot, and I watch in fascination as he carefully moves my foot out of the way so he can collect my dress. His lips touch my ankle, sending sparks up my legs, directly hitting my sensitive core.

"You're so beautiful," he muses, placing my cocktail dress on the back of one of the chairs. "Now, the underwear, but leave the heels on." He winks at me. I unclasp my bra, letting the straps fall, then I throw it to him. He catches it with a smirk on his face. "Cute, Liv, real cute." I shimmy out of my tiny G-string and do the same, sending it in his direction. He takes it to his nose and smells it briefly before putting it with my other clothing items. I think if it were any other man who had done that, it wouldn't have been a turn-on, but with Axel, everything he does is so sexual, primal, raw, and I love it.

"Now, Liv, do you trust me?" he asks.

"Yes, of course."

"I know you do, darlin', but I mean in here, this room, with the things that we might do here."

My heart is racing. My body is a flutter of nervous anticipation. "Yes, I trust you, Axel."

"Even if I bring in people to watch us?"

My body stiffens, a little taken aback by his statement. "Depends on who they are and what they'll be doing." My newfound confidence slightly wavers.

Axel walks toward me, understanding the nerves that have suddenly hit me. "I'd never bring in anyone we didn't trust, Liv." My shoulders relax a little. I knew he wouldn't, but this world is still so new to me. "I was thinking of maybe exploring things further like we did in Monaco."

My eyes widen in surprise. "With Stacey, Oscar, and Jackson?"

"Minus Jackson this time." Axel touches my cheek with his hand. "I thought maybe we could explore that request Stacey asked months ago."

I gasp. "You want to have sex with Stacey?" Slight insecurity hits me.

Axel grabs my face tightly. "Never. No one will ever compare to you. I don't have to touch Stacey at all tonight. I can sit and watch as Oscar and Stacey take their turn pleasuring you if that makes you feel more comfortable. Stacey is a friend, nothing more. You never have to worry about her." He kisses me, showing me exactly how much he loves me. When he pulls away, my lips are swollen from its intensity.

"I trust you. I was just a little shocked, that's all…"

"I can call off the whole thing. I just thought because this was our bachelor and bachelorette party, that this one time, we might do something crazy. I want you to explore those fantasies that you have locked up in this pretty little mind of yours. I know how much you loved it last time, so this time I thought maybe it would be easier as a foursome. I know you trust them."

I nod in understanding. "And you would be okay with Oscar touching me?" I need to clarify things.

"Honestly, I'm not sure. I think there will be pangs of jealousy, but the difference is we're here at The Paradise Club. For me, it's like a switch gets flicked in my mind, and all I see is the act, the fun, the desire more than the insecurity and jealousy. Does that make sense?"

"I think it does," I say.

"Mind you, I have never shared the woman I love before, so maybe it might be a disaster, but I do trust both of them. Stacey and Oscar are tight. I know they are secretive about what goes on between them, but I also know that he's not sleeping with anyone outside of The Paradise Club."

"I know the same is true for Stacey as well," I add.

"I know Oscar would never touch you outside of what goes on here. He understands the rules and requests the same courtesy in return."

"I'm nervous," I confess.

"Is it a good kind of nervous?"

I look up at him, and my cheeks turn pink. "Yes, yes, I think it is."

A brilliant smile crosses his face. "We'll all go slow and test the boundaries to see what we're all okay with. How does that sound?"

"It sounds like fun."

48

AXEL

I'm actually nervous but in a giddy kind of way. I understand Olivia's hesitation—most people wouldn't share their partner with one of their best friends, especially not when you're about to marry them. For some reason, tonight feels okay. I'm pretty sure once I put that wedding ring on her finger, this will stop. Maybe not visiting The Paradise Club—we might save that for special anniversaries—but having another couple join us will stop.

There's a Saint Andrew's Cross in the room, and I have just finished tying Olivia to it. God, she looks beautiful with her brunette hair falling over her creamy shoulders. Her toned body and her perfect tits look divine, and those killer legs in her high heels—wow. I love the pink flush that's currently making its way over her skin, illuminating it.

A light tap sounds at the door, and I answer it with excitement. Oscar and Stacey smile at me when I open it. We greet each other like we normally would, and they enter the room. They both stop and take in Olivia spread out against the cross.

"Liv, you look beautiful." Stacey smiles at her friend, and I notice Olivia's blush increase.

"This is a beautiful sight. We're so honored to be here," Oscar says to me, being courteous of my relationship with Olivia, which I appreciate.

"Sweetheart, would you like to be blindfolded this time, or would you like to watch?" I ask, holding up the black satin blindfold.

Olivia thinks it over, sucking in her bottom lip as she does. "I think I'd like to be blindfolded this time." She smiles at me.

Her answer surprises me, but I love that she's feeling more confident with her sexuality around me. For someone who says they are so inexperienced, she has blossomed. She has become adventurous, and I think there are many fantasies stuck in her head that she hasn't told me about yet. I have a feeling that they are dirty and kinky. I'd give her anything her heart desires, in and out of the bedroom.

I look into her hazel eyes. "You ready to have some fun?" I ask before I slip the blindfold over her head.

"Yes, yes I am. I trust you to keep me safe." Those words tighten around my heart, she trusts me that much.

"I'll always keep you safe."

I slip the blindfold over her eyes and kiss her lips. As I step away, Olivia flinches as all her senses work overtime trying to decipher what's going to happen next.

"Relax, Liv, just enjoy it."

She nods and relaxes against the leather of the cross. I turn and look at Oscar and Stacey, who are in the middle of a steamy kiss. Obviously, the sight of Olivia is turning them both on. I kick off my socks and shoes, then unbutton my shirt and lay it on one of the chairs. Oscar has done the same, but we have both left our pants on for the moment.

Oscar is now working the zipper of Stacey's cocktail dress and pulls it down her body. It's not long before she's standing in front of us in her lace underwear. Stacey is a beautiful woman, there's no denying that, but she is not the woman for me. Stacey drops her bra and steps out of her lace panties as she takes a couple of steps toward Olivia, her tight ass swaying as she walks.

Olivia is still straining to work out what's going on, but all she can hear is Stacey's high heels against the cement floor as she gets closer to her. Stacey stops in front of Olivia, bends down and takes one of Olivia's pert nipples in her mouth and sucks on it. Olivia gasps at the surprising touch but settles in against Stacey's lips. My dick instantly stands at attention, pushing hard against the zipper of my pants. Fuck it, this scene is too hot not to enjoy. I unbuckle my belt and unzip my pants and kick them to the floor and palm my dick. I hear rustling beside me, indicating Oscar is doing the same.

We both watch from a distance as Stacey sucks Olivia's nipples until they are rosy peaks, giving her skin an instant flush. Once Stacey has given them enough attention, she leans in and kisses Olivia. We watch as they both get lost in the kiss, and fuck me, my dick twitches with jealousy. I give him a quick couple of strokes to calm him down.

"So beautiful." Oscar groans beside me as Stacey moves from Olivia's lips and down over her collarbone. She makes her way down through the valley of her breasts, spreading feather-light kisses over her toned stomach and out to her hip bone. Stacey is now bent over, her legs stretched out, showing off her glistening pussy. This is so much better than any porn channel. She continues further down Olivia's thighs, teasing her. I can see Olivia is arching against her restraints, her chest heaving with excitement. The first stroke of Stacey's tongue against Olivia's clit nearly makes me come. The moan from both women is a sound I could never get sick of hearing.

"Fuck me dead, this is hot," Oscar grumbles beside me, his large hand slowly stroking his cock. "I can't stand watching anymore." Oscar stands up and stalks toward Stacey's exposed rear. He slaps it hard a couple of times, making her moan between Olivia's legs.

He's right, I'm sick of watching.

There's a lever that moves the cross from standing to laying, and it might make it easier for all of us to join in this way.

Stacey moves away from between Liv's legs, and she lets out a little shriek as she starts moving backward.

"It's okay, sweetheart, we're just moving you into a better position." My voice instantly calming her.

Olivia is lying on the cross which is now like a bed. Luckily, it's made of cushioned leather and not a traditional one made of hardwood. That would make things rather uncomfortable for Liv after a while. Olivia is still blindfolded, but her legs are spread wide open. Both Stacey and I move toward her open legs. Stacey gives me a look, and she knows exactly what I want to do. Stacey resumes her position between Olivia's thighs, and I do the same. We both alternate, sometimes feasting at the same time, our tongues clashing against Olivia's heated center, Stacey tasting like Olivia's sweetness.

Oscar has positioned himself at Olivia's head, where his cock is buried down her throat, and he's feasting on her tits. I let my hand fall between Stacey's legs and find her drenched. She obviously loves eating out my girl. If I'm being honest, I love watching her too. My fingers easily slip between her folds, sinking deep into her, and she groans against Olivia's cunt. Olivia's strangled moans echo through the room. I can tell she's so close to coming. Stacey and I take turns giving her exactly what she needs, over and over again. A couple of well-timed strokes, and she's coming all over our tongues, and a couple of flicks of my thumb over Stacey's clit, and she's also coming, humming against Olivia's pussy.

Not long after, Oscar is pulling out of Olivia's swollen mouth, his dick is glistening from her saliva.

"Stace, I need you to sit on her face while you finish me off,"

Oscar growls. Stacey moves away from my fingers and walks to where Oscar is standing, and a heated look happens between them.

"Is this okay, Liv?" Stacey questions before she moves.

"Yes," Olivia says breathlessly, sounding as if she's far away even though she is just there. God, she must be so fucking turned on right now. Stacey gets up onto the cross and straddles Olivia's face before bending over and taking Oscar into her mouth.

I grab a condom and sheath myself. Even though Olivia and I no longer use them, we're playing with others, so it's a must. I sink my aching cock right between her glistening lips, and I hear her hum against Stacey's pussy. I notice as I thrust into Olivia that Stacey moves in time, and the friction is making her go crazy around Oscar's dick. His hands grip her hair tightly, pulling her harder against him.

It's the craziest sex I have ever had in my life. I swear I'm ready to blackout as I come inside of my fiancée. Not far behind me, Stacey and Olivia come in unison with Oscar coming seconds after the girls.

We're all too weak to move, still panting from the best sex I think we all have ever had.

I can't wait to do it all again, which we do, over and over again all night long until all four of us are quivering messes of goo, all wrapped in each other's arms, sated.

OLIVIA

"You're getting married today," Derrick squeals, rushing into my room and waking me up. We have been at my family's home in the Loire Valley for the past couple of days. Frieda has been working like a madwoman making sure everything is perfect.

Our long weekend in Paris for our combined bachelor and bachelorette party was so much fun, but now the serious party happens. We had a girly spa day the day after the bachelorette party and high tea at Ladurée, the famous French Patisserie. There was no awkwardness between Stacey and me the next day either, especially as we both spent the night exploring every inch of each other's bodies as well as Oscar's and Axel's—it's like our own little secret that nobody else needs to know.

My God, it was a fantasy come true, and Axel was right—that kind of sex happening inside The Paradise Club is different than the sex outside of it. I mean, if I had watched Stacey having sex with my fiancé outside of the club, I think it would kill me, but inside that tiny little bubble, it all seems natural—all hands, lips, and faces melded into one. It didn't matter who was who, we were all just going with the flow.

"I know, D, I know." I refuse to open my eyes. Last night's rehearsal kind of got crazy, and I may have had one too many champagnes, plus Axel kept me up all night sexing me because he wouldn't see me again until I walked down the aisle. That makes my stomach flutter with nervous excitement just thinking about it.

"Come on, princess, it's the day you marry your prince." Derrick pulls the covers off me, making me groan.

"We have cake," Ivy adds, which perks my ears right up.

"For breakfast?"

"Yep, I know that's your favorite thing, so why not have it on your wedding day?" I jump up and out of bed and head out to the parlor next to my room. It's all set up with a table of French delights—macaroons, pastries, cupcakes, fresh fruit, and tiny little breakfast canapés.

"Wow, this looks beautiful."

"Frieda did it all," my mother tells me, giving me a quick kiss on the cheek as I enter the room.

"You're getting married," Stacey calls out from her side of the room. I make my way around the room, saying good morning to all my friends and bridesmaids.

"So lucky that my dress is huge, so I can indulge on cake for breakfast." I eye off the beautiful little cupcakes.

"Morning." Camryn and Kimberly walk in, both of them greeting me. "Everything is under control. We have done a walk-through, and the flowers have arrived and are being set up in the chapel, the ballroom tables have been set up too, and more flowers and decorations have arrived. Charlotte will be down any moment to start taking photos of you and the bridesmaids getting ready. Anything else?" Camryn looks to Kimberly, her business partner.

"Sebastien and his team are busy in the kitchen, which is kind of interesting with Frieda hovering over them. I don't think she likes them being in her space." Kimberly giggles. I can just imagine.

"So just sit back and relax, your day is going to be perfect." Camryn smiles before taking a sip of her mimosa.

The day moves along quickly in a cloud of hairspray and makeup brushes and maybe one too many mimosas. We decided on getting married in the late afternoon because the heat of the day in the middle of summer would be a little too much for our guests.

"Olivia, you look beautiful." My father walks into the dressing room with tears in his eyes. I rush forward and give him a tight hug, which surprises him as we don't usually display affection publicly.

"This, this is what your wedding day should've been like," he whispers to me. I take a step back. I can see the guilt on his face from trying to force me to marry Eddie.

"That doesn't matter anymore, it's in the past. I'm so happy you're here to celebrate today with me." I kiss his cheek. He looks so handsome dressed in his morning suit, so traditionally English, but he couldn't be swayed.

"You look like a princess," Derrick gasps, entering the room.

Yvette has done a beautiful job. In the end, I embraced my title and decided on being a princess on my wedding day. She designed the perfect modern-day princess dress for me—a strapless top with a big, full tulle layered skirt in a creamy ivory color that matches my milky skin perfectly. The bridesmaids are dressed in a gorgeous blush pink V-neck top, embroidered with tiny, beaded flowers all over that meld into a tulle gown. It's beyond anything I could have ever imagined.

"Axel is going to be in a puddle at the end of the aisle when he sees you," Derrick states as he smiles at me. "He has asked me to bring this to you," he continues, handing over the red velvet box with the distinctive gold writing on the front. I open the box, and the most stunning diamond necklace and bracelet set appear. There's a card with a note.

Olivia,

There is no one in the world as precious as you are to me. Love, Axel.

I'm not supposed to be crying as it will ruin my makeup but damn him.

"I had better head back. Shall I tell him you liked the gift?" Derrick nudges me.

"Yes, of course… I love it. You can even give him a big kiss to show how much I appreciate it as well." Derrick's eyes light up.

"You know he'll do it, don't you?" Vanessa adds. "He's done it to Christian plenty of times."

"Hush, woman. This is my last chance with Axel." He kisses me on the cheek, a moment Charlotte captures with a snap of her lens before he disappears out the door with a bounce in his step.

Charlotte graciously offered her services to us for the wedding, and, of course, we said yes. We also know there's no way she would sell our wedding photos to the highest bidder. Charlotte's been taking photos of us while we've been getting ready, bouncing between the groomsmen and us.

It's almost time.

The hairstylist positions the vintage diamond tiara on top of my head, securing the cathedral veil to it. It completes my wedding look. I catch myself in the mirror and can't believe this is me, and I'm about to walk down the aisle to the man of my dreams. Never did I ever think this would happen to me.

"I remember the day I married your mother, she was wearing that exact same tiara," my father reminisces. "Best day of my life." He leans over and kisses my mother's cheek, surprising her.

"I can't believe you got our parents to be affectionate with each other. It's a miracle," Penny whispers to me as we watch our parents joke with one another.

"A wedding miracle," I respond, making us both laugh.

"Okay, it's time." Kimberly pops her head in, letting us know that we need to move. "The boys are all set. Axel looks like a bundle of nerves. All the guests have arrived, and we're just waiting for the bridal party."

"Let's get you married," Ivy squeals.

Slowly I make my way down the spiral marble staircase covered in many shades of pink roses and peonies. The smell is divine.

"Are you ready, sweetheart?" my father asks me once we make it down the stairs. I had this nightmare that I'd trip and fall down them on my wedding day.

"Yes." My stomach flutters with nerves as Charlotte takes our photos against the beautiful backdrop of roses along the staircase.

"Okay, this way." Kimberly guides us toward the chapel once we're finished with the photos. With the chapel being so small, we only have our closest family for the ceremony, the rest of our guests we'll see at the reception later.

"Oh my God, Ryder, you look adorable in your little suit." The gorgeous little boy is dressed in a mini version of the boys' tuxedos. Sienna is holding his hand as he plays with the pillow, which has our wedding rings on it. He is our ring-bearer and is going to *hopefully* walk down the aisle all by himself. He's only just learned how to walk, so fingers crossed he'll be able to make it—he'll look so cute waddling down the aisle. It didn't work out so well during rehearsals last night, he wasn't interested at all. I think he was pretty tired, poor little monkey. More photos, this time with little Ryder before we ready ourselves to walk down the aisle.

The wooden doors have been closed, and I can hear our

guests talking, waiting anxiously for me to walk through them. Kimberly arranges us in order—Vanessa will hold Ryder's hand and go first, so he isn't too scared, followed by Camryn, Stacey, Penny, and Ivy. The doors will then close, and it will be my turn.

I seriously need to pee.

Do I have time to pee?

The music starts, and the girls make their way down the aisle. It's already my turn. It went so quickly, and now my heart takes off racing. I think I'm going to throw up. That would suck, especially all over this beautiful dress. Imagine what a field day the press would have if I did. *I'm babbling to myself again.* I'm so nervous I can't make my hands stop shaking.

"Sweetheart, it's going to be okay," my father reassures me.

"I know. I know it will be. I didn't realize I was going to be so nervous."

"Once you see Axel at the end of the aisle waiting for you, all the nerves will disappear."

I sure hope so.

"It's go time. Good Luck," Kimberly whispers as she opens the doors to the chapel, and the wedding march starts. I take a deep breath and step forward. As soon as I pass the doors, my eyes fall on Axel standing at the end of the aisle, and he looks as handsome as ever in his tuxedo. He had decided to cut his long hair short for the wedding, much to Derrick's horror. Whatever makes him happy. I didn't mind that he had because the man is gorgeous either way, but if I'm honest, that man looks even hotter with short hair, if that's even possible.

I have no idea who's here because everything has faded away, and all my focus is on Axel and the tears cascading down his cheeks as he watches me walk toward him. *Damn him, why is he crying?* He's supposed to be holding it together, so he doesn't start me off.

Ugh, I'm going to ruin my makeup by the time I get to the end of this aisle.

50

AXEL

The doors open and the wedding march starts to play. An angel, that is the only word to describe what I am seeing right now, appears before me. She looks stunning. I never envisioned what she would look like walking down the aisle, but this, this is far beyond what I ever thought she would look like.

"Welcome to the club," my brother whispers to me, watching the tears fall continuously from my eyes. Goddamn it, I can't help it. I look into the audience and see everyone else is crying. My focus comes back to Olivia and she too is crying. *What is going on?* Her father squeezes her hand as she walks toward me, looking so regal, so beautiful, an absolute vision. Thank you up there for delivering this woman to me.

Olivia is now standing before me, hidden behind her veil and I can't stop staring at her, she is breathtaking.

"Who here gives this woman to this man?" the priest asks.

"I do," her father replies as he places Olivia's hand into mine. I give him an appreciative nod which he returns before taking his seat next to her mother who is trying not to show any emotion, but is failing miserably.

"Hey," I whisper to her as we hold hands.

"Hey." She looks up at me through tear soaked eyes behind her white veil.

"You look so beautiful," I whisper again. I know I should be listening to the priest, but he is talking about some religious stuff. I just need to know when I have to say I do and I'll say it.

"You look so handsome." *Seriously can we skip the ceremony? Let's just say I do, because I want to kiss the ever loving hell out of her and take her back to the honeymoon suite, discover what is hidden under all that material and ravage her. Shit, I am getting a hard-on at the altar on my wedding day in front of all our family and friends. I need to think of something, anything else to take away the images of my head underneath all those layers of material and eating her out. Shit! Abort those thoughts, abort those thoughts.*

"You may now kiss the bride." The priest finally says the words I have been wanting to hear all day. I lift up Olivia's veil, placing it carefully over her head making sure not to mess up her hair. I know what chicks are like, especially on their wedding day. Now, I know your wedding kiss should be polite as we are in a chapel and all, but I don't care, you only get one first kiss as a married couple and this is it, as I go in for the kill. I hear a couple of cheers from my friends and that's when I know I may have gone a little far.

"Let me introduce to you all, Mr. and Mrs. Taylor," the priest proclaims, and those words sound amazing. I take her hand, I give it a quick kiss as we make our way down the aisle, our family and friends congratulating us as we walk past.

"I can't believe we are married," Olivia squeals, exiting the chapel. I pick her up in my arms and kiss her once again.

"You better believe it Mrs. Taylor," I growl, sharing a quiet moment before we are inundated with well wishes. "You're stuck with me for eternity."

"I think I'm okay with that." She smiles back at me, warming my heart.

After what seems like an eternity for photos, we are finally being announced into the Grand Hall, where the ballroom is. Derrick is of course our MC. *Who else could do it better?*

"Please put your hands together for Mr. and Mrs. Taylor." The room erupts as we enter the ballroom. Wow, it looks like a florist has thrown up everywhere, there are so many pink flowers. I really can't complain, I did tell Olivia she could have anything she wanted for the wedding, as long as she turned up on the day, that was all I was worried about, but maybe I should have paid attention a little better in the planning stage, oh who am I kidding, the complete and utter look of happiness on her face means more to me than drowning in a million shades of pink.

We take a seat at the bridal table, which has two golden thrones. Apparently they date back to 1598 royalty and the French nobility have sat upon these thrones hundreds of years ago, just like we are today. That is kind of cool, steeped in such history is mind boggling, and now here sits a rock star and his Lady. This makes me grin. There are tables scattered throughout the ballroom, each one with a tower of pink flowers in the center. I think there may be two hundred people here for the reception. I'm pretty sure I know most of them, well I hope so anyway. Olivia had certain people she had to invite because of family protocol, which is fine, it makes her family happy, and if it scores me extra points with them then I am okay with that.

The table is set extravagantly. A tiny rush of nervousness fills me as I look at the many sets of cutlery displayed in front of me.

At least I know the food will be amazing as Sebastien is catering the event. He did my brother's wedding and our family Christmas last year, I still dream about the food, it was that good. A waiter comes over and pours us both a glass of champagne. "Sorry, can I grab a beer as well." I ask, he nods and rushes off.

Settled into our seats, I let myself finally relax for a moment and take in the day, as everyone tells you it goes by so quickly and it is. I catch sight of the California Bros. at their table and the Sons of Brooklyn boys too; they all look like they are having a great time. Then I hear someone tapping a crystal glass, it's Derrick.

"What are you doing?" I hiss at him.

"You're supposed to kiss the bride anytime someone hits their glass." He smiles sweetly at me.

"Is that true?" I ask Olivia.

"Yes, it is."

Derrick starts it again and many more people join him, I lean over and kiss my bride, I think I might like this tradition as the room erupts into cheers.

"Where's my bride?" I ask, looking around the dance floor.

"She's with her sister out in the garden I think." I head out to where Derrick points. What are they doing out here? It takes me a little longer to get outside due to well wishes stopping to congratulate me and when I do make it outside, I can't see them anywhere. I strain and look into the darkness and I notice a row of bodyguards standing in a corner. What is that about? And where did they come from? That's when I notice Olivia and Penny standing together, not looking happy, in front of some guy in a suit who has a deep scowl on his face. I start to head toward them until one of the guards stops me, halting me in French.

"Hands off, fucker, this is my wedding and that is my bride." I point to Olivia.

"Axel," she calls to me, hearing the commotion.

"What's going on?" I look at her with concern and see Penny is now crying.

"Axel Taylor, I am a big fan of Dirty Texas," the guy in the suit states, his accent is French, I think.

"And you are?" I growl, wondering who the hell this guy is interrupting my wedding and upsetting my sister-in-law.

Olivia tugs my arm. "That is the President of France," she whisper yells. My brows rise looking between Penny and Olivia. What the hell is going on?

"Julien Soucy." He holds out his hand for me to shake.

"I'm so sorry, Axel, for interrupting your wedding." Penny looks exhausted, defeated even, her make-up has run, her eyes are puffy and red.

"You haven't done a thing. But are you okay?" I don't care if this guy is the king of the moon, if he is upsetting my new sister-in-law then he is going to have to deal with me.

"He found out about the baby," Penny whispers, rubbing her hand protectively over her belly.

"I saw you in the press." He looks hurts by this. "You never told me." I can understand him being upset finding out he is going to be a father through the gossip magazines.

"Like I said, Jules, I contacted you. I contacted your office and left messages and no one returned them. So, as far as I am concerned I am going to be a single parent," Penny argues, crossing her arms defensively.

Julien runs his hand through his hair, a look of frustration mars his tanned face. "Like I told you, Penelope, I never got those messages. If I knew you were contacting me, I would have replied."

"It doesn't matter anyway, you know now. I promise nobody

knows except the two people here, your secret is safe." Julien looks a little pained by Penny's comment.

"I'm guessing you haven't been keeping up with French news then?" She shakes her head. "Marion and I announced our divorce last week. She fell in love with someone else and wanted to marry him." Penny looks pale. "It was announced that we have been separated for a while, that we both require our private space."

"I don't understand," Penny says. "What about your campaign? This scandal will ruin your chances."

"I never wanted to do a second term, the party pressured me to, that's why Marion and I decided to divorce." Penny gasps. "She was my excuse to leave politics."

"But...I don't understand," Penny says in disbelief.

"I've done my duty to my country, Penelope. Now I want to live life again. I owed that to Marion, she stuck with me until my term was up but she couldn't do another, we both were extremely unhappy putting on the facade. She is my best friend, but that is all. She is the one that pushed me to chase after you, told me I needed to tell you how I feel."

I squeeze Olivia's hand, not sure I am believing what I am seeing before me, it is like an episode of The Young and the Restless. Penelope shakes her head.

"I want a life with you Penelope."

"No, I ..." Her words trail away.

"You know that I've loved you from the moment we met," Julien confesses as Olivia squeezes my hand hearing his words.

"Julien, no. I can't."

He shakes his head. "Finding out that you are carrying my baby, Penelope, God, you have no idea how happy I am." This gets her attention.

"You are?"

Julien grabs her hand. "Of course, mon cheri, you are giving me a gift. One I never thought I would ever have." Penny stares at him and they are both lost in a moment together, I kind of feel like an intruder. Penny pulls her hand away from him. "You think that because you are now divorced that it changes everything?"

"Oui, of course. We can be together."

"But what about me, what about what is best for my daughter and I."

"We are having a little girl?" Awe fills Julien's face.

"No, there's no we."

"Penny," Olivia interrupts.

"No, Liv. There is no happily ever after for me, not like you. I'm sorry, Julien." She turns on her heels and runs back into the reception, Olivia hot on her heels after her. He looks utterly defeated watching the woman he loves run away from him.

"I am sorry I interrupted your wedding, Mr. Taylor."

"It's Axel," I say. "Do you mean it? What you said?"

"What?"

"That you love her?"

"With every beat of my heart. I understand you know the story of how Penelope and I met. It was unconventional but there was something about her. It was not a love match between my wife and I, it was always a political move. I'm not saying that I did not love her, she is my best friend, but she is not the love of my life."

"But Penny is?"

"Yes, she is. For the first time in my life I felt alive. Marion knew this, I mean she met the love of her life too, but we needed to finish my term as President before going our separate ways. When Penny married Edmund, it killed me, but I assumed she was happy, so I let her go."

"Until you found out the child wasn't his?"

"Yes."

"Then why did you not come to her sooner?"

"I had to wait, to do it right, make sure that the scandal

would make the party chose another, I needed to make sure that I was able to leave."

"And gatecrashing my wedding was the right time?"

Julien looks justifiably ashamed. "Ah no, I have only just found out she was in the country, and as soon as I did, I had to explain things to her."

"How did you get in? Security is tight."

"Remember I am the President of France." This makes me laugh.

"Give her time. These Pearce girls are awfully stubborn, so trying to change their minds is hard. She will eventually come around, I promise you."

"Merci, Axel, Merci." He shakes my hand. "Here." He hands me a white card with gold embossed writing on it. "This is my private phone number and email. Would you please just help me? Just, keep an eye on her for me, and if she needs anything, and I mean anything, please let me know. She will have full security detail around the clock looking after her."

"Of course, I can give you mine, if you like." He pulls out a fountain pen and another embossed card and I write my number on the back. "I guess this kind of makes us family now, huh?"

He chuckles, "I think it might. Congratulations once again, and I am sorry to invade your special night."

"Look, you are more than welcome to stay," I say and he shakes his head.

"That would lead to too many questions, but thank you." With that, he turns on his heel, his guards following him into the night. Seriously, did I just give love advice to the President of France on my wedding day? I shake my head and walk back into the party.

It's close to midnight and the party is in full swing. We are all standing out on the back terrace overlooking the gardens as the clock strikes midnight and fireworks start flying off into different directions from the top of the castle, lighting up the night sky. My arms are wrapped around my wife. *My wife,* I still can't get used to saying that. I look around and see my brother with a baby in his arms. He's looking down at the sleeping princess and Ness is doing the same with the other, only she is screaming at the fireworks display and Ness is trying to console her. My parents are cuddling, watching as the night sky lights up. Even Olivia's parents are holding hands, smiling, enjoying the pyrotechnic display. I'm feeling pretty damn lucky at the moment and I can't wait to see what the first year of marriage brings for us.

51

OLIVIA

Months later

"You're doing so well." I try and help Penny through another contraction.

"I can't go on anymore, please just pull it out," she screams at the nurse, who pretends she doesn't understand English. She also doesn't realize I understand French and can hear everything she's saying about Penny and the situation with her baby's father. I give Penny another cup full of ice and make my way over to the nurse's station.

"Just because we're English does not mean we don't understand French," I say in French, and the nurses all freeze. *"Exactly! I heard the things you were saying about my sister, about the former President. There's a strong chance that if I told him exactly what you have said about his baby's mother, that he'd fire you on the spot. That man loves that woman, and he'll not tolerate such gossip about her. He doesn't tolerate it from the media, and he sure as hell won't tolerate it from you."* They all nod their heads furiously. *"Now, do whatever you have to do to*

make my sister comfortable." And with that, I turn on my heel and head back into the birthing suite.

"Thank you." Penny smiles at me.

"Bunch of jealous bitches."

She laughs. "I like Olivia Taylor. She's a boss bitch."

"Damn straight I am. Those nurses are nothing more than Julien groupies. I'm used to women like them. I have to deal with Axel's groupies daily." Penny smiles, but it quickly turns into a frown as another contraction hits her.

"Mon chéri , I'm so sorry… I had to take that call," Julien apologizes.

She waves him off. "It's okay, the world doesn't stop while I push out a baby the size of a goddamn watermelon," she screams through another contraction.

God, I hope she hurries up and pushes my niece out.

This is torture.

Three hours later, little Genevieve Pearce Soucy arrives into the world.

Axel brought my parents to the hospital in Paris once I told him the good news. They were both so excited to meet their first grandchild. The look on my father's face staring down at little Genevieve was precious—he looked every inch the doting grandfather. Of course, my mother was beyond happy when Penny finally told them who the father of her baby was. Initially, they were shocked, but I know Mother was impressed that Penny had caught the eye of the President of France.

Of course, once news broke of their relationship a couple of weeks after our wedding, all of Penny's friends from London started to mysteriously connect with her again, but she quietly ignored their calls. Funnily enough, France was okay with the news that their president was having a baby with another woman that wasn't his wife, even though he divorced his wife only a few months ago. His ex-wife had already remarried and was extremely happy sailing in the south of France. She even sent Penny a baby hamper to congratulate her on the impending baby, which was nice of her I guess.

Penny is actually looking forward to moving back to England, to the cottage in the village of our estate. I know, I was as shocked as everyone else, but now that Julien is officially no longer the President of France, he's looking forward to stepping away from the spotlight with his new family.

Life works in mysterious ways.

"So, tell me, does this make you broody?" Axel quizzes me as I hold little Genevieve in my arms at her new home in Paris for the foreseeable future.

Penny was released from the hospital a couple of days ago, and I have been on aunty duty.

"Of course, it does. I mean... look at her." I look down at the sleeping little angel. "But I have to tell you, giving birth was pretty traumatizing, so I'm not sure."

"Is it really that bad?" he questions me.

"Much, *much* worse." I giggle.

"Well, when you're ready for me to knock you up, you know where to find me." He gives me a wink as he walks out the door.

I stare at the little baby in my arms.

Maybe I'm more ready than I think I am.

One month later

"Hello," I answer the phone groggily, looking at the clock. It's early in the morning in Los Angeles.

"Livy, oh Livy." My sister is crying into the phone, the sound of her voice wakes me up really quick.

"What, what is it? Is Evee okay?" That's our nickname for Genevieve.

"She's fine, it's Daddy."

My stomach sinks.

Axel is now awake beside me.

"He's dead, Liv. He is dead."

"No, no, no. You're lying, Pen, you're lying," I scream down the phone. Axel tries to comfort me, but I push him away.

"I'm sorry, Liv. He had a heart attack at the top of the stairs and fell down them. The ambulance arrived too late to save him."

"I'm coming, Pen. Tell Mother I'm coming."

THE END

ABOUT THE AUTHOR

JA Low lives on a faraway beach in Australia. When she's not writing steamy scenes and admiring hot surfers, she's tending to her husband and two sons, and dreaming up the next epic romance.

Come follow her

Facebook: www.facebook.com/jalowbooks
Twitter: www.twitter.com/jalowbooks
Instagram: www.instagram.com/jalowbooks
Pinterest: www.pinterest.com/jalowbooks
Website: www.jalowbooks.com
Goodreads: https://www.goodreads.com/author/show/14918059.J_A_Low

Come join JA Low's Block
www.facebook.com/groups/1682783088643205/

www.jalowbooks.com
jalowbooks@gmail.com

BIG THANKS TO ....

You - Another book done in the Dirty Texas series, thank you for still wanting to tag along on this journey with me.

My family – My wonderful husband and kids for understanding days when I have to lock myself away to get things done.

Trish – My book bestie and editor, thank you for helping me make this book the best it can be.

Jemina – As always your covers rock. Thank you for dealing with all my anal tendencies I have.

My wonderful proofreaders Heather and Kelly for helping me understand how American's talk.

My Blockies – Your love and support blows me away.

My Review Babes – Thank you for all your work getting your reviews up and helping me pimp to the masses, your support is amazing.

Robyn – Your tireless pimping of my work is amazing and I appreciate everything that you do for me.

Clique Tribe – You ladies rock! Thank you for all your support.

INTERCONNECTING SERIES

Reading order for interconnected characters.

Dirty Texas Series

Paradise Club Series

Playboys of New York

Hotshot Chef

ALSO BY JA LOW

The Paradise Club Series

Book 1 - Paradise

Spin off from the Dirty Texas Series

My name's Nate Lewis, owner of The Paradise Club.

I can bring every little dirty fantasy you have ever dreamed of to reality.

My business is your pleasure. I'm good at it.

So good it's made me a wealthy and powerful man.

I have one rule—never mix business and pleasure, and I've lived by it from day one.

Until her.

** WARNING: If you do not like your books with a lot of heat then do not read this book. **

ALSO BY JA LOW

International Bad Boys Set

Book 1 - The Sexy Stranger

Book 2 - The Arrogant Artist

Book 3 - The Hotshot Chef

ALSO BY JA LOW

PLAYBOYS OF NEW YORK SERIES

BOOK 1 - Off Limits

Chloe Jones is trying to put the scandal of leaving her Super Bowl legend fiancé at the altar behind her. No better way to escape than to turn her island honeymoon into a much-needed vacation with her girls. What she wasn't expecting was to meet a hot stranger. Don't they say to get over somebody you need to get under someone else?

Chloe's ready for a fresh start, shame her vengeful ex is making it difficult for her. That is until she lands the job of her dreams.

What she wasn't expecting was to come face to face with the hot stranger from her island escape—Noah Stone, New York's biggest playboy, and her new boss.

Chloe can be professional even if all she can think about is those lips. And the way he fills out his suit pants.

He's totally off-limits, and she's signed the paperwork that says so.

INTERCONNECTING SERIES

Reading order for Interconnecting Series

Bratva Jewels Series

The Sexy Stranger

ALSO BY JA LOW

BRATVA JEWELS DUET

An unconventional love is tested to its limits.

A beautiful woman is found bloodied and battered at their door.

Can Matteo and Tomas find out who she is before her past catches up with her.

This is a MMF dark romance.

Then

Round 2 with the Devil begins.

Manufactured by Amazon.ca
Bolton, ON